Dead Man Hollow

Suzanne Arruda

ISBN: 1533161526
ISBN-13: 978-1533161529

DEDICATION

This work is dedicated to Hershell and Chauncy who have
joined me in many hikes in the Arkansas woods.

ACKNOWLEDGMENTS & AUTHOR NOTES

Several people were of tremendous help in the research for this book.

I wish to thank Newton County, Arkansas Sheriff Keith Slape; Sheriff's office manager (retired) Pat Ramsey: and daytime dispatcher Maggie Metzgar for all their time and patience in answering my questions and teaching me about the ins and outs of the sheriff's business.

Equal thanks to Devils Den State Park Superintendent Monte Fuller and Assistant Superintendent Tim Scott for all their time and help in teaching me about running a State Park.

Thanks to Sheriff's Deputy Bob Peters for showing me how to load and operate a gun and Dr. D.P. Lyle for showing me how to "load a naturally toxic plant."

Thanks to Sandi Ault for all her hours listening to and advising on this story.

* * *

There is no Cado County, Arkansas, nor is there a Dead Man Hollow State Park. These are entirely fictional. For those who wonder where Dead Man Hollow State Park sits, it hovers in a fourth dimension somewhere between Devils Den State Park and Petit Jean State Park in NW Arkansas. Both parks are well worth the time to visit.

i

CHAPTER 1 – MAY, 1940

She reclined in the stall; an Ozark Aphrodite in a straw sea, the front of her yellow cotton frock unbuttoned to the waist, a wide, white collar framing a throat as creamy as fresh churned butter. One small breast peeked out, and the man stretched out a calloused hand to caress it. His other hand brushed away some flecks of hay that drifted down from the loft. He wore a working man's clothes, denim trousers and a long-sleeved shirt faded as an August noon sky. Presently, the shirt hung loose around his narrow hips and his suspenders fanned out beside him. His frayed denim jacket hung high on a nail close to a pitchfork.

"I'm sorry that we couldn't slip away to the cabin again," the man said. "I think of it as ours, and a stall's no place for the likes of you."

The young woman's cheeks took on the blush of a newly ripened peach, and the man looked as though he longed to devour her again. She felt the warmth spread again through her.

"But it is, Ben. My name is Agnes and that does mean lamb." She rolled to her side and faced him, one slender finger stroking his lips. "I'm glad the cabin was where I first loved you, because you built it, but I wouldn't mind if we were in the woods on a bed of ferns as long as we were together."

Ben grinned. "Soon you'll be my lamb legally, and I won't have to sneak around like a chicken thief. It was a lucky thing that you got permission to miss the prayer service, what with your mother helping that woman birth a new baby and all."

Agnes smiled. "Luck and a little bit of deception. I hate those evening services." Agnes sat up, bracing herself on her right hand. "But we can't stay here much longer," she said. "Father will be finishing his sermon about now and soon, after the last song, he'll be coming home."

"There's enough time for you to pack a bag," Ben said, his voice ripe with urgency. "Come away with me tonight. Now!" He reached into his trouser pocket, retrieved a brass ring with a glass inset, and pushed it into her hands. "I know it's not a real emerald or even real gold. But someday it will be."

She turned the ring over in her hands and smiled at some inward thought. "Oh, Ben. It's a beautiful . . . emerald. But I can't leave. I shouldn't." She kissed him again. When she pulled away, her face and chest glowed apple red, her lips lush and swollen, "Wait for me at the crossroads," she said in a breathy voice. "I'll come tonight after all have gone to bed." She slipped the ring into her dress pocket.

The man stood up quickly, as though his departure could speed up time and their reunion.

"Oh, Agnes. My own beautiful lamb. Do you mean it?" He extended his arms to her.

"Yes," She took his hands and let him pull her to her feet, letting loose a fall of straw from her auburn hair. Her slender fingers worked the tiny buttons of her dress while he tucked his shirt into his trousers, adjusting his suspenders. Ten seconds later, the clatter of hooves and a whinny startled them both, and they froze momentarily.

"Father!" exclaimed the woman, her eyes widening in panic. "He's early."

"You need to run to the house. Now! Before he sees you like this."

She hastily finished buttoning her shirtwaist and brushed

her hands over the skirt. "I can tell him I was waiting for him and fell asleep. It's you that needs to go. But stay to the woods and off the lane until he's in the barn."

"And you'll meet me at the crossroads?" He hesitated, as though afraid to leave her.

"Yes, now go!" she turned him by the shoulders and pushed him out the side door just as she heard Jepthah's heavy hooves clomp on the wooden planks outside. She ran her fingers through her hair once more, making certain all of the straw was out, and opened the barn door to greet her father. He slid down from the saddle, a tall slightly-built man garbed in flat, clerical black. Only his wan face loomed in the dim light. The horse, a huge, sway-backed roan, stamped one hoof, impatient for his stall and hay.

"Agnes! What are you doing here? Why aren't you in the house?"

Agnes blushed and looked down as though the scent of her tryst clung like a heavy mist about her, discernible to her father's critical eye. "All's well in the house, Father. But it felt warm to me so I came out to get some air and wait for you. I sat in the barn awhile to pray and I must have dozed off. I'm sorry."

"Prayer in a barn is not unholy," the man said. "Our Lord was born in just such a stable."

"Yes, Father," Agnes said, her head still bowed meekly. "Let me take Jepthah from you and get him into his stall." She took the reins from her father's hand and led the big-boned animal into the barn, as though to put distance between herself and her father's sharp gaze.

"Deacon Tanner asked after you," the minister said.

"Did he indeed, Father?" the reply was flat, less of a question than an acknowledgement.

"Indeed, child. It would please me mightily to see you two wed before the summer is over. He's coming this evening to speak to you. He'll be here as soon as he locks the church."

"Father, I do not love him."

"Marriage, daughter, is a woman's duty. Provided, of

course, that it is the right sort of man. I have seen the looks you've given to that stone mason from the park camp. But his job is temporary, and then he will move on. I would not have you waste yourself on a drifter, nor would I lose you from our community. He is not a member. I am not even certain he is a Christian."

Agnes opened her mouth to reply, but got no farther than "But, Father--"

Reverend Elwood held up a hand for silence. "And if you are thinking of your mother, do not. It is true that she is not always as well as she should be, but the Lord gives no burdens beyond what can be endured. She manages her roles in this church and that of her house. She will continue to do what is required of her. But she need not manage them alone. And you would not be far, daughter. Indeed, as the Deacon's wife, you could relieve her of some of her burdens in the church."

Agnes said nothing more, unbuckling the leather girth. She slid the worn saddle from Jepthah's back, displaying a strength that one wouldn't expect from her slender build. But Agnes, like most of the country women, had been used to manual labor and chores all her young life. She hefted the saddle and let it straddle the stall. When she turned to her father, she saw him staring at something on the opposite wall. Agnes followed his gaze and gasped.

Ben's jacket.

"What is the meaning of this, daughter?!" he demanded. He looked at her dress and his eyes opened wide. His right hand came up, an accusing finger pointing. "Your buttons are awry! Daughter, have you been whoring like some Jezebel?"

Agnes' hands flew to her buttons and clutched them, to hide the evidence. "Father," she began, but he gave her no opportunity to finish. His right hand dashed across her cheek, the slap echoing in the barn. She fell against the horse. In the commotion, neither of them heard or noted anything else but their own distress.

"Perverse woman, you are no longer fit to be his wife," yelled Elwood. "You shall be cast out and another will be given to Deacon Tanner." He lunged, as though to grab her by the arms, and Agnes leaped back, colliding a second time with the great horse.

Jepthah shied sideways, his sturdy rump shoving Agnes with tremendous force, pushing her as a hammer drives a nail.

Agnes shot forward, her arms bracing against her father.

He fell hard against the pitchfork.

Reverend Elwood cried out once, a piercing shriek as sharp as the tines. It died into a sputtering gurgle as a rivulet of blood dribbled from his open mouth. Elwood's body twitched, his arms jerking like a marionette, his eyes wide and staring. Then, with a raspy sigh, the minister's body relaxed. His head lolled to one side, eyes open.

Agnes stared in paralyzed disbelief at her father, skewered on the tines as easily as any hay bale. "Why?" Agnes' question lingered in the air along with the disturbed flurry of dust motes choking her. She ran from the barn.

CHAPTER 2 – MID-JUNE, 2012

"There is no way in hell that I can haul my carcass over that!"

For the past two days, the forest's trees had writhed like revelers in a frenetic orgy. Now one massive oak obstacle sprawled across Ranger Phoebe Palmer's path. The tree reminded Phoebe of her brother-in-law, Walter. He'd passed out on the dance floor at her wedding reception, creating the first hurdle in her marriage though not the last. Only there'd be no dancing around this monster. Or climbing over it for that matter. Phoebe's chest didn't even clear the tree's four-foot diameter. She put her fists on her hips, eyeing this latest roadblock.

"Crap!"

She pulled her GPS unit from her belt, brushing her Glock. Just touching the gun sent a shiver down her arms. After two weeks as an interpreter and ranger at Dead Man Hollow State Park, she still wasn't comfortable with its presence. It was a constant reminder of the other half of her job; commissioned law enforcement officer for the state of Arkansas. And while she hadn't yet rousted her first inebriated camper, she knew it was only a matter of time before she had to play cop instead of park interpreter.

DEAD MAN HOLLOW

The GPS acquired its satellites. Phoebe noted the coordinates on her notepad and put an FT for 'fallen tree' on her topo map. Since this giant blocked the trail completely, it would have to be sawed into movable chunks. According to the map, there was an old logging road running the ridge top south of the trail. A work crew could use it to haul in chain saws. Probably the same road the Civilian Conservation Corp had used to build this trail.

"Where's a four-wheel drive when you need one?"

To her left, the valley plummeted steeply down into the Little Sugar Creek, an open invitation for a broken leg if she'd ever seen one. To her right, the hill rose sharply through thick brush to the sandstone outcrops near the ridge top. Neither looked inviting. The uphill side and the spray of exposed roots won.

"At least we could drag Walter off by his feet."

Phoebe shoved the folded map into her hip pocket and massaged her legs. She hadn't hiked like this in years, and the Dead Man's Trail was a doozy. Skirting the little valley where the first settlers had found a mummified corpse in a small cave, it was mainly popular with serious backpackers and scouts in training for a high adventure outing. It offered ten miles of steep inclines through the spell-binding scenery of northwest Arkansas' Boston Mountains. Today it featured a generous serving of backsliding mud, loose rocks, and felled trees; all the fault of two days of spring storms that sent a deluge worthy of Noah's flood down these valleys.

She worked her way up the incline to the tree's base, testing each step before trusting her full weight. Above her sat layers of broken sandstone, inviting her to utilize them as stair steps. They lied. Many of the smaller ledges had been undercut. It wouldn't serve to count on any of them holding her one-hundred and thirty pounds. Six minutes and thirteen feet later, Phoebe's boots skidded in the mud. She pitched sideways and nearly collided with the radiating root system rising like a wall to her left.

A quick hand up saved her from a face full of muck and a

7

possible eye gouge. Phoebe clung to a thick root with a choke hold, her heart pounding from the near accident. Mere inches away from her nose, heaps of loam and detritus clung to the intricate system of rootlets and root hairs. The aroma hung heavy, ripe with decaying leaves and the promise of fertile nutrients, a reminder of how closely death and life were intertwined in a forest.

It mirrored her own world; her husband's death and her resurrection into this job. Two snails were tucked in a notch where a root branched, their outstretched necks intertwined, busily procreating, creating more life from the detritus. An entire earthen ecosystem had been upset in the oak's fall and a good portion of it was now on her left hand and chin. Only the snails, locked in the ardor of molluscan passion, seemed oblivious to the upheaval.

"Get a room!"

Phoebe searched for a better foothold. That's when she saw a fat root move mere inches in front of her right foot.

Snake!

Its thick, brown body, draped with darker cross-bands swelled from a wide, triangular head. A faint, rusty stripe ran down its considerable length. Phoebe traced the sinuous muscles from the head to the cluster of rattles at the end and estimated the timber rattler's length to be at least two feet.

Oh, shit!

She froze, unable to go backwards, unwilling to risk moving forward. Her heart pounded, and her breath came in short gasps. Phoebe felt her arm muscles turn to the proverbial jelly as her body sent more blood rushing to the legs, preparing them for flight. But any attempt to run on this muddied slope would pitch her headlong into danger no matter which way she fell.

The snake didn't coil or shake its rattle. Instead it pointed its head away from her, focusing its heat sensors on something else. Unable to take her eyes off it, she gripped the root system more tightly and inched her left leg back, feeling for a stout root to climb on. If she could put enough distance between herself and the rattler, she could take time to think of a way out of this. She hadn't even brought along a hiking stick to push it away.

Just shoot the damn thing!

Her right hand reached for her Glock. Her fingers brushed the holster snap and trembled.

You're a park ranger, you idiot. You're supposed to protect all the wildlife, not just the fluffy part. There was also the fact that she wasn't certain she'd hit the beast on the first shot and it wouldn't do to piss it off.

Her ankle brushed against wood and she stepped back and up onto the root. Not much distance, but a little. Somehow it felt safer than being on the ground.

The snake shifted again, edging forward. Phoebe watched, mesmerized and saw the woodrat, one paw twitching as the venom did its job. The hapless rodent had probably suffered extensive damage to its own house and had been collecting sticks to rebuild or repair when the rattler found it.

Remodeling is a pain, isn't it, buddy?

Phoebe waited while the reptile positioned itself near the rodent's head. The snake opened its mouth, unhinging its lower jaw, and gripped the rat by the face. Phoebe eased back down onto the ground, preparing herself for her brief window of escape. Once the snake had the rat half-way into its mouth, it couldn't strike her. The rear-facing teeth wouldn't allow it to spit out its prey. Down the gullet was a one-way trip.

Another ripple of muscles, a repositioning of the mouth, and the rat slid in past its shoulders, one little forepaw sticking out to the side as though it waved goodbye.

NOW!

Phoebe moved as quickly as she could around the tree's splaying roots, one eye always on the reptile. By now it had felt her vibrations and become nervous. Rat still firmly in its jaws, the snake edged backwards, dragging its prey with it to safety under the oak. But by then Phoebe had cleared the tree and made the other side. She didn't stop until she'd put a quarter mile between herself and the rattler. She collapsed, panting on a boulder in the area designated for back-country campers.

At least she was through with the serious climbing. Another mile of trail running parallel to and just below the ridge and she'd begin her descent on the other side of the hollow. Of course, there was no guarantee that going down would be any easier. She might just as well sit on her rump and slide.

Her stomach rumbled, and she glanced at her wristwatch. Twelve-thirty. Close enough. Lunch time! Fear gave way to hunger and she dug into her pack for the peanut butter on whole wheat bagel that she'd prepared that morning. Chewy and filling, it and the snack bag of raisins would hold her until supper. The rattler behind her, she reveled in the forest's beauty.

Wren doesn't know what she's missing. Phoebe mentally ticked off the pleasures of the trail: the fresh air, exercise, wildlife, not to mention the fact that she'd already lost six pounds since she'd joined the park staff.

Who am I kidding? Forget the snake. She'd have a cow over peeing in the brush.

For a moment, Phoebe dwelt on a happier time when her daughter had enjoyed the outdoors, before Lieutenant Charles Palmer had been blasted into bits in Iraq. It shattered more than his body. His last letter, a fat packet, reached her five days after she'd received news of his death.

She never opened it.

Phoebe's eyes moistened, and she swiped away a tear. "Stop thinking about it, you idiot!"

Her voice startled a bushy gray squirrel and sent him scurrying up a tree where he sat on a high branch and chattered invectives.

"I don't need any sass from you, buster. I get enough crap at home from my daughter."

She extracted her water bottle from her knapsack and took a long drink. Somewhere to her right a pileated woodpecker did his best Woody Woodpecker imitation, his reverberating cackle cutting the silence. She twisted around to catch a glimpse of its red crest as it flew from a lightning scarred pin oak. Phoebe watched the bird's roller coaster flight until it disappeared behind another tree and began drumming.

She wondered how Wren was faring at her summer job in the camp store. She'd ask Mrs. Gracehill later and thank her again for giving Wren the opportunity.

Wren will come around. She just needs time.

Phoebe stuffed her trash into her pack and consulted the map. One more bridge, a wooden one, as the trail rounded the top of the hollow. According to the contours, it looked like she'd cross over a narrow ravine on the bridge before beginning her gradual descent via switchbacks. One mile across the valley, as the crow flew, sat her cabin within the park. Her new home.

"Let's go girl, they're not paying you to spend the entire day out here."

She covered the trail at a brisk pace, made easier by the iron-laden rock outcrop that capped much of it. The path sat on rock, but years of fallen timber left a rich loam off trail. She inhaled its scent mingled with the occasional crush of juniper needles under her feet and once again her mind whisked away to their last camping trip as a family, before Wren took to wearing black and dying her hair to match.

A soft piggish grunt stopped her. She waited, listening. Something rooted through last year's leaves just around the bend near the bridge. It snuffled again as it pawed through the detritus.

Definitely not a squirrel.

Wild hogs sometimes wandered the hills, dangerous animals to stumble on. Phoebe stepped forward like she was walking on glass, watching where she planted her feet before shifting her weight in order to maintain silence. Her arms quivered and her heart pounded. Her spit retreated, turning her mouth to sawdust.

Phoebe's hand went to her side, again grazing the Glock. Suddenly, the weapon became a comforting presence. Her moderate skill as a marksman wasn't. Maybe the beast stood in the ravine under the bridge. She'd be past it before it could scramble up the slippery sides and charge her.

You fool! Thinking you could handle this job. Scared of a stupid pig.

But these were damn big pigs. And mean. The timber rattler had posed less of a threat than one of these. What the hell did she think she was doing, hiking alone in this forest? This was one of the less frequently used trails, too. She could lie out here for hours before anyone thought to look for her. Phoebe took a deep breath and steadied herself. A whistle hung around her neck. A good blast on that might scare it.

Or make it mad as a wet hornet.

She could see the near end of the bridge from where she stood. It looked undamaged. Just a few more feet and she'd be there.

And then you run like hell!

She didn't. The other side was partially blocked by a young hickory that had fallen. She could push past it, but not quickly and definitely not silently. And running suddenly didn't seem like such a good idea. It wasn't a feral hog rooting around amid the exposed roots.

It was a black bear.

Phoebe watched the animal for a moment. The bear was relatively small, either a young male or a female. She didn't see or hear any cubs nearby. That was good news. Nothing she could think of beat a protective mother bear for ferocity and tenacity. The animal sat in a side ditch, an offshoot that fed into the main ravine. It poked intently into the roots, probably looking for grubs. She could slip past it on the bridge and that same hickory would block its view of her.

Her fingers went to the lanyard around her neck and the whistle. Maybe she should try to scare it off first. Wasn't that what they taught her? Yell and make a lot of noise? It wouldn't do for a bear to feel too comfortable near this trail. Three scout troops were already scheduled to use it over the course of the summer.

"Hey, bear!" Phoebe let out a blast on the whistle and clapped her hands. "Get!"

The bear jerked his snout back, hitting his head on a root. Phoebe blew the whistle again and stomped her feet. "Go away, bear!"

The animal fell onto its back, his hind feet peddling an invisible bicycle as it struggled to right itself. Once it rolled onto its feet, it half ran, half slid on its rump down the ravine until it reached a valley floor and galloped off.

Phoebe hugged herself and laughed, more at herself for being such a fool than at the bear. She pulled her map, ready to mark the fallen hickory tree when she spied the long, dirty white object protruding from the root tangle.

It was a leg bone. And nestled farther back, peeking out from under a thin rock ridge was a human skull, an eyeless socket pleading with her for help.

CHAPTER 3

"Did you move anything? Touch anything at all?" The Caddo County coroner glared at Phoebe, as if she'd purposely knocked the tree down and disturbed the grave.

"I didn't touch a blessed thing. As soon as I saw the bones, I radioed park headquarter with the location. Then I stood guard on this spot." She pointed down at her feet, planted on the little bridge overlooking the grave.

The coroner knelt beside the skeleton, gripping a digital camera with an intensity that made Phoebe throat feel those fingers throttling her. Within minutes of meeting Leona Harper, her initial surprise at seeing a female in this job disappeared. The little wolverine of a woman with her flaming red hair looked to Phoebe as if she could stare down the angel of death while playing poker with him. Next to her squatted a deputy sheriff who carefully bagged and tagged items once they'd been photographed. He'd already sketched the overall scene.

"You swear you were here the entire time?" asked the coroner. "You never left?"

"I had to leave at first to radio in." Phoebe pointed to the rising slope beside them. "I'm on the backside of the ridge right here so I needed to go back around the bend a couple hundred yards to make the call. Then I came right back and stood guard. I wasn't gone for more than fifteen minutes, twenty tops."

"You touched something. These bones have clearly been disturbed. The debris has been shifted." Leona beat the issue like it was a rug she was desperate to get the bugs out of.

"That was because a bear pawed at them. You want to chew someone out? Go find the damned bear."

And no bear deserves to come face to face with that harpy. Phoebe turned her back on the woman to signal an end to the argument. She faced her supervisor instead.

In his immaculately clean and perfectly pressed uniform, Park Superintendent Burt McGowen looked every inch the classic poster ranger. His campaign hat exposed just enough of his silver-gray hair which, along with his hazel eyes, served to give his long face a look of wisdom and serenity; a man you could trust.

"Pay no never mind to Leona," whispered McGowan. "She doesn't get too many of these cases and she gets a might excited about them. It's actually the deputy and the sheriff that're schooled in crime scene investigation, but she doesn't like people to know that. If they're not complaining, then you're okay."

Phoebe looked down from the bridge at the fragile remains peeking out from under the root tangle. A thick tap root snaked through the pelvis, cracking it into two larger chunks and several shards. The long bones fared better, but mice or a chipmunk had discovered the shelter provided by the carefully positioned rocks and had built a nest nearby, gnawing down the finger bones for the calcium.

"Have other bodies been found in the park?" Phoebe asked. She spoke in a whisper, feeling that anything louder was disrespectful.

"Oh, a few over the years," said McGowan, his tone matching hers. "Mainly hikers that weren't in proper condition and had a heart attack on the trail. One college fellow down from Fayetteville died of alcohol poisoning last spring break."

McGowan looked at the bones tucked under a tangle of roots and rock. "Never found one this far gone. It takes a good long while for that much clothing and the muscle to disappear." He nodded towards a thin, dark chunk being deposited in a bag. "That might be a bit of rubber from a shoe sole."

"Maybe it was an old, historic grave site," suggested Phoebe. "Like that mummified body the early settlers found near here." She hoped so. It made her skin crawl to think of some poor hiker having collapsed all alone and his family never knowing what happened to him.

"Not in the sense that you're thinking," said the Caddo County sheriff as he picked his way up around the felled hickory to the bridge.

Sheriff Linus Boone looked to Phoebe like an athletic man, until she noticed the slight spare tire around the middle, straining a bottom of his uniform. He wore a black, collared polo shirt with the department logo, jeans, and a Sheriff's department ball cap which exposed enough of his brown hair to show a short, military-style haircut.

"Sheriff Boone, this is my new ranger-interpreter, Phoebe Palmer," said McGowan.

Boone extended his hand. "Call me Linus."

Phoebe caught the scent of Old Spice and shivered, transported back to the day she'd clung to Charles before he boarded the bus. He always used Old Spice. It was Wren's favorite Father's Day gift to him. Phoebe shook the sheriff's hand.

"What did you mean just then," she asked with a nod to the remains, "when you said it wasn't in the sense I was thinking?"

They moved to the far end of the bridge to talk, putting a respectful distance from themselves and the remains before continuing the conversation. "Oh, it's an old grave all right. But not from any cemetery or family burial plot. There may well be some of them around, but nobody ever buried anyone in this rocky mess unless they didn't intend for someone to find the body."

"Then someone died and tumbled into that little gully,"

suggested Phoebe.

The sheriff shook his head. "The body was pushed under that rock ledge and those other rocks were carefully placed in front of the body in a way that protected it from scavengers. The rocks in front look different, too. There are also scraps of a blanket here and there. Like the body was swaddled in it."

McGowan nodded towards the burial. "Those smaller rocks are limestone. Someone had to have carried them up from the creek bed. Everything up here must have been too massive to move."

"So this was a homicide?" asked Phoebe.

Sheriff Boone nodded. "Looks that way. There's a nasty dent in the back of that skull. We're recording this as death by blunt force trauma."

"Maybe a hiker fell and hit his head on a rock," she suggested, trying to find a more innocent explanation. "He was dazed but managed to crawl under that ledge for shelter." But as she voiced it, she knew she was fooling herself.

"Maybe, but he sure didn't stack those rocks in front of himself. No, someone buried him. If he'd stayed on the surface, scavengers would have dragged the bones all over." He pointed down slope. "They'd have eventually tumbled out of this little feeder depression into the main ravine and washed down into the stream."

"Then this is a crime scene," said McGowan. "Any idea how old?"

"You mean the age of the victim or how long ago he died?"

"He?" asked Phoebe. "You know it's a he?"

Boone twisted around towards the exposed skeleton. "Ethan," he called. "What can you tell me?"

Deputy Ethan Garnett didn't bother to look up. "Young. Maybe male. That's hard to say at this point. The tree roots are thickest around the pelvis and they've done a number on it. The skull's in better condition. Not as much root growth there." He deposited a soil sample into a vial and stoppered it.

"It's a male," said the coroner.

"Talk to me, Leona," said the sheriff.

Leona Harper peered at the skull from several angles. "Little bit of a brow ridge forming, and I found enough of a rubber sole intact to suggest large feet though so I'm saying male. I would guess he was in his teens judging by his teeth. The wisdoms hadn't descended yet. He doesn't have epiphysial union at his elbows, so I'm thinking younger than fifteen."

"About Wren's age," murmured Phoebe. "His poor parents."

"As to when he died," said Leona, "that hickory will give you a starting date if you count the tree rings. The body could have been here, oh, maybe up to a year before it started growing.

"You have one of those borers handy to take a tree ring sample, Burt?" asked the sheriff.

The Superintendent shook his head. "Sorry, Linus. Got both a chain saw and a crosscut saw in the back of my truck, though. Just slice it open and take a cut."

"It's odd to see a hickory here," said Phoebe. "There's plenty farther down the hollow, but they aren't common here." She looked around. "It's the only one I see."

"Squirrel?" suggested Boone. "Though why one would carry a nut so far is odd."

"The trunk lapped over the ledge and the tap root runs right into his pelvis," said Leona. "I'm guessing the boy had some nuts in his pocket and . . . Ah, hell, take a look at this!"

"What?" asked McGowan and Boone returning to the bridge.

The coroner sat back on her heels, camera in hand. "Your deputy just found what looked like a belt buckle tucked under part of the pelvis. I know who this is, Linus."

Garnett had just brushed away the dirt on top after taking his sample and had moved back for Harper to take a photograph.

"By the belt buckle?" asked Phoebe.

"If you'd seen this Star Trek buckle nearly every day at school, you'd remember it, too,"

said Leona. George Tanner was a year behind me in school.

I was a sophomore when he disappeared. He was a complete trekkie, what they'd call a nerd today."

"Caddo County's only cold case." Boone squatted down for a closer look. "That looks like a bloody print on it."

"So what happened?" asked Phoebe.

"You tell her, Burt," said the sheriff. "You know the case better'n anybody."

McGowan sighed. "That was late November, nineteen-seventy-six. Big Tanner clan family reunion over Thanksgiving. I was a young ranger then, relatively fresh out of college. They'd taken all eight of the cabins. One of the boys, George, and Ruthie, his little four-year cousin, went missing. It had been warmer, but the temperature dropped something fierce late that Thursday afternoon. We searched everywhere into the night, finally quitting when some of the trails got icy slick, and a few of the searchers nearly slid over a cliff. I'd hoped they'd just gotten lost in a cave. It would have been a miserable night for them, but they wouldn't have frozen to death."

Phoebe's stomach roiled at the implications. "You found the little girl then?" Hope edged her voice. She wanted that child to be alive, to be somewhere now with a family of her own and not moldering in some shallow grave.

"We found her on Friday. Unfortunately, she hadn't survived the night."

The sheriff returned with a body bag and laid it out beside the coroner. "She was curled up outside the Woodcutter Cave, wasn't she?"

McGowan nodded. "Clutching a little stuffed bear, like she'd passed in her sleep, which is likely what happened. We all knew that freeze was dangerous. That's why we worked so hard searching. Poor little thing didn't have on a coat, just some thin cotton dress."

"But Woodcutter Cave isn't on marked on any of the maps," said Phoebe. "How did the kids know about it?"

McGowan shrugged. "That's why we never even thought to look there. I had the idea after we'd exhausted everyplace else they could have gone. That poor little child, her face all blue, frost on her hair. No coat, no socks. My God, I'll never forget that sight." McGowan swiped a hand over his eyes, as though to sweep away the image.

"That's a good mile or two across country from the cabins," said Phoebe. "A rough hike for a little girl. For anyone for that matter."

McGowan sighed. "After I found the girl, I went into the cave, figuring the boy had gone in and hadn't come out, leaving his cousin to wait for him. Never found him. I swear, every time some researcher went into that cave, I expected he or she'd come back screaming about a body. But it never happened."

Boone stared at the gravesite. "Buried just before a big freeze," he said. "That explains how a grave only three feet deep escaped getting dug out by bear." He pointed to several flat rocks, clearly disturbed when the tree fell. "It took some work to cap the grave with those rocks. The ones protecting the skull must weigh ten pounds each. Whoever did this was no weakling, especially toting them up from the stream bed."

Phoebe hated the next thought that crept into her mind. The only way to get rid of it was to ask. "The little girl, she wasn't . . . he hadn't . . ."

"The girl wasn't sexually molested, if that what you're asking," said Boone. "She died of exposure, plain and simple. But she did show signs of bruising around her knees and calves. Still it was nothing that couldn't be explained by an active little girl making that rugged hike."

Phoebe exhaled, relieved. Bad enough the child was left to die, but she couldn't bear the thought that someone had abused the girl and abandoned her. "How was the case treated?" she asked. "Did everyone think this boy has deliberately left his cousin to die?"

"George was, by all accounts, a good boy," McGowan said. "Smart, funny. Interested in collecting things: leaves, dried scat--"

"Hickory nuts," finished Leona.

"Well, yeah, I guess so. He went on a nature walk with me

the day before Thanksgiving and asked more questions than you can ever want in a single hike. Did the bats migrate or hibernate? Why do the oaks hold onto their dead leaves in the fall? That sort of thing. He was particularly interested in the bats. He kept trying to get me to take him to one of the bat caves. He knew we had some in the park. But then, his family grew up in this county."

"That sounds like George," said Leona. "All science and science fiction. We'd just gotten a new science teacher that year. George couldn't stop talking about her. Miss Meany this and Miss Meany that. Just like some kids talk about their coaches."

"Was Ruth with George on that hike on Wednesday?" asked Phoebe.

McGowan fingered his chin and looked up. "Yes, she was. I remember he toted her piggy back part of the way."

"So maybe when he went for a hike with whoever killed him, she followed after and got lost," suggested Phoebe. "George might not have even known she was behind him."

"That's the way the sheriff's department took it," said Boone. "Boy went out. Little girl followed. Boy fell in the cave and broke his leg in one of the off passages. Nobody thought of homicide or kidnapping." He looked at the skull. "I do now. If I was a betting man, I'd bet my paycheck on it. But," he cautioned, "no one says anything about the cracked skull. As far as the public goes, this was an accident."

Phoebe stared at the scanty remains and the felled tree. "Most of the boy is in that tree now. Somehow it doesn't seem right to cut it up and haul it off for firewood. Can't you just leave it to decompose beside the trail?"

"I never really thought of it that way," said Boone. "I promise I'll only take a thin sample."

"We have to take some of the tap root," snapped Leona.

"We'll treat the tree with as much respect as we can when we move it," said McGowan. "I'll leave it close by here."

"I guess that's all you can do. How can I help?" Phoebe asked. "Should I wait here, Burt, until the coroner is done and escort her out?"

"I came up this miserable logging road with the sheriff," said Leona. "You think my hearse has four-wheel drive? I left it parked at the bottom of the hill on the service road."

"I can take care of everything up here, Phoebe," said McGowan. "I need for you to finish hiking this trail. Who knows what shape the down side's in? And you still have a program tonight."

Phoebe gave one last look at the remains before starting down the trail. This boy would have been a man now, perhaps a husband and father. Did his parents still live? In their mind, he would always be a boy, a sapling full of promise. In one brief day he hiked out of their lives and his own. Suddenly the need to see Wren, alive and unharmed, overwhelmed her.

* * *

So the Tanner boy had been found. The knowledge stirred up old memories, older than the boy's death. Memories that harked back to youth and a warm, sweet-scented hay loft and the voices and vision of two lovers below. They hadn't known that their passion and confidences were overseen and heard.

The memory ended as it always did, with Reverend Elwood's gruesome death and the knowledge that it was no accident. Agnes' choking "Why?" had never been answered. There had been no need. The answer had been clear.

CHAPTER 4

Boone slid the last evidence box into the back of the midnight-blue Lincoln hearse and eased the kink out of his back. He spent too much time sitting at a desk and he knew it. Maybe it was time to get that old treadmill out and start using it. But he hated trudging on the dreadmill which was why it got shoved into the closet to begin with. He gazed into the forest which hugged each side of the service road. Perhaps he should try one of the park's trails sometime, but he preferred doing paperwork at his desk to spending days off alone.

"Hell of a way to spend a day, eh, Leona?" asked Boone. He slammed the tailgate shut. "Everything is bagged, tagged, and loaded up. Including," he added, "a slab of tree root, a slice of the trunk, and every blasted rock that somebody laid over the body and any others we found within Olympic throwing distance that could've been used to hit the boy."

He handed her the clipboard and a pen, waiting while she signed the chain of custody form.

"Where'd your deputy go in such a hurry?" asked Leona. She tossed the signed form on the passenger seat and fumbled in her bag for a cigarette.

"Call came in as we were loading up," said Boone. "Someone robbed Dick Cooper's hardware store. The list reads like a meth head's shopping cart. Looks like you're stuck driving all this to the crime lab."

"Not a problem," she said. "You know, it always amazes me how someone who couldn't have passed high school chemistry thinks they can mix explosive chemicals at home. Idiots." Leona sat sideways in the driver's seat, the door open and her feet propped up on car's frame. She inhaled deeply before puffing out the smoke in one long breath.

"Yeah, I know what you mean." Boone looked at the hearse's rear. It didn't ride too low, and the tires looked well inflated. But then, Leona needed good suspension in order to haul full caskets. "Can you get it all to Little Rock by yourself?"

"I don't have any customers waiting, if that's what you're asking," Leona said.

Boone leaned against his Tahoe which was parked on the other side of the access road and waved away the smoke. To him the coroner resembled a little red dragon. The story went that when she was a nurse at the Evening Breeze nursing home, she's started covering the gray that crept into her naturally auburn hair. Claimed the old folks didn't like to see their nurse getting older. Made them nervous, she'd said. But since she'd retrained as a mortician and taken over her father's funeral home, the red had gotten a little more vibrant. Today it was nearly orange, a flame against the green trees.

He wondered how many of her old patients she'd seen on her table after they'd permanently passed out the doors of the nursing home. Boone didn't care to ask. Morticians made him nervous, and Leona was no exception. She was far too comfortable with death. He made a mental note to make any advance arrangements for himself with another funeral home. Preferably in another town.

"Try as hard as we may, we're not going to keep this a secret for long," Boone said. "Hell, word's probably out by now. Everyone at the park headquarters knows that the new lady ranger found a body. If Burt hasn't already filled them in, that ranger probably will. There are a few houses on the near side of the valley that can pick up our radio, too. I know some of them listen in."

"Yep, I call it Scannerville," said Leona. "Folks with nothing else to do for entertainment I guess."

Boone fanned away another plume of smoke. "We'll need confirmation of identity with dental records, Leona, but we're all certain enough that I think I should go ahead and notify the boy's next of kin."

"Suit yourself, sheriff," she said with a wave of her cigarette. "I never liked that part of the job, but I don't know who you're going to tell."

"His parents."

"Dead."

"Dead? Since when? I thought they moved away. Waited a couple of years and left the county."

Leona dropped the cigarette butt on the gravel and stretched out a leg to grind it with her heel. "You got that much right, but that's not the end of the story. You were probably too young at the time to know much of the details."

Linus waited in vain for her to enlighten him. Like a pump, she sometimes needed to be primed before the information started flowing. "Do you know the details, Leona?"

"Yep."

"Care to fill me in?"

Those two promptings appeared to be enough as the coroner crossed her polyester clad legs and settled herself more comfortably on the seat. "I guess Reuben and Prudence held on here for two years after their boy disappeared. They did their best to see their second girl through school." She looked Boone over. "You know George had sisters? Elverna was the oldest. She got married to Jasper Keefe right out of school in sixty-eight or nine. Moved down to Louisiana I think. Lit out like the devil was on her tail. Then there was Betty. She was the same age as me. Quiet girl. The type whose main aspiration was to get married so she wouldn't have to make any more decisions. Know what I mean? I think she worked as a secretary for Drew Wallace for a while."

"Didn't he have that used car lot down on Main?"

"That's him. Anyway, she may have done more for Drew than just be his secretary if you catch my drift, 'cause he left his wife for Betty. Last I heard, they went somewhere out west together." She stopped and stretched. High overhead, a crow cawed and was answered by another farther up the road. "Anyhow, those two sisters are the only next of kin to tell."

"You still haven't told me what happened to George's parents."

"Well, that's the sad part, not that this whole mess ain't sadder'n a toothless dog trying to crack a bone. They hung on for a while, long enough to see Betty graduate, then they cleared out. Reuben had lost his job at the market. He'd always been a drinker, but once George disappeared, he started hitting the bottle hard and I mean hard! After Betty left town with Drew, no one really kept up with them until a notice showed up in some out-of-town paper about a single-car accident. Reuben and his wife went off the road one night. Took several bad tumbles before landing in the Buffalo River. Both bodies were beat to hell in the crash."

"Had Reuben been drinking then?"

"That's the story. But I don't know the truth behind it. It was a closed coffin funeral. Elverna came back for it, but we never saw Betty. Not sure she ever knew. I got the impression that Elverna came just to make sure the old man was dead."

Boone pondered the news before pushing himself off the vehicle. "Then I guess I'll have to track down Betty and Elverna."

"Yeah, well good luck with that." Leona shook her right leg. "Damnation, my foot went to sleep. Hate it when that happens." She limped around in circles behind the hearse, working out the numbness. "You know, Linus," she said when she'd climbed back into the hearse, "with no family to push this, you're going to have a hell of a time solving this one. If I were you, I'd cut my loss and forget about it." She waved goodbye and drove away.

Boone watched her turn off the dirt access road onto

paved county highway. In a matter of seconds, the surrounding trees masked the hearse's engine noise, leaving him immersed in a thick, palpable silence so complete that he could imagine that he was the last man on earth. He looked up and saw a half-dozen vultures, riding an updraft in lazy circles.

Carrion eaters can afford to be lazy. Death always served up dinner.

Boone waved his arms, trying to shake off the desolation.

A perfect place to commit murder and hide a body.

Suddenly a rapid drumming cut clear and sharp across the ridge. Boone jumped, startled. Only a woodpecker.

He thought about the abandoned logging road near the ridge. Anyone familiar with the park then would have known about it and used it to dump the boy. He might not have been murdered here and, to Boone's eye, the indentation in the boy's skull looked like it had been struck with a heavy tool like a crowbar rather than a hiking stick or an irregularly-shaped rock.

Leona said he should cut his losses. He couldn't do that. Even without family to push him, he'd see this case solved and he'd start by talking to McGowan.

He owed it to George Tanner.

CHAPTER 5

"Phoebe! You're back. Lordy, what did you do? Take the trail on your stomach?"

"I nearly did, Shirley." Phoebe moved deeper into the park store, edging past a postcard rack and stacks of assorted souvenirs. Wildly-colored kerchiefs with maps of Dead Man Hollow State Park printed on them, coffee mugs, teddy bears holding little hiking sticks, and decks of cards with a photo of the Sugar Run falls sat on a shelf above a stack of T-shirts. Beyond the souvenirs was the store's camping and food section. Above shelves of Dutch ovens, lid hooks, long-handled forks, and sandwich irons rose shelves of Vienna sausages, graham crackers, chocolate bars, marshmallows, and other more nutritious comestibles. In the far corner stood a battered Hotpoint refrigerator that had seen the Kennedy administration.

Phoebe took out a grape soft drink and set it on the counter. "I want two of those kerchiefs, too." She chose an orange one for herself and a yellow one for Wren. "If I let Wren pick, she'd complain that you didn't sell one in black." She fished into her hip pocket for her wallet.

Shirley Gracehill took Phoebe's money and rang up the charge. The storekeeper reminded Phoebe of Santa Claus' little

28

sister. Pushing sixty-five, her rounded face and berry-shaped nose lent a congenial look to what otherwise was a very business-like build. At five foot, five inches and one-hundred fifty plus pounds, she bordered on plump. Yet her upper arms, visible in her sleeveless cotton shirt, showed no sign of developing jiggly bingo sags and probably wouldn't as long as she continued to stock her own shelves and drag rental canoes around. She was the closest Phoebe came to having a personal friend.

"I'll tell Wren that you're back," Shirley said. She smiled broadly, a clue that Wren hadn't been too much of a bother.

"Please don't call her just yet. I want to know how her first day went." Phoebe twisted the cap on the bottle and took a long pull, savoring the natural concord-grape flavoring and the tang of phosphoric acid.

"Wren did fine," said Shirley. "I put her in charge of getting people in and out of the canoes and paddle boats. When that girl tells a kid to put on a life vest, they do it." The woman's hazel eyes shifted under her thin white bangs as she handed back a quarter and gave Phoebe the once over. "Looks like you met up with more of the trail than you'd intended. How bad was it?"

"I guess it could have been worse but I'd hate to imagine how. A few big trees down but the bridges were intact. I managed to scramble over the first tree but that last one..." she shook her head and chugged her drink. "I am beat. I started at five this morning and would've finished it in seven hours if there hadn't been for some . . . interruptions."

Shirley leaned on the countertop, one elbow touching the assortment of locally made fudge. "You know," she said, dropping her voice to a near whisper, "I have a radio in the back. I heard your call in to Burt. I can also pick up the radio from the sheriff's department."

Phoebe sat the empty bottle on the counter. She should have known. With no cell phone reception within the park, radios were often the only means of communicating to each other. There was one in every building and in each of the rangers' homes as well. It kept everyone in the park informed of everything from the need for a toilet plunger in one of the cabins to storm alerts and other danger. As if to give evidence, the store's radio crackled to life.

"18-1 to 18-2."

"18-2 here."

"I'm heading into town to talk to Sheriff Boone. Should be back tonight, but I need for you to do the drive through the campground for me. You copy?"

"Got you covered, Burt, but it's going to cost you. You owe me a Danish from Chelsey's bakery. Cheese filled."

"You got it. 18-1 out."

Shirley put a comforting hand on Phoebe's arm. "Must have been hard, finding a body like that. But don't worry. Wren was outside when the call came in. I don't think she heard. What happened? Did some hiker get hit by lightning in that big storm?"

Phoebe shook her head. "No. This happened a long time ago. The sheriff and Burt both think it's some boy that disappeared over Thanksgiving in seventy-six."

Shirley sucked in her breath. "The Tanner boy!"

"You know about him?" As soon as she said it, she knew it was a dumb question. Shirley had owned and worked this store for the last eleven years. Surely the topic would have come up.

"Of course I know about him. I grew up in this county," Shirley said. "I guess you didn't know this, but it was my mother who owned the store back in seventy-six. She'd had the store for years and got it grandfathered into the park when all the other parks took over ownership. I was a science teacher down by Little Rock at the time of the disappearance, but I kept up with the news. Mother, of course, was my main source, but I also had the daily Wayside Whistle mailed to me." She shook her head. "So you finally found poor little George Tanner. My lord, what was he doing on that trail?"

Phoebe shrugged.

"Oh, that was just a rhetorical question, dear. And Burt is sure it's him?"

"Yes. His belt buckle was apparently unique."

"Star Trek."

Phoebe nodded.

"You know, his little cousin was found frozen to death the day after those kids went missing. She was supposed to be slow, you know, a special child. Almost five years old and couldn't tell her colors, trouble counting, barely spoke a word beyond yes or no. That sort of thing. Said to be a pretty little creature. Her mother had had her rather late in life and sometimes that can cause problems." Shirley crossed her burley arms on the counter and leaned on them. "Well, I'm glad the poor boy's finally been found if only for his own sake. And to think he was lying dead near the trail all those years and no one ever found him before."

Phoebe saw her questioning look and felt the expectancy in the silence. But this was now a murder investigation, and friend or not, she couldn't divulge anything extra without the sheriff's permission. "That storm washed out a lot of land. But I'm glad it was me and not a hiker that spotted him," Phoebe said. "The sheriff's in charge of the case now. Hopefully the trail will be reopened in a day or two. And Wren was no problem? I feel like I should be paying you to babysit her."

Shirley seemed to accept the change in topic. "Nonsense. She was a big help today. She knows that, since she's under sixteen, I can't hire her for a full day, but she was happy to help out here for a few dollars an hour, and I suggested she could bus lunch tables in the café for a share of the tips if she wanted."

"I appreciate it. It's been tough for her since her dad died. She loved him so much."

"At least she knew hers. My father was one of those wounded World War Two vets. Mom had been hired to care for him and I guess they fell in love. But he passed before I was born."

"I'm sorry. Is your mother still alive?"

Shirley nodded. "She is. Spunky soul, too. If I didn't worry about her driving, she'd probably be out here telling me how to run her store. But at eighty-four, I don't want her taking these hilly roads. And I don't really want to share my store with her." Shirley looked long and hard at Phoebe's face. "Look," she said finally, "it's not Wren that I'm wondering about. I know how hard it is to be newly widowed. Went through it myself. Your married friends dump you and everyone else tells you how lucky you are that your husband died before he could cheat on you."

Phoebe nodded, grateful that someone understood, suddenly anxious to spill her guts to a friendly ear. Once Charles died, she became a non-entity: a piece of furniture, a tool, something to be used. With no husband to make demands on her time, it was free for the taking. Parents, students, principal, colleagues, and especially Wren sank roots into her soul and drank deeply just as the trees did in the forest. Only no one gave back. She'd been rapidly sucked dry until she hadn't the strength to cry out.

"I thought it would be easier since he was deployed overseas," Phoebe said. "You know, that I'd have been used to it. But I have to tell you, there were times during his deployment where the pain of separation felt like I was seared with a hot brand. I used to cry in my pillow so Wren wouldn't hear me. But within a month, I'd get a letter from him and everything would be better." Her lips curved in a thin smile. "He'd relate some humorous anecdote about a poker game with the men, or describe a sunset. He made it sound like he was never in any danger. I got his last letter a week after he died."

Shirley put her hand on Phoebe's. "What did he say?

Phoebe shook her head. "I never opened it. I locked it away in the fire safe with the insurance papers." She peered into Shirley's eyes. "Every time I open that damn safe I swear I hear the thing calling to me. I'd burn it, but someday Wren will want it. When she's ready."

"When you're ready. And you're adjusting to life in the park okay?"

"Sure," said Phoebe. "Better than Wren is." She wondered

if the lie showed. Getting used to silence was one thing. Silence punctuated by animal movement outside her window was another. She still wasn't sleeping well. "I mean, it is a lot different than living in Wichita, more so than I anticipated, but it's so peaceful here."

"Helluva change from teaching school in Wichita. You never did tell me what brought you all the way out here."

Phoebe smiled. "You're better than a shrink, you know that, Shirley? Can you believe that I had Wren in mind? I don't have any family myself, but Charles' parents live in Fayetteville. I thought that if Wren had grandparents close by, it would help her through the loss of her father. I didn't consider how she'd react to no cell phone covering and one television channel. And Fran and Jack aren't helping. They not only agree with Wren that living in the park in a cabin is stupid, but have suggested that Wren should live with them." She snorted. "Over my dead body."

Suddenly Phoebe felt guilty for wallowing in her own grief. "How did your husband die?"

"Suicide. Four months after we were married. He . . ."

The store's screen door opened accompanied by the tinkling of the shop's bell. Phoebe turned in time to see the angel of death's little sister come in. The slender sprig of a girl wore black pants and t-shirt brushed by shoulder-length purple-black hair.

"Hello, Wren," said Phoebe, trying her best to not show her revulsion for her daughter's appearance but it was like looking for a fresh bud on a treasured rose and seeing a sooty canker instead.

"Oh, so you're back," Wren said. Her surly voice screamed 'go away.'

Phoebe kept her smile. "Good to see you, too. Mrs. Gracehill said you've been a great help and that you can even get some extra tip money busing tables."

"Like there's anything to spend it on." Wren muttered. She stared at her mother's filthy uniform. "You look awful. Not that those uniforms ever look good."

"The trail was muddy, and I had a run in with a fallen tree. Come on, get your stuff and let's go home. I need to clean up before I do my evening program."

Wren rolled her eyes and went into the backroom, emerging a moment later with a black backpack, and an mp3 player.

"Burt's making you do a program after you had to hike what's supposed to be an overnight trail in one day?" Shirley shook her head. "Slave driver. What's the program tonight?"

"Bats."

"Bats?" Wren perked up "Really?"

"Sure. You'll enjoy it," said Phoebe.

The fleeting interest vanished like a sunbeam behind a cloud, and Wren lapsed back into the sulky teenage mode. "Whatever." She shoved earbuds in her ears and turned on her player.

"Goodbye Mrs. Gracehill," said Phoebe, waving.

"Goodbye Shirley," said Wren.

Once in the park's mini-van, Phoebe turned to her daughter. "I don't want you to call Mrs. Gracehill, Shirley."

"Why? That's her name. You're not fooling me, with that Mrs. Gracehill stuff. You only do that when I'm around."

"I'm trying to teach you to be respectful. She's old enough to be your grandmother and she's your employer."

"She's cool. She's got internet. She lets me use her computer on my breaks and when I'm just hanging around . . . waiting."

Phoebe ignored the pause, laced with the unspoken accusation about ruining Wren's life bringing her into the park. "Which is nice of her, but still no reason to call her by her first name."

"You call your boss, Burt. I don't see why I can't do the same."

"Because I said so."

"Whatever."

Phoebe decided to let the matter rest. She drove the mile up the service road to their five-room cabin, searching for some way to connect with this stranger sitting beside her. Maybe it was true that space aliens took over teenage bodies, returning them when they hit twenty-three.

"I want to take you into town tomorrow," Phoebe said.

"Fayetteville?"

Phoebe heard a note of anticipation in Wren's voice and knew her daughter was going to be disappointed in her again. "No, Wayside Springs." She saw Wren slump further down into her seat and fold her arms across her chest. "I want to get you registered for school. It might be fun to see it together, you know, that way it won't be so new and strange to you next fall."

"No, just strange. Why can't I go to school in Fayetteville?"

"Because we don't live in Fayetteville, and I don't want to hear about that anymore."

"Whatever."

Phoebe tried one more attempt at civilized conversation. "I saw a pileated woodpecker today."

Wren stared at her player, her fingers working a central dial.

"I saw a bear, too. I think it was a young male."

"Was that when you found the stiff?"

Phoebe nearly skidded in the mud. "How did you know about that?"

"I hear stuff." She looked at her mom from under half-lowered lids. "So was it all creepy?" Her voice held a note of ghoulish anticipation. "Were there, like, maggots?"

"No. Just bones. Just very . . . young bones."

"Young? How do you get young bones? I mean, if it's just a skeleton, it should have been there a long time."

"It had been, but that's not what I meant." Phoebe paused to handle the sharp turn into their lane. "The bones belonged to a child. Someone about your age."

"I'm not a child. I'm going to be fourteen in two months."

"Whatever," said Phoebe, imitating her daughter's

35

favorite response. She felt Wren bristle beside her. She knew that as soon as they reached the cabin and she shut the engine, Wren would bolt like a deer, heading straight to her room. Anything that needed to be said, needed to be said now. She slowed the vehicle.

"Wren, I just meant that it's always a shock when a young person dies. And finding this boy made me feel so sad for his parents, wondering all those years what happened to him. It made me think about you and me and . . . well, I don't want us to have regrets about things we say or do."

"Like you getting daddy killed?"

"Wren! I had nothing to do with that. How can you even think such a thing?"

"You didn't make him quit the Guard. You didn't even try."

"Your father loved the Guard. Nothing I could have said or done would have made him leave it."

"That's a lie! He told me once that he did it for the extra money." Her voice broke. "If you'd gotten a better job than working at that stupid school, maybe he wouldn't have felt that way." A tear ran down Wren's cheek, dragging a black mascara line behind it.

Phoebe parked beside her personal car, a smaller crossover vehicle. "Honey, your father had --"

"Don't talk to me about daddy! And don't tell me how great it is to live out here. It's horrid," she screamed. "There's no cell phone, no internet, no malls. It's like you think I'm supposed to become some stupid, prancing nature girl." Wren swiped the back of her hand across her nose. "Well, I'll live in this stupid park with you and go to your stupid programs because I have to. But only until I can make other plans."

"Other plans? What--?"

The car door's slam interrupted her. Wren stomped off to the cabin alone.

Phoebe watched her daughter unlock the front door and go in. For five minutes she sat alone in the driver's seat, staring at the cabin. Beautiful in its simplicity, the rectangular structure rose from a sturdy stone base, turning into a classic log structure three feet above ground. A rugged stone chimney climbed up on the narrow, northern side. A sugar maple and three towering short-leafed pines shaded the long, western backside which included a cemented patio with barbecue grill and picnic table. The view should have filled her soul with joy and peace. It was her dream home, a place that she and Charles had talked about. But instead of laughter and love, the house held pain and unspoken anger. Mostly unspoken.

Phoebe followed her daughter to the house, stopping as a flurry of movement near the foundation caught her eye. She waited, motionless, and was rewarded in a minute by the emergence of a chipmunk from a slender gap in the stonework.

"Hey, little buddy," she said softly, noting how small the animal looked. She reckoned it to be a newly weaned youngster from an early April litter. It watched her, too young to have enough sense to hide. "Spunky, aren't you. Bet you're hungry. Wait there."

She went inside. As she expected, Wren's bedroom door was closed, a tangible reminder of how the girl had shut her mother out of her life. Phoebe went to the cupboard and took out a can of raisins. After grabbing a small handful, she added it to a cup of breakfast granola and poured it outside a few feet from the hole. "Dinner's on me," she said.

Phoebe went back in to take a quick shower and change into a fresh uniform before

heading into the combination kitchenette, dining and living room to prepare supper. She had to be at the campground amphitheater at dusk to give her talk on bats. By then, Wren should have settled down and would dutifully sit through the presentation. Phoebe didn't feel comfortable leaving her home alone yet.

Bad enough she had to walk to her first day of work. The Arkansas woods held dangers for the unwary; the occasional black bear and timber rattlesnakes to name a few. Mother chipmunk didn't have any problem kicking the kids out after six weeks. Why am I so overprotective?

The answer came easily. While their home wasn't visible from the road, she had no idea who might come by the house. The access road was clearly marked, Employees Only, but a curious day hiker might stroll down to take a look. Mothers of teenage daughters viewed every male with suspicion.

You're being stupid! You're safer here than you were in Wichita. It's little Spunky Chunk out there that should be worried.

Phoebe had no sooner thrown together a salad when her own radio crackled.

"18-2 to all available rangers. Emergency. Shooter in campground B. Repeat shooter in campground B. I need backup. Now!"

"18-5 to 18-2," Phoebe responded. "I'm on my way."

"Wren," she yelled. "I have to leave. There's an emergency. Stay in the house!" She raced out the door, the weight of the Glock pressing against her body.

CHAPTER 6

"Hope you like barbecue sauce and bacon on your roast beef, Burt." Sheriff Boone held up a paper sack bearing the label of the local diner, What's Your Beef? above the image of a pugnacious steer standing on his hinders, front hooves on his hips.

"Bacon's one of the basic food groups, Linus. Just don't tell my wife. Deb's trying to make me watch my cholesterol and my waist." McGowan lightly patted his flat stomach.

"I hear you. Guess you're stuck more behind the desk than you are outside. Gets that way for me too, sometimes." He handed over a foil wrapped sandwich. "Coffee? Water? "

"I've had your coffee before, Linus. I don't make the same mistakes twice. Don't you have a soft drink machine around here? Where the hell are my taxes going to?"

Boone chuckled. "Take it up with the quorum court. They control my budget." Then he hollered out the office door. "Gabe." The deputy popped his head around the door frame. "I need you to make a drink run." Linus pointed to Burt and raised his eyebrows in the silent query.

"Sprite," said McGowan.

"Bring me a Coke, and make sure the cans are clean this time."

"Clean?" asked McGowan.

Boone unwrapped a sandwich. "Gas station on the corner. Last time whoever stocked had oily hands. Black goo everywhere." He bit into his sandwich, savoring the sweet and spicy flavors. As far as he was concerned, the bun and the beef were just there as an excuse to eat the sauce. "This cold case is going to be a mess, Burt. The boy's parents are dead, the oldest sister hung up on me, and the next oldest is proving impossible to locate. Not to mention, my resources are limited and getting tighter every year."

"So what happens? Do you just bury the poor kid and let it go? Unsolved mystery?"

Boone shook his head. "Nope. The boy deserves justice, and I intend to see he gets it." He punctuated his statement with a big bite of beef. Both men concentrated on their food, each polishing off a sandwich before unwrapping another.

"I know you didn't invite me down here just for supper, Linus. What can I do to help?"

Deputy Wells hustled into the office with two cans of soft drink on a box lid. He set the lid down on the desk and handed a can of Coke to Boone. "Sorry it took so long, boss. Had to wait for someone buying sixteen lottery tickets."

"Thanks, Gabe." Boone reached in his pocket and extracted a pair of bills. "Here."

The deputy took the money and went back to his own desk out front as McGowan reached for the Sprite. Boone pulled the tab on his Coke and took a drink. "I need for you to tell me everything you remember from that night. Hell, from that day and the day before. Who was with the boy when you last saw him alive? Were all the family on friendly terms with each other? Any arguments, plans, gossip. Anything at all."

McGowan took another bite, chewing slowly, chasing it with a drink. Boone watched him with the practiced eye of long years of experience interrogating people. He'd known Burt for years, working several searches together for lost hikers. A quiet man, the Park Super seemed to be arranging his thoughts in a logical order, separating fact from supposition.

"I figured you'd want to know all about that time, so I made some copies of the records. I spent an hour with them in my office, trying to pick my own brain." He pulled a folded legal envelope from his hip pocket and held it up for Boone to see. "Most of the families came in for the reunion on Wednesday. Reuben and Prudence Tanner got in first."

"George's family," said Boone.

"Right." McGowan opened the papers and read from them. "Then Jessup and Daisy Hawley arrived. That's the little girl's family. The other brothers dribbled in during the day." He paused to take a drink. "Benjamin made it in before dark. That pretty much left Martha and John Benton. They arrived early Thanksgiving morning from Eureka Springs." He folded papers and tossed them on Linus' desk

Linus took the copies and studied them. "So these were all brothers and sisters?"

"Yep. I asked one of them. They were the children of Agnes and Noah Tanner."

"And you were there Thursday?"

Burt nodded. "I was the green kid on the staff so I got the holiday duty in the office. I was supposed to work the desk until one o'clock. After that I had the afternoon off. During Thanksgiving morning, a few of the fathers and some of the older kids came in picking up maps to the trails. I didn't see too many of the mothers. Probably all busy doing cooking in their cabins. I remember John Benton, mainly because he looked the least interested of the group. But then he just married into the clan."

Linus looked at the names on the registry copy, noting the Tanners but also the other last names. "Like Jessup Hawley did."

"Correct. Near as I could make out there were three brothers and two sisters. And they had a passel of kids. They were in and out of the office, shrieking at one of the rat snakes in the terrarium. The usual. I can't think of anything out of the ordinary. By one o'clock, I closed up the office and went on home. It looked like I'd be free and clear. There weren't any tent campers in the campgrounds to check up on."

"No tent campers? Nobody in the campground?"

"Nope." Burt looked down and crossed his legs.

"So you were off enjoying your Thanksgiving dinner when the boy and girl went missing? When did you get the call on your radio?"

McGowan picked a piece of bacon out from the remains of the second sandwich.

Boone caught the movements and recognized them as a nervous attempt to avoid the question. "What?" he prompted.

"That was when Deb was pregnant. She was in her first trimester and sick as a dog. She was lucky to keep a can of soup down her on a good day."

Linus searched his memory for any information on Burt and Deb's kids. He came up nearly empty. As far as he knew they had one son somewhere in Colorado. He wondered if that was the child Deb was carrying at the time. It surprised him that he didn't know the answer. Burt looked uncomfortable enough to be reliving bad memories, but Boone read more guilt than sorrow on his face. "Tell me about that hike on Wednesday."

McGowan fished into his hip pocket and pulled out a tattered leather diary with a piece of paper sticking out of it for a bookmark. "I kept a notebook back then. I wrote down the number of people on the hike, age range, the questions they asked, anything interesting we saw, that sort of thing. I think I intended to consult it at some point and use it to improve my talks."

"I take it you don't do that anymore."

"Hell, I quit doing that after four months. I still write down interesting things I've seen, first warbler, stuff like that. That boy, George, is probably why I quit keeping so many details about each hike. He asked more questions than any twenty kids I've had since. I couldn't remember them all to write them down."

"Did your notes give us any clues as to what happened to the boy? Can you tell me who else was on that hike with him?"

McGowan opened the book to the marked page. "No, all I wrote down was two women, one man, and five kids. But the notes do help tickle my memory. Maybe it's because of what happened afterwards, but I can picture them all as clearly as if I'd seen them this morning."

Linus took a pad of paper and a pen from his desk drawer. "Okay, shoot."

Burt leaned back in his chair, eyes closed, hands folded on his stomach. "George addressed both of the women as aunt. And the man was a tall, lanky fellow. A beanpole with limbs. I think he was Isaac. Never said a word, but he had commanding eyes. One of the kids must've been his. I remember him snapping his finger, and that boy towed the line immediately."

"How old was his son?"

"Seven or eight."

"What about the other kids. You said there were five."

"George, of course, and that little girl, Ruthie. Her brother, and some other little boy."

Boone noted the details. "Tell me about Ruthie's brother."

"He was about the same age as George. Maybe a year or two older. He kept making fun of George, calling him a stupid Trekkie, but I got the impression it was good-natured. At least George didn't seem to mind."

"Do you remember the boy's name?"

McGowan closed his eyes again and appeared to concentrate. "I know George called him by name, and I'm trying to re-create the scene in my head. Something with a T. Tim? Tom? I think it was Tom."

Boone made a note on his papers. "I'll check the original files. I think all the family is listed in there. What else you got there in those notes? Do you mind if I make a copy?"

McGowan handed over the leather booklet, his index finger marking the page. "Be my guest. But as you can see there's really not much there."

Boone took the little journal and read aloud. "November 24, 1976. Sunny, 53 degrees. Afternoon hike from nature center up Rocky Crest Trail. Three adults, two women, one man. Five children ranging from preschool to fourteen. One of the boys is named George Tanner. Very intelligent, asking a lot of questions about plants, geology, especially interested in bats. Wants to visit some of the bat caves. Told him they're hibernating. Very persistent. Found one little brown bat fifty yards into the Devil's Larder cave at the top of the trail. Only the man and three boys went in with me."

He flipped past the page and looked at the notes on the top. Burt had recorded finding some bobcat claw marks on a tree and a few white tailed deer tracks closer to the creek. There was nothing regarding the search that night or the next day.

"Gabe," Linus called. When the deputy popped his head in the door, Linus handed him the note book, his finger marking the page. "Make a copy of this page here for me, please."

"What do you remember about that little girl, Ruthie?"

"She was a quiet little creature, as I recall. Wouldn't even make eye contact with me. Maybe four years old. I thought she was George's little sister at first but she called one of the women, Mommy, so I figured she was his cousin. He was good with her. Toted her part of the way on the trail when it got steep. She seemed to cling to George more than to her mother."

"And this Tom, what was he like?"

"I frankly don't remember much about him other than his making fun of George. I guess he didn't make much of an impression on me."

"Sullen?"

"Dull might be more accurate. Certainly wasn't interested in the hike."

Boone made another note. All of the adults had been interviewed at the time the children went missing, he didn't think any of the children had been questioned. At least he didn't remember seeing anything in the file. If he could locate them, he'd see what they remembered. The boys would be easier to locate than the girls. He wouldn't have to deal with married names.

"Anything else about that hike that you remember or about that Wednesday or Thanksgiving, Burt?"

McGowan drained his drink and shook his head. "I only remember that much because of what happened later. We see a lot of people in the park, Linus. Most go in one eyeball and out the other." He set the empty can on the box lid, using it in lieu of a coaster.

"Okay, let's get to the search. If the park office was all locked up, how did the parents notify any of you that the kids were missing?"

"Same as now; emergency contact number on the outside of the office door. The only difference is, today there are phones in each of the cabin. Back then there was just a pay phone outside of the office."

"And the number? Who were they reaching? The sheriff?"

"Nope, the visitor's center actually. But after hours the phone was sent to ring in the park Superintendent's house or, if he was gone, the Assistant Super's house. Now it patches into whoever has the night phone call duty. We rotate it."

"And the Super was close by?"

"McGowan nodded. "The Super always lived next to the visitor's center. Course, now that's the Assistant Super's house. When they built a new home next to the National Park land, we all shifted. My new ranger that you met, she lives in my old house."

"So the Super got the call that night and then radioed the rest of you in your homes. What time was that?"

"I actually got the call on my truck's unit."

"You weren't at home?"

"Deb had fallen asleep so I took a drive through the campground. Like I said there wasn't anybody camping there that night, so I got out of the truck and just spent some time sitting on one of the picnic tables, listening to the evening sounds. I had the unit in the truck on, but I was far enough away that I didn't hear it. It may have been closer to six-thirty when I got the call. But that's all in the original report, Linus."

"Yeah, it is. But you know law enforcement. We have to

document everything twice." Linus looked up from his notes. "About the search. Who was on it? Who else was working as a Ranger back then?"

"Jack Sanford was the Park Super. He's deceased now. I think he took one of the men on the Rocky Crest Trail. They thought the boy might have gone back to see if any of the bats would come out of the Devil's Larder cave there. Charlie Pugh was one of the Rangers. He took some of the other men down to the lake and the dam. Pete Wallace was the Assistant Super. He went on Sugar Run Trail. They had me scouting out the CCC Trail, the amphitheater, and the campgrounds."

"You know how I can reach this Charlie Pugh or Pete Wallace?"

"Pete and his wife retired in eighty-eight and moved to Eureka Springs. I think Charlie took a job over at Devil's Den."

"Wasn't there another ranger there? I seem to recall reading something about a Hodges."

"That would be Russ Hodges. Most people call him Rusty. He was gone that weekend."

Boone detected the edge in Burt's voice, saw the sudden tightening of his jaw. It was clear that there was no love lost between him and Ranger Hodges. "Do you know where?"

"Hunting, so I heard. He hunted every chance he got. Went down to the Ouachita Mountain area."

Linus wondered if that was why Burt didn't like the man. Some rangers didn't approve of hunting. "So he didn't take part in any of the searches?"

"Nope."

"Do you know where he is now?"

"Got a job as a Superintendent in one of the other parks. Don't recall which one. I wasn't exactly interested in keeping up." Burt's words were clipped, his tone and posture suggesting a deep-seated anger. Linus waited, giving Burt a chance to explain or elaborate. He didn't. Linus let it slide. There were other ways of finding out why there was bad blood between the two men.

"Anything you can remember about the search? Something unusual on the part of, oh, say one of the uncles?"

"What I remember are a lot of very worried and desperate people. Especially when the temperature started to drop. The women were crying, and the men were just stoic."

"Well I do thank you, Burt, for taking the time to come in here and talk with me. I can read reports but it helps me see things more clearly just speaking with you. I'll try to run down some of those kids that are grown up now and any of the surviving uncles. See if anybody remembers anything and cross check their stories. The state takes an interest in cold cases when something new breaks open, but it's not going to give me very much time on this one if I don't come up with something soon. Add to that, the crime lab is backed up with work so it could be a while before I get anything specific back on the cause of death. "

"I wish I could help you out more, Linus, but for the life of me, I can't figure out who would've killed that kid. But more than that, why leave that little girl out in the cold to freeze to death? All I can imagine is that there was some tramp wandering through. Some pervert."

"I suppose that's always a possibility." The sheriff stood and extended his hand. "Thanks again Burt. I'll let you know if I need anything else. I appreciate your bringing in those copies."

McGowan shook the sheriff's hand. "Thanks for the sandwiches. I know I shouldn't tell Deb, but I suspect she's going to smell the barbecue sauce and figure it out." He took two steps towards the door.

"Oh!" exclaimed Linus, "I did have another question for you. Two actually."

Burt stopped in mid-stride and turned around. "Yes?"

"The old notes are a little hard to read. Faded typewriter ribbon. Anyway, I can't quite make out the name of the park's office manager from that time."

"That would have been Beulah Ingram, but like I said, she had Thanksgiving off. I was the only one around."

Linus penned the entry in his notebook. "Beulah Ingram. She works part-time at the library, doesn't she?"

"I think so, yeah." McGowan grimaced, put his hand to his chest and belched.

"That barbecue sauce gets me every time, too," said Boone. "But Ms. Ingram was there on Wednesday when some of the others checked in, right?"

McGowan. "You think maybe she overheard something?" He belched again and sidled towards the door.

"Could be. I'll talk to her first chance I get. Right after I run down some of these relatives. Oh, hang on a moment more." He held up an index finger to signal one more thought. "I had some other names I wanted to verify. Sorry."

"No problem, sheriff."

"The store owner. That was?"

McGowan rubbed his hands across his eyes. "That was Tabitha Campbell. Her daughter, Shirley Gracehill, owns the store now. Mrs. Campbell lives in some condo for the elderly I think. She'd be in her eighties by now."

"Housekeeper?"

McGowan let out an exasperated sigh. "Ah, hell, Linus. We had an executive housekeeper and two maids working under her in the winter, but I couldn't tell you who they were. Do you know how many people we've had working in the park since then? Too many of the help has come and gone and their names sometimes go with them. Now if you don't mind, I need to get back to the park and check in before I can get home."

"That's okay, Burt. I may be grasping at straws here. Thanks and say hi to Deb for me."

Boone watched McGowan leave and leaned back in his chair, hands clasped behind his head. He thought about Burt's murder hypothesis, some transient pervert. It had been the seventies and there were the rare instances of Vietman vets wandering about trying to survive as squatters in the Boston Mountains. And while the forest didn't look like a hot jungle, he could imagine one of the less adjusted vets flashing back to

Nam and seeing the kid as a threat.

He ran the scenario in his mind, imagining an overly inquisitive kid hiking and spooking a nervous man. He could see the boy telling the girl to run back to the cabins, only to get lost. The murderer, fearing discovery but facing a personal shame, dragging the boy to this out of the way spot and carefully, respectfully, burying him. It played out but it was too pat. One didn't always need to look too far, and family members were not always innocent. There were enough other people to look into without making up an unknown bogeyman.

With families busy going back and forth between cabins on a holiday, someone could have easily slipped away and come back without being noticed. What had him stumped was why. What motive would anyone have for hitting that boy over the head? He could almost believe it was an accident except for that little girl. Or did she innocently wander off looking for her favorite cousin? No. A child that small didn't wonder that far. Not alone, and not up and down those steep, rocky hills. She'd have tired long before she reached the Woodcutter's Cave. He wasn't sure exactly where that was, but he knew it wasn't close by the cabins.

Linus pulled out his folder on the park, fished out the topographic map and look for the cave. To his surprise it was only a quarter-mile as the crow flies from where they'd found George's body.

"Convenient," he murmured softly. The closeness of the two bodies did a lot to dispel any notion that these were two unrelated, tragic deaths. Had any of the uncles been in the corps?

He had another thought. Any of the rangers would have known about that logging road. Was Hodges hunting that day? Had he been hunting illegally on park land and been seen? He thought about Burt and his unease when questioned about Hodges. He'd been hiding something, Boone was sure of it. He'd also reacted strongly when questioned about the office and housekeeping help. Odd that the man couldn't recall the name of the head housekeeper – someone that he dealt with every day - but he remembered the name of George's male cousin.

Boone pulled an evidence bag from his desk drawer and, using his pen, picked up McGowan's soft drink can and dropped it in the bag. He'd seen what looked like a bloody fingerprint, brown with age, on the boy's belt buckle. He wasn't sure if it was readable, but if Little Rock found a print on the belt buckle, then he'd need to give them prints to check against. Burt was holding something back. In Boone's experience, a man with something to hide was often dangerous.

A minute later, a call came into dispatch about a shooting in the park.

CHAPTER 7

Phoebe took the park's curved roads as fast as she dared without risking a rollover, all the while maintaining radio contact with Assistant Superintendent Bob Sloan. She learned that the call initially came in from campers who reported a man staggering around the campground, waving a gun. By the time Sloan arrived, the man had shot at two sycamores, screaming that the trees were talking about him and planning to kill him.

"I'm at the campground, Bob," Phoebe said. "Where is he now?"

"He just ran into the men's showers by campsite twelve. I'm going to position myself in front of it to hold him in there. This guy's about five bottles short of a six-pack, and unpredictable means very dangerous."

Phoebe raced past a huddle of terrified campers to the campground's upper end. If the pounding in her chest and the nausea was any indication, she felt as frightened as they looked.

"Careful. He's got a gun," shouted a man shepherding a woman and two children in the opposite direction.

She stopped the van next to Sloan's truck and got out, her hand on her holster. She saw Sloan crouched behind the dumpster in front of the facility and ran to him in a crouch.

"Thanks for getting here so fast, Phoebe," Sloan said.

"Burt's in town and Phillips took his wife into Fayetteville. Pierce is working with maintenance at the horse camp on the other end of the park."

"Is this guy holding any hostages inside?" Her hand shook as she unsnapped her holster.

Sloan shook his head. Two men ran out when he went in. They said they were the only ones in there. If there's anyone on the women's side, they're staying put."

"So what do we do?"

Before Sloan could answer, they heard a shout from the restroom. "Stop it! I see you at the window. You think you can get me that way?" Two more shots and the sound of shattering glass followed.

"This guy's got to be strung out on something," said Sloan. "Screaming about trees trying to kill him. That kind of paranoia goes right along with drugs. My money's on meth, and there's no reasoning with that. All we can hope is that he shoots enough to run out of bullets. Then together we can pin him down."

Phoebe struggled to keep her knees from buckling completely. "Hopefully Pierce will be here by then to help," she said.

Sloan shook his head. "Probably not. If they're finishing up on that last washout, he's probably out of radio contact. And if not, it would take him a half hour at least just to get back here."

"Then we should call for the sheriff," she suggested.

"Someone probably has, but, Phoebe, we're the law here."

You're the law. I'm a measly interpreter. What if he doesn't clear his weapon? What then?

She recalled her training for this job and visualized aiming for the center of the human-shaped silhouette, firing repeatedly. Her instructor drummed it into the candidates over and over. "Fire until the assailant drops. None of this 'shoot to wound or warn' crap," he'd said. "You shoot to neutralize the threat and you keep shooting until the threat is down." That was a polite euphemism for 'shoot to kill.'

That was the part that made her sick to her stomach just thinking about it. Surely it wouldn't come to that.

She took a deep breath. "How will we know when he's empty? Did you see what kind of gun he had?"

"No, unfortunately not. But it may be that he'll just pass out in there. If we don't hear anything more from him after a while, we'll go in, weapons drawn. Understand?"

Phoebe nodded. The Assistant Superintendent had been at this job for sixteen years. Surely he had enough experience to keep this from getting ugly. They waited behind the dumpster for another fifteen minutes without hearing any sound from the restroom.

"We're going to go quietly up to the door," said Sloan. "I'm going to try to talk to the guy, see if he's still with us or if he's passed out. Maybe try to talk him out quietly. Are you ready?"

"Yes," she said, feeling anything but.

She gripped her Glock, her left hand cradling the right, and followed Sloan to the brick facility. A woman and a small child poked their heads out of the women's side of the building, and Sloan waved him back inside.

Once outside the men's door, Sloan called in. "Hey, buddy. I'm a park ranger. You all right in there?"

At first all they heard was a low groan. A moment later the man answered. "Are they still out there?"

"Nobody out here but myself and another ranger," said Sloan. "Why don't you toss your gun out the door and then come out?"

"Can't. They'll get me. They're after me."

"Who's after you? I don't see anyone else here."

"Those trees, man. I heard them talking. They're gonna kill me."

"I won't let them," said Sloan. "I'm the Assistant Superintendent of this park. Those trees have to obey me. Otherwise they'll get cut down."

"I don't know, man. They sounded pretty pissed."

"Why are they pissed at you?"

"I don't know." The man's voice quavered, riddled with

fear. "Maybe they're not real trees. Maybe the Feds have experimented on them. Maybe it's all that genetic engineering crap. You know. Pollen blowing around and stuff." His voice rose in pitch. "I'm telling you man. I think they've got animal DNA. They said they were gonna kill me."

"Nobody's experimented with my trees. These are good trees. You can trust me." Sloan softened his voice. "Just toss out the gun. Then the trees will see that you don't mean them any harm."

"They hate me, man."

"It's okay. My partner here has her gun trained on them. Any tree that tries to get you would get hurt. Toss out the gun. Then come out slowly with your hands in the air. I'll get you into my truck and you'll be safe. I'll even drive you out of here."

There was no reply.

"Is it a deal?" Sloan asked.

Another pause. "Okay. I'm gonna come out."

"Toss out the gun first."

Sloan motioned for Phoebe to be ready on the other side of the door. Her palms were slick with sweat and her breathing came in short, ragged bursts.

"Toss out the gun, buddy. That's the only way this will work."

The steel door opened slowly, the hinges squealing. Phoebe shifted right a few steps to clear the door and waited, her shaky legs spread for stability. She saw a young man, possibly in his twenties, hair awry where he'd tugged at it, his clothes covered in filth. His right hand held the door open, a pistol dangling in his left. His eyes twitched nervously from side to side.

Just drop the damn gun!

"That's it," said Sloan softly. "Toss the gun on the ground. It'll be all right."

The man's jaw worked back and forth, as though he was trying to say something. Suddenly he screamed.

"You're in league with 'em. They sent you to kill me." He

raised his left hand, firing once.

Phoebe heard Sloan's sharp cry of pain, saw a dark, wet stain on his right thigh. "Shoot," he yelled. But her finger froze.

Sloan's didn't. He fired repeatedly until the man dropped.

Phoebe turned and retched.

* * *

"Why the hell didn't you shoot?" McGowan ran a hand through his hair and paced in agitated circles. "Sloan could've been killed!"

Phoebe had nothing to say. By now the question was rhetorical. Burt had been asking her that same question for the past ten minutes, ever since the ambulance took the Assistant Superintendent and the dead druggie away.

Her boss stopped and pointed at her. "You've got Sloan's duty for the rest of the week."

"Are you punishing me?" Phoebe asked.

"Punishing you? I'm short a man now. And this will have to get reviewed. My own ass is on the line now. Punishment? I thought I hired a ranger."

She went on the defensive at that. "Burt, you hired me to be an interpreter. I'm supposed to inform people about birds and bunnies, not shoot people."

"You knew full well that the state needed a ranger as well. That this was a combination job. You went for the training eyes open. You can't pick and choose now."

"I'm sorry, Burt. It's just that . . ."

"I'm sorry, too, Palmer. But if you can't handle the full job, then maybe I need to look elsewhere. You're on probation."

CHAPTER 8

"Would you try to find at least one good thing about your new school, Wren?"

Wren, dressed in black nylon cargo pants and black t-shirt with a pink sequined skull on the t's front, swiveled slightly on her diner stool, avoiding eye contact with her mother beside her. Instead she ran her finger around the rim of her water glass. "They're called the squirrels, mom. The squirrels! How lame is that? Nobody calls their mascot the squirrels." She waited for her mother to say something predictable, like 'squirrels are cute and so energetic.' She took a sip of her cola. Here it comes.

"Well, you simply don't mess with squirrels. The little buggers could chew the other team's nuts off."

Wren gasped, her cola spurting up and out her nose. Did her mom really just say that? But ever since her mom came back from that emergency last night, she'd been acting weird, her eyes kind of blank and distant. Wren wondered if she had to shoot that crazy dude. Maybe she accidentally shot the Assistant Super in the thigh. I bet old Burt is pissed at her!

She grabbed a napkin and blew her nose, using the opportunity to recover herself and hide her smile. Wren had no intention of forgiving her mother, not only for making daddy reenlist, but for dragging her out to the middle of some technologically-forsaken forest. Honestly, no cell phone coverage, some ancient antenna that picked up one television station unless the wind was blowing hard, and now this absolutely lame small-town high school.

"I thought you wanted me to go to college. I can't imagine anyone from Wayside Springs managing to graduate from any college. It's one step up from a one-room schoolhouse. It's attached to the freaking grade school."

"They actually have a good program there, Wren. You saw it. Debate, all the sciences, computers better than the one we have. And, yes, everyone gets a lot of one-on-one time with the teachers. Students from there go on and do very well in college. I'll be doing nature programs for the elementary school. Maybe you can help me. Would you like that?"

Wren shrugged, a non-committal gesture that she knew maddened her mother.

"It's almost like a private school with all of the individual attention that you'll be getting," said her mom. "I thought their Arkansas history project looked very interesting. Imagine having students research the county's history for a series of books."

"Oh, yeah," said Wren, her black-painted lips curling in a sneer. "And now I've got homework for this summer because they started this in the eighth grade. Thanks for nothing."

The waitress brought their orders and placed them in front of them. "Here ya go, ladies. A roast beef ranch with coleslaw and a What's Your Beef burger deluxe with fries." She slid a Red Gold ketchup bottle in front of them. "Will there be anything else? Mustard? Mayo?"

Wren shook her head 'no.' Her mother added a verbal "no thank you."

"You're making a wall out of a single brick, Wren. It's not much work at all. You just need to pick a topic and find two sources of information. The rest gets done in school."

"Like I know anything about this stupid county to even pick a topic," said Wren as she grabbed the ketchup bottle and slathered her fries with it. "Everyone else's families lived here for, like, twenty-thousand years. Probably have a family history of hunting mammoths." She shoved a fry in her mouth. They were waffle cut, crispy on the outside, soft on the inside and tasting of salt and grease, just the way Wren liked them. At least this diner isn't a total waste. If it wasn't for the two old geezers on the bench out front, it would be kinda cool.

"It won't be so bad, Wren. This town used to be a very popular health resort back at the turn of the century. Trains brought in a lot of guests. Famous people visited here. After lunch we'll go over to the library and get cards for both of us. The librarian will have ideas. An hour, maybe two at the most, and you should have what you need or at least a good start. If that doesn't work out, we can see what's in the little historical society museum."

"Whatever." Wren attacked her hamburger in an attempt to close the conversation. There was no use arguing with her mother, especially when Wren didn't even really want to talk to her at all. She finished her meal, slurping noisily on her straw whenever her mother started talking, which wasn't often. Twenty minutes and several heavy sighs later, Wren was alone in the library, her mother finally taking the hint and declaring she would come back in two hours.

Two hours. It wasn't very much time, but it would have been an eternity with her mother breathing down her neck making stupid suggestions for topics. Wren already had an idea, one she was sure her mother wouldn't approve of. Somehow that actually made this assignment better.

The building, with its entrance cutting across the corner at an angle, had clearly been a bank in its prime and not a very large one at that. A white-haired woman in a powder blue pantsuit sat in a plush armchair, perusing a book on gardening with wildflowers. Behind her, a flight of narrow stairs led to a mezzanine crammed with bookshelves. At the base of the stairs were two rods, hung with newspapers, like flags. The librarian sat hunched over a stack of books at the main desk. When Wren first saw her, she thought she looked like she could well have been one of the bank's original tellers, but discovered that her face was merely sun-hardened making her look like a dried apricot.

Wren continued her survey of the library, mildly surprised to see new computers against one wall. Next to them was a handmade poster listing "Teen Summer Fun Projects." Wren scanned the list: sketching, knitting, scrapbooking, photography, teen book talk. The sketching sounded remotely interesting but she imagined some perky leader having them draw fruit bowls. She moved on to the magazine rack. Seventeen, Cobblestone, Boys' Life, American Girl. The choices stunk but she didn't expect them to carry anything like Night Walkers or Gravesite anyway. She'd get her grandparents to subscribe to those for her.

She ignored the Summer Fun Project's brochures and turned her attention to the polished granite walls. Wren ran her palm across one, feeling the coolness, and wondered if that's what a headstone felt like. She decided she preferred black marble instead. A slight snort from a dark, secluded corner startled her and she turned to see an aged man wearing house slippers asleep in a wingback chair. Another old man with wisps of white down fluttering atop his head sat in a second chair, having a quiet conversation with the wall.

Aren't there any young people in this place? At least the librarian had been friendly enough. Wren found herself drawn back to the woman.

"Did your mother abandon you?" the librarian asked.

"It's hard to work with her around," said Wren.

Apricot Woman nodded, the soft blue-gray curls atop her head fluttering. "Mothers can be like that. So you're new to our community? I imagine you're disappointed, too. I can read it in your eyes. It's hard living out at the park. I know. I used to work there."

Wren felt the woman's gaze run across her, like she was being wave scanned at the airport, her innermost thoughts exposed. Before she could think of something suitable to say in reply, the librarian took her hand and patted it.

"Don't worry," she said. "Everyone is welcome at the library. It's the last bastion of egalitarianism. You should sign up for some of the classes. Meet some young people. We do have them, you know, though you can't tell by today." She shoved a brochure in Wren's hand.

Wren jerked her head back, wondering if the woman had read her earlier thoughts. "I'm supposed to do some report. For the school's history project."

"So your mother said. Good for you, getting a jump on it. What's your name, again?"

"Wren Palmer."

"How pretty. I'm Beulah Ingram. You may call me Beulah. Do you have any idea what sort of topic you might be interested in?"

Wren licked her black painted lips. "Yes. I want to write about a murder."

* * *

Burt McGowan regretted several things. Eating those two sandwiches in the Sheriff's office last evening was one of them. He'd been into the antacids most of the night, and Deb was furious at him for it. More than that, he regretted trying to keep the cause of his heartburn from his wife. She would've been less angry if he'd just admitted to eating the sandwiches to begin with, rather than trying to pretend he hadn't. Deb was a stickler for honesty, and one of these days he'd remember it.

He also regretted telling the Sheriff that there hadn't been any campers in the park that night. He saw how Boone looked at him when he told him he'd patrolled the campground and sat and watched the sky. What if he found out that there'd been a couple in an Airstreamer in the campgrounds? It wouldn't be hard either. Verl and Vivien Keck still made regular visits to the park during the summer, sometimes acting as campground host and hostess.

And what if he checks the desk records that I gave him against any copy already in his files? What if he talks to the executive housekeeper. He never knew if Ruby suspected anything or not. She still lived in Wayside Springs.

He felt another pang in his chest and reached into his pocket to unwrap a couple of antacids chews. Somehow he didn't think the sandwiches and hot barbecue sauce were entirely to blame. It was the situation. It came on him when they'd found the Tanner boy's skeleton. Every mistake, every action from thirty-five years ago kept replaying in his head. By the time he'd left the sheriff's office early last evening, he felt like a pack of dogs were closing in on him. That meth-crazed shooter didn't help either and he'd roared at Ranger Palmer when he found out she hadn't even fired one shot in defense of Sloan. He purposely avoided looking for her today, too. At least Sloan's injury was superficial. He'd be back at his desk tomorrow.

The park office phone rang, and Burt started. From the desk inside his personal office he heard his office manager, Sherry Tucker, cheerfully greet someone on the other end of the line. He listened carefully for a moment, waiting for her to call to him. She didn't. Instead she recited campground fees.

Why did they have to find the boy? I never should have hired that woman.

CHAPTER 9

"A murder? My dear, I don't know that we've had any murders to write about."

"There was a kid that disappeared a long time ago. A boy."

"Do you know when . . ?" The librarian stopped. "Oh, you must mean George Tanner. I heard that your mother found him. She didn't say much when I asked her about it. I suspect it will be in tomorrow's newspaper, though. But that wasn't a murder. The boy and his little cousin went hiking and got lost."

"There was a cousin, too?" Wren couldn't believe her luck. She actually knew next to nothing about the skeleton her mother found, only that it was a boy her age. But by pretending to have information, she managed to trick this woman into revealing what she knew, including the boy's name and the existence of a second victim."

"Yes, a little simple-minded girl named Ruthie Hawley. They found her frozen to death outside of one of the caves in the park, poor little thing. She probably died in her sleep waiting for George to come out of the cave, only he never did."

Wren leaned over, bracing her hands on the desk. Her voice dropped to a conspiratorial whisper. "He never went into the cave."

62

"He never. . . ? Are you certain?"

Wren nodded, enjoying the old woman's interest. "I know because my mom found the skeleton yesterday somewhere on Dead Man's Trail."

Beulah looked around the room as though to make certain no one else could overhear them. The elderly man in the plush reading chair appeared to be dozing, his companion chatting with the wall. "But why do you think he was murdered? He could have died somewhere on the trail. It got awfully cold that night as I recollect."

"I overheard that the Park Super had to go in to see the sheriff last night. Now why would he have to do that unless the kid was murdered, and they were investigating?" It was a wild supposition, and Wren knew it. She was betting on Beulah buying into it.

"Of course Sheriff Boone would need to speak with Superintendent McGowan," countered Beulah. "There doesn't need to be any suspicion of foul play. A body was found in the park, and Burt is in charge of the park. There are always reports to be filed even with accidental deaths." Her eyes took on a far-away look. "I worked at the park back then. I was the office manager. I wonder if someone from the paper will interview me?"

"So you were there when it happened?"

Beulah shook her head, no. "I had Thanksgiving day off, but I was there the Wednesday before and the Friday after. It was on Friday that they found the little girl."

"Then you can help me with my report. There must be newspaper stories about it."

"Newspapers, yes, but you'd want to interview people, and I don't even know if any of the Tanners are still alive. That Tanner family!" Ingram sucked in her breath. "Now they were an odd bunch. Did you know that they had their own church and it was headed up by a woman?"

"Really?" Wren felt a twinge of curiosity. "Wasn't that, like, kinda odd back then?"

"A little, but from all I ever heard, Agnes Tanner was a very remarkable woman. Now she would be someone to write about for your report. You should focus on her, not two accidental deaths. I know a woman that knew her personally. Her name is Viola Hargitt and she lives at the old rectory now. She's also very interesting. She knows all about herbs and medicine. Many, many years ago when Burt was doing your mother's job, he talked to her about herbs for medicine and food. I think he was doing a program on it. I'll tell your mother about her."

Wren felt her initial plans start to crumble. For a moment, she had this woman interested in what Wren was sure was a murder, maybe two. Then, as quickly as March weather, the librarian changed. Writing about a stuffy woman preacher did not appeal to Wren anymore than writing about some old weed woman.

"You don't want to talk to Miz Hargitt," said the white-haired woman who'd been sitting in the plush chair. She'd set her gardening book aside and walked over to join them.

"Wren," said Beulah, "This is Mrs. Campbell. She used to own the park store. Now her daughter runs it. And this," she said indicating Wren, "is Wren Palmer. Her mother is a new ranger-interpreter at the park."

Mrs. Campbell extended her hand and smiled. "How do you do, Wren? So nice to meet you."

Wren took her hand, surprised at the strength of the woman's grip. She'd expected something clammy and cold. If this town didn't produce anything else, it sure had its share of healthy old women. "You're Shirley's mom?" Wren blurted out. "I work for her."

"I am. And I take it that the store isn't going under at the moment if you work there," Mrs. Campbell said. "I ran that store for nearly thirty years, but just try to give her a bit of advice and see where it gets you." She nudged Wren with her elbow. "You know, technically, I still own that store. Didn't know you worked for me, did yah?" She chuckled. "I could fire my daughter, except I kind of enjoy being retired."

Ingram frowned. "Yes, but I don't understand why you say

that Wren shouldn't see Ms. Hargitt. She's still alive, isn't she, Ms. Campbell?"

Mrs. Campbell flapped a hand in the air dismissively. "Oh, she's alive, but she's crazy as a bedbug from what I hear. Comes from living alone in the woods half your life." She grinned and winked at Wren. "I doubt you'd get any sense out of her and if she confused her herbs, you could get worse. Some of that stuff'll set you loose outa both ends." She laughed, then spied the clock. "Oh, look at the time. I've got a card game to get to. We play Hearts cutthroat style. Nice to meet you, Wren." She waved and hurried out of the library.

"She's funny," said Wren. "I like her. I like Shirley, too."

"Oh, they're a couple of characters," said Ingram. "Fight like cats and dogs, though. You know mothers and daughters, right? Mrs. C. can't admit that her daughter knows how to run the park store. But I still think either Agnes Tanner or Ms. Hargitt would make a fine topic for you."

"But wouldn't someone else in the town already be writing about this Agnes Tanner? She's probably got grandchildren or great-grandchildren running all over the place."

"Not so many anymore," said Beulah. "After Agnes quit running the church, the family drifted apart. That's why they had that big reunion back then. I don't know that any of the great-grandkids are attending our school. Don't think any even live in the state."

"Then who am I supposed to talk to?" Wren had to own that she was curious about this unusual woman. But more than that, she was realizing that the only way she was going to find out about what happened to the two dead kids was to learn about them indirectly, by researching their family. If only she could be certain that she'd find out something good. *If I don't then I'm going to have to start over again for this stupid project.*

Another idea elbowed its way to the forefront. *Figure out how to get out of this hick dump and you won't have to do this stupid report.*

"I don't know," Wren said. "I really wanted to write about

something more exciting than a female preacher."

Beulah leaned forward and beckoned Wren to move in closer. "You want something exciting? Did you know Agnes' father was speared on a pitchfork?"

Wren was sold. "Where should I start?"

"Come with me," said Ingram. "With the death of Agnes's father. I think that was in nineteen-thirty-seven."

* * *

"Your call's on line four, sheriff. She sounds pissed."

Boone took a deep breath, preparatory to punching the phone button.

"Mrs. Keefe? This is Sheriff Linus Boone in Wayside Springs over in Caddo County."

"I know what damn county Wayside Springs is in. I lived there long enough. What the hell are you harassing me for?"

"Ma'am, I apologize if my first call and the two messages sounded like harassment. I assure you this is important. It's about your family. Am I correct that your maiden name was Tanner, and your parents were Reuben and Prudence Tanner?"

Linus listened to a long pause and wondered if she was going to hang up on him again.

"That's right." The voice came through with less certainty now, the bluster replaced by a nervous edge.

"Well, Mrs. Keefe, I called because I have news about your brother. We found him."

"You found George? Where is he? Wait . . ."

Linus heard the faint glimmer of hope disappear as reality set in. Another long pause followed and he imagined the woman struggling to accept the truth. He didn't keep her waiting.

"We found his body, ma'am."

* * *

"This folder has everything connected with the Tanner family. Obituaries, news stories, photos." Beulah cradled the worn manila folder in her left arm and opened it. "But I'm surprised that there is so little in here. There should be a record of her mother's death. I could have sworn I'd seen an obituary for Rachel Elwood in here."

Beulah gently shuffled through the remaining papers. "Ah. Here's an article about Agnes' father's death. August, nineteen thirty-seven. Very tragic. Pierced by a pitchfork. Tsk tsk." She set the yellowed news clipping on a table.

The thought of some man getting skewered on a pitchfork like a shish kabob had caught Wren's attention. She snatched up the paper and read aloud.

"Reverend Joshua Elwood died tragically last Sunday evening. The pastor of the Church the Blessed Carpenter had returned home from the evening prayer service and was unsaddling his horse. The details are not known, but it appears that the animal, a sturdy beast, shied and pushed Reverend Elwood. He fell backwards into a pitchfork which pierced his lungs. The minister was found by his daughter, Agnes, who came running to the barn when she heard his scream. His wife, Rachel Elwood, was away at the time, tending to a parishioner with a new baby. Deacon Noah Tanner will assume the mantle of Reverend for the church."

Wren set the article aside. Gruesome, yes, but the fact that it was an accident disappointed her. She was on the hunt for a crime.

"I don't think Mrs. Elwood took the news well," said Beulah. "It shocked her out of her senses from what I recall hearing, though she lingered for nearly a decade after that. I'll have to find out what happened to her mother's obituary notice." The librarian spoke more to herself than to Wren. "And there should be one for her father, too, not just this article. I think I know where I can get another copy to replace the one that's supposed to be in there."

Wren only half-listened. She'd become engrossed at the moment in another clipping. It showed a young woman in a frumpy, flowered dress handing a slice of pie to a man dressed in what looked like heavy blue jeans and a denim work shirt. The caption read, Ministering to the workers at Dead Man Hollow. Agnes Elwood, daughter of Reverend Joshua Elwood, offers a piece of homemade pie to Ben Owen, chief mason for the Civilian Conservation Corps.

The man, who wasn't bad looking, clearly seemed more interested in the girl than in the pie. Agnes, who might have been pretty if she wasn't wearing that feed sack excuse of a dress, looked equally interested in this Ben. In the background stood a middle-aged man garbed in black trousers and a jacket. His dour expression suggested that he didn't approve of the way Ben and Agnes were looking at each other.

"I'll bet seeing that in the paper set her old man into a fit," said Wren, fishing for some dirt. "Look at how she's looking at this guy."

"What? Oh, the photo? The church groups all used to provide for the men at the work camp. My eldest sister met her husband that way. This was seen as charity."

Yeah, right. Wren looked at the man's eyes again. He'd take her charity for sure. "I don't know," she persisted. "The old man looks pretty mad."

Beulah took the clipping from Wren and studied it. "Hmmm, that man in the background isn't Reverent Elwood. That's Deacon Noah Tanner."

"That's Tanner?" said Wren a little too loudly for a library. From where she stood, she saw that the old man, who'd been dozing comfortably in the big chair, had stirred and was staring at her. His companion began pacing in her direction, continuing his conversation with an invisible somebody. Wren dropped her voice a notch and pointed to the photo. "Isn't that this Agnes' married name? Did she actually marry that guy?"

Beulah nodded. "Noah Tanner took over as minister immediately after Reverend Elwood died. He and Agnes married shortly after that, too."

"But I thought you said that she became the minister?" This was looking less and less interesting to Wren. Bake sales, stuffy ministers, backwoods communities; none of it was what Wren had in mind. She looked up at the clock. Her mother wouldn't be back for over an hour. Maybe she could just skip out and go back to the What's Your Beef Diner for a Coke.

"She did become the minister, after her husband died. He maybe died in nineteen forty-nine, fifty? Anyway, his obituary should be in here somewhere. I'll leave you to look at the folder. If you want to make copies, the machine is over there." She pointed to the back wall. "It's ten cents a copy."

Wren thumbed through the few remaining collection of newspaper notices for potluck dinners to benefit polio victims or some other charity. "Hey, there's no obituary for Agnes Tanner either."

"What? I'll take a look at the folder later and see if I can figure out what's missing."

They were interrupted by the aged wanderer's conversation. "You're right, Roosevelt was a good man, but it was Eleanor that really cared for us poor folk."

"Oh, dear," said Beulah. "Now Mr. Henries," she cooed. "You must sit down." She guided him to a chair nearby. "Will you watch him for a moment, Wren?"

Wren's eyes opened wide in horror. "What? I don't know anything--"

"Just talk to him, or listen and nod while he talks. I need to call the care home for someone to pick him up."

"Don't they know he's here?"

"Mr. Henries and his friend sit in the garden on a sunny day and sometimes they take it in their head to go for a walk or for ice cream at the diner. Usually Mr. Henries is pretty lucid, and we don't mind, but sometimes, he likes to argue about who started the Civilian Conservation Corps." She dropped her voice to a whisper. "I think he has a soft spot for Mrs. Roosevelt."

Beulah scurried to her desk and picked up the phone. Wren faced the old man and smiled weakly. The only old people she'd ever known were her grandparents and they were still relatively youthful in their sixties. Here you couldn't take a step without tripping over a geezer. "Hello," she said to the old man. She hoped the people from the home came soon. Wren wanted to make her copies before her mom got here. Not that there was much here to copy.

"Hello," replied Mr. Henries. "Do you know Eleanor?"

"Um, no." A thought came to her. "Do you know Agnes Tanner?"

"Girl. Come here."

Wren leaned back and peered around the shelf at the other old man in the slippers, the one that she'd awakened when she'd spoken too loudly. Something about him looked vaguely familiar. "What?" she asked.

"You want to be careful," he said.

Wren nodded, wondering how many of these old men had escaped. "Okay. Uh, why?"

"Looking for Tanner is dangerous. He's the devil incarnate."

CHAPTER 10

In the course of his seven-year career as sheriff, Boone had contacted six people to tell them that someone in the family was dead. Once was for a teenager who'd been driving too fast after a party, another had been someone's husband who'd been shot in a hunting accident. Elderly heart attack victims rounded out much of the list. His most recent came a year ago when a mail carrier told him that an old man hadn't picked up his mail for three days. Boone had made that call to a son living in California. It was no easier breaking the news over the telephone than in person. He knew he'd never get used to those long pauses where the party struggled to grasp the reality. He waited patiently through another one now.

"When?" the woman at the other end finally asked.

The question could have meant a couple of things. Boone answered both. "We found his remains two days ago near a hiking trail. He'd probably been dead since the day he went missing. Mrs. Keefe, I'd like to drive down to Shreveport and talk to you in person." He glanced at his watch, did the mental calculation for drive time. I could be there this evening."

Elverna Keefe agreed to see him around six-thirty. After five and a half hours of driving down US 71 and a couple of quick burgers at a fast food place, Boone pulled his Tahoe up to an aging ranch house and was ushered into the Keefe's living room.

The room and the furniture resembled Mrs. Keefe; clean but worn out. Boone sat on the edge of a faded lazy boy facing Elverna and Jaspar Keefe seated on the tattered sofa. A chipped plate of Oreos sat on a fifties-style coffee table next to a mug of coffee.

"Is George's body still in the truck? Should we get him to the funeral parlor?" asked Mrs. Keefe.

"I'm sorry, Mrs. Keefe," said Boone. "Your brother's remains are in Little Rock with the State Crime Lab. But I can have them released to you as soon as they've finished with him."

"I don't understand," she said, reaching for her husband's hand. "Why would he have to go to a crime lab? Didn't he just get lost and freeze to death like cousin Ruthie?"

"No, ma'am. It appears that George suffered an injury."

Elverna's right hand jerked up to her mouth, her left hand clutching her husband's. "Oh, my sweet lord," she said.

"Sheriff," asked Keefe, "are you saying that George fell on the trail and hurt himself? Or that someone struck him?" His wife gasped again.

"Well, Mr. Keefe, that's why his remains are in Little Rock. They'll determine that. But until I do know otherwise, I have to treat this as a homicide. I know this is difficult for you, but I need to ask you about George and the family. Try to get a picture of who'd want to hurt the boy."

"We always sort of hoped he'd just run away," said Keefe. "At least Elverna did. Me? I never held out much hope."

"George talked about running away?" asked Boone.

Mrs. Keefe shook her head. "No. It was just wishful thinking. What do they call it? Projecting your own thoughts?"

Keefe squeezed his wife's hand again and then released it. "You see, sheriff, Elverna's grandpappy, Noah Tanner, was a real piece of work. Do you know he had the church painted red as soon as he took over? Said it reminded him of the blood of the lamb. He was real strong on Paul's statement that wives be submissive to their husbands but somehow he always neglected Paul telling husbands to love their wives as their own body. Big on the Old Testament admonition about sparing the rod and spoiling the child, too. For a preacher, he clean forgot all about what our Lord taught. How his wife survived was beyond me. It was a blessed thing for Grandma Agnes when her husband died. Anyway, my father-in-law learned from the master and when Reuben went on a bender . . . well let's just say it was best for all concerned to hide."

"What about Ruthie's parents?" asked Boone.

Mrs. Keefe shrugged. "Aunt Daisy drank and when she did, she yelled. That woman could screech and curse to make the devil blush. I think she took the switch to the kids sometimes, but most times they could outrun her. But Uncle Jessup? There weren't no harm in him. I think he may have started drinking to cope with his wife, but he'd just pass out quiet like."

"Ruthie was found holding a teddy bear," said Boone. "Someone loved her."

"Didn't come from her parents. What didn't go to booze went to food. More than likely it came from George," said Keefe. "Right honey?"

Mrs. Keefe nodded. "It sounds like something George would do. He was such a good soul, but I don't know where he'd have found the money. I don't think he had a paying job."

"Was all your family this way?"

"Some more'n others. The youngest of Grandma Agnes' kids came out better'n the others. Grandma Agnes was a saint and as long as she was around, we were safe, but once she started to decline . . ." She raised her hands in a gesture of hopeless surrender. "I always thought my father would be the death of one of us." She pulled a tissue from a box and wiped her eyes. "Maybe he was."

* * *

The paddle boat bobbled alongside the dock as the two boys scrambled inside. The oldest, a teenager, used his life vest as a seat cushion.

"Hey," called Wren, "You have to wear the vest like I showed you. Look at your little brother. He's got it right."

"Ah, chill, Lady Dracula," said the kid. "It messes with my tan. Just cause you'd probably die if you stayed out in the sun too long, doesn't mean I can't. Besides, I can swim. Come on, cast off our line so we can get going."

Wren folded her arms across her chest. "Yo, butt-for-brains, you're not going anywhere until you have that vest on correctly. Geez! If my boss sees that I let you go without it, I'll get fired." She hadn't intended to work once she got back from town, but her mother seemed to think that just hanging around was one step shy of delinquency.

"Come on, Danny," whined the little brother. "Put the vest on before Mom and Dad see you and make us both quit."

"All right, all ready." The boy yanked the bright orange vest over his head and snapped the buckle in front. "Satisfied?"

Wren unlocked the paddleboat's rope from the dock and tossed the line to the boys. "You've got it for one hour." She watched them backpedal from the dock, the younger boy striving to keep up with his brother, before she turned and walked back to the store.

"Hey, Shirley, we may have to keep an eye on those guys. The older one'll probably have his life vest off as soon as he sees I'm not looking." Not getting an answer, Wren stopped and looked around the store. Her boss was nowhere in sight which meant she was probably in the back office. A quick scan told her there were no customers waiting. She went to the map rack and reorganized the ones put in the wrong slot by browsing customers. "Shirley?" she called, raising her voice. "I wanted to ask you what you know about that dead kid my mom found."

Wren heard movement in the office behind her and turned, colliding with a man in blue jeans and a white t-shirt. "Sorry, mister."

"Not a problem. My fault." His voice had a soft, nearly undetectable southern accent, coming out only in the word 'my' which sounded more like 'mah' to Wren's ears. For northwest Arkansas, it wasn't unusual.

Wren moved aside to let him pass, wondering who he was that Shirley allowed him into her little office. Thinking he might be her boss' boyfriend, Wren sized him up. Decent butt, strong shoulders, well-muscled, not bad looking in a rugged old-guy sort of way. With his little chin cleft and the gray hairs at the temple, he reminded her of some of those older movie stars like Peck or Clooney that her mom preferred. Somehow, Shirley didn't seem his type.

"Catch you later, Shirl," he said.

"Bye, Joe."

"Who was that?" asked Wren when her boss came out of the back room.

"Joe? He's a contractor. Did you get those two boys off okay? Are they wearing their pfd's?"

"Yeah, but I had to make the older one put on his. My bet is he's got it off already."

"Well, if he falls in and drowns himself now, that's his fault. All I care is that they had it on before you let them paddle off. Otherwise the family could sue us."

"Really?" Wren was a little taken aback by Shirley's callous remark. She'd assumed that her boss was so insistent on the kid's wearing the life preservers because she didn't want to see anyone get hurt.

"Now what were you hollering about when you came back in here just now?" asked Shirley.

"I was wondering what you knew about that kid mom found. The skeleton?"

"Why would I know anything about that?"

"But weren't you here when that kid disappeared? I thought this was your mom's store."

"It was, but I lived in Little Rock."

Wren frowned. "You didn't come home for Thanksgiving?"

"Sure I did, but why would I come here? For one, the store was closed. For another, I didn't get in until Thursday morning. I went to mom's house."

"I met your mom at the library today. She's funny."

"Oh?" Shirley cocked her head and studied Wren. "Why are you so interested in this dead kid anyway? Is this part of that whole fascination with death that teenagers seem to have?"

Wren saw Shirley's eyes focus on her black t-shirt and leather choker and felt her defenses rise. "You sound like my mom. How should I know what other teenagers are fascinated with?"

"Well, to answer your question, Wren, I don't know anything more about that boy than he disappeared around thirty-five years ago on Thanksgiving. Kids do silly things." She pointed towards the lake. "They go off into boats without life preservers and into the woods without telling anyone where they're going. Poor kid must have fallen and hit his head on a rock or something." She handed a stack of bandanas to Wren. "Here, see what you can do with these so that they catch people's eye and make them want to buy some."

Wren took the bandanas and thumbed through them. To her surprise, they were each stamped with a sketch of the park showing the dam, the lake, campgrounds, and the most popular trails. A little canoe dotted the lake along with a smiling, jumping fish. Cartoon raccoons, deer, chipmunks, and various birds made up the border. "These are kind of fun," she said.

"Glad you like them, cause your mom bought one for you. And quit focusing on the dead kid. It's not healthy."

* * *

When the phone rang in Phoebe's living room, the last person she expected to hear on the other end was also the one she least wanted to talk to, her mother-in-law. "Hello," she said, waiting to hear one of the ranger's wives on the other end.

"We have to talk."

Probably wondering why Wren hasn't called them.

Phoebe's cabin came equipped with a land line but in order for her to dial out of the area code, she needed a calling card. Next month, she hoped to sign up with a phone provider, but it was not in her immediate budget.

"Oh, hello to you, too, Fran. I'm fine, thank you."

"Don't get cute with me. I'm calling because we think Wren should come and spend a week with us."

"You just spent three months with her while I did my training."

"And it's a good thing we were around to care for her. Imagine, running off like that to shoot guns. Nonsense."

"I'm a park ranger, Fran. I had to get training to get my law-enforcement commission. I didn't abandon my daughter, so quit worrying about her. As a matter of fact, she even has a part-time job here." She put her mouth over the speaker and called for Wren. "Honey, would you please set the table?"

"Still," said Fran, "we think this move has been hard on the child and we think she should spend some time with us in a real home. Not some shack in the woods."

Phoebe sighed and sank down onto the floor, knees drawn up. "We don't live in a shack. This is a very lovely, modern home. I even have indoor plumbing and a microwave oven." And it might not be mine much longer. Probation!

"Very funny, but--"

"But nothing, Fran. You and Jack should come here if you want time with Wren. You could see for yourself that's she's in a good house. But she's never going to adjust to living here if you keep hauling her off to Fayetteville. Give her a chance for Pete's sake."

"You know, we have rights as grandparents, Phoebe."

"Yep. The right to come visit. I've got a pull out couch and I'll even sleep on it and give you two my room when you come. But Wren's not leaving here until she's settled into the park and her new school. Especially," she added in a lower voice, "after you encouraged all this Goth crap. We'll visit you over Christmas. Now if you don't mind, I've got to get supper and then do an evening program. Good-bye."

She hung up before her mother-in-law had a chance to argue her point any more.

How two such odious people could have raised anyone like Charles is beyond me.

She just hoped Wren hadn't eavesdropped on this end of the conversation.

* * *

"Plug the projector in for me please, Wren." Phoebe hunkered over an old laptop, searching for a Power Point file.

Once again the girl wore unrelieved in black; a gangly crow in pigtails. Phoebe refused to buy those clothes for her daughter but her in-laws seemed to relish their granddaughter's rebellion with a full checkbook. Just the thought of Fran's insistence on Wren visiting them made the hairs on the back of her neck tingle like a riled junkyard dog. Phoebe quickly scanned the images in the laptop's file, refreshing her memory while she tried to ignore her daughter's exasperated sighs.

Wren crawled under a table to plug in the projector. Phoebe heard the machine hum to life and mentally calculated how long before the bulb glowed and she could see how the images looked on the far wall.

"Thank you, sweetie. I don't know what I'd do without you." Phoebe smiled at Wren who returned the compliment by turning her back. Phoebe decided not to take the bait. "I'm really glad that you found a topic at the library that interests you. What's this woman's name again?"

"Agnes Tanner."

Phoebe shuddered. When she'd picked up Wren from the library, her daughter told her that she was going to write about a woman preacher. But Wren hadn't given the woman's name. What was it about that name that made her react so strongly? Then it came to her. Tanner was that dead boy's last name. She wondered if Wren knew. "What made you pick her? Aside from the fact that Mrs. Ingram suggested her?"

Wren shrugged. "I told you I don't know anything about this place. How was I supposed to pick a topic on my own? I asked Beulah--"

"Beulah? Wren, you can't go around calling your elders by their first names."

"She told me I could. Jeez! What is your problem?"

Phoebe held her tongue. It wouldn't do any good to

provoke her daughter, not when she'd actually volunteered two sentences towards an answer. "Well, then, what did Beulah tell you about this lady?" The projector light came on, and she studiously avoided looking at Wren lest the girl take it as a challenge. Instead, she called up her first image and concentrated on moving the projector farther back to enlarge the picture of a great horned owl. The banner across the photo read: Creatures of the Arkansas Night.

"She said she was some sort of preacher or something like that."

"Well, that is interesting." Phoebe relaxed a fraction. At least her daughter didn't know of any connection to the dead boy. Maybe there wasn't any. The name might be as common as tadpoles in a spring pond. "Do you think you can get enough information on her for a report?"

Wren shrugged, then poked the mouse, advancing the slide show to an image of a bat.

"You, know," said Phoebe, "Ms. Ingram called the office this afternoon and left a message for me. She said there's a woman named Viola Hargitt that I should take you to see at someplace she called the old rectory. I asked Shirley if she knew her, but she said she wasn't sure. But Mrs. Tucker took the message, and she said that my boss used to ask this lady about using wild plants and stuff for his nature program. She's actually on the next ridge south. Would you like to meet her? Maybe she'd be better for your report."

"Did Beulah say why I should talk to her?"

Phoebe could feel Wren watching her for a reaction, waiting for her to pounce on the familiar use of Ms. Ingram's first name. It was a challenge along with Wren's implicit dismissal of her mom's help. Phoebe didn't take it. "No. She didn't. Maybe she knew your preacher lady? That would be interesting. And I'd be interested in learning about herbal lore. We could go together."

She decided not to press the issue too much. Often Wren quit doing things as soon as Phoebe showed any interest. It was like trying to catch a cat. Sometimes, if you ignored them, they got curious and came to you.

"Anyway if you talked to her, you might not have to spend too much time in the library."

"Yeah, about that," said Wren. "I'm still going to need to go into Wayside Springs."

Phoebe clicked through the next dozen slides, checking on the pictures of fox, opossums, and raccoons. "I'm sure I can get you there again. I'll have another morning off next week."

"That won't work."

Phoebe clicked on a picture of a flying squirrel. "Why not?"

Wren started to roll her eyes in her usual exasperated manner then stopped. It was the first exhibit of self-control from her daughter in weeks, and Phoebe waited hopefully for Wren's next words.

"There are teen classes at the library. I wanted to take the one on drawing." She fished into her back pocket and pulled out a folded up brochure. "See."

Phoebe stifled an enthusiastic outburst and the urge to hug her daughter. "Oh?" Her brain scrambled to come up with a solution. Somehow she'd make this work. "When are the classes?"

Wren opened the brochure and ran her finger down the list. "Uh, Tuesday and Thursday afternoons. They started this week already."

"This Thursday?" asked Phoebe?

Wren nodded. "I missed the first one on Tuesday, but Beulah said it was mostly just introductions."

"Ranger Phillips' wife works in town. I could drive you in on my lunch break and maybe she wouldn't mind bringing you home. Would that work? You might have to stay at the library longer than you'd planned. It would mean changing your work schedule at the store."

Wren shrugged, her head turned so that a flop of purplish-black bangs hid her eyes. "S-okay. Like maybe I could get more information for that school paper while I'm in town.

Gotta be better than hanging out here."

Phoebe couldn't wait. What if her daughter changed her mind between now and when they got home? As she'd told Shirley, Wren could go from apathy to angst in zero point five seconds.

"Let's find out." She pulled her portable radio from her belt. "Phoebe Palmer calling for Marsha Phillips. You there, Marsha?"

The radio crackled. "Hi, Phoebe. What's up? Did you get your land line yet?"

"Next month. Hey, I wanted to ask a favor. Wren needs to go to the library in town on Tuesdays and Thursdays starting tomorrow. There's a sketching class, and she's also catching up on a school report. I can take her to town at noon, but I can't get her home."

"I can bring her home. She can stop by the bank. What's she doing her report on?"

"Some woman preacher. Agnes Tanner."

"Tanner? Any relation to that dead boy you found?"

Ah hell! If Wren didn't make the connection before, she would now. Phoebe glanced at Wren who seemed to be intently studying the image of a flying squirrel. "Don't know."

"It's fine by me. Just have her stop by the bank sometime before four. I don't leave for another fifteen minutes, but the doors are locked to the public at four.

"Thanks, Marsha. I owe you."

"Bake me a pie."

"Will do. Phoebe out." She slid the portable unit on to her belt and ran her hand across her waist, tugging the belt into place. "You're good to go, girl," she said. "And considering everyone in the park can eavesdrop on any of our calls, if anyone else knows something about this Agnes Tanner, they'll probably let you know. They're a pretty helpful group of people."

"Somebody I met at the library will help me," said Wren. She clicked back to the opening slide.

Phoebe was about to reply when a family of five came

into the meeting room. "Welcome to the evening program," she said. "I'm Ranger Phoebe and this evening we're going to talk about creatures of the night."

To the side, Phoebe watched as her daughter's eyes shone with an anticipation she couldn't credit solely to a lecture on night animals. *What is she up to now?*

CHAPTER 11

"How was your trip yesterday?" Grace Leawood, Boone's office manager, leaned against the door jam, arms folded across her chest. "Productive?"

Boone plopped into his chair and surveyed the pile of paperwork. Grace had taken over the administrative job at the same time he became sheriff, and had been responsible for the department's solvency by tackling the back fines. A slim, petite woman with deep, coffee skin and short, wavy black hair, she packed more determination into her small frame than most people Boone met. She and her husband, Gil, a successful lawyer, moved here from Little Rock to retire, but Grace quickly decided work was more fun. Boone had come to trust her judgment and regard her as a friend.

"I didn't get a confession or find an eyewitness who could say who killed the kids, if that's what you mean." He put his hands behind his head and leaned back. "I learned that George's father, some of the uncles, and at least one of the aunts had it in them to kill the boy in a drunken rage. Apparently the family's patriarch was a difficult man to live with, a spare the rod and spoil the child sort of man, and his children learned the lessons well."

"That happens," said Grace. "You'd think kids would say;

'hey, I'm not going to be like my old man,' but instead, they usually pick up where he left off. And little girls who were abused generally go looking for a man like daddy."

"Yeah, I guess baby skunks imprint on the stink, don't they? But, in this case, the eldest daughter, Daisy, didn't marry a mean man, but she drank and provided enough mean for the both of them. She was the little girl's mother."

"So what you're saying, Linus, is that someone in the family could have struck out at the boy in anger, then took him and buried him to hide what they did."

Boone nodded. "Yep. Impossible to prove which one, and it still doesn't answer what happened to the little girl."

"She went wandering off looking for the boy? Didn't you tell me the other day that she was partial to him?"

"She was and that may be it, but there's not enough of the family left to talk to and look for inconsistencies. After Ruthie died, Daisy drank herself to death. Her husband, Jessup, was supposedly a quiet drunk, but he died in a timber cutting accident. Elverna didn't know what became of her cousin Tom, but then, she wasn't even sure where her own sister, Betty is. The rest of the uncles and aunts scattered off into Tennessee and the Carolinas. Most are dead now and a lot of their kids were too young at the time to have noticed anything."

"Looks like Betty is your next best bet," said Grace. "But there may be another way to hear from those dead relatives."

Boone sat up straight and folded his hands on the desk. "What do you mean, Gracie? And don't tell me to conduct a séance."

She chuckled, low and throaty. "Shoot, no. Have you ever stayed in one of those cabins in the park?" Boone shook his head. "Well, Gil and I have. They have this cute idea of leaving notebooks and binders of paper in the desk drawer for the guests to write in. Cabin diaries, I think they call them. And they leave the last four or five year's worth in there with them so you can read what people have seen or been up to over the years."

"So if they had those notebooks back then--"

"Then you can read what any of those relatives saw fit enough to write down. I don't know where they keep the really old ones, but I can't imagine they'd just throw them away. There's history in there."

"Gracie, you are a treasure. Remind me to tell the quorum court to give you a raise."

* * *

Secrets were meant to stay hidden. Why the hell did everyone else need to know? What was it about today's society where every bit of dirty laundry was aired for all the world to see? Prancing around with their underwear exposed, sharing personal dirt on the internet like it was something to be proud of. It was sickening. Putting a chapter in some school's book that said Agnes Elwood Tanner was a sainted woman was fine. It could even be laudable. But digging too deeply into the events of thirty-five years ago was going to expose more than physical skeletons. And digging deeper into Agnes' past was worse. This girl didn't need to know any more.

Too nosy. Just like that other child.

For a moment, time slipped. The two teenagers melded into one before they emerged as separate beings again. The boy was long gone. Maybe this girl would give up and lose interest before it was too late.

Or maybe not. Makes no difference. I'm bound for hell anyway!

Hell. That's where Tanner was now. Satan was nothing compared to him.

"I'll keep your damn secrets, Tanner!"

A work-hardened hand removed the lily of the valley leaves from the oversized glass vase and tossed them in the trash. They'd steeped overnight, far more time than needed. While the flower stalks were preferable, all of the lilies had finished their bloom over a month ago. No concern. All the parts were equally deadly and as a bonus, they made the water sweet.

Such pretty little white bells, shyly peeking out of the foliage, just like Agnes' breast had peered out of her dress, a symbol of innocence. Who would have thought that they could be so deadly? It was one of many such tidbits that had passed from mentor to student.

It was time to pour the water into an empty soft drink bottle and set it on a shelf in the back of a closet, out of view. In the event that some was needed, a squirt of concentrated lemon juice or the addition a bag of green tea with ginger would make a tasty drink. The last that someone would ever enjoy.

A sudden thought forced its way to the front. Were all parts equally deadly? Did it make a difference that the plants weren't new grown?

It might do to test the batch first to be certain.

CHAPTER 12

"How are you feeling today, Dad? Not still napping are you?"

Ben Owen stirred in his chair and raised his chin from his chest. "Huh? Oh, good, morning, Joe. What'cha doing here so early?"

"It's not early, Dad. It's nearly five. Time for dinner."

"It is?" The old man searched his mind, struggling to clear it of all the cobwebs that had taken over during the day. "I guess I didn't sleep well last night."

"Too much exercise, yesterday. I heard all about how you and Mr. Harries left the grounds and walked to the library."

"And what of it?" snapped Owen. "I'm fed up with the molly coddling attention here. All the rules. Can't do this. Can't do that. Up to two years ago I lived well enough in my own place and kept garden. I worked hard all my life. That's how I managed to live to be ninety . . ." he paused, trying to remember just how old he was.

"Ninety-seven, Dad."

"Darn tootin! You think you get to live to be this age a sittin' around on your butt? What is this place, some sort of prison?"

"It's not a prison, Dad."

"Then why'd you put me in here?" Owen didn't really know why he was snapping at his own son, his only living relative. He couldn't help it. It was those blasted dreams. "I never wanted to come back to this town." He saw her face in those dreams; young and vibrant, fresh as a spring daffodil. Maybe his son was right. Maybe he shouldn't have gone to the library yesterday. Seeing that strange girl did it. Talking to her didn't help either.

"Dad. You know I put you here so I can be closer to you. You can't live alone anymore. Not after you fell last winter. And there are too many steps up to my house."

"I'm all right, son." He waved a gnarled hand, heavily knotted from years of hard work. "Forgive a cranky old man."

"Nothing to forgive, Dad. Shall I see about your dinner? Are you hungry?" His son rose and went to the door, his hand poised on the open doorframe.

"Joe," called Owen. "I . . . I did care for your mother. You know that, don't you? She was a good woman."

His son smiled and nodded. "I know that, Dad. I'll go get your food.

Owen let out a deep breath. Why was it so hard to let go of the past? Why fight so hard to hold on to secrets? What was done, was done. Choices were made that couldn't be undone. And yet, they were a part of his life now. A body couldn't just toss them.

Such an odd girl all dressed in black.

For some reason she remind him of another girl but he couldn't remember who. The cobwebs crept back. Was Joe bringing dinner? Did I dream that, too? His stomach rumbled. Didn't I have lemonade and cookies today? No, he remembered. He'd given them away.

As if on cue, his son returned, carrying a tray. He set the tray on the little table and wheeled it in front of Owen. "Here you go. Chopped steak, mashed potatoes, peas and carrots, cherry pie, and prune juice. Looks good."

"I wanted fried chicken. Don't these people know I still have my teeth?" He stuck a fork into the pie. "I better eat this first. One of the damned orderlies here steals our food when we're asleep. But does anybody listen? One of these days I'm gonna pretend to be asleep so's I can catch the sonofabitch in the act!" Owen swallowed the first bite and grimaced. "Crust is dry. And why can't I get ice cream on my pie?" He poked off the remaining crust with his fork. "I guess Harries and I'll just have to get that ourselves."

His son frowned. "Dad, about that. I just found out that your friend, Mr. Harries, passed away early this afternoon. I'm so sorry."

Ben Owen's eyes misted over and a lone tear spilled down his cheek. *Maybe I shouldn't have given him my cookies and lemonade today. It was too much sugar for his diabetes.*

* * *

"There was no sign of forced entry?" Boone sat up straight, his hands clasped on his desk. He knew the store didn't have a security camera. Hell, most of the business in town didn't. Budgets in this economy were tight to begin with and tourism decreased with each passing year. This hardware store case was just one example of how his own thinly stretched department was struggling to do their job.

"None," said Deputy Garnett. "Whoever got into Cooper's hardware store did it with a key. And nobody's reported any keys missing. Cooper's not even sure when he was robbed. He discovered it when inventory didn't check out this morning."

"You've talked to all the employees? Seen their keys?"

Garnett nodded. "He has two regular employees, Hazel Bell and Tom Clarke. Tom's been with him for twenty-four years and Hazel for eleven. Cooper himself tends the bookwork and sometimes works the floor. Everyone had their keys."

"What about the part-time help?"

"I asked Cooper for a list of everyone working full or part time, and he keeps saying he'll get it to me. Claims he doesn't issue keys to the part-timers anyway. But, Sheriff, here's the thing, having your key doesn't mean a lot in a hardware store when there's a key master machine right there on the premises."

"Someone made a copy and gave it away?"

"Could be. Clarke's the one that makes keys, but once you've watched him a few times, it wouldn't be hard to figure out."

"So someone could slip a key from Hazel's purse for instance, make a copy like it was for a customer, and put her key back before she knew it was missing." Boone leaned forward. "You're right. It looks like an inside job. You interviewed both Bell and Clarke, asked them if anyone else has used the machine?"

"Yes, and they both claim that the only keys made recently were two house keys for Mrs. McDermid and a Ford pickup truck key for Ted Holder. Both were made last week by Clarke."

"Someone could have made a key weeks ago and held on to it, planning this," said Boone. "Judging by the list of stolen items, our other angle of investigation would be the meth operation." He thought about the man who'd been strung out on meth in the park. Was it him? Other than a nearly empty bag of crystal meth in the man's car, there hadn't been anything to link him to manufacturing the drug, or to the robbery.

"There haven't been any suspiciously large purchases of cold and sinus meds recently. At least not here in town. But then, making it by shake and bake doesn't take much. I'll take that dead druggy's photo to Cooper's store, see if anyone recognizes him. And I'll check other spots in the county, but . . ." Garnett shrugged.

"Yeah, he could go out of county for that," said Boone. "It's a crap shoot at best."

CHAPTER 13

Phoebe recounted the little fish nets and still came up one short. She'd already policed the creek bank three times after releasing the two darters, and several dragonfly and mayfly nymphs they'd captured during the stream study. Where else could it be? Maybe one of the tiger cub scouts took it with him. They were certainly an enthusiastic bunch of boys if her sopping wet trousers were any indication. Next time, she'd wear her uniform shorts to lead the Life in the Stream program instead of trying to roll up the trousers.

I need to find that net. I'm in enough trouble with Burt without losing equipment. She plopped on the picnic bench and pulled off her pool shoes, reaching behind her for a towel to dry her feet. Fatigue from another late evening driving the campgrounds wore on her. At least all had been quiet.

She touched something wet instead and held up a white sock, sized for a child's foot. As she examined it, a drop of water splashed on her head. Phoebe looked up into the sycamore tree and spied the second wet sock, caught high on a branch. Just below it hung the missing fish net.

Definitely a very enthusiastic group.

Someone must have tossed the wet sock in an attempt to knock down the net. Why the net was up the tree was another matter that didn't bear questioning. Six and seven-year old boys were a force of nature. Phoebe stepped onto the picnic table and yanked the net by the handle. It came free, carrying part of the sycamore's twigs with it. The movement was also enough to free the other sock which landed with a smack on the table.

Fifteen minutes later, Phoebe had rolled down her trouser legs, put on her shoes and loaded up her gear. She felt good about this program. Tired, but good. The scout leaders had been pleased and that meant that she'd probably get calls for more specialty programs. Each one helped the park justify to the state why they needed to keep a full-time interpreter on staff.

I need all the good reviews I can get to make sure it's me.

As long as she didn't have to deal with any more drug addicts she'd be fine.

And what about your first obstinate drunks? What then?

"Cross it when you come to it," she told herself.

Phoebe looked at her watch. Three o'clock. She could get Wren from the park store and surprise her. She'd found out that Viola Hargitt's home wasn't far, just south on the other side of Dead Man Hollow. They could drive there and see if she was amenable to talking to them. Of course, getting there meant locating and maneuvering several winding dirt roads, but that could be fun, too.

She parked close to the store and trotted to the entrance. Locked! Why was it locked? The store didn't close until five during the week. That's when she saw the note.

Store and bathhouse closed due to water leak. Sorry for the inconvenience.

Phoebe stepped around to the backside of the store which was attached to the restrooms and noticed the yellow 'caution' tape across the doorway. At least two maintenance workers, judging by the voices, were hard at it inside the men's restroom.

So where's Wren?

Phoebe made a quick stop at the visitor's center to look.

"Haven't seen her, hon," said Jeanne Newcomb, the daytime desk clerk. "But the store's been closed since eleven. She probably went on home."

Since lunch time? Phoebe hadn't realized that she'd been busy away from the visitor's center for so long. Sure, she'd heard the radio call for maintenance to the restrooms, but she figured it was just a clog and ignored it. Wren had been on her own for most of the day. Phoebe was nearly out the door when McGowan stepped out of his office and called to her.

"Palmer!"

Palmer, not Phoebe. "What'cha need, Burt?" she asked as she stood in his doorway. She felt like she was a kid called into the principal's office all over again.

"Shut the door a minute, will you?"

She did, wondering if Sloan's leg wound had gone sour. Did the state decide she wasn't competent for the job? Was she getting fired already? Wren will be thrilled. No! I will not live with my in-laws!

"How is everything in the campgrounds, Palmer?"

"Fine, Burt. Quiet. Is Sloan okay? I saw him come in today."

"He's fine, but I want him sitting at a desk for at least a week.

"Is he going to be in trouble with that man's family?"

"No. The tox screen on that man came back with high levels of at least three different controlled substances. The man was a ticking bomb. Sloan is in no trouble at all."

But I still am. "I'll be happy to do his campground duty for a while longer, Burt."

"Damn straight you will. But I didn't call you in for that. The news about the skeleton is in today's paper, and that means that people will start talking and bother you with speculations. They'll try to pump some information out of you. I was in town today and three different people stopped me."

"Nobody's bothered me, Burt. I don't think anyone knows that I was one that found the remains. Didn't the paper just say 'found by a park ranger'?"

"It did. But folks talk and if people do find out and start to pester you or regale you with old gossip and tired speculations, you ignore it. Understand? No comments.

"I understand, Burt. I won't say anything. Oh, and have you seen Wren recently?"

"Wren? No. I saw Shirley drive off shortly after the store closed, though. Said she might as well get some errands done in town while she had the chance. Wren probably went on home. You want some advice?"

No. "Sure."

"If you plan on doing your job, you're going to have to give your daughter some room. I need your head on the job when you're on the job."

* * *

Beulah Ingram felt the tiredness seep into her bones and sap her muscles. She never thought that being a librarian could be so exhausting. It didn't help that the summer story time had started up. There must have been two dozen of the little monsters running in and out of the library this afternoon, and all of them wanting to check out videos. Whatever happened to checking out picture books? This wasn't a video rental store.

Then there were the usual patrons in for some socializing. In many ways, Ingram reflected, she was the tee-totaler's equivalent of a bartender. People who had little family or fewer friends often came into the library just to talk and be less lonely. They came with their tales of sciatica, ungrateful children, tiresome spouses, or photos of their pets and distant grandchildren. Shirley Gracehill, of all people, had even dropped in, looking for her mother. Ingram had just finished taking stock of that Tanner family folder at the time and told her she'd just missed her. Then later Joe Owen came in with news that Mr. Harries had passed away. It was sad news, but at least she wouldn't have to worry about him wandering around in the library and falling.

As a result of all the commotion, she hadn't gotten around to calling in a request for copies until just before closing. There was no doubt about it, she thought as she massaged her aching calves, it was time to think about retiring again.

* * *

Phoebe didn't bother to unload the stream equipment from the back of the van. She just wanted to get home and make sure that her daughter was safe. That she hadn't done anything foolish.

One of these days you're going to have to let her stay at home alone. She's nearly fourteen, for heaven's sake. What are you so afraid of?

Phoebe couldn't really put an answer to that last question. But there was a general feeling of uncertainty surrounding the girl. Phoebe had already lost so much; her husband, control of her daughter, her daughter's affections. She might even lose this job. But the thought of losing Wren terrified her.

It's that damn Goth crap. That's what it is. Kids shouldn't be focused on death.

Her fingers tightened on the steering wheel and she inadvertently skidded left, narrowly missing a sassafras sapling. Visions of Wren lying in a pool of her own gore popped unbidden in her mind. *Stop it! You're being an idiot. She's fine.*

The house was unlocked, but her daughter was nowhere inside. *Okay, she went for a walk. Good. That's healthy, right?*

But this was the girl that declared she wanted nothing to do with hiking and nature. She stepped back out when the resident chipmunk poked its head from its den. "Hey, Spunky Chunk," said Phoebe. *You haven't seen Wren have you?"

Phoebe was about to go in search of her when she heard footsteps. *She's okay. Stay calm. Keep your head, girl. No use in antagonizing her any more than necessary.*

"Where the hell have you been?!" Phoebe yelled, as her daughter walked into the house. The girl looked even more disreputable than usual, her hair askew, a few stray twigs and leaves clinging to her shirt and hair.

"Jeez. Chill, Mom. Next thing you know you'll be putting those ankle things on me like parolees wear." She held up her hands in a gesture that said, "back off." A crimson rivulet dribbled down across her palm.

CHAPTER 14

"That is so typical," snapped Wren. "Yell at me right off. Jeez!"

"What happened to your hands? You've got blood all over them." But this time when Phoebe looked, the stains appeared more purple than red.

Wren examined her hands briefly then licked them, enjoying the look of confusion on her mom's face. "It's just berry juice. I found a big patch of wild raspberries down the hill." She wiped the remaining juice on her black pants which elicited on a fresh pained look from her mother.

"Not on your pants."

Wren shrugged. "Like it's going to show."

"Look," said Phoebe as Wren walked to the kitchen sink, "I'm sorry I yelled at you. I was worried, that's all. I couldn't find you, then I learn you've been on your own all day, next you aren't home and then I see you with . . . red stuff running down your fingers."

"Yeah, well you can chill. It's not blood." Wren lathered up her hands and washed away the excess juice, leaving a faint purple stain behind on her fingertips and palm. An interesting color. She wondered what would happen if she used it to stain her hair. Behind her, her mom tried to make friendly small talk.

"So you had a day to yourself to explore. Was it fun?"

Wren shrugged and reached for a dish towel to dry her hands.

"There might be some really interesting trees or ferns to sketch," continued her mom, "you know, to practice drawing once you start your lessons tomorrow. Or maybe you'd like to try watercolors. I could talk to your instructor tomorrow and see what she recommends."

"Yeah, about that idea, mom. No! Okay? Just drop me off at the library with a check for the class and supplies. I can ask my own questions." She couldn't believe it. Her mother definitely put the 'mother' in 'smothering'."

The resulting silence was palpable, but Wren didn't turn around to see if she was angry or hurt. She hoped she was angry. She was counting on it. It would make things better if her mom was so aggravated that she wouldn't care when Wren moved out, maybe even glad. It would be less painful for her mom that way. What did adults call it? Oh yeah, tough love.

"If that's what you want," began Phoebe, with a tone reminiscent of a scolded puppy.

Damn. What does it take to make her really furious?

"Yeah, it's what I want. Look, I'm gonna go to my room. Call me when supper's ready."

Wren walked away without looking back. Tomorrow she'd sign up for the sketching class, but she had no intention of hanging around drawing circles or practicing perspective. She'd met someone the last time she was at the library, someone she needed to see again.

"Wren wait!"

Wren stopped and turned around, arms folded across her chest. "Now what?"

"There's someone I want you to see. Come with me."

* * *

"What's this, Sherry?" asked McGowan. He held up a square of memo paper. "Don't tell me old Mrs. Hargitt called. Last I ever knew, she didn't even have a phone."

"Oh, that?" said Sherry. "No, that was a message for

Phoebe from Beulah. She was recommending that Phoebe pay Mrs. Hargitt a visit."

"Really? Well, that's good, I guess. Boy that brings back memories of some of my old grade school programs. 'The forest: nature's pantry and drug store,' he recited as if reading a poster. "The woman was a wealth of information, that's for sure." McGowan poured a cup of coffee. "I didn't know she was still alive." He turned towards his office.

"I guess so," said Sherry. "But I think Beulah was meaning for Phoebe to take Wren to see her. I didn't understand all of it, but I guess Wren is interested in writing about the Tanner family and Beulah thought that Viola could shed some light on them."

McGowan stopped. "Wren's doing a report on the Tanners? What for?"

Sherry shrugged. "Some school history project. But considering Wren's interest in the macabre, I'd bet that she's actually interested in them only because we found that missing boy."

McGowan went to his desk and pulled a packet of antacids from the drawer. It wasn't over yet.

* * *

"I think you'll find this very interesting, Wren," said Phoebe as she steered her car around the turn. Technically, since she wanted information on herb lore, she could have driven the park's mini-van, but she didn't want to get in trouble for bringing Wren in it. "This woman is pretty amazing."

"What's so amazing about being old? All you have to do is not die."

"It's not her age, Wren. It's how she's lived. How she probably still lives. You think you have it rough at our house? She's lived without electricity or central heating. If she taught Superintendent McGowan about herb use, she might once have been a healer for people who couldn't get to a doctor. I'd like to learn about those herbs."

"Why don't you just ask Burt, then?"

Phoebe thought about Burt's new attitude towards her and her probation. She hoped showing this initiative would give her a few points in his favor. "I could, but I want to meet her, too. She's living history." Phoebe glanced from the road to her daughter. "You might be able to get some interesting information from her, too. You know, for your history project."

"Whatever."

Phoebe stifled her frustration and the urge to stop the car and shake her maddeningly pissy daughter. Instead, she forced her attention onto the road and to the hand drawn map in her left hand. She'd made it after calling the library and getting the directions from Beulah. Even now she wasn't sure she was on the right route. Should've asked Burt.

"There should be a right turn coming up soon." She slowed from forty to twenty miles per hour and scanned the surrounding woods for a break in the trees. She found it and took it, immediately switching from blacktop to a rutted dirt lane.

It was amazing how someplace only three miles away as the crow flew took fifteen minutes of winding roads to reach. The same could be said for her current dreams. It should've been so simple; quit one job, sell the house, move, start new life. But every day presented a fresh obstacle to go around, taking each one as cautiously as she did these mountain curves. Even the stupid house couldn't get a buyer.

Phoebe spied the nearly obscure little side road and took it, marveling that someone lived all alone out here. She loved the woods, but every night she still felt a little overwhelmed by the absolute blackness and silence, both broken only by glowing eyes and stealthy rustlings. How does little Spunky Chunk handle it?

"Geez, and I thought our house was in the middle of nowhere," said Wren.

"There used to be a church out here, and Mrs. Hargitt lives in what was the old rectory."

Wren sat up straighter. "The church that Agnes Tanner

went to? Did she live out here?"

"Could be. Mrs. Ingram--"

"Just say Beulah, mom."

"Fine. Beulah told me what little she knew of her after I prodded a bit. It seems that your Agnes Tanner had treated Mrs. Hargitt when she was a girl and had contracted polio. Anyway, as this lady grew up, Mrs. Tanner taught her about herbal cures, too. But you must call this lady Mrs. Hargitt. Old-fashioned people have old-fashioned ways. If you offend her, she cut you right off."

They bounced slowly over the rough, narrow lane, startling two hen turkeys that had been picking at something on the road side. Phoebe watched them run into the tree line.

"I'm hoping you'll find her interesting, Wren, so please try not to roll your eyes and sigh even if you're bored."

Wren answered by doing both.

After another five minutes, they pulled up to the house. Phoebe was surprised to see a burned shell of a barn not far from the rectory. Judging by the size of the trees growing out of it, the fire had happened long ago. Nature had done its best to cover the old scars. Phoebe wished it would work that same magic in her job and her little family. The house, she noted, had been made of thick stone as high as the entire first floor, and looked solid enough.

"So, does she know we're coming?" asked Wren. "What if she's not home?"

"No, she doesn't know. She may not even has a phone. I was just hoping." Phoebe peered through the driver's side window, suddenly uncertain about this trip. If Mrs. Hargitt wasn't here, she doubted that she could drag Wren back for a second try. "I'll try the house."

Phoebe got out of the car. "Wait beside the car, honey," she told Wren. "At least until I see if she'll take visitors. Oh, and hand me that box in the back seat, please. I brought a pound cake that I'd made yesterday. My mom always said that bringing a gift was better than coming with a hand full of gimmee and a mouth full of much obliged."

She took the box from Wren and walked up on the front porch. Before she could knock, the screen door opened and a slender woman stepped out. She had gray and black hair pulled back in a bun and wore a blue pinafore-style wrapped dress. Her pendulous breasts hung loose and swelled the fabric just above the waist tie. Below the knee-length dress sprouted one sturdy leg and one withered one encased in a metal brace. Both legs ended in white ankle socks and worn sneakers. But the woman's face and arms still spoke of health and vigor in spite of her years and her hard life. This was no fragile flower, Phoebe thought, but a sturdy oak nurtured in the mountain soil.

"Do I know you?" The woman's dark brown eyes were fixed on Phoebe's uniform.

"No, ma'am. I'm Phoebe Palmer and I'm a new ranger-interpreter at Dead Man Hollow State Park. Do you remember Beulah Ingram or Ranger Burt McGowan?"

The woman reflected a moment and nodded.

Encouraged, Phoebe continued. "Well, Ms. Ingram thought you might help me put together a talk about herbs for food and for medicine, just like you did once for Mr. McGowan." She held out the box. "And I brought you a pound cake. I made it myself."

The woman's sun-reddened face creased in an expansive smile. "Well, isn't that sweet of you." She motioned towards an old wooden church pew on the porch. "Have a seat. And who is that child standing out there like some little crow bird?" She waved for Wren to join them. "Come on child. I don't bite."

"That's my daughter, Wren."

"Wren. And Phoebe. Like a family of sweet song birds," said Mrs. Hargitt. She studied Wren for a moment. "Though this here wren is dressed more like a raven."

Phoebe winced. At least her daughter didn't have on one of her metal-studded dog collars.

"Well, as you must already know, I'm Viola Hargitt. Would you like some lemonade?"

"Yes, thank you," said Wren.

"Fine. I'll be right back with it." She took the cake inside, cradling it in her left arm and gripping a stout, walnut cane with her right hand. A few minutes later she returned, cane hooked over one arm as she balanced a tin tray with three, brightly-colored metal tumblers, a bowl of sugar, and three spoons on it. Wren jumped up and took the tray from her, setting it carefully on a low wooden table without spilling anything.

"Your girl has good manners e'en though she dresses a might queerly." Mrs. Hargitt sat on a bentwood rocker and handed around the tumblers. "Lemonade is always good, but I don't sweeten it. I'll just let you add what sugar you like. It's better that way."

Phoebe spooned in two heaped teaspoons and passed the sugar bowl to Wren who dumped in five. Mrs. Hargitt took none. "Don't care for sweet drinks much myself," she explained. Mrs. Hargitt drank deeply then placed her blue tumbler on the tray. "Though I do sometimes enjoy my own root beer."

For a moment, Wren seemed to forget everything else, evidently taken in by the concept of someone actually making root beer. "You make root beer? Like you buy at the store?"

"Not like you buy at the store. You kids today have no idea what real food tastes like. Homemade root beer has yeast in it, which makes a little alcohol while it bubbles the drink."

Wren thought about it for a moment. "I guess that makes sense. I always thought calling a soft drink 'beer' was kind of stupid, but if the real stuff is beer... Can I try some?"

"It's not for children," said Mrs. Hargitt. "Now, you two want to know about wild herbs for food and medicine, do you?"

Phoebe nodded. "If it's no trouble."

"Wait here then." She hoisted herself to her feet with the aid of her cane.

"I can come in and help you carry something," offered Wren.

"Sweet of you, child, but my house isn't fit for company

right now. I'm fine." She limped into the house.

"Thank you for being so polite, Wren," said Phoebe.

Wren shrugged and drank her lemonade. When she finished, she put her green tumbler on the tray. "That wasn't too bad, but I can't see how she could stand it without sugar."

"Maybe she's diabetic," suggested Phoebe.

They sat in silence, listening to a cardinal call "sweet, sweet, sweet," from the far side of the house. A few minutes later, they heard a door shut somewhere inside followed by the woman's uneven steps. Once again, Wren was at the door, holding it for her.

Mrs. Hargitt held several bundles of dried plants in her arms. She plopped into her chair and lifted one of the bundles.

"Now this here is sassafras root. You know the sassafras tree?" She put the thick root in Phoebe's lap. "It's got three different kinds of leaves all on the same tree. You make a tea from the root and it builds up the blood. It's good in my root beer, too. And this," Mrs. Hargitt said placing a slightly hairy-stemmed plant on top of the sassafras, "is boneset. You can see the leaves are opposite each other and have lots of teeth. They're fuzzy underneath, too. Helps to identify it. Flower tain't much to look at. Little white things."

"Bone set," said Wren. "You mean it heals broken bones?"

Mrs. Hargitt chuckled. "No. when people got the flu real bad so their bones ached, they called it a break-bone fever. In small doses this is very good to halt the fever. Makes a body sweat it out. But you don't want to take too much or it will make the bowels too loose and maybe make you vomit. A good dose of blackberry juice will set the bowels free, too."

Wren smooshed her lips up to her nose in an expression of disgust. "Ick." Phoebe wondered just how many wild berries the girl had eaten and if that was on her mind.

The old woman continued with red horsemint for coughs, willow branch bark for headaches and general pain, and wild mint to sooth the stomach. "Did you know you can eat violets, child? They say the flowers make a grumpy old man happy."

"I didn't know you could eat flowers," said Wren.

"You can't eat all flowers, child. Violets are safe, but there are others that could kill you." I guess I like them 'cause their name is close to mine. And I think they look pretty in a mess of spring greens. I prefer young dandy-lion greens. They make my blood strong and stop the scurvy. When I was married, my husband gave me a yellow canary bird. That bird loved dandy-lion greens. Sang to beat the band."

"So the dandelion leaves must have vitamin C and iron," said Phoebe as she wrote furiously on her notepad. This woman was amazing. She'd have to try for a grant to make video recordings of all this knowledge before it was lost to the ages. Burt had to like that. "What is that last root? Is that ginseng?"

"Yes it is. Good for you. You know about it?"

"Only a little. Do you harvest it near here?"

"A body has to walk too far to find wild ginseng anymore. I do walk a might but there is a limit. So I grow my own. Took a lot of patience harvesting berries. Need lots of shade and leaf mold to make them happy. And you can't plant them. No, you have to let them drop on the ground like in nature. I can show you if you'd like."

"Did you learn all this from Agnes Tanner?" Wren asked.

Mrs. Hargitt stared at Wren with an expression bordering on astonishment; her eyes wide open, mouth agape. For a moment her sun-hardened face paled then flushed. "How do you know of her, child?" The 'her' was spoken with a soft reverence.

"Beulah . . . I mean Mrs. Ingram told me a little about her. We thought she would be an interesting person for me to write about for a school report. She seemed to think you knew her. Didn't she used to live here? Wasn't this the rectory?"

"I knew Ms. Tanner, yes. She's the reason I can walk. I caught the wasting disease when I was a girl younger'n you. I was lucky."

"Lucky?" asked Wren. "How's it lucky to get sick?"

"Lucky not to die. Four others took ill that summer. For three of them, it got so that their whole bodies were paralyzed.

Three could barely draw breath. It only wasted my leg, but even then, Sister Agnes saved it. She put many a healing poultice on it and massaged it daily. Saved my muscles from breaking down and forgetting how to move."

"Did she save the others?"

Mrs. Hargitt shook her head. Only one boy, the one her mama helped birth the night that Reverend Elwood died. The boy's family moved on a year after the sickness. The other three, well she did her best but it was beyond her skills. Still she'd stay with them and tell them of God's merciful heaven and give them water or tea by the spoonful when it became hard for them to swallow. Eased their minds and their pains."

"She sounds like a wonderful lady," said Phoebe.

"She was. Took over the church preaching when her husband died. And never stopped ministering to the sick. Birthed many a baby as did her mother. She taught me about plants and healing, though I later learned a few things she didn't know from my mother-in-law. Things for women's woes and herbs to keep from getting with child. Things that a good Christian woman like Agnes wouldn't think right."

"What was Tanner like?" asked Wren, eagerness edging her voice.

Mrs. Hargitt glanced up at the sky then turned her gaze to the shadows. "It's getting on in the day. I expect you two have things to do. But I do thank you for the cake."

Phoebe blushed. "Oh, Mrs. Hargitt. Please forgive Wren's question. She has it in her head to do her report on the Tanners, but I told her that you would be a much more interesting person. Don't be angry."

The old woman smiled. "Anger is a weed I choose not to cultivate, Mrs. Palmer. But I promised to show you my ginseng bed. It's just to the back of the barn. You can't miss it." She pointed the way. "I'll just sit here, and Wren can keep me company."

* * *

Mrs. Hargitt waited until Phoebe was out of earshot before she spoke again. She held up the ginseng root. "Did you see how the root looks like a man? Look." She pointed to the branching roots at the side and bottom. "Two arms, two legs. It's God's way of showing us simple folk that this is good for us. But not everything comes with such a clear marker, child. How old are you?"

"Um, I'm almost fourteen. I will be on August thirtieth."

Mrs. Hargitt nodded. "Old enough to know some things but young enough to think you know all. I remember. I was that age too, you know. You think that there's some wicked story about Reverend Tanner and Agnes that is just waiting for you. I can see your ears a-growing just straining to hear of it." She shook her head and made a few clucking sounds with her tongue. "I suspect it's that way because of what everyone reads nowadays in the papers, airing all the dirty laundry, but it isn't always true."

She watched Wren's face carefully and saw a hint of dismay in the downturned mouth and slightly raised brows. "Now this was the parsonage and Miss Agnes grew up here and when she married the Deacon after her daddy died, then he became the minister. My mother died when I was a young'un, and my pappy remarried. His new wife had no call for another woman's girl child underfoot, so he sent me to live with Reverend Elwood and his wife. I grew up in this house till I went to work for a family down in the hollow." She twitched her head to the north. "The one they call Dead Man Hollow. I got married to them folk's son. He was a good man that didn't mind that I wasn't whole. Later when the church kind of broke up due to family's moving away, we came and lived in this house. The land was better and the park helped us buy the land in trade for the old. No scandal. Just families making a living."

"Where was the church?" asked Wren looking around. She pointed to the ruined barn growing out of a hillside. "Was that it?"

"No. That's a barn." Mrs. Hargitt shook her head. "City girl." She pointed to a faintly visible trail leading east, deeper into the woods. "That was the way to the church. It was about a half mile. Reverend Elwood used to ride a horse and the family walked."

Wren stood up and leaned on the railing, looking out. Suddenly she squealed and pointed to a slithering shape below. "Snake!"

Mrs. Hargitt hoisted herself to her feet, slipping the ginseng into her pinafore pocket. "Don't be a ninny. That's a king snake. He won't harm you. He keeps the mice away from my house as well as other, nastier things. I call him Henry. That was my late husband's name."

Wren had leaned over the porch to see the snake better. "He's pretty," she said. "I like the speckles. Can I go see the old church? Is there a cemetery there?"

"You don't want to walk in the church yard, child. There's a timber rattler that lives under the foundation stones and he doesn't take kindly to visitors. But he knows my Henry could eat him so he stays where he is."

"Oh!"

Viola heard the disappointment in the girl's voice. "There's nothing to see there. You won't find any curious verse or tales on the few headstones that are there. Can't even read most of them, they're so worn. Like I said, we were just ordinary people living our lives. But if you want to write up what you learned about me and my herbs, you go ahead and do that. And you can tell how Ms. Agnes saved my leg and ministered to the people here-abouts."

She heard the lady ranger come back from the ginseng bed and stood.

"You have a wonderful garden started, too," said Phoebe. "Thank you for sharing your information."

"You're welcome and you can keep those herbs. Use them to make a school lesson."

"Thank you. Is there anything you need? Anything we can do while we're here?"

Mrs. Hargitt put up her hand. "Nary a thing. I'm used to doing for myself and there's a body or two that comes by with groceries or things I need from town."

"Thank you, Mrs. Hargitt," said Wren. The girl's eyes,

Viola noted, didn't reflect the gratitude spoken by the mouth.

"You're welcome, Wren. You all be careful on that old road, now."

She stood a while on the porch, watching the car drive off. She remembered being that young. When someone told you not to do something, you did it. That's why she didn't tell Wren how dangerous it could be to pry into the Tanner's past. Instead, she tried to make them seem so dull that the girl would give up the idea. That's also why she didn't tell Wren that she called the rattler, Noah.

"That child's tenacious, Henry," she said to the snake who'd crawled back out into the sunlight. "That one will be trouble."

* * *

Shirley Gracehill shoved the butter pecan ice cream into her little freezer, nudging a package of peas aside. If she opened it now, she'd eat the entire quart so it was best to hide the temptation, at least until she'd eaten supper. Tonight's menu consisted of a microwave chicken alfredo dinner and a half can of Pringles. Bob's IGA in Wayside Springs had a limited selection of frozen cuisines, and her initial plan to drive later into Fayetteville for a serious grocery run was curtailed after she spent half her afternoon catching up with her mother.

Shirley started by dropping off some cookies for Ben Owen at the Evening Breeze nursing home. She didn't stay, those places made her feel uncomfortable. After that, she drove into Mountain View to the Golden Days Retirement Village. Shirley couldn't honestly claim to be close to her mother, but it didn't do to ignore her for too long. If she didn't make the effort to go to the retirement home, then her mother might eventually take it into her head to drive to the store, and that was the last thing she wanted. Shirley said it was because an eighty-three year old woman, no matter how healthy she was, had no business on those curvy roads. But the truth was she didn't want her in the store any more than she wanted moldy hot dog buns on the shelves.

My store!

Technically her mother still owned the store, but Shirley had managed it for her mother for so long that she thought of it as hers. Besides, when her mother came, she micromanaged everything and, when her mother headed to the office, the older park personnel started talking about the 'old days' with her. Never a good idea.

Unfortunately, her mother wasn't in her little bungalow, and inquiries from the office staff didn't reveal any specifics.

"You might try the library in Wayside. She reads a lot. Or see if she's at the church. I think she volunteers in their Goodwill shop."

Shirley tried the Goodwill store in Mountain View first with no luck. Rather than drive all the way back into Wayside Springs, she first cruised up and down the main street, looking for her mother's black Chrysler New Yorker. When that failed, she returned to Wayside Springs to the library.

"You missed her. She was here this morning," said Beulah. "She likes to read the magazines here, but you might try the nursing home. I know she volunteers there to read to what she calls the old folks." Beulah laughed. "Your mom is a real pistol. Most of those 'old folks' are younger than her. I wish I had half her energy. I'm only seventy-two and this job just about wears me down." An unsupervised toddler ran past them as if to emphasize the latter statement.

Shirley made three more stops before she finally caught up with her mother back at the retirement village. And after all that aggravation, her mother laughingly informed her she didn't have time to visit as she was due to play hearts in the village's rec center.

At least if she's so busy, she can't be too upset over the sheriff finding that kid. So why do I still feel like I'm walking on eggshells? How long before they just give up on this case and sweep it back under a rock?

She opened the cartoon of butter brickle, picked up a spoon and dug in.

CHAPTER 15

Beulah Ingram unlocked the library door early the next morning and went into the back genealogy room. She plopped into the chair behind the desk with a deep sigh. That girl, Wren, created problems like it was a hobby, upsetting her usual routine. Beulah believed in ignoring first impressions, so she'd overlooked the girl's clothes, the tiny skull earrings, the ghoulish black nail polish. And she'd done her best to steer the child away from some supposed murder into a more positive history of one of the community's little known, but more interesting women. The girl should have just photocopied the information in Agnes Tanner's file, rewritten it in two pages, and turned it in. No one was expecting college level research here for pity's sake.

But Wren was so persistent. And she'd asked so many questions. Was it true that Agnes' granddaughter, Ruthie, was retarded? Where was the mother's obituary? I thought you were going to find another copy? How did Reverend Tanner die? Did anyone ever look into her father's death? Don't you think it's odd that her father dies in a freak barn accident and two of her grandchildren died during a reunion? Was Agnes a serial killer?

Beulah had shared her frustration with some of her regular

acquaintances until her supervisor scowled at her for gossiping. She deposited her handbag in the bottom desk drawer. What made it all more than a little unnerving was that she'd started thinking about those questions herself.

Had Agnes been more than what she seemed?

"Hi, Beulah."

The librarian looked up to see a familiar face watching her with concern. "Hi. I didn't know anyone else had come in." She rubbed her eyes. "You really shouldn't be here, you know. We're actually not even open yet." She'd been told in the past to relock the door after she came in, but that meant fishing the keys out a half an hour later to unlock. And the few patrons who knew about her habit never took advantage of her.

"Oh, I'm not staying. I was wandering around town early while it's cooler and saw you. Thought I'd say hello. I must say, you look tired."

"I am tired. That girl I told you about has me running in circles. I created a monster." She chuckled and patted the phone. "But I think I can finally surprise her later today. I know where I can get all the Elwood and Tanner obituaries. I just have to make a call to the college library once they open. You know, it's the oddest thing. I could have sworn we had copies, but they're gone, and the newspaper's missing some of their older back issue."

"Well papers do get lost, especially old ones."

"That's true." Beulah sighed. "Oh, if we only had a grant to put our history on microfilm. So much history gets lost every year."

"You work too hard, Beulah. Always have. I hope that girl appreciates what you're doing for her. But it looks like you could use a pick me up. Here. I brought a travel mug of green tea to drink later with my lunch. I hear it's got those antioxidants and other healthy things in it. Why don't you take it?"

"Oh, I couldn't. That's yours."

"Nonsense. You need it more than I do today."

Ingram took the capped tumbler. "Why thank you. How

very kind. That would be better than a cup of coffee this morning, wouldn't it." She took the lid off the container and took a sip. "Mmmm. It's good. And cold."

"Drink it down before your get to busy to enjoy it. Well, I just wanted to see how you were. I'd better get going before I get you in trouble for being here."

"But your cup."

"Don't worry about that. It's nothing special. I can pick it up later. You just enjoy. I'll close this door so no one bothers you."

Beulah took another drink as the door shut. It wasn't locked either, but since this room was only open to the public on Mondays, she doubted that anyone would disturb her. "Mmmmm." The sugary sweetness hit the spot, especially as a wave of heat washed over her. I'm supposed to be through with hot flashes. Three more swallows followed.

She picked up a book club flyer and fanned herself with it left-handed as she downed the rest of the tea. In another few minutes she'd call the University library. She'd talked to one of the reference librarians there yesterday afternoon, a Carol Ann Robb, giving her the approximate dates for the town newspaper that might hold the missing obituary. Ms. Robb said she'd do the search and see if she could find it. Robb told her to call back in the morning and see if they'd had any luck. It was the reason she'd opened up fifteen minutes earlier today.

Her head throbbed and an uneasy queasiness hit her stomach. She wondered if she was coming down with the flu. She handled so many books; books touched by any number of people. And who knew how long germs stayed around?

Beulah set the tumbler on her desk and rose unsteadily to her feet, fighting dizziness, her arms clammy under her cotton blouse. A shadow dashed by the corner of her eye, just out of vision. Then another. Mice? We don't have mice. Maybe someone was in the library. "Who's there?" she called out, but her voice had little strength. I'm seeing things.

"I don't feel well," she said to no one in particular. Her chest fell tight as though her longline bra was constricting her.

"I think I need an aspirin." Beulah fumbled for the bottom drawer and her purse. Her head pounded and her lungs clenched. She couldn't get any air. Beulah yanked out her purse and wrenched it open. In front of her was a small, white bottle, but the darn thing wouldn't stand still. It kept evading her grasp.

The door opened again, a figure in the doorway.

"Help me!" Beulah croaked. "Call 911."

Her fingers clenched the aspirin bottle, but she couldn't' open it. Beulah fell to the floor.

"Don't just stand there," she pleaded. "Please . . . help. . . me."

Then her vision blurred and the last thing she remembered was seeing Ben Owen watching her before he turned away and stumbled out the door.

CHAPTER 16

Sheriff Boone stood to one side of the ambulance as Beulah's body was loaded into the back. Doctor Thaddeus Flynn finished signing papers and handed them and the clipboard back to Leona Harper, before joining Boone. The ambulance drove off without running the siren or lights, Leona following in her hearse.

More business for Leona. Some days this job is just too damned depressing.

He'd been in his office, going over the budget, trying to figure out where to pare down costs without firing anyone when he heard the call come into dispatch. He sent Deputy Chapman to look for signs of foul play.

"See what you find with the autopsy, Doc," Boone said. "So far we haven't seen anything unusual but you never know."

"I understand," said Flynn. "An unattended death. You know, I might have been able to do something for her if we'd gotten to her sooner, but the plain fact is, sheriff, that she probably lay on that floor too long before anyone found her. She had bottle of aspirin in her right hand. My impression is that she was trying to mitigate a heart attack. She'd have done better to dial 911 instead. The town's at least on it, even if the rest of the county isn't."

Boone considered Flynn's heart attack hypothesis. Beulah was found on the floor in a back room marked as off limits to patrons. Unless a person walked in there looking for her, no one would've known to call for help.

And that person happened to be Anita Holmes. Boone glanced her way. The thirty-something-year-old grade school teacher wore lime green pants and a white tunic style shirt covered with large, gaudy purple blossoms. She stood against the library like some artificial flowering vine, hugging herself, waiting for Boone to tell her she could leave. He would, as soon as he talked to her. Not that this mattered too much. According to the doctor, this was a simple case of natural death and he'd seen enough heart attack victims to know. "You can go back inside, Ms. Holmes. I'll be with you in a minute."

Boone turned back to Dr. Flynn. "I didn't think Beulah was old enough to have a heart attack."

"Well that's where you're wrong, Linus. Anyone can have one. Beulah spent her life behind one desk or another. I talked to her about exercise and diet, but she didn't care to listen. Hated walking. Kind of ironic considering she worked all those years in that gorgeous park." He looked pointedly at Boone's waistline. "You could be a candidate yourself. When was the last time you had your cholesterol checked?"

Boone waived the doctor away and joined Ms. Holmes inside the library. A teenage girl dressed like a crow stood by the genealogy room door, hand poised to knock.

"Sorry, Miss. That room's closed," Boone said.

The girl started visibly and scurried off towards the magazines.

"Sorry to keep you waiting, Miss Holmes. I needed to hear what the doctor said."

Holmes straightened and ran one set of manicured fingers through her short brown hair. "That's quite all right, Sheriff. I didn't mind waiting for you. And you can call me Anita."

Boone flipped open a notebook. "I know you talked to my

deputy, but tell me what happened."

"I was in the library, browsing the cooking magazines. I'm a very good cook, so people tell me. And my cakes have won several ribbons."

"And Ms. Ingram? She was helping you?" Boone knew she wasn't, but he needed to keep this one on track.

"No. I didn't see Beulah. Hadn't seen her when I came in, either. That would have been around nine-thirty. I came in just as Burt McGowan was leaving. I asked him if the new park naturalist would be doing the children's school programs next year. I teach third grade, you know. I love children."

"Anyone else in the library?"

"What? Oh, yes. As I told your deputy, old Mr. Granger was asleep in one of those easy chairs." Ms. Holmes put a painted forefinger on Boone's arm. "You know, Sheriff, something should be done about him. I don't think most of us mind that he sleeps in the library chairs, but he always takes his dentures out and leaves them on the table beside him. Sometimes he forgets them. It's really very disturbing and unsanitary. Can't the people at Evening Breeze keep him in his room? I hear that their residents are always wandering off."

"I'll look into it. Now, just when did you find Ms. Ingram?"

She pulled her hand back. "I wanted to make a copy of a recipe for burgundy beef medallions, but the copy machine was out of paper. I looked around for her. I mean the library does have its slow days but it's not a good idea to leave it unattended for so long. She didn't even come when the phone rang so I answered it."

Boone looked up from his notes and arched his eyebrows in disbelief, but the teacher apparently took it for an unspoken question.

"It was someone from the University of Arkansas library named Robb. She was calling to say that she found one of the obituaries and would fax a copy to the library."

"And that's when you found Ms. Ingram?"

"Yes. As you can imagine, I was becoming concerned. Beulah is never away from the desk that long. At first I wasn't even sure that she'd come in, but of course the door was unlocked, so she must have opened up. I looked in the break room and even the storage room. I finally I decided to try the genealogy room. I know Beulah did research for patrons. The door was shut, but it wasn't locked so I went in."

"And you found her slumped at the desk?"

Ms. Holmes shook her head. "No. She was lying on the floor, her face flushed. I thought she'd passed out, but, sheriff . . ." once again, her fingers touched his sleeve, "she was dead! I couldn't find a pulse. I called 911 as quickly as I could."

"And that was at eleven-fifty-three. Boone closed his notebook and slipped it into his shirt pocket. "Thank you, Ms. Holmes. That's all I need. You can go home now."

"But I haven't copied my recipe. The machine still needs paper."

"That may have to wait. I need to talk to Ms. Kent now and I believe she's the only other librarian here at the moment."

Ms. Holmes let out an exasperated sigh and walked off. Boone stepped towards the front desk where he was met by the head librarian, Helen Kent. She'd just finished talking with the goth girl and waited patiently for Boone to begin. A quiet and unobtrusive woman, she was the opposite of Ms. Holmes.

"Should I close the library, Sheriff?"

"No, just keep the genealogy room locked. When did you come in?"

Boone couldn't have told anyone just what he was looking for, but something felt wrong. He hadn't known Mrs. Ingram socially but with the library a half a block from the sheriff's office, there were few days when he didn't see her come and go over her lunch break, each time with a friendly wave. Somehow he just couldn't imagine her keeling over like that. Then he recalled the doctor's pointed comment about his own health. Maybe he should have his cholesterol checked.

"The same time that the ambulance arrived. This is usually a slow morning since there's no children's story time today and the teen classes don't start until the afternoon. So Beulah would open alone and hold the desk until noon when I'd usually get here. I only came in earlier today to finish processing some new books."

Boone found Deputy Chapman, making his final observations in the genealogy room. Boone stood in the doorway so as not to interfere with his investigator, his gaze again taking in the scene. The rolling chair was four feet from the desk. The bottom desk drawer was open as was her purse, a huge aqua-green, fake-leather monstrosity. There were no loose files or papers about. On the desk top was an aspirin bottle next to an uncapped travel mug with the logo: "Dead Man Hollow State Park" emblazoned in copper-colored letters. In the corner stood a coffee mug that read "librarians do it by the book." Boone walked in, taking care to touch nothing. He leaned over the desk and peered into the tumbler. A bit of liquid sat at the bottom.

"Who picked up the aspirin bottle?" Boone asked. He turned and saw Mrs. Kent. "Did anyone else come in here?"

"Just Anita and then the doctor," she replied. "And of course the EMT's."

"In other words," said Chapman, "everyone."

"She'd just finished drinking something," Boone said, "but I don't see any paperwork or files on the desk. I don't understand what she was doing in here. Just sitting and drinking coffee? Doesn't make sense."

"I don't think it's coffee," said Chapman. "Too weak looking."

"We'll bag it and send it off for analysis," said Boone. He put on a pair of latex gloves, picked up the tumbler and gently let one drop hit his index finger. "Sweet tea," he said after tasting it. "One of those green or white kinds." He placed the tumbler and its lid in the evidence bag that Chapman held open.

"Why do you need to analyze her drink?" asked Kent. "Surely you don't think--"

"Just following procedure," said Boone. "Maybe she was trying a new brand and had an allergic reaction. More information to help the doctor."

Mrs. Kent returned to the main desk and Boone followed after leaving final instructions with Chapman. As he approached, the fax machine on the back shelf chimed twice followed by the whirring of tiny gears, feeding a sheet of paper.

"It's an obituary," said Mrs. Kent, as she scanned the papers. "Must be something Beulah requested for the genealogy room." She handed the first one to Boone.

"Reverend Noah Tanner," he read aloud.

Tanner!

The obituary was dated May tenth of nineteen forty-nine.

Reverend Tanner, head of the Church of the Blessed Carpenter passed away on Saturday afternoon. The well-known minister, a powerful face in the community had been sitting on the parsonage porch, drinking tea, and working on his sermon when he sickened and died. Doctor Oscar Hunt declared the death to be due to a heart attack even though the reverend had been in seemingly good health. He is survived by his wife Agnes and five children.

"Who requested this?" he asked.

Mrs. Kent took the fax and studied it. "I have no idea. Must have been someone that Beulah was working with. The second paper says that they are still looking for copies of Rachel Elwood's and Agnes Tanner's obituaries."

"Well, if you find out, give me a call and let me know."

"I can't do that, sheriff. It's a violation of our patrons' first amendment rights. Now if there's nothing else, I'll just put this in the Agnes Tanner folder. I'm sure that's where it goes."

Boone stopped. "You have a folder on Agnes Tanner?"

"Why, yes, she's a bit of a local celebrity around here. Reputed to have been a very caring and hard-working lady."

"Who sent this fax?"

"A research librarian at University of Arkansas, Fayetteville. Carol Ann Robb."

Boone thanked her and left the library wondering why the sudden interest in the Tanner family. What bothered him the most was the irony of Beulah's death. She was drinking a sweet tea while waiting for a fax about a man who died drinking tea.

Coincidences bothered him. Especially since the skeleton they'd just found was also a Tanner.

He pulled his phone and called Doctor Flynn. "Doc. Send Beulah's body to Little Rock. Tell them to check her stomach and blood for whatever might cause or simulate a heart attack."

The travel mug had the park logo. True, Beulah had worked there for years so it could have been hers but Anita Holmes had said that Burt McGowan had been in the library that morning.

CHAPTER 17

Wren pocketed the receipt for the art class and stuck the complimentary sketch pad and two pencils into her backpack. The older cop had already left, but there was a younger one still packing up. What were they doing in here? Jeez, this town must really be backwoods if the library had to call out the sheriff just because someone didn't return a book. Maybe one of those old dudes that hung out here the other day got sick or had a fit. She hoped not. She wanted to talk to that one again.

"The class won't start for an hour," said the librarian.

"Yeah, I know."

"Then did you need something else, miss . . ." the librarian looked at the name on the class list, "Wren?"

Hearing her name made Wren refocus her attention. It looked as if Beulah only worked in the morning today or that she had the day off. She felt disappointed. She actually had looked forward to seeing her today. "Uh, yeah. Mrs. Ingram was trying to get some obituaries for me for a school report. I was wondering if she'd found them and left them for me. It was the for the Tanner family."

"Oh? Yes. Actually, one came in via fax this morning." She retrieved the sheet with Noah Tanner's obituary on it, copied it, and handed the copy to Wren. "The librarian that sent this from the college said she's still trying to locate some others. That will be twenty-five cents for the fax and ten cents for the copy."

Wren fished a quarter and a dime out of her pocket and handed them to the librarian. She was about to ask what the cops were doing when the phone rang and the woman answered it. The librarian looked as if she was doing her utmost to hold herself together.

Something big happened.

Whatever went down, she knew the librarian wasn't going to tell her. With the curiosity held by every teenager who felt everything was their business and what they did was no one else's, she looked around for a likely person to ask. She settled on a plump woman browsing the romantic suspense shelf.

"Excuse me, but did something happen here? I mean, what's with the sheriff?"

The woman did a double-take when she saw Wren's black clothes. "You're a bit too late for the job, aren't you?" she said.

"I don't understand."

"Your outfit," said the woman. "You look like an undertaker. What I mean is that someone died. I don't know who. Nobody'll say."

Gross. Must have been one of those old men that was in here the last time.

She just hoped it wasn't the one she was going to go see.

Might as well go and find out.

* * *

Wren took one whiff of the hallway and wrinkled her nose in disgust. Underneath the layer of pine-scented cleansers and baby powder was the scent of age: wrinkled bodies laced with fungus, the hint of soiled adult diapers, all overlain with the aroma of institutionalized food.

I am never growing this old!

"May I help you, miss?"

The words were polite, the tone frosty. Wren turned and faced a middle-aged woman in a navy-blue business suit with the skirt stopping an inch below her knees. She reminded

Wren of a school principal, carrying her authority balanced on her upturned nose.

"Yes, please," said Wren in a voice that would have made her mother proud. "I came to see one of your residents. I'm supposed to interview him as part of the Arkansas History project at the school. And I'm combining it with my church's youth group good will program. They ask us to visit the sick and elderly." She shifted the weight of her backpack and waited.

The woman stared at her, her arms folded across her chest, her lips pursed. Crap! I probably shouldn't have added that church bit. She's not going to buy it.

"Who did you want to see?"

"Oh! Uh, a Mister Owen. Ben Owen? I think he once helped build the park. Part of the C.C.C corps."

"The last C in C.C.C. stands for corps. You don't need to repeat it at the end. That's redundant."

"Oh." Wren waited, doing her best to smile sweetly at the frosty woman. For the first time she felt conscious of her clothes. Maybe, she should have gone undercover as some cutesy girl instead.

"I think it will be all right for short while," said the woman. "Mr. Owen does have a few visitors, but outside of his son, they rarely come more than once a week, and I think he gets very lonely in between. But mind you, he is ninety-seven years old. He tires easily and sometimes his mind fails. If I think he's wearing out, I'm going to ask you to leave." She pointed at Wren's pack. "You'll have to leave that in the office. Security rules, you understand."

Like I'm packing a weapon. But at least Mr. Owen wasn't the stiff in the library.

Wren opened her pack and pulled out a red spiral-bound notebook and a pen before handing the pack over to the woman who deposited it on the floor just outside the office door.

"You can simply pick it up on your way out." She turned and led Wren down a short hallway and then right into another brightly lit corridor painted pale blue. "What is the name of your church?" she asked.

"Uh, the Church of the Blessed Carpenter," said Wren, remembering the church that Agnes Tanner had led.

"Oh, I'm not familiar with that one. But how nice that they are getting the young people involved." She glanced over her shoulder at Wren's clothes. "I wouldn't have expected someone dressed as you are to be in a church youth group. I suppose that should teach me not to judge people, am I right?"

Cripes, she even talks like a school principal. "We're encouraged to blend in with other kids. It's part of our missionary outreach."

"How interesting. Ah, here is Mr. Owen's room. And you're in luck. He appears to be in his room and awake."

Wren peeped into the room and spied the white-haired man sitting in a chair, staring vacantly at a magazine. He wore in gray sweatpants and a green t-shirt. "Where is he if he's not in here?" She imagined him in some community room playing bingo or making egg-carton sculptures while a perky blond in butterfly-print scrubs commended them on how good they were doing like they were preschoolers. Suddenly she empathized with this man. Bad enough being treated like a baby at her age. But at his?

The woman dropped her voice to a whisper. "He used to sit in the garden with another resident until we discovered that they tottered off for ice cream or to sleep in the library. He's actually incredibly agile for his age. Now he's not allowed to go outside unless a family member is with him. But that friend passed away so I doubt Mr. Owen will leave now. Sometimes he wanders off into another patient's rooms. Usually he's just visiting a friend he's made here. But other times . . .? Other times he seems to be looking for someone." She made some sympathetic "tsks" and added "Very sad."

"Did you say his friend died?" Wren looked at the old man with fresh eyes. Coping with death was something else she understood.

"He did. Heart just gave out. But," she added in a perkier

voice, "a young visitor like you could be just what he needs. Now don't stay beyond a half-hour." She rapped on the doorframe three times. "Be-en," she sang out, "You have a visitor. A nice young lady."

The old man looked up, his face hopeful. "Ruthie?"

CHAPTER 18

Phoebe sat at her patio picnic table, the dried herbs to her left, each with a paper label twist-tied to it. She'd just finished labeling the plants that Mrs. Hargitt had given her and had her nose deep in a copy of Ozark Wildflowers, studying a picture of horsemint. To her surprise, she recognized the flower as bee balm and wondered if she could find some in bloom.

"Afternoon, ma'am."

The slow, gravelly-voiced greeting came from behind. She responded by dropping her book, trying unsuccessfully to jump to her feet only to be caught by the picnic bench, and crying out in what could only be described as a squeaky "aah!" By the time she'd freed herself from the bench, the stranger was at her side, picking up her book. He wore a workman's dark green trousers and shirt with the words "Dilman's Pest Control" printed on his cap.

"You scared the hell out of me," said Phoebe, her heart beating so hard she could feel the pulsation in her gums. "Where did you come from? What are you doing at my house?"

"Sorry, ma'am," he said touching the bill of his cap in a deferential greeting.

He handed the book back to her. His words came slowly

and evenly-spaced, reminding Phoebe of a dripping seep in the rocks, each drop plunking down to patiently and inexorably erode the stone below.

"Didn't mean to scare you," he continued. "I'm just here for the quarterly check on the termite traps around the house."

"Oh. Well, I'm sorry I responded so badly. I just didn't expect to see anyone out here."

"Tis kind of lonesome at that," he said. "Rebaited the traps, ma'am, but I noted that you got a little varmint infestation."

"An infestation?" Phoebe imagined a family of raccoons lodging in her chimney.

"Just a leetle one," he said, holding his right thumb and index finger an inch apart. "Leetle bitty chipmunk has moved into your foundation. I can trap it and seal the hole if'n you like."

"No! That's Spunky Chunk. I'm kind of making a pet out of him."

The man shrugged. "Suit yourself. Take care no fox nor snake gets him." He touched the bill of his cap again. "Twon't bother you no more, ma'am. Be back in three months, though."

Phoebe gave a half-hearted wave goodbye as she watched the man plod silently around the house. She'd never even heard his vehicle.

Thank heavens Wren wasn't here alone when he came.

* * *

"Mr. Owen? My name is Wren – like the bird." She glanced behind her to make sure that the woman was gone and not eavesdropping. "We talked in the library. Remember?"

Owen's head drooped, his eyes downcast. "Oh. I thought . . ."

Wren paused in the act of walking towards his chair, caught off guard by a sudden twinge of sympathy for this old man facing yet another disappointment. The feeling was supplanted by one of embarrassment at having witnessed his frailty. She turned to leave when he spoke again.

"You may come in, Wren. I don't bite. I remember you.

You're the girl interested in the Tanners." His tone sounded cautious, the way adults were when they hadn't quite decided if what you were doing was dangerous, wrong, or interesting.

Wren found a plastic chair in a corner, pulled it closer to Mr. Owen and sat down, her notebook on her lap. She studied the man seated in front of her, taking in the remnants of what had once been a handsome face. Yes, the features were all there just as they were in that photograph; the square jaw, the high cheekbones and brow. His nose was large, but not bulbous or hooked. Anything smaller, she decided, wouldn't have fit his face, and Wren wondered if the man carried some Indian blood in him. At least, the face reminded her of a picture she'd seen of Crazy Horse. Owen's eyes, once a rich, deep brown, were partly clouded with age, but he examined her features, not with an air of confusion, but as one trying to see in the dimly lit room.

"Are you okay, Mr. Owen?" she asked, unable for once to use an adult's first name. "You look a little . . . tired."

The old man took a deep, shuddering breath. "Child, I'm as good as anyone who keeps company with the angel of death. He and I are nearly on a first name basis."

"Oh. . ." Wren recalled that his friend had just died. Once again she felt self conscious. The woman at the library said she looked like a mortician. Probably not a happy reminder for anyone out here. She decided not to launch right into asking him about Agnes or Reverend Tanner. "I, um, wanted to talk to you about when you worked for the C.C.C.; when you were building the park. Do you remember that?"

Owen looked down at his hands, now gnarled and knotted with arthritis. "I was a stonemason. I worked with stone."

Wren avoided saying, "That's right," or anything that might sound condescending. She hated when adults did that to her. She couldn't imagine how it felt to be this old and be treated like a child again. "I think I know what a stonemason does, you cut stone and build walls, right? Is that what you did?"

Mr. Owen seemed to perk up a little. His eyes took on a clearer focus, less distant. "Other men rough cut the blocks for the dam on Sugar Run. That was hard labor. We called that team Pharaoh's men." He chuckled softly. "I didn't work on the dam but I did make some bridges on the trails."

"I thought the bridges were all made of wood."

"That's just the part you walk on. Look underneath and you'll see the abutments that hold up the wood. The wood eventually rots but if the stone is put together right, it will last to hold more wood. I took the rough cut and worked it to make tight fits that held even without mortar. And I hand cut the shelves that the wooden braces fit into."

Wren made a few notes inside her tablet, maintaining the pretense that she was researching his work in the corps.

Owen reached for her notebook and pen. He patted the cover. "You're like me. I always liked green, too." He opened the book and sketched a basic wall with overlapping stone then drew an arch below it. "That's called a keystone," he said, tapping the center stone in the arch. It holds everything together. I did one of those in a little drainage bridge but I doubt you'd see it unless you got on your knees and peered over the edge." He handed the book back to Wren.

She decided it was time to broach her real subject of interest. "In the library, you told me that searching for Tanner was dangerous. That he was the devil incarnate. Did you mean Reverend Noah Tanner?"

Owen's head snapped up, his cloudy eyes suddenly burning with an inner fire. "Tanner? What do you know of Tanner?" His fist clenched and Wren knew that once the man's hands had been capable of great strength.

Wren's pulse raced and she scooted her chair back. "I . . . I don't know anything except that he was a preacher and married to Agnes Elwood. I thought you could tell me about him."

At Agnes' name, the old man's face softened, his mouth and brows drooping. "My Agnes. She was going to marry me, you know. Her father didn't approve." His head dropped again. "He wanted her to marry Tanner cause he was a deacon and I was a nobody. And then," his voice trembled, "then that same day her father died and I . . . I lost her."

Wren placed a comforting hand on the man's gnarled one. "I don't understand. With her father gone, she could have done what she wanted, right?" Even as she said it, she thought of her own situation, being dragged into no man's land by her mom. But Agnes had been older. Surely that made a difference.

Owen shook his head slowly. "Tanner had some hold over her. He suspected that there was more to her father's death." His chest swelled as he took in a deep breath, releasing it in a long, sorrowful sigh. "I think she married him to protect me. She didn't want him to accuse me of killing her father. I should've known that no one escapes from him. Not then, not ever.

CHAPTER 19

"Russ Hodges speaking."

"This is Sheriff Linus Boone from over in Caddo County. You're a hard man to get a hold of, Superintendent Hodges. Do you have a few minutes to talk?"

"What do you need, sheriff? Don't tell me that there's a fugitive heading all the way across the state towards my park."

"Nothing of the kind, Superintendent. I'm working a cold case. Hoped I could pick your brain."

What he really wanted was to interview this man in person but the Tahoe decided to lose the muffler in a pothole earlier in the day. Plus the park was three-hundred miles away. Hodges wasn't a suspect, and Boone already had the county quorum court breathing down his neck about cutting his expenses. He knew who was the main instigator there. Dick Cooper, one of the justices of the peace, had been most vocal at the last meeting. At least his deputy had finally gotten the list of Cooper's hardware store employees including the ones who had keys.

"Okay. I can probably spare you five minutes. What do you need to know?"

Boone noted the man's officious tone of voice and that, unlike most professionals he talked to, Hodges didn't invite him to call him by his first name, Russ, or his nickname, Rusty. He imagined the man's body language, sitting ramrod straight in his desk chair like he had a poker shoved up his backside. In Boone's experience, some people were strictly stiff and formal all the time. Others reacted that way when speaking to law enforcement, guilty or not. And others had something to hide. The question was, which of these fit Hodges?

"What do you remember about Thanksgiving nineteen, seventy-six?"

"You must be working a case on those kids that wandered off from Dead Man Hollow. I'm guessing you found the boy?"

His response, while evasive, could have been a simple desire for clarification. "Yeah, we did. What can you tell me about that weekend or anything you remember later?"

"As I recall, I wasn't on duty that Thanksgiving weekend. But then, if you'd read the files, you probably already know that."

"But you were called in on the search, right?" Boone knew that Hodges was away from the park until late Sunday, but he wanted to hear it from the horse's mouth.

"I was kind of unreachable, sheriff. I'd gone hunting. The first I knew of any of this was some folks talking about it down in Mansfield at a diner. Said a girl had just been found frozen to death and her brother was missing."

"Cousin," corrected Boone. "He was her cousin. Do you remember what day that was?"

"Nope."

"Would your wife remember?"

"How the hell would I know? You'll have to ask her. We're divorced."

"Okay, tell me where to find her."

There was silence on the line, broken only at the end by a muttered curse. "I send the alimony checks to Fayetteville." He recited an address. "Look, sheriff, I'd like to help you, but I wasn't there until the aftermath. But I'll tell you who you should look at."

Boone noted the choice of words, "look at" and not

"ask." "Who's that?"

"Burt McGowan. The guy was around, he had access to the kids, and he just happens to be the one who found the girl in some out of the way spot where no one would think to look, but too late to save her. I never liked the guy."

No kidding. "That's a pretty strong accusation to make, Superintendent. What makes you think that it was anything other than an accident?"

"'Cause someone recently heard on the radio channels that a possible homicide was being taken in to the crime lab. And they told someone who told someone who told me. And why the hell else would you be asking around if it was just an accident? Now if you'll excuse me, I've got the governor's wife coming to my park and I need to put on a nice welcome."

"Sure. If you think of anything else, Superintendent, give my office a call." He repeated the desk number and hung up, thinking about the man's self-righteous attitude and his story.

Ruthie was found on a Friday, so it was possible that her death might have made the Saturday papers, at least locally, and other Arkansas papers by Sunday. The search for the boy went on intensively for a week and everyone kept an eye open for weeks after that. So why hadn't he taken part later? For that matter, once he knew that something so horrific as children missing had happened, why didn't he hustle his butt back and pitch in?

"Jack!"

Deputy Chapman popped his head into Boone's office. At twenty-three, he was Boone's youngest deputy but his face was the kind that would get carded in bars until he was forty-five at least. The freckles didn't help. "Yeah, boss?"

"I need you to do some legwork for me. Get a hold of Game and Fish. Found out what kind of hunting license Russ Hodges had back in nineteen seventy-six. And get a photo of him, preferably from around then. Send it to the sheriff in Mansfield. See if they'll run it around to any of the diners, motels, and gas stations down there. Find out if anybody remembers this guy."

"From seventy-six? You're kidding."

"Unfortunately not. I know it's a long shot, but there may be somebody that remembers him. If he hunted in that area regularly, maybe he had a cabin or something. He had to buy some groceries and gas somewhere. Hell, if he was hunting something big, then check with any taxidermists or meat processors in the area. See if he took his business there rather than haul it all back here."

"You got it. I may have to promise somebody down there a six-pack or something."

Boone chuckled. "Take it out of petty cash." After the deputy stepped out, Boone opened his notepad. Below McGowan's name he wrote "Russ Hodges" and drew and arrow connecting the two. There was bad blood between them, but Burt hadn't hated Hodges enough to accuse him of killing two kids. Was Hodges simply trying to get even with McGowan for something? Or was Hodges trying to throw out the proverbial red herring to pull the investigation away from him. Where was he all that time? Could anybody provide him with an alibi after all these years?

Or did the man actually have a justifiable reason to suspect Burt?

The Tahoe was surely finished by now. Tomorrow morning, he'd head to Fayetteville, talk to the research librarian and to Sharon Hodges. In the meantime?

Boone felt like he was slogging through heavy brush. It was difficult enough to track down the living relatives after thirty-five years. Maybe someone with a larger staff could have done it, but not county sheriff's department with four deputies and a dispatcher in one of the more impoverished counties of Arkansas.

All he had so far was his conversation with George Tanner's oldest sister, Elverna. The other relations seemed to have dropped off the face of the earth or six-feet into it. That one interview pointed to a troubled childhood for just about everyone with a Tanner name and all thanks to a brutish patriarch, Noah Tanner. According to Elverna, if it hadn't been for the matriarch, Agnes Tanner, things would have been far worse.

What was it Elverna said? The reunion had been Agnes Tanner's idea and she was there.

It was no far stretch to imagine that either the boy's father, or one of the uncles struck the boy in anger, killing him, then sought to cover up the crime by making it seem as if the boy got lost on a hike. But then, why leave the little girl to die out in the cold?

The likely answer was that Ruthie had witnessed George's death.

Could it really have been George's father? Reuben Tanner had died in a car crash due to driving under the influence, taking his wife out with him. Linus could easily imagine how killing your own child and an innocent little niece would drive even a hardened man to become desperate; hoping to drown his demons in liquor only to have them come roaring back instead. And Reuben apparently had a head start on alcoholism.

Such a scenario would certainly be a tidy end to a black day in Caddo County history. A cold case closed, a sort of justice if only in giving the victims their due. But there was nothing other than a general allegation of alcohol-induced brutality for a basis. Boone needed some evidence. He hoped the M.E.'s report from Little Rock would help.

In the meantime, if the living weren't speaking, maybe the dead would. Gracie had told him about the quaint tradition of placing notebooks in each of the cabins for the guests to write in. Perhaps there was something in one of those cabin diaries.

But what if it wasn't one of the family?

That didn't mean that someone didn't make a comment relevant to the case. It only meant that Boone had to be more surreptitious in his investigation. He couldn't go into the park office and demand these cabin diaries, not if he wanted to hold his cards close. That new ranger, Phoebe Palmer, didn't have any involvement back then. He could talk to her.

Boone felt a fresh eagerness rush through his veins and

wondered if it was entirely due to a new attack on the case, especially when he caught himself checking to see if his uniform shirt wasn't too tight around the middle. Had he lost a pound or two since the start of this case? Would he if he exercised more? Linus pinched at his middle. So far he'd pulled the treadmill out of the closet but he had yet to set foot on it. Maybe if he moved it in front of the television. Maybe just hauling it from room to room was exercise enough.

"Jo," he hollered to his daytime dispatcher. "Is the Tahoe back yet?

"Yep."

"Then I'm heading up to the park."

"Want me to call them for you? Make sure Burt's in his office."

"No. I want to surprise them."

Boone drove the Tahoe along the twisting county road up to the park, one part of his mind alert to any hidden dangers beyond the next bend whether it was a startled deer or someone taking the curves too fast. Even in his off hours, he was always on patrol when he was on the road. His county was by and large a peaceful one. Some drunk and disorderly on a Saturday night, the usual domestic abuse case when the monthly paychecks were running on empty. Up to this week, the drug-related violence had passed them by. Unfortunately, it looked as if that was changing. The stolen items from Cooper's hardware and the man in the park proved that.

Each of the hollows that he drove past could harbor a hidden meth lab - modern day bootleggers cooking up a more dangerous brew. Greed and poverty, it seemed, made better chemists than the high school did. Hell, it didn't even have to be a permanent lab anymore. In neighboring Missouri, more and more meth was made on the go in the back of someone's van or car. The damned stuff was concocted in a two-liter pop bottle or some other big plastic container. The shake and bake method. Boone had advised his deputies to look for tossed containers.

He crested the last rise, put the Tahoe in second, and began the steep, serpentine descent into the valley that housed most of Dead Man Hollow State Park, pulling in at the park office as the sky began to darken with thickening clouds. Looked like they were in for more rain tonight.

"Linus, good to see you," said McGowan, extending his right hand. "What can we do for you?"

Boone shook hands, noting that McGowan actually didn't look all that glad to see him.

"Hi, Burt. I actually came to see that new lady ranger of yours. Ranger Palmer."

"Yeah, she's around. What do you need her for? The paperwork on that campground shooting is done."

Boone put his hands behind his back and walked casually around the room, inspecting the enlarged photos of the C.C.C. during construction days. "Just routine follow up on the kid's skeletal remains. I thought she could take me back out to the crime scene, help me understand the lay of the land better."

It sounded lame to Boone. He obviously had driven to the scene before so why would he need a ranger now? And why Palmer and not McGowan? But he noticed that Burt didn't make the offer to accompany him. Too busy? Or something else? He turned. Burt didn't look happy, but then, who would with a murder case tied to the park followed by a drug death?

"I'll radio her for you. But don't keep her too long. She's got some of Sloan's duties along with her own."

In a matter of minutes, Boone was back in the Tahoe, a nervous-looking woman in the passenger seat.

"I appreciate your taking the time to talk with me," he said.

Her "no problem" sounded like it was a big problem. How hard was Burt riding her?

"If it makes you feel any better," said Boone, "I really don't need to see the grave site again. I just needed to be able to speak with you where no one else was going to eavesdrop."

The ranger's head snapped up and around at that, curiosity vying with wariness in her eyes. "What about?"

Boone turned into the start of the old logging road and stopped the vehicle. "The park," he said. "Come on. Let's walk a bit. I've been sitting too much anyway."

He eased out of the driver's side, put his hands on his back and arched out a kink. "Got bottled water in the back." Boone opened the rear door and pulled two plastic bottles of "Ozark Springs" from an opened case. He handed one to Phoebe before cracking the seal on his own and taking a swig.

When he started up the logging road, the woman fell in step beside him, but didn't say a word. Boone found that interesting. Most people, guilty or not, felt uncomfortable and talked. It was like they got diarrhea of the mouth. But not her. She knew when to hold 'em.

"I'm having some trouble getting in touch with living relatives of the Tanner boy. People who can tell me about that reunion."

Phoebe glanced up at him before turning her visual attention back to the road and any possible obstacles in their path. But Boone saw her shoulders relax a little. *What did she think I was going to ask her to do?*

"In fact," he continued, "the only person I've managed to talk to besides your boss is the boy's oldest sister, and she wasn't at the reunion."

Phoebe stopped and faced Boone. He expected her to protest, saying that she didn't know any of the relatives, wasn't from this county, any of the usual arguments against an assumed request. Nothing. Most interesting.

"I understand that the park puts notebooks in each of the cabins for guests to write in," Boone said.

Phoebe nodded, the faintest trace of a smile on her lips. Boone could tell that she was already anticipating where this was going.

Smart lady.

"As far as I know, they've been putting notebooks in the cabins since the cabins first opened," she said. "What I don't know is where all the old ones are. And that's assuming that they still exist. We don't exactly have them archived. If anyone would know, it would be Superintendent McGowan. You already know, Burt. Why are you asking me and not him?"

Very smart lady.

Boone laid it out straight. "Because everyone from that time period is suspect."

Phoebe blinked rapidly, a clear sign of surprise and some agitation. What Boone couldn't read was whether she was more disturbed by her boss being considered a suspect or the possibility that he might actually be a murderer. Boone knew her next statement would tell. If she defended him, said the usual blather about how he couldn't have possibly done something so vicious as to strike a boy and leave a little girl alone to freeze to death. . . And if she doesn't?

The only sound that disturbed the extended silence was that of a woodpecker hammering in a distance. It was answered by a distant rumble of thunder. Drumroll, please.

"I see," she said.

"You're not defending him." Boone was floored. The two had been friendly enough when they'd found the Tanner boy. Apparently, the Sloan-meth-head shooting had created some serious bad blood between them.

Phoebe's eyes met his. "I wouldn't read too much into that, Sheriff. What you have to consider is that I'm the mother of a teenage girl. Once she hit ten, I stopped fully trusting any man other than my husband. It goes with the territory whether I like it or not."

"But if you didn't have a daughter?"

"I'd say that you were stuffed full of week-old baloney."

"Understood. And if I didn't have a thirty-five year old case that involved a green ranger, I'd agree with you."

Phoebe chuckled. "Okay. We understand each other. If I'd been alive back then and in the park, I'd be a suspect, too."

The woodpecker ceased drumming, and the ensuing stillness again struck Boone as palpable. George Tanner had rested in this silence for thirty-five years. But Phoebe broke it first which surprised him. He'd have bet that she could withstand it longer than he could.

She needs to get back to work. Burt's probably holding her job over her head.

"So you want me to find these old diaries for you, is that it?"

"Yes. But don't let anyone know that I want them, or that you're doing this as part of the case if they catch you at it."

"I may have a way out of that. Wren, that's my daughter, has to do a report on some aspect of Caddo County history for school. If anyone catches me looking for them, they'll think that she's using notes from the books to write about the park. Again, that's assuming that these books still exist."

She grinned and Boone was struck by how attractive she was, even wearing that smokey bear hat and badly tailored uniform.

"So, am I a temporary deputy or something now?" she asked.

"Do you need to be? I mean, as a park ranger you're already commissioned law enforcement." He nodded towards her belt and the holster strapped to it. Too late he remembered her part in the recent park shooting – she'd frozen with her gun drawn.

The smile dissolved immediately. "I need to get back to work. I've still got an evening talk to prep for."

"What's the talk about?"

"The role of predators."

* * *

After Boone dropped Phoebe at the visitor's center, he turned the Tahoe towards the park store to talk to Shirley Gracehill. She'd been home that Thanksgiving and might have remembered something her mom had said. And, as he'd told Phoebe, he wasn't ruling out anyone that was alive back then. He went inside, the bell above the door jingling.

He'd never been in the park store before. Funny how growing up in the country near the little logging town of Oakwood, his family never spent time at the park. But then, they were a rural family and driving somewhere to visit someone else's woods always seemed foolish, especially since his dad had worked as a logger. He'd claimed he seen enough trees to last him a lifetime. Instead, his idea of relaxing was fishing. Boone imagined his dad out in his john boat near

Broken Bow, Oklahoma where he and mom had retired.

"Be right with yah," called a woman from a back room.

"Take your time," Boone replied. He surveyed the goods, souvenirs for tourists, foods, camping supplies, firewood, and cast iron cookware. The place reminded him of an old general store. The refrigerator caught his eye, a near antique as such things went. He opened it, retrieved a plastic Coke bottle by the cap, and wiped it down with his pocket handkerchief.

"What can I do for you?"

Boone turned around, holding up the soft drink by the cap.

"Sheriff," said Shirley. "I didn't recognize you from the back." She held out her hand. "I'm Shirley Gracehill. I even voted for you last election."

Boone set the bottle on the counter and shook hands. "Appreciate that, Ms. Gracehill."

"So what brings you out to the park today? That dead druggie?" Suddenly her face stiffened, the smile disappearing. "Oh. I'll bet it's about that Tanner boy, isn't it?"

Boone nodded. "I was in the area and decided I should talk to you. I understand your mother kept the store in seventy-six."

"She did. I was teaching high school biology near Little Rock at the time." Shirley rang up the soft drink. "Not sure what I can tell you."

"I'm hoping you can tell me how to reach your mother or maybe your father. I really need to talk to them about what they remember."

She folded her arms and leaned on the counter top. "My dad died before I was born. He was injured in World War Two, Pacific arena. Mom worked with rehabilitating the soldiers. I guess they fell in love straight off and got married, but six months later he took a bad turn."

"Sorry."

She shrugged. Can't miss what you never had."

"And your mother?"

"Mom lives over in Mountain View in one of those

retirement villages."

"I grew up not too far from there. Oakwood. One of the last to go to that high school before it closed up. Had a graduating class of nine." He smiled, but received no answering smile or comment. "Do I need to check in with her doctor before I talk with her?"

"Mom?" Shirley snorted. "She has her own cottage. Spends her days running around bossing some committee or another. She may be eighty-three, but she's spunky."

"It's good when they keep busy," said Boone. "Keeps them healthier."

"Well yeah, as long as she's not trying to run my business. But, sheriff, I have my doubts about what good it'll do you. The store was closed over Thanksgiving, and when she came in on Friday, the search was already underway. I know it disturbed her greatly, especially when they found that little girl all froze to death. I'd just as soon you didn't get her all upset."

"I understand. But she must have said something to you. Didn't she ever talk about it?"

"Nope. I drove back to Little Rock on Sunday and, anytime I brought up the subject before that, she just changed it right back to restocking or cleaning shelves. But that was nothing new for mom. Every time I came home it was that way. Work came first."

"And you didn't observe anything odd about the Tanner family? Anyone that seemed less than worried or just the opposite, overly anxious to be helpful?"

"I don't know how anyone could be overly anxious, and I didn't see much of the search. I came in with mom on Friday to work. I recall some people came in early for maps, a few candy bars to fuel up while searching, that sort of thing. No one talked. The girl's parents left the morning after she was found."

"Do you remember anything else?"

Shirley shrugged. "Who can remember? I didn't know those people by name and back then, it was a cash business. No credit card receipts or i.d.'s to check." She eyed Boone.

"You must be thinking foul play to be questioning this after so long."

"Just dotting my i's and crossing my t's." Boone changed tactics and gestured at the store. "Guess you've seen a lot of changes over the years."

"Yeah, times change. I don't carry as many tent camping supplies as mom did. People RV more and have most everything they need. I still keep some spare tent stakes on hand and some tarps. And I'll never stop carrying marshmallows, hot dogs, or those two-pronged fireplace forks."

Boone looked over his shoulder and spied them stacked beside the dutch ovens and sandwich irons. "Bet you go through a lot of graham crackers and chocolate bars. This store's probably seen a lot of different park people, too. I think Burt's the only one left from back then. Do you remember a ranger named Russ Hodges?"

"Trusty Rusty? Yeah. A bit of an operator. Always trying to charm my mom out of a free soft drink or candy bar. Me too, if I was here."

Boone lightly slapped the countertop. "Well, thanks for talking to me. It was good to meet you." He turned and headed for the door.

"Hey, sheriff," she called. "You forgot your Coke." She picked up the bottle and held it out to him.

"Oh, thanks." He snagged hold of it by the neck and walked out, careful not to handle the places she touched.

CHAPTER 20

"Stupid old coot! Passed his drink on to that other old geezer." Not that it mattered. It still proved that the mix was potent as Beulah's death evidenced. But now the old man was talking, telling tales out of school as it were. This time, he needed to die and make no mistake.

And Tanner's specter loomed larger every day, always threatening. "Keep my secret or suffer for it."

"Be damned if you think you can get me for this, Tanner. I'll keep your secret, and when I get to Hell, you can fear me!"

The old man wouldn't be a problem much longer. He had a fondness for cherry-flavored drinks. That was something he wouldn't pass on to someone else. It meant yet another trip into town, but it had to be done.

* * *

Thunder peeled outside, and Phoebe heard the gentle patter of rain turn into a beating drum on the roof. Nobody was going to leave their dry cabins or RV's to attend a ranger talk on predators on an evening like this. She'd waited fifteen minutes in the A.V. room just in case before deciding that this was the perfect time to search for those old cabin journals. If her assistance ended up being key to solving the cold case, then maybe that would strengthen her status as park law enforcement. Maybe Boone would speak up on her behalf.

It can't hurt.

She shut the outside door and unlocked the back storage room.

The park, like any other state run bureaucracy, never discarded anything. 'Lost but never tossed' was the old adage. Phoebe had only to look at the shelves and see the antiquated film-strip projector and cassette players to verify it. In a place where budgets were tight, you never knew when those items might actually be needed again. Plus, there was always the possibility that they could be used in trade with another, equally strapped park. In addition, every scrap of paperwork was kept in case some bean counter demanded an account. So if any of those older cabin diaries existed, they'd probably be in one of the boxes shoved into the corners. Not that anyone could actually tell her what was in here. The other adage, 'out of sight - out of mind," also held true.

Two boxes of moldering cassettes and aged mimeographs later, she found what she was looking for; stacks of spiral-bound notebooks, jammed into an oversized box. Phoebe knelt on the floor, her back to the open storage room door. She reached for the top notebook gingerly, her eyes alert for any resident brown recluse spiders. "Cabin 6" was written on the cover in bold black marker. She opened to the first page to see the date. June 16, 1987. Phoebe set it aside carefully and pulled out another. Twelve notebooks later, she hit one with "Cabin 8 – 1976-77" printed on an orange cover.

Now we're getting somewhere.

She silently read the first entry. Monday, Nov. 29, 1976. Day two of our anniversary. So romantic, all except for the resident mouse. The Ranger brought over some mouse traps this afternoon to set in the cupboards. Think we'll pass on that. Don't want to open a door and find a dead mouse anymore than a live one."

Phoebe closed the book. Honeymooners. It's a wonder they even noticed a mouse.

Without bothering to look at the remaining time stamps,

she removed each notebook one by one, setting them aside until the box was empty of all but one resident spider which Phoebe dispatched. Orb weavers were one thing, but she had no intention of taking home a brown recluse to the cabin. Then she repacked them, putting the most recent ones on the bottom.

I'll take these home and read them there. Somehow she doubted that there would be anything in them that would help the Sheriff Boone, but she had promised to help. She'd also promised to keep it quiet. As if you could do anything around here without someone knowing about it. The park was like any small community.

A deep rumble broke the stillness, reminding her of heaven clearing its throat before beginning its concert. A check of the amplifiers; testing - one, two, rumble. Perhaps a little more bass. The next rumble was deeper, more rolling and closer. With the ground still wet from that last storm, most of this rain would run off from the saturated watershed, swelling Sugar Creek. Burt had already closed down Campground A, the one closest to the river. At least she didn't have campground duty tonight.

She slipped several of the more useful looking mimeograph handouts that she'd seen on top of the notebooks. One depicted animal tracks and others were of bird feet and beaks. She could make paper copies and possibly use them with the grade school kids in the fall.

"Phoebe? Is that you in there?"

Phoebe yelped, startled by the unexpected intrusion. Jeez, second time today.

"Sorry, didn't mean to scare you."

"It's okay, Shirley." She quickly closed the box, and got to her feet. "I was sort of lost in listening to the thunder and sorting through this crap. Can you believe the junk in here?" She picked up one of the film-strip canisters. "Our friend the beaver. I bet that was a favorite."

Shirley spared a momentary glance at the canister before peering at the other boxes. "Are all these full of film strips?"

"No. There are some insect-infested mammal pelts, too."
Shirley made no motion to go so Phoebe dusted off her
trousers and acted as if she was leaving. "No one showed
tonight, so I thought there might be more mammal skulls in
here and maybe some useful handouts. But I haven't been
through everything. I'll bring Wren in here to help me. You
know, give her something useful to do besides gripe. Maybe in
another month or two I can afford to get satellite tv and
wireless internet. Until then . . ." she rolled her eyes.

"Yeah, well, good luck with that." Shirley leaned against the
door frame and crossed her arms over her chest. She became a
fixture in the doorway and looked as though she'd be as hard
to dislodge as the clay muck jammed into the cleats on
Phoebe's boots.

Go away!

"So what keeps you in the park so late, Shirley?" She
wondered just how you pried a woman from a door jam.

"I was doing inventory, that's all. Saw the lights on in
here. Thought I'd catch you."

"Was there something you wanted to see me about?
Something about Wren?" Phoebe felt her stomach clench.
What had the girl done now?

"Actually, I was wondering if she was coming to work
tomorrow or not. I could use her to help me finish restocking.
That leak ruined a rug and I want to go into town and get
one."

"I'll be sure to bring her by, Shirley. She signed up for a
teen art class on Tuesdays and Thursdays. Did she tell you?"

"Tell her what?"

Both women jerked at the sudden male voice.

"Oh, hell, Burt. You gave us a start," said Shirley. "You
shouldn't sneak up on a woman like that. No telling how she'll
react."

Phoebe thought the same thing could be said about
Shirley's unannounced intrusion a moment ago. How many of
these could she survive a day? "It's nothing, Burt. I was just
telling Shirley that Wren's taking an art class at the library." She

glanced at the box beside her. "And since no one was coming out for my talk tonight, I was just taking the opportunity to look for something useful for future programs. You know, anything to hold down our budget."

McGowan looked from one to the other, as if trying to decide whether or not to say something.

"What is it, Burt?" asked Shirley. "You look like you have bad news."

"Actually, I do. I just found out that Beulah died today. Heart attack."

"What?" both women exclaimed. "When did you hear that?" asked Phoebe.

"Boone told me today. Just before he left the park."

"I wonder why he didn't say anything to me," said Phoebe.

"Maybe he didn't figure you knew her," said McGowan. "I thought I should tell you."

"I didn't know her well, having just met her at the library earlier this week, but she seemed like a really nice lady. So helpful and thoughtful. Not only did she take Wren under her wing for this history report, she told me about that fascinating lady, Viola Hargitt."

Phoebe couldn't believe it. It was true she didn't have any deep friendship with Beulah, but there was something terribly unsettling about someone you'd just interacted with passing away. It was like the thunder outside. Most of the rumbles were growing distant, but occasionally, a boom meant a lightning strike close by and reminded her of her own frailty.

Wren will be very upset.

"You're not going to have any people come by tonight, Palmer," said McGowan. "Go home."

"I'm heading there." She made no move to leave before the others.

McGowan checked his watch. "You're running late today, too, Shirley. The plumbing got fixed didn't it?"

She nodded. They finished this morning. "I ran a few more errands in town while they cleaned up," she replied. "But putting everything back took me longer than I'd planned and

I've got warped drywall in my office now. Whole blasted wall needs to be rebuilt."

Phoebe wished they'd all just leave. Good lord, they're a convention of buzzards waiting for the last call on roadkill.

As if he read her mind, McGowan's gaze swept over the boxes. "Can't imagine there's anything worth salvaging in here. Ought to just haul it all to a landfill."

"Well, you never know what might be useful someday," Phoebe said, making her tone as light-hearted as possible. "Though there is a box of old animal skins that weren't mothballed and they definitely need to go." She kicked at the offending box with her foot.

"I'll get maintenance to haul it off later. Find anything useful?"

Apparently, she'd need to serve up some roadkill if she wanted to get rid of them. "I saw some old mimeographs in this box. I might be able to use them. Thought I'd take the box home and sort through it tonight, see what I can find."

"It looks heavy. Let me help you with it." He squatted down and slipped his hands underneath the box.

"Really, Burt. You don't need to--"

The bottom of the box broke through, spilling the notebooks like the day's catch on a trawler deck, an array of red, blue, green, and floral spiral bounds.

Shirley retrieved one and flipped it open. "These are old cabin diaries." She stared at Phoebe under lowered eyelids.

Phoebe felt both sets of eyes boring holes into her. "There were some old mimeographs on top. A match the bird feet with what the feet do." She left the offered explanation hang in the air, hoping no one would press further. She couldn't keep the existence of the old journals a secret anymore, but she could protect Sheriff Boone's interest in them as well as his request for her assistance. If they'd leave her alone, she could still salvage this. Phoebe snatched some mimeos from the pile and held them up as evidence.

"Shoot! Only a few worksheets out of that whole box. I guess I should've dug further." She knelt down and started collecting the sprawling notebooks. "I'll take these home anyway. It will give Wren something to read. She might find them amusing."

Both McGowan and Shirley squatted on either side of her, gathering notebooks.

"I can do this," protested Phoebe as she reached for another book.

"What you need is another box," said McGowan

"Or this one taped up," said Shirley.

Phoebe heard both of them hurry away. By the time they returned, Phoebe had the books in two neat stacks with the mimeo sheets atop one.

"I found a box in the office by the copy machine," said McGowan.

"And I had duct tape in my truck," said Shirley.

"Let's reinforce Burt's box with the duct tape so it doesn't break, too," said Phoebe.

Thirty minutes later, she was home and had arranged the notebooks chronologically and by cabin.

Cabin 8, 1976-77 was missing from the pile.

CHAPTER 21

Phoebe pushed the box of cabin journals into a living room corner. After going through them quickly in an attempt to find the orange one, she suddenly decided she was in no mood to look at them tonight. Outside, the rain hammered the roof. The storm had come in with a cool front and Phoebe wanted a cup of hot tea. When she'd locked her Glock in the fire safe, she'd brushed against Charles' last unopened letter, which depressed her. Maybe Wren would join her.

"Wren? Come on out for a moment."

"Why?" came the surly answer from Wren's room.

"Just come out. Please."

Wren's door opened and the girl came out, wearing gym shorts and t-shirt, both black. She plopped on the couch, her arms folded across her boyish chest.

"Mrs. Gracehill wants you to work early tomorrow. You'd even be in charge for a while."

There was no answer beyond a slight nod.

"Are you hungry? I can make popcorn. Would you like to play a game of cards or something?" Phoebe asked.

"No." She started to get up.

"Wait," said Phoebe, putting on a brave smile. "Come on. Talk to me. How was your first art class?"

Wren shrugged. "s-okay."

"Can I see what you did?"

"It's nothing. We drew shapes."

"Did you make friends with some of the other kids in the class?"

"No."

Phoebe sighed. "Wren, this is supposed to be a conversation, not an inquisition." Her daughter made no reply. "Did you hear what happened at the library today?"

Wren stirred on the couch, drawing her feet under her, knees out. "I saw the cops there but nobody said anything." Her voice sounded questioning, hopeful.

"It seems that the nice librarian, Mrs. Ingram, died today. She had a heart attack."

"Crap." The word was flat, expressionless.

"Crap? That's all you can say? Have some respect, Wren."

"Jeez, what am I supposed to say? I mean, I hardly knew her and she was like . . . old. But she was helping me with that stupid history report. She was gonna find some stuff for me."

Phoebe watched her daughter for a moment. To be truthful, she wasn't sure how she'd expected Wren to react. What she said was true. She didn't know Beulah and, from her perspective, the woman was old. All the girl saw was yet another disappointment in a series of disappointments.

"I'm sure one of the other librarians will help you. Or wait until I get a week day off and I can help you."

Wren unfolded her legs and stood up. "I don't need your help so quit pushing." She stomped off to her room, closing the door behind her.

Phoebe went into her own room, the tea forgotten. She slipped into a pair of cotton knit gym shorts and a soft t-shirt, suddenly wanting nothing more than the oblivion of sleep. Worrying about her job and her daughter grew more oppressive with each passing day. Neither Burt nor Wren responded to any of her efforts, and Sloan had studiously avoided her.

The counselor in Wichita had told her to be patient with

Wren, that youth dealt with death at a different rate than adults. But how long, she wondered, could she hold out before the gulf between them was unbridgeable?

* * *

Wren pulled the sketch pad out of her backpack and flipped it open to the first page. Cripes, that was a close call. What if her mom had insisted on seeing her work? She'd have to remember to draw something on class days, just in case. She sat cross-legged on the bed and drew a cube followed by a circle. After shading them, she added a cone and two lines merging as an example in perspective. That much she remembered from a middle-school art class.

When she'd finished, she tossed the pad onto the floor with the pencil and flopped back on the bed, staring at the knotty pine ceiling, her hands behind her head. She knew her mother was angry, but more than that, she was probably hurt.

Good! It wasn't that Wren wanted to be cruel. Well, maybe at first when her dad died, but not anymore. It's for her own good. It'll make it easier for her in the end.

She already knew her plan was at work and, with any luck, she'd be out of this place before summer was out. Her mom would get over it, but Wren knew she'd get over it sooner if her mom actually wanted her to leave. And to that extent, she was working to be as bitchy as possible. It was a kindness.

Still, it was a shame about Beulah. She was kind of nice.

CHAPTER 22

It had been many years since Boone had been back on the University of Arkansas campus. What made him feel like an interloper were the students. The guys were all 'dudes' in multi-pocketed cargo shorts, t-shirts, and hair moussed into a bed-tousled look. The girls, no matter what their body shape, invariably wore low slung short-shorts and tight cropped t's. He saw more fanny cracks in an hour than he'd seen his entire four years in college. Half of the guys went sockless in size-gigantic athletic shoes. The other half and nearly all the females, wore flip flops. Boone felt like he'd strayed onto a beach.

He'd never stayed for summer school. His summers were always dedicated to working his butt off to make enough money to pay for the next year, so maybe nothing had changed. Maybe the summer co-eds had always been this casual and exposed and he just never saw them.

A cuddly pair, walking with arms around each other's waist stared at him and his uniform. The guy whispered something in the girl's ear. She giggled and they moved on. Boone picked up the pace and headed towards campus center and the David W. Mullins Library.

A petite, forty-something woman, professionally but

comfortably dressed in tan cotton slacks and a short-sleeved pale yellow blouse met him at the reference desk. Boone studied her with an eye to reading personality. Her short brown hair was styled with little fuss, attractive without looking frivolous. An efficient, neat, practical woman.

"Ms. Robb? I'm Sheriff Boone from Caddo County."

She held out a hand. "Please, call me Carol Ann."

"Linus," he added, shaking her hand.

"Now I'm a little confused Linus. You didn't say much on the phone, but I can put two and two together. It's no coincidence that I just sent information to a librarian in your county."

"You're correct. It's not a coincidence." He stopped speaking as an international student headed for one of the nearby computers. "Is there somewhere private that we can talk?"

"My office." She gestured towards a small room behind the desk.

Boone followed her inside and shut the door. "The librarian who requested that obituary, Beulah Ingram, died before your fax came in."

Robb leaned back, her eyes widening. "Oh, dear. What happened?"

"Heart attack." He felt safe saying that. The question was what caused it.

"I'm sorry to hear that."

"Yes, she was a nice lady. Normally I wouldn't think anything of a fax coming in with some requested material, but this fax also pertained to an open murder investigation in our county. It's an old case so I'm trying to catch any leads I can get my hands on.

"A murder investigation? But, Sheriff, that obituary I faxed in was from the nineteen forties. Just how old in your case?"

"Not that old, but it's a piece of family history that might help me understand the rest of the family. I'm hoping you can help me find more information and maybe tell me why Ms.

Ingram requested it to begin with."

Robb frowned. "She just told me that their genealogy folder was missing some papers and that they were also gone from the stacks at the newspaper office."

"So this obituary was the only one she requested?"

"No. She requested others for Rachel Elwood, Joshua Elwood, and one for Agnes Elwood Tanner. We have a very complete set of newspapers from our county and the surrounding counties. Our special collections section has been very gifted. But some of these people may have died without anything being reported in the papers. And, without a year of death, it's been a challenge to locate anything. I've got a grad assistant still searching."

Boone held up a folder of papers which he'd copied from the Wayside Springs library. "This is all I have so far. What else do you have on the Tanner family?"

Two hours later, Boone signaled to the special collections librarian that he was finished.

He'd learned a few things in that time. One, librarians lived for this and, if you weren't careful, they'd bury you alive under information. The other tidbits dealt with the park, its construction, and the Tanner's Church of the Blessed Carpenter. Reverend Joshua Elwood died in a tragic accident in his barn and was said to have been survived by two daughters. Neither girls were named in the article. Boone knew that Agnes was one of them. Agnes had married Deacon Noah Tanner one week later. Her mother, Rachel, survived for seven years, but her obituary only listed Agnes Tanner and five grandchildren, all Tanners, as surviving relatives. Rachel Elwood's obituary touted her as "a paragon of women, always putting her hand to the plow." It went on to lament that she'd suffered a stroke on learning of her husband's horrific death and was cared for by Agnes Tanner in her final years.

He'd browsed the scanty church record. The congregation was small, but active, especially the women's group. Agnes was there at every turn; cooking, quilting, and caring for everyone. Her duties stretched beyond that of the church members and must have kept her constantly on the move. Even before her marriage she'd been involved with outreach to the camp workers, building the park. When polio struck down a few members, the paper reported that Agnes was there at their bedsides, helping them to heal or, if the case was too severe, "providing them with spiritual comfort at their passing."

Reverend Noah Tanner, on the other hand, held his involvement to running his parish. He took charge of the older children in the bible studies and the Little Marthas and Marys work group, leaving the younger ones in the care of his wife. When Noah died in 1949, after a spring church festival, Agnes took over the parish which lasted for another three years before a fire reduced the building to ash and the congregation scattered, including her family.

Boone found nothing that helped him with George murder. He jotted down the names of the Tanner children and their date of birth to compare with the list of aunts and uncles in the park's records. Then he remembered that a woman still lived at the former rectory. Perhaps she knew the family and could tell him if any of the others were still alive.

What Boone found most interesting was that both Rachel Elwood and Reverend Noah Tanner both died of heart attacks on warm spring days. Both obituaries praised how the Lord had taken them quickly as they enjoyed a glass of sweet tea and the song of spring birds.

He wondered what the M.E. would tell him about Beulah Ingram's last drink.

CHAPTER 23

Ben Owen had nestled back in his easy chair, a crocheted afghan in variegated blue zig-zags draped over his lap. He closed his eyes and mimicked sleep. His visitor had left him a plate of homemade gingersnaps and a big cup of cherry-limeade from the local drive in. These sat on his end table, a plastic lid on the drink and a straw sticking out of it. As much as he enjoyed gingersnaps, he was willing to risk losing some of them to catch that thieving orderly in the act. Gingersnaps were dry so he saved the drink, one of his favorites, to wash down the ones left behind. It would be a victory treat. But the easy chair was comfortable, and it wasn't long that he fell asleep for real, his jaw dropping open and a gentle snore rumbling from his throat.

Ned Martin, the orderly, made it a habit to do rounds after any visitor left. He peeked in and saw his opportunity. With a practiced soft tread, valued for not disturbing the residents, he walked into the room and eased the door closed. Then he proceeded to stuff his face with cookies. He'd leave one on the plate and drop a few crumbs on Owen's shirt to make him think he'd already eaten the rest and fallen asleep before he'd finished.

Hell, these old codgers could barely remember what day it

was much less what they'd eaten or even if they'd eaten. And Ned had a big metabolism. He needed the fuel. He was what his high school football coach had called 'a big boy,' husky. The doctor said he was fat, but what the hell did he know?

Three cookies later, he realized that they tasted a little salty which was weird. Some cook messed up the recipe and added too much salt to the batter. Not a problem. He'd just help himself to whatever was in the foam cup.

Ned took a long pull on the drinking straw. Cherry-limeade! Now that was tasty. Sweet and tart at the same time. The old man wouldn't miss it. He finished the drink and left the room as quietly as he entered, feeling a little tight in the chest.

Maybe he should cut back a bit on the sweets. It wouldn't do to get sick.

By the other end of the hall, he'd collapsed dead in front of a shocked nurse's aide.

* * *

Sharon Hodges had agreed to meet the sheriff over her lunch break. Luckily, when Boone checked into the office after his library stop, nothing else was pressing. Aside from a call regarding two loose horses blocking traffic on a county road, the dispatch call board had been relatively quiet. Boone knew the horses. Ethan Burdett's paint and bay were adept at opening their paddock gate and taking a leisurely stroll. And the paint dearly enjoyed blocking traffic. Jo had sent Deputy Wells over to Burdett's house to help the old man collect the animals. The trick was to get Burdett to put a padlock on his gate.

Boone pulled up to the Powerhouse Seafood and Grill a few minutes before noon and went inside, showing his badge to the maître d' and assuring him that he'd contacted the Washington County sheriff to let him know that he was in his county and armed. "I'm meeting someone here," he explained. The maître d' responded with an insincere "very good, sir" and left him to wait in a corner.

He'd been in the restaurant once before, but was still intrigued by the place. Built inside an old power plant, the building exuded history. If his stomach's memory served, they specialized in Cajun recipes.

Mrs. Hodges arrived a moment later. She could easily have passed for a woman in her early forties, rather than fifty-seven. Her brown hair, the color of well-polished walnut, was cut shoulder-length with a whisper of bangs that brushed her thinly plucked eyebrows. She wore a short-sleeved blouse in something that looked to Boone like silk the color of a fresh peach. Her close-fitting, knee-length skirt was a deeper shade of the blouse and showed off her tall figure and legs to perfection. Boone wondered what would possess a man to throw off a woman this attractive.

Must have been one hell of a divorce.

They sat at a corner table. Boone ordered a cup of baked potato soup and coffee, and Ms. Hodges ordered lobster bisque, a crawfish salad and sweet tea.

"Okay, sheriff, you've got me. I'm assuming this has something to do with my worthless ex-husband. What did he do?"

"Nothing that I'm aware of, ma'am. I need to talk to you about something that happened a long time ago, back when you lived in Dead Man Hollow State Park."

She made a shudder which struck Boone as being well rehearsed. "Horrid place."

"How is that, ma'am?" Boone asked, thinking that it seemed peaceful and that a woman who married a park ranger must have had some love of the outdoors. Yet the former Mrs. Hodges looked "all-city" as his grandmother used to say.

"Don't ma'am me, please. I'm not that old. But to answer your question, it was so primitive. Stuck in those woods. Bugs, those horrid owls hooting all night long, raccoons coming into the house. And what was I supposed to do there? Play Rachel Carson?"

She sipped her tea, studying Boone over the glass. "I know what you're thinking," she said with a silvery laugh. "You're wondering why I married a park ranger to begin with." She made a graceful shrug with one shoulder. "I suppose it sounded romantic at first. Big strapping outdoorsman for a husband. But I swear, I thought they commuted to work and we'd live in town." She leaned closer and dropped her voice to a near whisper. "Do you know how often he left me all alone in that god-forsaken place for days at a time?"

"Where did he go?"

She shrugged again. "How in the blazes would I know. Hunting – he said."

They paused while the waiter returned with their lunches and topped off Boone's coffee.

"So your husband liked to hunt," said Boone, prompting her to continue.

"You have no idea. If it wasn't deer season it was duck season or turkey or wild boar. At first, I thought it was kind of interesting. You know, my man the provider. But I can't stand the taste of wild game. It wasn't long after that he quit bringing home the meat. Just hauled back some hideous head to stick on the wall. I put a stop to that. Bad enough listening to who knows what prowling outside the windows at night, but getting up and seeing those glassy eyes staring down at me." She shuddered, this time more convincingly. "No, thank you."

Boone sampled his soup. It was hot and good, laced with bits of bacon and topped with shredded cheese and fresh chives. He allowed the woman to eat some of her lunch, too, giving him a chance to watch her behavior. She seemed perfectly at ease, betraying no nervousness.

After a minute of silent eating, she looked at him. "I still don't know what this is about."

"I'm following up on an old investigation, Mrs. Hodges. Some children that disappeared from the park over Thanksgiving in nineteen seventy-six. I was hoping you might remember something that could help after all these years."

The fork slipped from her fingers and she made a hasty snatch for it. Too late, it struck the salad plate with a clatter and tumbled to the floor. "Clumsy of me," she murmured.

Boone signaled for the waiter and asked for another fork. He noticed that she no longer made eye contact, preferring to study each sprig of lettuce or chunk of crayfish. Her bisque went untouched.

"I remember that. Russ had Thanksgiving day off as well as the two days after. He'd put in for that vacation time a year in advance, working all the other holidays just to get it. I thought we were going to go away together. You know what that bastard did? He went hunting without so much as a by-your-leave. Just left me there with nothing. Not even a damned turkey." She stabbed a crouton and sent part of it flying off her plate. After that she put her fork down and placed her hands on her lap. "He could've at least shot something for me to eat."

"Did you go anywhere? Maybe one of the other wives invited you for dinner?"

"The Super's wife did. But I didn't want to . . .to barge in on some other family's dinner." She kept her gaze on her hands, now fiddling with the napkin in her lap.

"So you stayed in your house?"

She nodded, not looking up. "I think I took a stroll one time, but I'm not absolutely certain. It was a long time ago. I did hear the call in on the radio of course," she said. "We had radios in the houses." She glanced at Boone to see if he understood. "Everyone was supposed to report to the office. Of course, I had no way of knowing where my husband was so I couldn't get in contact with him. It was late Sunday before he came home."

"Was your house close enough to see the search party form?"

"Not really. Ours was at the top of the ridge. It wasn't much more than an oversized house trailer. But," she hastened to add, "I couldn't see the visitor's center from there" She signaled the waiter by waving a hand. "Can I have a to-go box for the salad? Thank you."

"Did you see those children the day before? Maybe during one of your strolls? I'm trying to find out who they were with and what those relationships were like."

"I have no idea. I knew there was a big family in the park,

but I didn't pay any attention to them. Look, sheriff, I'm sorry I can't help you."

"There's one more thing," Boone said. He opened a file folder with a black and white photo of a scruffy-bearded man. "Do you remember seeing that man in the park then?"

Mrs. Hodges picked up the photo and studied it. "What a mean looking derelict." She shuddered. "Is he a suspect?"

"Did you see him?" pressed Boone.

She shook her head. "No. I certainly would have remembered a face like that."

Boone held out the open folder for her to replace the photo. "Thanks anyway," he said, putting it aside. "It was a long shot."

The waiter returned with a clamshell box and Mrs. Hodges scooped her remaining salad into it. "I really must be getting back," she said, gathering up her purse and the box. "I'm sorry I couldn't be more help." She quickly turned her back on Boone and walked away, her heels clacking a rapid tattoo on the floor.

Boone thought about her behavior. How it had changed from mildly flirtatious to nervously secretive once he'd asked about her movements during those days. But he had a good thumb print on the picture to send to Little Rock along with the bottle that Shirley Gracehill had held and McGowan's soft drink can. Amazing how a fine man like his own dad could look so disreputable at five a.m. on a camping trip before his morning cup of coffee. It was Boone's most useful and possibly his favorite picture of his dad.

He wondered which one of the present guest cabins had been the site of her home and what could she really see from there.

* * *

"Did you need me to do anything else, Shirley?" Wren waggled the duster over the stack of coffee mugs for the second time. Last night's rain had subsided to a steady drizzle, which kept people out of the park on a Friday. There would be no one renting canoes or paddle boats today.

"Oh, there's always something else, but you've already put in as many hours as I can work you today. I'd send you over to the café to bus tables but there's nobody in the park. I do appreciate your watching the store earlier today while I went into town."

Wren felt a stirring of hope. "Then can I use your computer for a while?"

The radio squawked in the corner. "Shirley, Phoebe here."

"Yeah, Phoebe. What'cha need?"

"Is Wren there? Is she still working?"

Wren clamped her lips together and glared at the radio. Couldn't she get any time for herself around here? She clasped her hands together and mimed pleading.

"Uh, she's in the bathroom right now," said Shirley. "but, yeah, I need her for at least another hour."

Wren turned her pleading act into a thumbs-up.

"Okay. Tell her I'll pick her up in an hour. Better make that two hours. That is, if you don't mind letting her play on your computer for a while. Poor kid deserves some fun time."

"That'll work, Phoebe. I'll tell her. Over." Shirley replaced the handset. "Looks like you have a reprieve, kid."

"Thanks, Shirley. I'll never forget it. And thanks for saying I was in the bathroom. I really don't want to talk to her right now."

Shirley shrugged. "Just a white lie. Sometimes they're less harmful than the truth."

Wren ran into the back room, slipped into the desk chair, and logged into her email account. If her grandparents had come through, there'd be a password for her to connect onto a paid ancestry website where she could hunt down some information on Agnes Tanner's family. Then, maybe there'd even be time for a game or two of zombie death warrior. Time, she knew, made possible by her own mom's thoughtfulness.

She pursed her lips. Her mom was not making this any easier. Why can't she just be bitchy? Why does she always have to make everything including hating her so hard?

CHAPTER 24

Boone hadn't been back in the office ten minutes before his day went south faster than a northern retiree outrunning a snowstorm. It started just after he got a mug of coffee and stopped at the dispatch desk.

"Been this quiet all morning, Jo?" Jolene Bright, the daytime dispatcher, had formerly been a juvenile detention center matron. At five-foot, one-inch and one hundred and ten pounds wet, she'd been a surprisingly good one, too. She moved to Wayside Springs eight years ago in preparation for marrying a man intent on starting up a resort. Neither the resort nor the marriage worked. He left, Jo stayed. She loved law enforcement and hated being bored. Most days the phone and the radio kept her busy. Not today.

"It's been dead dull," Jo said. She had her nose in a paperback.

"Watcha reading this time, Jo?"

"Blood Rustler. It's about a cattle rustling vampire."

"You read the strangest stuff." Boone glanced up. "Ah, sh--"

"Sheriff!" warned Jo. She reached up for the cuss jar on the shelf and shook it.

"Shoot!" finished Boone, staring through the dispatch

window to the outer door.

She looked to see who was coming into the office. "Dick Cooper."

"Before he dick's you," added Boone. He pushed a dollar in the cuss jar before she could scold him.

The outer door opened with a heave hard enough to smack it against the outer wall.

"Sheriff! Where the hell have you been all morning?" shouted Cooper.

Jo plonked the cuss jar onto the window ledge. "No cussing, Dick. Pay up."

"Oh, shit!" muttered Cooper.

She shook the can. "Uh oh. Double fine. Five bucks."

Cooper pulled his wallet and extracted a five dollar bill. "You told me last time it was a dollar a swear. I should get three bucks back or else I've got three cusses coming."

"Double swear in less than a minute is five bucks," she said. "Always has been."

Boone sipped his coffee, using the mug to hide his smile. He'd never heard of a double cuss rule before, but then Jo disliked Cooper more than he did. Her opinion of him as one of the duly elected justices of the peace was that it was a good thing his head was stuffed far enough up his backside to at least see out his belly button. Add to that, she was determined to buy a new deluxe coffee maker for the break room. By the time she was done with Cooper, she just might have enough.

"What can I do for you, Dick," said Boone.

"I want to know why you haven't solved that break-in into my store."

"As I recall, there was no actual break-in involved. Whoever got in, did it with a key."

"I was robbed."

Boone extended his hand to direct him down the hall. "Come into my office."

Once Boone was behind his desk and Cooper was seated on the other side, Boone began.

"I've had Deputy Garnett go over the store with the

proverbial fine-toothed comb, Dick. He's dusted the doors for prints which, as you can imagine, are a complete hodge-podge of half the town except for the perp who likely wore gloves. And it took you a couple of days to give him a list of everyone who has a key to your store.

"What we don't have," countered Cooper, "is your personal interest in this case." He stabbed his index finger at Boone's desk.

"You have my interest. That's why I put Garnett on it. The man's a trained crime-scene investigator. Now the materials taken included," he paused and opened a case file, "three cans of Coleman's fuel, cans of acetone, starter fluid, and ten instant cold packs among other things."

"You should be looking at some of these college kids camping and floating on the river."

"Dick, those items I listed did not include six packs of beer, packs of beef jerky, and condoms. We're not dealing with drunken kids on a float trip. We're dealing with methamphetamine manufacture. Maybe making just enough for their own use and not to sell."

Cooper rose from the chair, his face red. "You know, you've spent way too much time driving around the state recently, and not enough time in your own county. Oh yes," he added, "I've seen the mileage statements. And don't think I'm not going to bring it up at the next quorum Court."

`Boone closed the file and folded his hands atop his desk. "You're a Justice of the Peace, Dick. It's your call what you bring up at the monthly meetings. But yours is not the only case on our books."

"Yeah, a thirty-some-odd-year old death that no one gives a flying crap about," snapped Cooper. "I want some satisfaction soon, Boone. Otherwise come next election, I'll personally finance your opponent's campaign. Now I want to see the asshole that robbed me behind bars!"

Cooper turned and stormed out of the office. Boone hoped the man was mad enough to cuss once more on his way out. Jo's coffee pot fund needed the money. This one made awful coffee. He was about to turn his attention to the paperwork on his desk when Deputy Wells came in, proudly holding up an evidence bag containing a filth encrusted two-liter bottle.

"Sheriff, you are not gonna believe what I found."

"A soda bottle with methamphetamine residue." Boone motioned to the chair across the desk. "Take a load off, Gabe, and tell me about it."

Deputy Wells sat down, grinning, and handed the bag to Boone. "I went out to Ethan Burdett's place before noon. His horses were blocking traffic -- again. Between Ethan and I, we got the paint back in and the bay just followed. Then, as I was leaving, I spotted this bottle in the ditch."

Boone turned the evidence bag over in his hands, examining the residue inside the bottle. "Did you test it?"

Wells jerked his head towards the door behind him. "Garnett did just now. Positive for meth. And here's the best part. There are prints on the bottle. Maybe they'll match the park shooter's prints."

"Good job, Gabe," said Boone. "Do you think whoever tossed this has been using Burdett's barn to manufacture? Is that how the horses got out of the paddock this time?"

"Nah. That paint is just an escape artist. I watched him go right back to the gate after I latched it and start working the bolt with his lips. So I twisted some baling wire around the gate. I'm going to go buy a padlock and chain and take it on up there after my shift, install it, and trust that Ethan won't lose this key like he did the last time and then go cut off the lock. But I did tell him to keep an eye out for suspicious activity."

"No need to wait for your shift to end. Go on and take the money out of petty cash. It will save us that much and more on gas and time rounding those blasted horses up again." Boone looked at the three prints visible on the one side. "All I need now are prints to run against these."

"But we'll send it on to Little Rock and they'll run it against the dead shooter's, right?"

"Of course. But what if they don't match. Maybe that

fellow only purchased but didn't manufacture. And what if our manufacturer isn't in the data base?" asked Boone. "We haven't seen any sign of meth production in the county for months. Then Cooper's store is robbed of meth making supplies. Next you find this bottle."

"So," summarized Wells. "You think the guy that robbed Cooper's hardware is the one that made this batch of meth and you think it was someone local."

Boone set the evidence pouch down and shrugged. "Hoping. You know how it is. I hate coincidences." He picked up the evidence bag and handed it to Wells." Get it signed into the evidence locker and get that padlock out to Burdett's place."

Wells left just as Deputy Chapman knocked on the door. "Got some information on that Ranger Hodges, boss." He set a sheet of paper on the desk and waited, hands behind him in a military at ease stance.

Boone quickly read through the report once, then twice. "This is all you found?"

Chapman's mouth drooped until he resembled some kid scolded for something he didn't do. "I worked hard for that, boss. I--"

Boone waved a hand for silence. "No. I didn't mean that. You did well. I just want to be sure that it's all here." He held up the single sheet.

"That's all I got so far. I got a photo from the state's human resources office. A deputy friend of mine is taking the picture around to a taxidermist he knows that's been in the business so long, he probably stuffed mammoths for cave men."

"That's a good job, deputy."

Chapman's face brightened. "Really? Can I drive the Tahoe?"

"Nope. You're still stuck with the Crown Vic, kid."

Chapman stuck a finger in his mouth and feigned gagging as he left the office. Boone couldn't blame him. No one wanted to drive that old Crown Vic, but they were stuck with it in the motor pool. He turned his attention back to the report – all three lines of it.

In seventy-six; deer, fur-bearers, squirrel, and rabbit were the only legal animals to hunt in the fall and Hodges hadn't owned a license to hunt any of them. But a realtor did recall him renting a cabin for three years running. She remembered because she thought that he and his wife made such a sweet couple with her petite frame and pretty red hair.

Sharon Hodges was a tall brunette.

CHAPTER 25

"What are you looking for in these filthy old books?"

Wren slumped on the couch like a limp rag doll. It was the first sign of life Phoebe had seen since they'd moved to the cabin. Unless Wren was eating, which Phoebe insisted was at the table, she shut herself away in her room.

She's curious. That's a good sign.

"I'm just reading them for fun. There's a lot of park history in these notebooks." Phoebe knew that the journals were supposed to be a secret between the sheriff and herself. Well, that train left the station the moment both Shirley and Burt saw them. But she reasoned that as long as she kept the purpose secret, no harm was done.

And yet that one diary was missing. At first she thought it was an oversight on her part when she quickly sorted the box of books. But now, a day later and another more careful sorting, she still couldn't locate it. She could have sworn she'd seen November 29, 1976 on the first entry. Was she mistaken about the date? Had it been wishful thinking? She was sure of two facts: one; the opening entry had been written by honeymooners plagued by a mouse and two; the notebook was orange. The only other orange notebook didn't have anything like that. Which cabin was that? Phoebe closed her eyes and tried to picture the cover. Cabin Eight.

Wren stirred on the couch. "History, huh." She reached for a notebook, scanning the cover. "Maybe there's something in one of these about those kids' deaths."

"Oh, honey. Don't be foolish. What do you expect? That someone's going to write 'today I killed a boy and dumped a little girl out in the cold?'" Phoebe kept her tone as light as possible, but inwardly she felt something akin to panic. The girl's too clever by halves. Damn!

Wren scowled. "I'm not stupid. But there might be something about an argument. Or the kid might have written how he hates his life and wants to leave."

No, Wren. That's what you would write.

"I think the boy really liked the park," said Phoebe. "Oh, I left one of the park bandanas for you in your room. There's a map on it, you know, in case you decide you'd like to hike one of the trails during the day." She slid over a stack of notebooks, ones she'd looked at already.

Wren ignored them and picked up another with a particularly ratty cover. Phoebe glanced at the cover date. 1991. It was far too recent to have anything useful for the sheriff.

"Those cabins didn't have phones or tv's or any of the good stuff they have now," Wren said as she flipped through the pages.

"No, they didn't get any of those things including hot tubs until five years ago. Superintendent McGowan says there was pressure on the state from the local resorts and hotels to upgrade, but I think they redid the kitchens and put in microwaves in nineteen-ninety. Superintendent McGowan said there'd been a lot of construction that year and the next."

"Mom, you don't have to keep saying 'Superintendent McGowan' to me. Like this whole first name business with adults is some secret club you have to be old to join." Wren looked at her from under lowered lashes. "Speaking of Burt, I heard him talking to you the other day and he sounded kind of pissed. Are you, like, gonna get fired cause of that druggy?"

Phoebe didn't take the bait. She was fed up with this game of 'try to aggravate mom' and hoped that, by ignoring or down playing some of these verbal jabs, Wren would get tired of playing. "I'm not going to get fired," Phoebe said as calmly as she could muster. She changed the subject and read aloud from her current notebook. It didn't apply to the sheriff's request, but she needed to at least maintain the appearance of reading all of these or Wren would get suspicious. "Listen to this, Wren. It was written June twenty-fifth, nineteen eighty-two from cabin three. 'Up early this morning and saw a doe with her spotted fawn.' Isn't that something?"

"Mmmhmm."

Phoebe saw that her daughter was thoroughly engrossed in her own notebook, and she could tell by Wren's furrowed brow that the girl wasn't faking to avoid talking to her. Phoebe turned back to her own stack, putting down the one and picking up another, wondering if she'd ever find anything useful. Cabin 5 – 1985. The opening date was May eleventh.

She scanned comment after comment on how lovely the park was, how much they enjoyed the cave, or the Rocky Crest trail. There were a few notes in the winter months on meals cooked in the fireplace. Skewered hotdogs won out second only to the expected smore's. Nothing! Phoebe paged over into the spring and felt her fingers tingle. Here was something!

Our C. C.C. reunion yielded a smaller group than I'd hoped, but after fifty years, I suppose it is to be expected. Most of the twenty-three men that attended came only for the day, but I could not imagine being back in this beautiful park without staying in one of the very cabins that I built, or walking on a trail that I helped bridge. Proudly took my grandson and showed him every stone that I put in place in the dam and the bridge abutments.

The biggest surprise came from seeing Ben Owen again. He'd been our foreman and a key man in setting the stones for the cabin fireplaces. There wasn't a man around that could touch Ben when it came to fitting stone, but he'd left in the spring of '37 of a sudden. Some folk said he'd been spurned by a young woman from the area - a minister's daughter. Others whispered darker tales, of running from the law, but I never believed that idle gossip. Ben was always a good man. What I remembered the most about him was his trouble with colors. He'd have on a green shirt and swear it was red. Most of the fall leaves were wasted on him.

When I saw him, he was sitting on the chair outside of Cabin 8, staring down at the lake. He always loved that cabin best. I wanted to visit a spell with him, ask him how he'd fared, and show him my grandson. Not sure if he ignored me when I hallooed to him, or if he was wandering in his mind to earlier times. Figured he was wanting some peace right then, so I left him alone. Went over to see if I could find him later, but he was gone.

Phoebe set aside that notebook and pawed through the others, looking for a Cabin 8 from the same date in the hopes that Ben Owen wrote in it. He seemed interesting and the name sounded familiar though she couldn't put her finger on where she'd heard it.

* * *

Wren would never have admitted it to her mom, but parts of the journals were kind of interesting. Not the sappy stuff about how much closer they felt to God in the park, but some of the personal stories weren't bad. Some woman was alone in the cabin while her husband took their two foster-sons on an overnight hike. The woman didn't know what to do except write and plead for more foster parents. Wren remembered camping with her dad. It had been fun. Then. She didn't think she could ever do it again. It would hurt too much, and the last thing she wanted was to feel anything. Anger was the only emotion that felt comfortable. All else felt like a lie.

She turned the page, flipped past drawings of two deer rendered in a blue crayon by some kid followed by the words 'Cabin 8 Rocks!' The deer looked like dachshunds with coat racks on their heads. Wren stopped at the next story and pulled her knees and the notebook closer. She heard her mother babbling on about someone seeing a fawn and ignored her.

June 30, 1991. Rainy morning. Doesn't seem to be too uncommon this time of year. We played every board game that the park office had, but the kids had more fun rolling the checkers across the wooden floors than anything else. Not sure how much more of this family time I can handle. Ooops. Got to go. Billy let one of the checkers roll into the broom closet. And guess who gets to go look for it.

(later) The sun is finally out so I sent John off with the boys to the pool so I can have some quiet mommy time. I'm worn out from looking for the silly checker. Once I got a flashlight, I found it stuck in a closet in the bedroom. It seems that the closet is a new addition and hides some of the fireplace stonework that also makes up part of the bedroom wall. Saw 3 of the cutest stone shelves there. They were tannish-white with a small stripe of brown.

I was looking for fossils in the stone when I saw something carved into the stone at the base. I couldn't make it out at first so I took some paper and did a rubbing. It looked like B. Owen. + A. Ell. I assume they must be the stone masons signing their work like the concrete men did when they poured our sidewalk. I showed the boys but you know kids. No interest. Oh, dear. Must go. John is back with them already.

Wren's arms tingled as she reread the initials. This silly woman was half right. One of them was the stonemason: Ben Owen. But Wren knew that would have bet anything that A. Ell stood for Agnes Ellwood. The remaining letters were either worn away or the woman just didn't look carefully. She had to get into that cabin. Not only did she want to examine the carving in the closet, but she wanted to find out if that brown stripe was really a bit of iron in the rock or if it was a smear of old blood.

George Tanner's blood?

CHAPTER 26

To Phoebe, the dam that formed Dead Man's Lake resembled a monument built by the Egyptians. It wasn't just the massive stone blocks, some a foot and a half tall and twice as long. It was the pattern of construction, stacked in cascading stair steps reminiscent of the pyramids. Definitely an impressive structure, and after the recent thunderstorms, the lake flowed over in a series of mesmerizing staggered waterfalls.

But today it was not the dam, the lake, or even Big Sugar Creek feeding it that drew Phoebe's attention. It was the monument to the C.C.C. workers and the bronze tablet containing their names. Her finger ran down the lists, sorted by their hometown. She had no idea what town to look for and so began at the top with Alexander and continued on. She hit pay dirt at the entry for Eureka Springs and her finger traced the name.

Ben Owen.

That was the name in the journal. It had finally come to Phoebe where she'd heard the name before. She'd met a Joe Owen in Shirley's store once, a contractor. Perhaps they were related. But what intrigued her most was that Ben Owen had left the corps early because, if the rumor was true, he'd been in love with a minister's daughter.

Agnes Tanner had been a minister's daughter.

Phoebe shook her head. What difference did it make? He wasn't here when the Tanner family had their reunion so he wouldn't have known what happened to George or the little girl.

It's Saturday afternoon, you have the rest of the day and all of tomorrow off this week. Go home.

Still she felt drawn to the name on the plaque. She wondered what he'd been doing all alone during the reunion. He sounded as lonely as she felt. Face it, you're only interested because it sounds like the plot of some old romantic movie.

Phoebe got into the van and pulled out into the road back to the visitor's center. Then, at the top of the hill where the road forked, she impulsively took the right hand road that began the winding cabin loop. At Cabin 8, she pulled over and shut the engine. In front of her was the cabin complete with the stone patio and the heavy-timbered picnic bench where Mr. Owen had sat all those years ago and looked down at the lake. Maybe he'd helped build the dam. She got out and walked to the table, hoping to connect with the man by sharing the view.

There was no view of the lake from here. All she could see was the backside of the store.

CHAPTER 27

Boone spent most of Monday morning looking over the week's district court cases and seeing who'd be needed to testify. After that, old Bob Middendorf from the local VFW wanted to talk about this year's Fourth of July parade. Wiley and LeaAnita Okerman requested a deputy to do a property check while they drove off to Albuquerque. He spent his lunch break grazing on a pre-packaged salad from the IGA while he finalized next month's schedule. It wasn't until two that he could get back to the Tanner case.

He had two stacks of papers in front of him. One set contained all the notes and statements from nineteen seventy-six. The other, the new copies which McGowan had brought in as well as new statements that Boone had personally taken. He spent the next hour pouring over them, comparing details, looking for anything that might give him some insight into who killed the Tanner boy and left the little girl to freeze to death.

After an hour all he had was a stiff neck. That and he was hungry. Again.

That's what I get for eating like a rabbit.

He resisted the urge to go across the street and raid the gas station's snack aisle or, worse yet, buy one of their double cheese and beef burritos. His stomach rumbled, weighing in its own vote for a bag of barbecue corn chips.

"Shut up!" Boone went to the break room, filled his coffee mug, and used it to chase down two aspirin. He stopped in the dispatch room and listened to Jo field a call from one of the county's odder residents.

"And you say they're having sex in your attic, Opal? . . . I know. . . Yes, I'll send the undercover deputy in the unmarked car. He'll get them and you won't hear a thing. . . okay, dear." Jo hung up and then punched in a phone number from memory. "Wanda? Your mom is off her meds again today. . . Yeah, I'd appreciate it. . . Goodbye."

"Opal seeing space aliens again?" asked Boone.

Jo nodded. "Three of them and they're having sex. Wish her daughter would check on her more often."

"You handle her well. Any reply back from Little Rock on cause of death?"

Jo glared. An empty ball point pen tube dangled from the corner of her mouth. Boone knew she was on the patch and the plastic tube was her surrogate cigarette. Since she only used it when she was really dead set on a smoke, he also knew her mood would be on the sour side. And, excepting Opal's hallucinations, it was another slow day. Slow and Jo was not a good mix.

"You getting bored in there, Linus?"

"Just frustrated. Frustrated and hungry."

"Yeah? Well, your answer to your hunger is crossing the street, but it might just raise your frustration level."

Boone spied Anita Holmes, carrying a platter of muffins. "Oh, hell," he said. "Tell her I'm not here. Tell her I'm in conference." He hurried back to his office, calling over his shoulder. "And I owe you a dollar for the swear."

"That one's on me, Linus," she hollered after him.

Boone shut his door and sat at his desk. He felt like a fool for hiding from the woman, but the last thing he needed right now was one of her high-caloric baked goods and a half an hour of her letting him know what a good cook and homemaker she was.

That's what I get for taking a break. He forced himself to concentrate on the case files. He wanted to get through them before he drove out to the park. Ranger Palmer had called earlier and said that she'd found the old journals.

Twenty minutes later he found his first discrepancy. The campgrounds weren't entirely empty. True, there were no tent campers, but there had been one couple registered with an Airstreamer. The signature was barely readable. It wasn't a big discrepancy. After thirty-five years, no one could be expected to recall every detail. Maybe Burt didn't mention them because they weren't tent campers. Maybe checking the campgrounds back then didn't include RVs.

Boone made a note to see if anyone could read the name on the register copy. They might be someone to interview. He fell to reexamining the two sets of notes with fresh interest.

In another fifteen minutes he found a second and bigger discrepancy. Not all of the cabins had been taken that weekend. The reservation on number eight had been cancelled the day before Thanksgiving. It was vacant.

* * *

Wren tugged on her bathing suit top before she hauled herself out of the pool. The suit was last year's, a blue two-piece and it tended to ride up when she stretched her arms. It didn't help that, at thirteen pushing fourteen, she had the chest of an eight-year old. She still wasn't sure why she let her mom talk her into hanging out at the pool.

A surreptitious glance at the blond life guard sitting on his raised deck chair gave her part of the answer. Wren had seen him often as she went about her job. A few times she spied him leaning against a cottonwood, smoking a cigarette on break.

She'd asked Sherry Tucker about him and learned that his name was Ricky Cooper and he'd just graduated from Wayside Springs High School. Sherry said that he'd been a star quarterback and the center on the basketball team. He was eighteen. Four and a quarter years difference in age wasn't too much. Her dad had been four years older than her mom. She decided to swim back to the other side. Maybe he'd say hello this time.

Wren pushed off with her legs and glided across the short side, letting her arms rest against her side. As she popped up from the pool, water streaming from her short, purple-black pig tails, she heard him call to her.

"Hey, you're that goth chick that hangs out in the store. How come you're not in a black bathing suit? I thought goth's only wore black."

"It's last year's suit," she replied, suddenly wishing she'd thought of something more clever to say. Maybe something about fashion.

"Good thing you're flat and can still wear it. What are you, twelve?"

Wren felt her face burn. "I'll be fourteen in August."

"Hey, don't snap. I didn't mean anything by it. That hair and all is kind of cute."

Wren pushed her wet bangs from her face. "Really? You think so?"

"Yeah, it reminds me of that girl in the Adam's family movie. What was her name? Wednesday! That's it. I'll call you Wednesday."

Wren hauled herself onto the deck and stood, fists on her hips, her chin jutting out. "I'm not Wednesday. My name is Wren, and I dress that way cause my dad got blown up, but maybe you're too busy being a pretty boy to understand about war and death and grown-up issues."

"Hey!" he retorted, index finger stabbing the air. "I'm plenty mature and I could teach you a thing or two, kid."

"Yeah? Like how to pose?" She strode off with as much dignity as she could muster, grabbed her towel, and heading into the girl's bathhouse.

"Hey, Wrensday," He called after her. "Don't be mad. I said it was cute."

"Stupid boy. What does he know?" she muttered. But not all the water drops that she wiped from her face came from the pool.

* * *

Phoebe stood barefoot in the doorway in her uniform, socks in hand. The words to an old ditty his grandma used to sing popped into Boone's mind.

Shoes and stockings in her hand and her feet all over the floor.

Only the ranger's feet were small and delicately boned, and Boone noted again with admiration that she did more for the uniform than any ranger he'd ever seen.

"Sheriff," said Phoebe. "I just got off duty. Won't you come in? Can I get you something?" She tossed the socks onto a pair of leather hiking boots, padded into the kitchen nook, and opened the refrigerator. "I've got ice water, instant lemonade, and hummingbird nectar. If you're hungry, there's a blueberry yogurt in here."

"Lemonade sounds good, Ms. Palmer. I'm not much for yogurt." He stood in the entryway, noting the huge stone fireplace against the far wall and wondered what it would be like to sit in front of the fire on a cold night.

She returned with a glass of lemonade and two spiral bound notebooks. She handed the lemonade to him. "I hear you there. I'd be more inclined to eat the stuff if it came in bacon flavor." She indicated a sofa and seated herself in the adjacent slide rocker. "And it's not Ms. Palmer. You said you'd call me Phoebe." She passed a blue notebook to him.

"You said you'd call me Linus," said Boone. He sat on the couch and turned the cover of the notebook to the starting page. "I appreciate your letting me talk to you in your home. It's best to keep this as secret as possible until I know more of what's going on."

"No problem . . . Linus. That's why I left Wren at the pool. But it'll close at six and then Shirley Gracehill from the store will drive her here. It's only a mile from the office, but I'm still a little nervous about Wren walking off alone. Especially after . . ." She cleared her throat and looked at her wristwatch. "Anyway, that should give us at least an hour to talk about the case."

"Well, I'll make sure that I'm gone by then." Boone felt a pang of disappointment, but he wasn't sure why. It wasn't as if this was a date. He barely knew this woman. McGowan had explained that she was a war widow, and she'd already told him that she had a daughter.

"I suppose that would be best," said Phoebe. "Wren might be a bit taken aback to come home and find someone here. You see, she hasn't taken her father's death well at all. Just seeing a man here . . . well, she might get the wrong impression."

Boone thought he detected a similar note of disappointment in her voice and allowed himself the luxury of feeling flattered.

Phoebe nodded to the book in Boone's hand. "Most of the notebooks are pretty standard, comments on the scenery, little lists of birds seen, that sort of thing." She leaned forward and touched the cover. "But in this one, I did find something that might be interesting. I don't know if it means anything. I put a bookmark on the page."

Boone found the bookmark, read the entry, then reread it. It certainly didn't fit the usual entries as he understood them, and from a lawman's perspective, it was intriguing. "Most curious," he said. "What's your take on this?"

"I knew I'd heard that name before somewhere so I checked on it. He was a C.C.C man and Agnes Elwood Tanner was a minister's daughter." She rocked a little. "The date is way off, but that Owen sounds like a man with a guilty conscience. I just don't know what he's guilty of."

"You think he came to the Tanner reunion, killed the kids, then comes back nine years later to a C.C.C. reunion and feels remorse?"

"It does sound stupid when you put it that way. I guess criminals don't always return to the scene of the crime, do they? Do we even know if he was at the family reunion?"

"He's not on any registry, but it's not stupid. I would've picked this guy up on my radar. One more person for me to try to track down, but he must be well over ninety by now. Probably dead." He watched as she picked up another notebook, this one green. "Something else?"

Phoebe nodded. "I may have saved the best for last. But I'll leave that to you." She opened it and flipped to the appropriate page. "There's no date given, but the entry just before it was October twenty-eight, nineteen seventy-six and the next one after is January sixteen of seventy-seven."

She handed the notebook to him and wriggled back into her chair as though to get more comfortable. Boone felt her gaze lock onto his face, watching for any change of expression as he started reading silently. It made him anticipate finding a solid lead in the entry.

My secund day in this cabin. Went on a hike yesterday with some ranger. My cousin George is so stoopid een tho he thinks he's so smart. All he talked about this morning was some dum science fair thing like anyone cares about bats. That's all he talked about yesterday. I wanted to play football but he woodn't. Said he was going to visit the store again on account they had books there to look at. This morning, he just kept pointing to stuff like this notebook or his kerchief and asking me and mom and dad to describe them. His dad got real mad cause he thought George was making fun of my dad on account that he can't always tell some colors apart. Uncle Reuben picked up a fireplace poker and waved it George and said he was gonna wop his backside but good. George lit out like he was on fire but it was funny to see. I'm riting this while my dad is sleeping. Ma says not to wake him until it comes time to eat turkey dinner. Maybe I'll go on outside.

Boone's pulse quickened, beating fast in his neck and ears. This had to be that cousin, Tom, that had been on the hike with his little sister Ruth. It confirmed that George's father had a temper. If he'd threatened the boy in the cabin, could he have gone after him later on?

"This is an incredible find, Phoebe. Unfortunately, it does little more than strengthen the one hypothesis, that George's dad killed him in a fit of anger. The boy certainly seemed to have been different from the rest of the brood. More intelligent, thoughtful."

"And happier," added Phoebe. "Burt talked about what an engaging boy he was, always asking questions. Everyone else in the family seems pretty dour by comparison."

"And less educated. His cousin, Tom, certainly wasn't a very good speller." He paged backwards and forward from that spot. "It doesn't appear as if any pages were torn out. I don't see any fragments of paper stuck in the spiral wiring."

"No. That notebook is pretty much the full thickness," agreed Phoebe. She leaned forward in the rocker. "Sheriff . . . Linus, if his father did kill George, even accidentally, do you think the entire family might have been in on covering up his death?"

"You mean going so far as to wait and then report the kid was missing and conduct a search?" He shrugged. "Anything is possible. But it still leaves the question of the little girl's death. Surely her parents wouldn't have been complicit in that."

"It could have been an accident. Perhaps they had to take her along when they buried George and she really did wander off. You know, that cave where they found her is not far cross-country from where the boy was buried."

Phoebe clasped her hands, resting her forearms on her thighs. "We may never know who killed those children. It would help, I suppose, if you knew what the murder weapon was." She looked at him with upraised brows, an enquiring look.

"Should get a cause of death soon. Full autopsy will take longer, not that there's much to autopsy, but we sent a lot of soil and other materials down to the lab." He cleared his throat. "But you're right. Having a murder weapon could help narrow down who we're looking for."

"Have you found much of the family around anywhere?"

"Just one older sister. I'm still trying to locate this fellow," he said, indicating the author of the journal entry. "Tom Hawley is not an easy man to find. He never finished high school. I found out he enlisted in the army and spent time in Germany. Got dishonorably discharged and since then, he's been under the radar."

"I know I'd like to see this case solved," she said. Poor kids. I can imagine that you feel it even more so. I mean," she added hastily, "being a real law enforcement officer."

"You're a real law enforcement officer," Boone said.

"Not according to my boss. I'm on probation, and I never wanted to be a ranger. I just wanted to be an interpreter, but this is a smaller park and its needs and budget meant doubling up two jobs. You know how I froze with that shooter. Your deputy took Sloan's statement and mine." She waved towards a small, locked fire safe. "I hate that Glock."

"You can't let that first time affect your performance on the job, Phoebe. Chances are there won't be another and in most cases, just seeing it strapped on your belt is enough to make most miscreants get in line. If you want, I can take you to the range, help you practice."

"How can you help me overcome a loathing for shooting someone? Killing a person. Actually, Charles had wanted to teach me to shoot. He loved guns, and I sometimes suspect he was addicted to danger. I think that's why he stayed in the reserves."

Boone watched her hug herself as though she suddenly felt a chill. He changed the subject, flipping the journals to a random page. He read aloud, "Saw a bobcat sitting on the deck while drinking bourbon and smoking a cigar." Boone closed the book. "Wow, I didn't know bobcats smoked or drank. You could have a real wildlife problem here."

Phoebe laughed.

He finished the lemonade. "Say, you might be able to help me with a few other things."

"Sure, I mean, if I can. What is it?"

Boone extracted a pocket notebook and took out a folded sheet. "I've got a record that someone was camping in an RV over that Thanksgiving, but I can't make out the name."

Phoebe held the paper close and examined the signature. "That's Vivian and Verl Keck."

"Do you know them? Could you check some records, see when they last showed up, get an address for them."

"That's easy," Phoebe said. "The Keck's practically live at the park. From what I've been told, they've been regulars every summer for years. Nice people, too. Always bringing up some of their homemade stew or cobbler to the office."

Boone perked up immediately. Here was a break at last. "And they're in the park now?"

She nodded. "They showed up mid-May and will probably stay through most of the summer, although," she added, "they do sometimes drive off for a couple of days to a week. But surely they'd have already reported everything that they knew. What can anyone remember after so many years?"

"There's nothing in the old file from them which means they were never interviewed. Remember, until now, no one treated this as a crime. Just two missing kids. I'll stop by the campgrounds on my way out and see if they're around."

"That was one thing," said Phoebe. "You said you needed help with a few other things."

"I need to get fingerprints from a boy named Richard Cooper. I understand that he works part-time in the park."

"He's a life guard. But why do you need his prints?"

"Just to rule him out as a robbery suspect," Boone said, making it sound simple. He'd heard the note of nervousness creep into her voice when he'd asked for the prints. "You see, his father's store was robbed, and I know he helps out there."

"Oh? Can't you just ask him for his cooperation? I think he's eighteen."

"You know kids and cops. They'll refuse for the heck of it. And I know you're an officer of the law, but he won't see you that way. To him, you're just the friendly park interpreter. I can let Burt know that you're assisting me here. Maybe that will help you get back in his good graces."

"I'd appreciate that. Really. So what do you want me to do?"

Boone took out a manila envelope and let a color photo slide out onto his open palm and away from his fingertips. "Ask him if he's seen this guy around. Tell him it's a vandalism matter or something. Get him to hold it. If you have to touch it, just use the edges. Can you do that?"

She nodded. "The man looks awful. Who is he really?"

"My dad camping. I keep copies in color and black and white. Been very useful."

Phoebe laughed again, and Boone noticed how her eyes sparkled. He slipped the photo back in the envelope and handed it to her, searching for an excuse to prolong the interview. It was nice sitting in this woman's cabin. "So, how old is your daughter?"

"Wren'll be fourteen in August."

"Pretty name."

She smiled. "It was my husband's idea. You see, Phoebe is also a kind of bird. I think he liked having another bird name for his daughter. Wren seemed prettier than Robin."

"Or turkey," added Boone. "Sorry about your husband's death. Burt told me he died in Iraq. You're pretty gutsy building a new life for yourself out here."

Phoebe sighed. "Thanks. I wish Wren saw it that way." She looked at her watch.

"I should go. You're worried that your daughter will be upset if she sees me here."

"Everything upsets Wren anymore. But, yes. Sorry."

"You could always say that I was doing follow up questions. What's important is that we keep anything you found out about the cabin notebooks secret."

"Oh, hell, Linus. I'm afraid I couldn't quite keep the notebooks a secret. Both Burt and Shirley saw them. But," she added quickly, "I told them I thought reading them might give Wren something to do. Help her with the school's Arkansas history project."

"Did they buy it?"

"I think so." She looked at her hands resting on her lap. "You know, I may be imagining this, but I could have sworn I saw a notebook from just after the crime's date. But when I got them home and went through them, I couldn't find it. It was orange. I distinctly remember that."

"You think one of them took it?"

"That's all I can come up with. You see. They were in an old box. I threw some mimeo handouts on top that I thought I could use some time, and when Burt and Shirley showed up, I kind of hinted that I thought that the box was full of them. Then Burt insisted on helping me carry out the box and the bottom fell out."

Boone grimaced. "That's when they first saw them?"

"Yes. I'm sure of it. I acted as surprised as I could and then said I'd take them home anyway for Wren to read. They helped me gather them. I hate to think anything bad of either of them, but I was sure I saw one that covered the time period. At least the opening date was November the twenty-ninth of that year. I didn't actually read the entire book to see if there was anything useful in it."

"But you read enough to know that it was missing from your stack?"

Phoebe nodded. "It started out with some honeymooners writing about a mouse."

Boone leaned forward, his forearms resting on his thighs, hands clasped. "Thanksgiving was on the twenty-fifth that year. Do you have any idea which one of them might have taken it? Did you see Shirley or Burt hurry outside or rummage around in a far corner? Someplace where one of them could have stashed the book to come back for later?"

"They both went out to get a good box and some duct tape. It was raining and they had jackets so either one of them could've slipped it inside a coat and taken it. But why?"

"That's why I hoped to keep this all secret."

She gasped. "You really suspect them? I didn't think you were serious about that."

Boone held up a hand to caution calmness. "I honestly have no idea, but I'll admit, this looks suspicious."

"But Wren is with . . ."

"Your daughter will be fine. As long as she doesn't know anything either and doesn't suspect anyone, then no one has any reason to harm her."

"Maybe, but I'll feel better once she's here at home.

Maybe I should radio down to Shirley and tell Wren to come home now. It's only a mile walk."

"No! That might only arouse suspicions. Better that you just show up and get her."

"I'll tell her I forgot hot dog buns for supper. Shirley stocks those."

She hustled to retrieve her hiking shoes and balanced on one foot, pulling a shoe onto the other without benefit of the socks. As she tried to put the second shoe on, she tripped on her untied shoelace and stumbled forward. Boone caught her and held her by her arms to steady her. Her cheeks blushed a pretty rose color before he released her.

"Thanks." She kept her eyes averted from his face and promptly sat down in the rocker to finish putting on her shoes.

"Slow down," he said. "You've got time. I wouldn't want you to have an accident on the way to get your daughter because you were distracted."

She brushed a stray lock of hair from her forehead and smiled. "I'm fine now. Really."

"Okay then." He held up the notebooks. "Thanks for these." He opened the front door.

Phoebe held up the envelope. "And I'll get that Cooper boy to touch this photograph."

A flurry of black rushed in. "The pool was contaminated with an annoying turd brain so I left early and caught a ride with Burt." Suddenly the black blur stopped and stared at him. "Who the hell are you?"

"I'm Sheriff Boone. And you must be Wren." As he studied the defiant face, the dyed hair and dead black clothes, he knew he'd seen the girl before.

She'd been in the library, trying to get into the genealogy room the day Beulah died.

CHAPTER 28

"What the hell was he doing here!" yelled Wren. She stormed back and forth in the living room like a skinny thundercloud, her arms folded tightly across her chest. "Daddy's only dead a little over a year and you're already hooking up?"

"You watch your language, young lady!" snapped Phoebe. "How dare you speak to me that way. And for your information, I am not hooking up with anyone. That was the sheriff."

Wren pivoted and glared. "You're going out with the sheriff? Oh, that's rich. It's not enough that you carry a gun now? You have to chase a man who carries one? I mean, is that what gets you off?"

Phoebe resisted the urge to slap her daughter across the face, struggling to calm herself before speaking again. "I'm not going out with him or anyone else. I found a dead body, remember? It's his job to ask follow-up questions. And don't you ever speak to me that way again!"

"Whatever. I mean, if honoring daddy's memory means that little to you." Wren turned her back on Phoebe.

Phoebe felt her rage explode as though the bomb that killed her husband blew up inside of her. She grabbed her daughter by the arm and spun her around.

"How dare you talk to me about honoring my husband!" Her voice rose to a shriek. "What the hell do you know about it? You lost your father, but I lost my lover, my best friend, and my partner in raising you, you ungrateful little . . ." She stopped, biting off the word before she went too far. She released her daughter and wrapped her forearms over her head. "I'm trying to build a fresh life for both of us here, Wren. The type of life your daddy would have loved."

"You just keep on telling yourself that, mother. At least one of us will believe it. And don't bother dragging me to your little program tonight, either. I'm not going."

Phoebe was too stunned to argue. What energy she'd had in her had already been spent. She felt hollow. "What are you going to do?"

Wren shrugged. "I know what I'm not going to do. I'm not going to watch TV or play games on the computer." She looked around the cabin in a mock search for anything of interest. "We live in pioneer land, remember?"

Phoebe heard Wren's door slam and collapsed onto the couch. What had she done? Why did she ever imagine Wren would approve of living here? She'd intended to have a satellite dish by now and wireless internet, but they cost so much and her budget had been tighter than she'd imagined. Why couldn't someone buy her house in Wichita? Right now there wasn't even a renter in it. Why hadn't her husband taken out a bigger life insurance policy? Why hadn't she insisted on it? In her heart, she knew why. To do that would have meant admitting that he might not come back. It had all been a complete denial.

Maybe if I put it on the credit card? She hated to go deeper into debt, especially if Burt still canned her when her probation was up. So many of the utilities had been in Charles' name so her credit score wasn't the best in the world. Still, if it meant making the home more palatable for Wren, it might be worth it. One thing was certain, she absolutely refused to ask her in-laws for help. She only had to see what happened to Wren when she left them in charge during the three months of her law enforcement training to know why.

They turned her against me and into a freak. They'd love to know that we're struggling.

Phoebe went into the bathroom and splashed water on her face. She had an evening program to do in forty-five minutes: 'Build a bat' started with the participants putting together a model bats using felt, chenille wire, and styrofoam balls as they tried to figure out all the adaptations that bats needed to succeed. They finished in time to watch the bats fly over the lake, catching insects on the wing. It was a family program in which Wren had once participated and it was one of Phoebe's favorites. Tonight her heart wasn't in it. It didn't matter. She was expected to do her job and do it with a cheerful grin. Afterwards, it was her turn again to drive through the campgrounds and give one last check on the park before retiring for the night. Now more than ever she needed to be on top of that aspect of her job.

"I'm heading out now, Wren," she called at her daughter's door. "There's chicken salad in the fridge and popcorn if you want to some."

Her only reply was a mumbled "not hungry."

It was at least a reply, thought Phoebe as she locked the door behind her and got into the park's mini-van. And when she got home, she'd go into Wren's room and try to talk to her.

And what if she's not here when you get back home?

CHAPTER 29

"Anything in yet from Little Rock?" Boone asked when he went in the next morning.

"Actually, yes." Grace said. She looked up from a ledger and handed him a set of papers.

"Quiet morning otherwise?"

"Laurel Danvers came in with a half dozen blueberry muffins."

Boone shook his head. "Just what we all need. More food."

"I had Gabe put them back in the break room. He ate two in front of Laurel which did not make her happy. She gave him a look that could curdle milk and told him to save some for you."

"I wish people would quit doing that. Bringing food I mean."

Grace cocked her head. "It's not people, Linus, it's Laurel and Anita. You know why they're doing it. They're trying to impress you with their homemaking skills. Now if you were to just be seen in company of some nice woman, maybe all of these others would get the hint and lay off. You're considered a prime catch around here, you know."

"Uh huh." Boone said, only half paying attention. He'd

already started scanning the report on cause of death by the state crime lab. The medical examiner had brought in a forensic anthropologist to examine the bones.

"Of course," continued Grace, "if you ¬were to get married, you'd lose all the women's votes in the next election. On second thought, better just smile and play the field with them."

"Right," He walked off slowly to his office, his nose in the report.

"Were you even listening?" she hollered. "Heck of a husband you'd make."

Boone sat at his desk and reread the report. They confirmed what he'd already surmised. The deceased was male, young, most likely fourteen to sixteen years old. Height was estimated at five foot, five inches. Dental records confirmed him as George Tanner.

None of the rocks he'd sent to the lab matched the impression in the boy's skull. Instead, the blow was most likely made by a heavy, narrow rod, one that likely had a blunt hook at the end of it. Analysis showed that the back was struck with the straight end of this implement but that the top was dented by a rounded end.

There were no traces of wooden splinters, but they picked up one burr of cast iron in the skull and a few more in the soil beneath it. None of the other remaining bones evidenced any severe trauma at time of death, although the right radius had been broken at some time. There was no perimortem damage to the vertebra or ribs, nothing to show a passing of a bullet or knife. Because the injury to the skull was severe, cause of death was officially ruled as death by blunt force trauma to the back of the head.

Cast iron! That suggested something other than a stick or a crowbar. And considering the boy had been in a rustic cabin, Boone's mind leaned towards a fireplace tool, possibly a poker. But those generally had sharp points. Could the murder weapon still be in the cabin where George stayed? The cousin, Tom, wrote that George's father threatened him with a poker.

But by now, after being inserted into innumerable fires to push and shove burning logs, there wouldn't be any trace of blood or hair left on it. Neither would he get any fingerprints after thirty-five years of handling.

It was a break and not a break. He could get the poker from George's cabin and send it to the crime lab. They could tell him if it matched the head wound, but he doubted there'd be a shred of evidence left to mark it as the actual weapon.

His phone rang. "Sheriff Boone here."

"Sheriff Boone, this is Sheriff Lester Tucker over in Bentwood. I got your request to locate a Tom Hawley, early fifties. I think we have him here. He goes by T.J. Hawley, but I'd bet dollars to donuts it's your man."

"That's good news. Can you give me his address and contact information? I'd like to come over there and talk to him. It's about a cold case we have here. Hawley was the victim's cousin. He may have information that could help."

"No trouble at all, Sheriff. He's in our lockup right now. Got into a fist fight while he was drunk last night. He's not going anywhere for a while."

* * *

"The sooner we get started, the sooner we can all get going." McGowan stood at the front of the Audio-Visual room, tapping his pen on a yellow legal pad. The seats were occupied by the rest of the park rangers, chief of maintenance, the office manager and one full-time desk clerk. Each was talking noisily.

Phoebe thought Burt seemed especially edgy today. He was usually very laid back at these staff meetings, cracking a few jokes with the male rangers. Sloan replied to her inquiries about his thigh with a cool, "It's fine," and walked away. The other rangers treated her politely, but without any warmth. None of them would make eye contact with her and she knew she wouldn't be welcome sitting next to any of them. They can't depend on me.

She took a seat beside the door and next to Sherry Tucker, burning from the sting of her co-workers' behavior. They exchanged quiet good mornings. Even though she never wanted the law enforcement side of the job, she coveted their respect and acceptance. Her summer intern, Wade, slipped in and joined the other men, receiving several pats on the back as he sat down.

"Geez, quiet down," McGowan scolded. "You all sound like a bunch of school kids after a holiday. We should've had this meeting yesterday, but let's just say that things came up. Okay. Now that I've got your attention, let's begin. The White Nose Fungus hasn't hit Arkansas yet, but we're still keeping our caves closed to the public to keep it from hitting. That's already made some of our guests a bit upset. They really like taking their kids into the Devil's Larder Cave. So I need everyone to be polite, but firm. And keep an eye on those gates we put over the openings. They're not all that strong, and someone with a mind-to could break in easily." He looked at Phoebe. "Educating the public is your department."

She decided she'd better address his concern and stood. "Wade and I," she said with a nod to the part-time summer interpreter, have made up some new signs to post around the visitor's center, the trail heads, and by the restrooms at each of the campgrounds."

McGowan nodded. "Good job, Wade. Appreciate the help. Now the sheriff gave us leave to get out on Dead Man's Trail and cut those fallen trees. Dave, that's your department."

Ranger David Pierce shifted in his chair. "You want anything in particular done with the wood? Leave it in place, haul it off to cure for building a bench, or what?"

Phoebe cleared her throat but McGowan beat her to the punch. "The oaks are fair game for firewood, but leave that hickory lie in peace. It wouldn't seem proper to do otherwise with it considering how it got there and how it was nourished. That seem okay to you, Palmer?"

"Yes, thanks, Burt." Palmer, not Phoebe. He's still shutting me out. She felt a rush of jealousy towards Wade. She'd designed the new signs and personally saw to their lamination.

"All right then, reports, people."

One by one, the other full-time rangers briefly spoke of any issues that they saw coming up that week. Ranger Pierce was in charge of the maintenance staff and Ranger Greg Phillips had charge of the cabins and housekeeping. Phoebe was supposed to oversee any park volunteers.

She waited her turn after Assistant Superintendent Bob Sloan's report on next month's bike race to announce that the Friends of Dead Man Hollow were cleaning trash from the campgrounds and some of the trails later this week. "I'll make sure we hit the bike trails, too."

"We've got a leak in Cabin 4 roof again," said Alan Mahoney from the maintenance staff. "If anyone is booked for that cabin this week, you may need to switch them into another."

"Is this a big leak?"

Mahoney shrugged. "Depends on the storm. If we're lucky, it'll stay dry."

Phillips raised his hand. "I've got it on the books for a new roof."

"Well then we pray for a dry June or what remains of it," said McGowan. "July starts our new fiscal year. But unless any of you have got a major problem to report, it looks like we'll make it okay. That means you all did a good job planning this last year's budget and I hope to heavens you turned in equally good ones for this coming fiscal year."

Phoebe saw him look at her and she sat up a little straighter. "Palmer, you came on after all the budgets were put together so you didn't get a chance to request anything this year. You should be okay though. Have you had a chance to look over the numbers?"

"Uh, Burt, I haven't even seen anything yet."

"Well why not?"

"Because no one's given it to me yet?"

McGowan rubbed his hand over his chin. "You should've asked for it. Go get it now. I want your take on it. It's on my desk in a blue folder. Maybe you should get Wade's take on it, too."

"I can look over the budget myself, Burt," she snapped. "My job, remember?" She went next door into the park office before Burt could respond, said a quick hello to Judy, a twenty-two-year old college student who worked part time at the desk, and slipped into McGowan's office. His desk had a precarious stack of binders and folders, several of them blue. She hated to rummage through the pile, but there was no way to know which folder was hers unless she did.

"Include Wade, my fanny," she muttered.

Phoebe lifted the top of the stack and set it down on the desk, exposing the first blue folder. It held Incident Reports for last month. Carefully setting the next pile aside, she opened the second blue folder. It contained budgets. She set the folder on the chair and restacked the pile. Everything suddenly slipped. Phoebe made a grab at the papers before they spilled onto the floor.

That's when she spied an orange spiral notebook.

The missing Cabin 8 journal.

CHAPTER 30

Boone didn't think it was possible, but the interrogation room in Bentwood was worse than the one in Wayside Springs. This one had a chair bolted against one wall for the prisoner and a free standing chair for the interrogator. A small camera mounted above the door recorded everything. Boone's room was at least large enough to hold a table and it didn't smell like stale vomit and urine.

He sat in the free chair, holding a notepad and pen. The man handcuffed to the other chair looked more like sixty-five than fifty-one. His dingy white, thinning hair rose up in unkempt patches like wisps of smoke, and the deep lines creasing his gaunt face only served to intensify his bulbous nose which had been broken at least once in the past. A purplish bruise the color of a ripe prune plum covered his right eye and cheek. The man's arms were well-muscled, but his abs had gone to a liquored paunch.

"So, T. J., when did you quit going by Tom?"

"I ain't been Tom since the Army. Who the hell are you?"

"I'm the sheriff from Caddo County."

"Caddo? Then what the hell you doing here? I ain't lived in Caddo since I was a kid. Anyone tell you that I done something there is full of green shit, sheriff."

Boone kept his eyes on Hawley, not saying anything until the man settled down. "Are you done cussing, Hawley. There's no need for that, you know. No one said you did anything wrong in my county. I just want to talk to you, that's all. Ask you a few questions."

Hawley squinted for a moment, as though trying to force his brain to work. Suddenly his brow cleared, and he sat up straighter. "You're here about my dumb ass cousin, aren't you? I read somewhere that you found him."

"That's right. I'm hoping you can shed some light on when he disappeared."

"I don't know anything about that. George was a jerk and if he was dumb enough to go wander off to find a bat cave, he deserved to die."

"Did Ruthie?"

At the mention of his little sister, Hawley's face contorted into a mask of pain and grief. Two tears rolled down his cheeks. He started to wail, his voice cracking in high-pitched sobs. "Ruthie was all kinds of slow and backwards, but she didn't deserve to freeze to death. After she died, momma just quit living, like she froze up inside, too. Pa took up drinking in a fierce way."

He struggled against the handcuffs and settled for stomping his feet on the floor, anger replacing his grief. "It's all George's fault!." He spat on the floor. "Ruthie followed him everywhere like he was her big hero."

Boone heard the jealousy in Hawley's voice and wondered what he'd ever done to protect or befriend his little sister instead of calling her slow.

"I read what you wrote in the cabin journal that Thanksgiving morning," Boone said. "Do you remember?"

Hawley screwed up his face again, his eyes closing to thin slits. "Yeah, kinda. Something about George being a pain in the ass, bugging everyone. I can't recollect what about, but I do remember his dad chasing him outa his cabin with a poker." He snorted and his shoulders shook. "Funny as hell." He stopped in mid-laugh, his head snapping up, his eyes locked on

Boone's.

"Wait a minute." His unbruised eye opened wider. "You think someone killed George, don't you. That's why you're here. You think maybe his old man actually beat him to death?"

"Why don't you just tell me what you remember."

Hawley's head drooped. Boone waited while the man got control of himself. A moment later, the man looked up. "You got a cigarette?"

Boone shook his head, then looked up at the video camera and made a slight nod towards the prisoner. A minute later, a deputy walked in.

"No smoking in the building, but if he cooperates, we'll get one for him."

"How about we walk him outside, Deputy, and let him have a smoke on your back porch while he cooperates," countered Boone. "You come with us and between the two of us, we'll have no problems." He looked at Hawley. "Will we, Hawley?"

"No, sir. I sure could use a cigarette."

The deputy left to confer with his boss and returned in another five minutes with a pack of Camels. He unlocked Hawley from the chair, relocking his cuffs in front of him. Then he led the way out the back, Boone following the prisoner.

Hawley sat on the wooden picnic bench and took the cigarette from the deputy who lit it for him. After drawing in one deep drag, he exhaled with a satisfied sigh. "Ah, man, I needed that in a bad way."

"Thanksgiving, seventy-six," said Boone by way of a reminder.

"Yeah. Hell of a time," said Hawley. "Mom was hitting the booze early. I don't think dad knew she'd brung any. But she was good at sneaking it past him."

"Your mom was an alcoholic?"

"Do fish swim in their own pee? She needed whiskey like I needed this cigarette. You know what I mean? It was in her veins running with the blood."

"And your dad tried to stop her?"

"Sometimes, but me? I helped her. Gave her places to stash it. See, if mom needed a drink, she got mean. Yelled, cussed, burned my arm once. And when she had one drink, she got meaner. So it was easier to just let her get good and smashed and then we were safe for a while."

"Did she ever hurt your sister?"

Hawley shrugged. "Slapped her a few times. Mostly screamed at her. Like being slow was her fault. I remember her shouting that Wednesday because we came back from a hike and tracked dirt in the cabin. She made us clean the floor then stay outside and clean our shoes top and bottom."

"Was she also angry with George? You wrote that he was asking everyone to describe things." Boone didn't say what things, hoping to gauge how much George really remembered and how much he was making up to sound cooperative.

He took another puff, letting the smoke out slowly. "He had some pocket handkerchief, the kind that farmers use. You know the type. Big. The kind you tie on the back of a load that sticks out behind your pickup so nobody runs into it. Tell me what this looks like, he'd say."

Hawley tried to wave the cigarette in the air, but stopped short as the handcuffs held his right hand back. "I told him it looked like he was stupid, and he just grinned. You know, I think he was trying to do some science experiment on us."

"Like what? See how fast he could make you mad?"

Hawley laughed. "That's a good one, sheriff. You're all right. Naw. I figured he was trying to see how being drunk changed how you saw things. Cause he pestered my mom and dad with the thing and mom was already getting corked. His own dad, he drank, too. Only his dad tore after him with a poker and chased him outa the cabin."

"What happened after that?"

"Not much. I went down to the creek and threw rocks. When I came back, Ruthie and dad were gone and mom was near passed out. I thought Ruthie was with dad. I guess she must have followed George again. It's all his fault that she died."

"Did she have her stuffed toy with her or did she come back for it later?

"Stuffed toy?" Hawley snorted. "Ruthie didn't have no stuffed toy that I know of. You think we had extra money for crap like that? Mom drank it all." He shook his head and took another drag on the cigarette. "If she had one, likely Gramma gave it to her. She had a soft spot for Ruthie maybe cause Gramma used to take care of sick folks and other losers."

"Did your grandma get out much during the reunion?"

"Naw, she mostly stayed in Uncle John's cabin. Like she was holding court. I think she walked down to the store once, and maybe once to look around the cabins, then she sort of lost interest in the whole place."

"So when did anyone notice that George and Ruthie were both missing?"

A fly buzzed around Hawley's right ear and he tried, ineffectually, to swat it away. "You still haven't told me why you're asking all these questions, sheriff." He took one last long drag on the cigarette and dropped the butt on the ground, snubbing it out with his shoe.

Boone knew that, with the nicotine craving satisfied, the prisoner would likely resort to being uncooperative, but he wasn't inclined to play any game of upping the ante. The man had talked and probably told him as much as he actually knew.

"You're a clever fellow, Hawley. You seem to already have it figured out." Boone nodded to the deputy. "We're done here. You can take your prisoner back inside."

Hawley resisted the deputy's attempt to haul him to his feet. "Wait a minute. Don't you want to know when we knew they were gone? I don't want to go in that cell just yet. It stinks."

"Funny," said the deputy, "it stinks out here right now."

Hawley's lip twitched in a mocking smile. "Funny man. Seriously, five more minutes and I'll tell you all I know." His head drooped for a moment before he began again. "Dinner was supposed to be around two. We were all eating at the big cabin, the one that Uncle John and Aunt Martha had on account of all there was an extra room for Gramma. Everyone shows up. Dad even got mom awake and poured some coffee in her. He told me to fetch Ruthie and head up to the dinner. Only I couldn't find her anywhere. George neither."

"Uncle Reuben, he was real mad. Swore a blue streak about George ruining dinner by gallivanting off somewhere. Told everyone the boy could go hungry if he didn't have the decency to come eat. Dad was more worried about Ruthie going hungry, but mom started scolding so he stayed, mainly to keep her quiet. It was after dinner they got worried. Gramma insisted we start looking." He hung his head. "Never did find them."

"That was Grandma Tanner?" asked Boone.

"Hell yes. She's the reason we all got together at that damned park. It was all her idea."

* * *

For several seconds, Phoebe stood rooted, staring at the battered notebook. Burt took it. Why? Her head knew that either Shirley or Burt had removed the journal while they were busy gathering them. Her heart didn't want to accuse either. Shirley had been a friend, helping Wren cope. And Burt was her boss, a man she trusted. Not anymore. Not completely.

And Wren was alone with him in his truck, coming home from the pool.

She shook her head and tried to find a reason for Burt taking the journal. You've got it all wrong. Burt probably just wanted one to look at and . . . And he just happened to pick up one from seventy-six? Just after the kids disappeared? It was too much of a coincidence. Maybe he took it intentionally, hoping to find a clue that would help the sheriff?

That had to be it. He didn't know that Boone had already solicited her help. Then why didn't he take the journal to Boone right away?

Phoebe restacked the rest of the pile, trying to reconstruct the original order. She hurried to the office copy machine and, while she photocopied the previous interpreter's budget, slipped the notebook behind the stacks of board games and puzzles on the shelf above. Before the cabins had televisions, the games had been in high demand. Now they gathered dust. She'd retrieve it after this evening's program. Then, assuming Burt's office door was open as usual, she'd replace the original after making copies.

"What's taking you so long?" McGowan hollered from the adjoining AV room.

"Coming. Just making a copy of the budget."

She hustled back and handed the original folder to her boss. "Sorry. You had two blue folders. I grabbed the wrong one at first." She sat, wondering if she looked as guilty as she felt.

"Palmer, you need to work off of that budget for this coming fiscal year. And use it as a guideline for putting your own together by first of December. Have Wade help you."

"Wade'll be back at school, Burt. I'll have it to you before Thanksgiving."

"Okay. Only thing else to bring up is vacation time. I want everyone to give me their first and second choices for the coming year. Not guaranteeing anything. Do it by next week."

Each of the staff went their separate ways to meet with their own work-related groups. Phoebe and Wade stayed in the A.V. room to run over the week's schedule.

"Can you tack up these posters, Wade?" She handed a stack of 'We Love Our Bats' papers to the college intern. "Put these in all the men's restrooms and in all the glass cases by the trailheads. I'll put up the laminated copies in the unprotected areas by the caves and picnic areas and the ladies' rooms."

"I can do that," he said. "Oh, do you want to switch evening programs with me this week? I can take tonight." He grinned. "I kind of have a date lined up for Friday and I thought maybe if I did tonight, then you could, you know. I mean I normally wouldn't do this, but she's pretty special and I'm trying to impress her by taking her to this new club that's opening up Friday night in Fayetteville."

Phoebe felt a momentary panic. She didn't want to leave

that folder off of Burt's desk any longer than she could manage. What if he looked for it today? "I'll be glad to trade with you, but not tonight. I've already got some arrangements for Wren and I'd hate to have to juggle those." She looked at the schedule. She only had a morning program on Friday. "How about if you take the morning bird watching on Friday and I'll do the night program?"

"That'll be great," Wade said. "I'll owe you."

"Yeah, well, try to arrange your dates according to the schedules from now on, though. I may not have much of a life, but I still have one. Or at least I'm trying to give one to my daughter." She looked at her watch. "In fact, I need to drive her to town in a little bit. She's taking an art class at the library."

"You're the best, Phoebe. Thanks. I'll get right on posting the posters."

Phoebe watched him trot off, full of youthful exuberance. Had she ever felt that buoyant when she was that age? Would Burt really fire her and hire him in her place? So far Wade hadn't evinced any desire to be a ranger, but that could change.

As she gathered up her papers, her mind returned to the notebook hidden behind the games and what would have possessed Burt to take it. Maybe there would be something in it that she could use as leverage to keep her job if it came to that.

CHAPTER 31

Boone left Bentwood for Wayside Springs, but as soon as he crossed the Caddo County line, he took the road to Mountain View. He hoped that Shirley Gracehill's mother would be receptive to talking to him. He radioed his new destination to Jo. If Shirley had her police scanner on, she'd know where he was going.

The county road climbed higher into the hills, twisting and turning in a series of sharply cut switchbacks. It must have been hell driving this with a full load of timber during the town's logging days. But where other logging towns like Oakwood had withered away when the timber industry ended, Mountain View thrived by attracting craftsmen and artists. Most were seasonal, but it was enough to secure the town's future. Lately it had become a popular retirement spot.

Boone found the Golden Days retirement village, a series of twenty individual cottages laid out along a horseshoe-shaped drive with the office and community center set in the shoe's center point. He parked in a visitor's spot in front of the office, a sprawling white, stuccoed building with forest green trim and the usual closely cropped hedges around it. One large blue hydrangea lent a splash of color. He radioed his position before going into the office.

The receptionist at the desk stared at him. "Is there something wrong, sheriff?" she asked.

"No, ma'am. I just wanted to visit one of your residents. I understand that you have a Mrs. Campbell living here? Could you please tell me which residence she's in?" The receptionist didn't answer. In the background he heard excited voices followed by an exuberant, "bingo!"

"Or perhaps she's in the game room?" he asked, making a move in that direction.

The action had the desired effect of loosening the woman's tongue. "Mrs. Campbell doesn't play bingo though she does participate in the Monday book club."

Since it was Tuesday, Boone didn't know what to make of that statement, but he nodded anyway, encouraging the woman to talk.

"Mrs. C. is such a gadabout that it's hard to tell where she is. Every Thursday she volunteers for her church group."

"To your best knowledge, where might I find her today – on a Tuesday."

"I really don't know. Maybe in her cottage?"

Boone avoided sighing. "And which one is hers?"

"Bungalow D. When you pulled in and started the drive, it was the fourth one. If her car is parked out front, she's home. It's a black Chrysler New Yorker."

Boone thanked her and drove around to Bungalow D, parking in the guest spot next to the shiny, clean New Yorker. Along one side of the cottage grew the remains of this spring's tulips and other plants. One rose struggled nearby. He rang the bell and a minute later was met by a short, white-haired woman. She was dressed in purple cotton pants and a loosely-fitting flowery overshirt that hung past her hips. The garb of a typical active older woman. She had no stoop and her eyes looked clear and lucid. He wasn't sure how old she was, but she had to be at least eighty. At least she'd avoided the blue highlights to her hair.

"Mrs. Campbell? I'm Sheriff Linus Boone. May I speak with you a moment?"

"Is Shirley hurt?" There was no nervousness, just a down to business attitude.

"No, ma'am. Your daughter's fine. This is about something that happened a very long time ago."

"How long ago?" She stood in the doorway, one hand holding back the wooden door, the screen door still between them.

"In nineteen seventy-six," said Boone. "Please, may I come in?"

She hesitated a moment, then unlatched the door with a flick of her finger. "Come on in."

She led him into the living room and gestured to a gold love seat, taking the matching recliner opposite him. The rest of the room consisted of a floor lamp, a television set with VCR and DVD players, and an end table with an empty blue vase on it. There were no photos or paintings on the off-white walls, and Boone wondered if the retirement village rules didn't permit it. He imagined that the turnover rate was high enough that management wouldn't want to rill in nail holes and repaint after each resident.

"Seventy-six, you say?" said Campbell. You must want to talk about that boy that got lost. I read in the paper that you found his remains."

Boone detected curiosity in her voice. She wanted to know details that the brief article didn't mention. What struck him as odd is that she read about it in the paper and didn't hear it from her daughter first. But Shirley did seem protective of her mother. "You're correct, ma'am. We found George Tanner's remains, and I'd like to close the file on this. I was hoping that you might remember something."

"I already spoke to a sheriff back then. Don't you people keep records?"

"New building, things get lost," said Boone. "I could really use your help, ma'am. I came across this photo." He held a black and white print of his father by the corner. "Nothing written about it, though. Does he ring a bell? Maybe you saw him around the park?"

She took the picture, frowned, and handed it back. "Means nothing to me."

"I figured as much," said Boone, slipping it into the envelope. "I hoped he might be the boy's father or an uncle. Can you tell me anything about that time?"

She chuckled. "Sheriff, you flatter an old woman's memory. I do recollect that there a big family reunion. Lots of them came in on Wednesday before Thanksgiving. I remember them because they were a cheap, penny-pinching lot, at least they never spent much money in my store. Now the boy, he did come in on Wednesday, but he mainly read all the books in the shop. I'd hoped he'd choose a favorite and come back with pocket money to buy one, but he didn't. Treated the place like a personal library."

"I understand he was particularly interested in bats."

Campbell nodded. "Yep, that sounds right. I teased him that he had bats in his belfry. Nice enough boy. Friendly with a mouth running a blue streak. But talk doesn't pay the bills, you know. Can I get you something to drink? I think I have some Coke."

"Thank you, no, ma'am. What about the little girl? Was she with him?"

"Like she was glued to him. Silent little creature. Just the opposite of the boy. Her fingers always tight on that boy's trouser legs. Pretty little child." She smiled at the memory.

"That's a little unusual for a boy of his age to tolerate a little girl underfoot."

"I suppose, but then never having raised a boy, I wouldn't know." She cocked her head and fixed her dark eyes on Boone. "You should be talking to his kin, not to me, sheriff. If I recall correctly, the children disappeared on Thanksgiving day. I didn't keep hours then."

"No, I know you had your daughter home. Those lucky students of hers must have gotten out early. When I was in high school, we only got a half day off on Wednesday. As if the poor teachers could try and teach us anything when all we could think of was a long weekend off."

"Well, Shirley didn't actually teach at one of the big schools in Little Rock. She was at a littler school closer to Sweet Home, and I guess the furnace broke down so they just shut the school up Tuesday to work on it. But like I said, you need to talk to the family."

"I wish, but there's not many of them left. That's why I was hoping you might remember hearing an argument between the boy and his dad or uncles or cousins. Something that would make him upset enough to wander off so far on Thanksgiving."

"So he did wander off, then? I thought you were angling for a murder since you were so set on knowing the family's mood." She cupped her chin in her left hand and rubbed it while she thought. "Sorry," she said finally. "If they didn't come into the store, and few did, I didn't see or hear them. But like I said, he was inquisitive. I can see him walking off in the woods just for curiosity. Some rugged places in that park. One slip and a body could fall and crack a skull on some of those rocks." She started to rise from her chair, indicating that the visit was over.

"One last question if I may," said Boone. "Did you see or hear any mention of the family's matriarch there? I think her name was Agnes."

Campbell stopped half-way out of the chair. "Oh? Was she there? I wished I'd known. I've heard a lot of stories about the lady they called Sister Agnes."

Boone waited a moment to see if she added anything and stood when she didn't. "I thank you for your time, Mrs. Campbell. I hope I didn't keep you from anything."

She patted his arm. "Not today, sheriff. But I do try to keep active. I've no wish to end up in a nursing home."

Boone left, knowing that Shirley Gracehill was home at least a day earlier than she'd claimed. Had she simply forgotten that after thirty-five years? Or had she been holding back?

CHAPTER 32

"Did you build any of the cabins?" Wren sat close to Ben Owen, keeping her voice low and soothing.

Owen studied his hands again, intertwining his fingers. "Some of them."

"The fireplaces?" prompted Wren.

"Fireplaces," repeated Owen. His eyes took on a distant look. "Putting that yellow firebrick in correctly is very important.   Firebox size is important, too." He frowned. "Johnson made his too shallow. The smoke goes out the front and not up the flue." His hands began laying down imaginary brickwork. "I told him not to do it again."

Wren persisted. She'd been in her for twenty minutes, and that office woman might come in early and chase her out. She had to direct him. "Did you build the fireplace in cabin eight?"

Owen blinked twice. "Cabin eight," he repeated, his voice barely a whisper. "I remember cabin eight. A big cabin. I made a bigger fireplace. Such pretty stone in the mantle. I wanted it to be my best. I wanted her . . ."

Wren leaned forward. "Who did you want to see your best work, Mr. Owen?"

"I brought her there, showed her where I carved our initials in the stone." His fingers traced the air, caressing either the remembered letters or a treasured face. "It was like when a writer dedicates a book to someone. I'd dedicated the fireplace to her."

"To Agnes?"

"Ah!" Owen inhaled sharply and released it in a slow sigh. "Do you know her?"

Wren reached for the old man's left hand and held it. The poor old creature was so lonely, it made her throat tighten and ache. "Not as well as I'd like to. Please, tell me about her."

He blinked at her for a moment. "Do you still have the emerald I gave to Agnes?"

Wren shook her head, wondering who he thought she was. "No. Was it pretty?"

He grinned, the creases of his face stretching taut. "Not a real one, you know. I gave it to her in the barn after we'd . . . pledged ourselves." He blushed. "It was just as bright as that pretty notebook you had the other day." His lips relaxed into a blissful smile. Then just as quickly as a frost kills a bud, his mouth contorted into an anguished frown, quivering as he fought for self-control. Wren stroked his hand. "She never came to me that night. I waited. Oh, how I waited. I heard why, later."

Wren felt a lump grow in her throat over the old man's agony. Part of her felt this was too cruel, but there was still something she needed to know. "Can you tell me about Ruthie."

As she asked, Wren thought she heard someone gasp out in the hallway.

* * *

Boone returned to find a stack of phone messages and three people waiting to see him. He took the people in order, listening patiently to each one's concern, giving them all the time they wanted. Whether or not they'd voted him into office, and he knew in one case that the person had actively campaigned for his opposition, he worked for them. When the last one left he recorded the fingerprint for Mrs. Campbell into evidence then answered the phone calls, mostly political in nature - invitations to some fund raiser. Finally he read through the two arrest reports; one drunk and disorderly, and a couple brought in for domestic violence.

It wasn't until he was ready to close up that he saw the document sent from Little Rock.

Beulah Ingram had ingested a cardiac glycoside, enough to cause a fatal arrhythmia.

* * *

Wren folded her notes and shoved them in her cargo pocket, picked up her backpack in front of the office, glancing up at the clock. Crap! I'm going to be so late!

She had twenty minutes to get back to the bank and act like she was just hanging around, waiting for Mrs. Phillips to take her home. It took her twenty-five minutes to get from there to the nursing home. Add to that, she hadn't sketched anything yet. I can run.

She turned and collided with a man. "Sorry," she said.

"Not a problem. My fault."

Wren glanced up at the man as she edged past him. He wore a blue work shirt and blue jeans. He seemed familiar, but she was in too much of a hurry to look twice. Instead she yanked open the door, slung her pack over her back, and took off running.

Six blocks later she turned down another street, cutting it on the diagonal. The route took her just past the sheriff's office with a Crown Victoria and a black Tahoe parked in front. Much as she didn't care to be this close to the cops, she knew this side of the street had fewer shops and therefore less people to try to avoid. Even the same old geezers were enthroned outside the diner.

Wren made a hard right at the next corner and jogged the remaining blocks to the library. She arrived, panting, at the door and plopped onto the sidewalk in the shade. According to the electronic sign outside the bank down the block, she had six minutes to spare. Time enough to pull out her sketchpad and make a quick drawing in case her mother wanted to see her artwork. She'd draw the bakery window across the street before heading to the bank.

She shouldn't have stayed so long. After Mr. Owen admitted that he'd carved Agnes' name into the fireplace, he said very little. Instead, his eyes glazed over and he murmured unintelligibly until he fell asleep.

Her fingers found the pad and pulled it out. Wren pulled her knees up and balanced the pad against her thighs, flipping past her first two drawings to a blank page.

Only it wasn't blank. Someone had scrawled a note in her sketchbook.

You're asking too many questions. Stop before you end up like the other two kids.

CHAPTER 33

The evening's Creature Feature program was a success, at least in terms of attendance and enthusiastic questions. Phoebe made a game of busting many misconceptions about bats, toads, vultures, and other beasties. She handed out four posters of Arkansas wildlife to the children in attendance, pretending that they were prizes for correct answers or for asking a question that could stump her. That question was the popular, 'how many leaves are on the trees.'

It was inevitable that someone would ask who was the park's dead man and why he was hollow. This time, however it came out as 'why did he holler?' Phoebe assumed the family had asked directions from someone with a strong country accent, pronouncing hollow as holler. Once again she explained that the first known settlers to this area found the remains of a man tucked in a small cave in a valley or "hollow." This time it brought on a suite of questions about the recent skeleton found in the park. Phoebe simply stated that they'd have to ask the sheriff.

After the campers left the outdoor amphitheater, she packed the projection equipment, policed the grounds for stray gum wrappers or abandoned water bottles, and drove towards the campgrounds. She had patrol duty, but she itched with anticipation, wondering what was in the hidden journal. She was anxious to get it back on Burt's desk before he decided to go look for it.

Everything was in order in campground A, but in B, a young couple flagged her down. The girl stood on the picnic table, hugging herself and whimpering, while the guy stood guard gripping a tree limb like a baseball bat. He informed her that a wolverine had gotten into their tent and tried to attack. "You need to shoot it," he said.

Phoebe took one look at the soiled paper plates and open soft drink cans that littered the site messy campsite. Tortilla chips lay strewn on the ground like candy from a broken piñata. At least she didn't see beer cans or bottles. "Open food attracts animals. You should keep your food locked away. And that trash belongs in the trash can. Did you have food in the tent?"

"Yeah, you know, in case we got hungry in the middle of the night."

"Never a good idea," she said, inspecting a ragged hole where something had chewed its way inside.

"The park better pay us for the tent," said the guy.

"Um, No! That's not going to happen." Phoebe pulled her flashlight and turned it on. Then she gently moved the unzipped tent flap aside and burst out laughing. There on a sleeping bag, lay a plump groundhog, sound asleep on his back, a cream-filled cupcake in his front paws.

"Let me have your stick," she said.

Phoebe moved around to the back of the tent and slipped the stick underneath. Then she flipped it up, jiggling the sleeping bag. The newly roused groundhog whistled once in alarm and raced out of the tent, his fuzzy round rump waddling fast enough to churn butter.

"It wasn't a wolverine. We don't have wolverines here. It was a woodchuck. Now clean up your mess before I cite you for littering." She took out her notebook and wrote down the campsite number and the names of the couple for her incident report. Then, after seeing that they did in fact clean up, she finished her rounds and went back to the visitor's center. Her pulse accelerated as she contemplated sneaking out the notebook.

Finally, now I can see what's in that journal. She hoped it was still there, that no one had glimpsed it. She'd shoved it far enough behind the games.

She unlocked the office door and bumped straight into the Superintendent.

"Burt! What are you doing here?" For a moment, she thought she'd been found out and her boss was waiting to fire her – or worse.

"Just getting some work done. Deb had a book club tonight. Why?"

"Nothing. Nothing at all. I just never expect anyone else to be in here after hours. You gave me a fright." Phoebe was getting tired of people startling her. She edged past him and went behind the counter to the desk she shared with Wade. "If you were getting ready to leave, Burt, go ahead. I'll lock up when I'm done."

He followed her. "What're you doing here?" The tone was accusatory, suspicious.

She yanked open a file cabinet and pulled out a blank incident report sheet. "Had an incident in B campground. Need to write it up. Part of my job as a ranger, right?" She forced a smile.

When is he going to leave? Why is he even here? It was impossible to do anything secretive around here without tripping over a colleague. She had more privacy at the Wichita high school where no one gave a rat's backside what she did.

"Anything serious?" he asked, suddenly interested.

"Huh? Oh, no. Wildlife annoying slovenly campers that's all. The thought the park should pay for a new tent because a groundhog chewed a hole into theirs to get their food. Thought it was a wolverine." She turned in her chair. "Seriously, Burt, go home."

"Were you firm with them?"

Was I supposed to shoot them? "Yes, I was firm. We

don't need people getting bitten by frightened animals and the animals shouldn't be eating that crap. I didn't give them a citation, though, since they cleaned up their mess."

"Yeah, . . . good job, then." He looked through his open office door. "Deb'll probably be home now. Okay. You convinced me. But don't stay too long. I'm sure Wren is waiting for you, too."

She wondered if Burt was trying to bait her. It felt like it. "You told me to keep my mind on my job when I'm on my job. I am. Wren can wait. I want to do a good job on my first incident report. Oh! Would you please turn on the copy machine on your way out." She held up the blank report page. "I need to make copies for the files and one to frame for myself. I'll call it, the wolverine incident."

"Sure," McGowan said. Phoebe heard him click the power switch for the copier and the resultant hum as the machine warmed up. "Be sure the doors are all locked when you leave."

"Will do," she said without turning her head. She was afraid if she looked at him again, she'd give herself away with a red face or some other nervous signal. When she heard the door close, she exhaled, letting her entire body sag. That was close. Was he here looking for that journal? Just in case, she kept her nose to the incident report, carefully filling in every detail lest her boss barge in on her just as she was fishing out the notebook. When twenty minutes passed and he hadn't returned, she went to the copier and made the requisite number of copies, keeping one for herself as stated. Then she retrieved the book.

It came out with a litter of dust bunnies. Phoebe picked off the dust wads and dropped them back behind the games. It wouldn't do for someone overly scrupulous to see them in the trash can in the morning and wonder where they came from. Then, without bothering to read any pages, she hurriedly copied the entire book.

Five minutes later she shut down the copier, collected her pages, folded them, and shoved them inside her shirt. Next she headed into Burt's ever open office to return the book. But where to put it? If he'd been through that entire stack, he'd know it was gone and notice its return with suspicion. Suspicion that would get placed squarely on her. The stack on his desk looked different, too. There was a green folder on top now. He'd shuffled items around.

"Blast it!"

Phoebe looked around his office. No good stuffing it in a file cabinet. That would be even more noticeably out of place. No, it had been on his desk. Burt's office might look messy, but she'd learned in her brief time in the park that he had a system and stuck to it. The only left to do was to make it look as though it had fallen beside the desk when she'd rummaged for the budget folder. She slipped the journal into the gap between the desk and the wall and let it drop. It landed spiral side down with a fraction peeping out from the space. It might take a while but he should eventually find it. If he asked her about it later, she'd admit that all the papers slid into a heap during the staff meeting and she'd tried to restack as best she could.

Feeling both guilty and pleased with herself, she turned off the lamp over her desk, left the office and checked all the doors. All the while, the copied manuscripts rustled inside her shirt like a guilty secret waiting to be spilled.

CHAPTER 34

"Good morning, Spunky Chunk," said Phoebe. She sat on the stone step outside her home and held a small ripe strawberry at arm's length. "Come on. You can trust me."

The chipmunk sat a foot away from her hand, his nose twitching. Phoebe set the strawberry on the ground and pulled back her hand. The tiny creature inched forward until it reached the fruit. Then it took the berry in its paws and bit into it.

"How are you this morning?" Phoebe asked, keeping her voice low and soft.

A noise from behind her startled the chipmunk. It shoved the berry into its cheek pouch and raced for the gap in the foundation.

"Jeez, mom. Is this what living out here does to you? Now you're talking to chipmunks." She snorted. "It's not like he's going to answer you."

"It never stopped me from speaking to you," Phoebe retorted. "I want him to get used to me, to the sound of my voice." She stood and dusted the seat of her trousers. "It's time for me to go to work. You coming today?"

Wren nodded and stepped out, her backpack slung across one shoulder. Phoebe locked the house, wishing she hadn't been so exhausted last night. She had yet to read the copied pages.

* * *

Boone turned the Tahoe onto the dirt track, taking the ruts and bumps slowly. The lane, no wider than the average driveway, had originally been designed for horse and wagon. One way in. One way out. It had never suffered to be widened even when some parishioners, including the then Deacon Tanner, purchased automobiles. There was no need. The only traffic would be members of the congregation either all going to services or all leaving it. The side track to the church all but disappeared as the lane wended another mile back to the former parsonage. Worn ruts made after the more recent rains showed that someone still drove this lane. Not the mail carrier. The box was out by the main road, a long walk especially if the box was empty.

He'd only been back this way once, not long after his initial election to county sheriff. It had been an endeavor to meet the rural people, let them know that he intended to take care of them. There had been an elderly couple living in the parsonage then. The man had seemed more frightened by having a sheriff visit him than comforted, so Boone left them in peace.

The old man passed on a year later and, since then, Boone had one of his deputies make a point of driving close enough to check on the property, once stopping by when a storm had knocked out power to the area. The widow assured him that she could do just as well without that electricity anyway and was just fine. Of course, his office had seen to it that her power was restored quickly. Now Boone hoped that she could tell him something about the Tanners, something that would point him in the way of George and Ruthie's deaths.

And Beulah's! At least Doc Flynn hadn't reported any other suspicious deaths, just one old man and a very overweight orderly.

The forest did its level best to reclaim the road. A thick stand of oaks leaned in, their branches forming a tight arch overhead. The cathedral-like aspect of the covered lane would have certainly put worshipers in the proper frame of mind as they went to their little church in the woods. Living in this seclusion was tantamount to being a hermit. There was no way in hell that he'd do it without a 12-gauge at hand.

Boone stopped the Tahoe fifty feet from the house, making certain that the county sheriff's logo on the side showed clearly to the door. He beeped the horn once, to alert the old woman that she had company, then stepped out of the SUV and leaned against the rear door, facing the house. He'd give the woman a few minutes in case she wanted to change an apron or run a comb through her hair. While he waited, he surveyed the property.

The original barn was a roofless ruin of blackened timber, but Boone could still spy the massive posts that had held up the loft. They stood as gaunt, blackened sentinels flanked by low limestone walls and the remains of the stall. Violets and lily of the valley grew riotously around the foundations, thriving in the shady location. To the east was a narrow path, the other side of the loop to the church. A galvanized outbuilding that had been thrown up behind the house showed the same signs of aging and disuse that came to all abandoned rural places. Trumpet vine and honeysuckle grew riotously over it.

Boone looked at the house. The foundation and first floor bore traces of blackening, where the barn fire had skipped over and tried to take hold, but with so much stone, the house had fared well. He didn't see any vehicle and wondered how the woman got her groceries.

The answer came in the multiple shallow ruts and bare soil which indicated that a vehicle drove here often enough to prevent much grass from growing. The tread didn't match his deputy's vehicle, so probably an unknown relative or someone from a church made routine stops.

Boone didn't have a chance to inspect anything in more detail before a thin woman opened the door and limped out onto the porch, leaning on a cane, metal leg brace gleaming in the sun. She wore a faded red pinafore style dress which wrapped across her loose, flopping breasts, the garment held snugly to her waist by a floral apron. The old-fashioned dress' capped sleeves left most of her sun-reddened arms bare, and Boone could see their strength in spite of the loose skin. Her hair, once a deep, rich ebony, held streaks of gray. She wore it clipped back from the forehead, bundling the rest into a tight bun. She dried her damp hands on her apron.

"Mrs. Hargitt, I'm Sheriff Linus Boone. Do you have a moment to visit?"

"Visit? I suppose, but I'm dampening my clothes. You'll have to talk in the kitchen."

Boone followed as she led the way down a narrow hallway papered sometime in the thirties by the look of the faded cabbage rose pattern. He glimpsed a parlor to the right, sparsely populated with an aged rocking chair and one mildewed horsehair sofa. A stiff backed wooden chair sat in front of a monstrous quilting frame made of thick oaken timbers. The nearest parlor window would shine light directly onto the patchwork quilt sometime around mid-afternoon during the winter. The doorway at the back of the parlor led into another room. Boone could just make out a massive dresser covered in doilies. He quickly looked to the left and saw a handmade oaken four-poster bed graced with a completed quilt in some sort of pattern of thin fabric strips. A radio receiver stood on a nightstand next to a hurricane lamp filled and ready to be lit.

An antique collector would have a field day here.

Ahead was the kitchen, and Mrs. Hargitt, retrieved a shiny blue tumbler from the cupboard. She handed it to Boone and pointed to a well pump inside the kitchen. "Help yourself, Sheriff. It comes out nice and cold."

Boone gave the handle one pump and filled his glass, letting the rest spill into the metal pot sitting in the sink to catch the remains. He drank deeply, enjoying the slight mineral tang to the well water, a taste heightened by the aluminum tumbler. As he drank, he noted four steps leading down from the back of the expansive kitchen to a heavy oak door.

"Pantry and root cellar," Mrs. Hargitt said in response to his look.

Boone set the empty tumbler on the sink. "Thank you, Mrs. Hargitt. Have my deputies been by to see to you?" He took a seat on a wicker chair next to a thick oak table that held an enamel basin and a faded green dress.

She dipped her right hand into a basin and flung the water over the dress. "Yes, they have. One in particular, the big one, he comes by every Friday." She repeated the dampening process on another part of the dress before rolling it into a tight log. She reached into her wicker laundry basket and pulled out a pillowcase, embroidered with purple and blue pansies.

"That would be Deputy Peters. Glad to hear he's been faithful about looking in on you."

"He's faithful all right. That's my baking day and he has a taste for my ginger cookies."

Boone's eyes opened wide . "Just wait till I speak to him," he began.

Mrs. Hargitt waved a wet hand in his direction, a few drops of water hitting him in the face. "It's perfectly fine, sheriff. He earns it. Last time he split some wood for me. The time before that he set up my quilting frame." She rolled the damp pillowcase and pulled out a cotton nightgown. "I appreciate the help. It's right neighborly. I have folks what do for me but none as strapping as him. But," she added with a piercing look in Boone's direction, "I suspect you're wanting something else than just to check on your deputy."

Boone was rendered temporarily speechless. It never failed to surprise him just how shrewd some of the elderly rural people were. He looked from the growing pile of dampened items to the wood stove where two old flat irons sat waiting. Perhaps living in these more austere conditions without a television to numb the brain kept a person more people savvy. Mrs. Hargitt's isolation taught her more than independence, it taught her to read people and coupled it with a strong dose of wariness. She'd make a good investigator.

"You're right, Mrs. Hargitt. I was hoping you could give me a history lesson."

"History lesson. Don't they have books in town to do that?" She dampened and rolled a second nightgown and started for the big ironing board standing against the wall.

Boone jumped up and grabbed the board. "Where do you want this?"

"Over here, by the light."

Boone set up the board beside the window where a patch of sun streamed through. Peters got cookies in return for doing chores. He decided that if he wanted information, he'd have to trade out in some work, too. "Need more wood in the stove?"

"It's fine, sheriff. Thank you." She tested the bottom of the flat iron with a drop of water. It sizzled and she attacked the first item to hand, a white apron. "What did you want to know?"

"I want to know about the Tanner family."

"The Tanners?" She shook her head. "What in tarnation for?"

Boone figured he wouldn't get anywhere holding his cards close. She'd take it as secretiveness on his part and respond with distrust. "There was a boy and a little girl, George Tanner and Ruthie Hawley, cousins, that disappeared thirty-five years ago. The little girl was found frozen to death. We found the boy's body recently. At least, we found his skeleton. He'd wandered pretty far from his family, and I'm trying to find out why. I thought it might help to know something about the family."

Mrs. Hargitt pummeled the apron with the iron with an intensity that spoke volumes. Clearly she had some issues either with the clan or speaking about them.

"I thought you might have known them since you live in the old rectory." Boone made the statement sound as innocent as he could. He took the finished apron from her and folded it carefully while she unrolled a bra and applied the iron to it, pressing out the cups. He wondered if it were her only one since, by the swaying of her breasts under the pinafore, she wasn't wearing one now.

"I knew them." The statement came out flat, without warmth, affection, or hate.

"You were a member of the congregation?"

"Yep."

Boone waited, taking the cooling iron from her and placing it on the wood stove to reheat. She unrolled a pinafore and picked up the second iron.

"Did you know Reverend Elwood or his wife?"

"Both of them. I know Sister Rachel was helping deliver a baby the night the reverend died. He died right out there in that barn. Probably the last time that poor woman left this house."

She set the iron back onto the stove, pulled out a chair, and sat down. "Reverend Elwood had come back from preaching an evening meeting and his horse shied in the barn. Pushed him right smack onto a hay fork. His daughter, Agnes, found him. When Mrs. Elwood got the news, she just went apoplectic. Face all purple. Couldn't talk. Agnes had her hands full taking care of her mother. She and Tanner got married the day after the funeral."

"Fast marriage."

"Folks always said it was for the best."

Something in her tone told Boone she didn't agree. "But you didn't?"

"Mind you I was just a child so my opinion comes from later years, but I think Agnes could've done better and if the whispers were correct, should've done better. There was talk that she'd had a beau at the work camp, but her father didn't approve. Not a member of the congregation. I believe he was a stone worker and they often have to go where the work is and then what with her needing to care for her mother and all . . . I do remember when her mother died, I helped Agnes dress the body for burial. Agnes opened a drawer in her bureau and out fell a brassy ring with a red glass setting. She winked and told me it was her emerald. Then she hid it away and said it was a secret and not to tell the Reverend."

"Emerald? That doesn't make any sense."

"I think it was some sort of secret joke she had."

"But you think it had something to do with that C.C.C man?"

She shrugged. "When she showed me that, I was a girl becoming a woman. It may just have been a romantic fairy tale I told myself. But like I said, there'd been some whispered talk. I know the reverend didn't give it to her. He wasn't a gift-giving man."

"Do you know if Reverend Tanner ever knew about this C.C.C. man?"

"You do ask a passel of questions, Sheriff. He might have. I don't know."

"Did you know that Agnes had a younger sister?"

Mrs. Hargitt fingered a tiny hole in her apron, as though weighing how much to say. "I remember someone helping with the children's Sunday school for a while. But she could've been anyone."

"Do you recall her name." Boone watched her face. For the first time, the woman didn't look him in the eyes, but kept her focus on the apron hole.

She shrugged, fingering her apron.

"Do you recall this sister getting married or leaving or dying? Anyone talk about her?"

She folded her hands on her lap and leaned back, looking at Boone from under hooded eyes. "Oh people always talk, Sheriff. But they don't often talk around children. I recall whispers and looks but that's all. And lots of people died around here back then. Life was hard enough, but we were hit with the wasting disease. It took several people." She touched her withered leg. "Left me for lame."

Boone studied her face. Her eyes jerked side to side and she blinked frequently as she apparently puzzled something out in her mind. He wondered if she was deciding what she could or could not reveal. Then her lips firmly clamped in what could be defiance, but he decided was more likely conviction. "But you have your own ideas as to what happened," he said.

Mrs. Hargitt nodded. "I do, but 'pon my soul I can't see how it has any truck with that boy and girl you found." Her eyes moistened.

Boone leaned forward in his chair. "Mrs. Hargitt," he said gently but firmly, "let me be the judge of that."

She dabbed at her eyes with her apron. "I knew that little girl what froze to death. Ruthie her name was. Daisy had trouble having children. She didn't have Tom until she was somewhere in her mid-thirties. She was forty-five when she had little Ruthie. I remember cause I was there mid-wifing her. Beautiful little girl, but her mind wasn't developing right. Her man, Jessup, tried to be a good man as did my Henry, but . . ."

Boone waited, sensing that to interrupt would be to end the interview just when it was getting started.

She let that thread drop and went onto another. "Daisy had been a close friend growing up. She was years younger than me, and being the oldest Tanner child, she soon spent more time watching her brothers and sister than anything else. But sometimes we all slipped away to fish. More often we tried to make our chores into a game. Guess the number of peas in the pod before we shelled them, things like that."

Her voice quavered and Boone got up and primed the pump, filling the metal tumbler with cold water. He held it out to her. She took it and drank it down in three gulps. Outside, some bird twittered a repetitive, three-note song.

"Thank you, Sheriff. It shouldn't be this hard. I gained my release many years ago."

"Take your time, Mrs. Hargitt. Nothing can hurt you or Daisy now."

"No. He's dead now. So is she. Tanner had a ministry group for the girls too old for the children's group and not old enough for the women's group. Or so he said. We were the Little Marthas and Marys. We cleaned the church and decorated it with flowers or what have you. It was one of those days that I was making a wild flower garland that he came to me. Told me I was beautiful, though with my wasted leg, I never gave much thought to my looks." She looked up from her apron. "I suppose I was pretty, though you can't tell to look at me now."

"I can tell," said Boone. "It shows through."

Her lips twitched at one corner briefly. "He mocked my lameness. Called me his gazelle. Named me Dorcas after the woman in the bible that Peter raised up. The name means gazelle, so they say. I never went back to the Little Marthas and Marys. But I never told anyone what happened either. I guess I should've."

"Predators have a way of making their prey feel guilty," said Boone. "Don't blame yourself."

"I never saw much of Daisy after that except at church. I still went with the family I worked for. Folks would've noticed if I hadn't. A year after my . . . after it happened, I noticed Daisy looking pale and sickly. She left the service. Her mother, Sister Agnes - that's what we called her - said she was ailing. It was in late April, as I recall. Next month, Reverend Tanner died when his heart quit. He'd been eating cake and drinking a glass of sweet tea right on that front porch when it happened. Folks said he was too young, but I reckoned that the devil just came for his own. I always figured that Daisy never had young-uns until much later cause she couldn't stand to have a man near her; not even her own husband."

"Do you think that Agnes' younger sister had been molested, too?" Boone knew the girl had existed when their father died and he gambled that she was still there for years afterwards. He thought this woman knew more than she was telling and waited to see if she would admit to it. Maybe she'd even been at the reunion in seventy-six. But first he needed a name.

"She'd have been the right age. Here one Sunday with us children, gone the next and never a word spoken to us about why. Most of us were young enough that we forgot about her. Sister Agnes took over the church and she was so kind we'd have wanted no one else."

It was an answer and not an answer. An admission that the younger Elwood girl existed, but not her name.

Boone considered all of this a while and decided to try another tactic. "How is it that you can live in this house where Tanner used to live?"

Again, the woman thought a while before answering. "My Henry never knew about the Reverend. I worked for his family, and we got married. Had a hardscrabble farm a few miles away down the hollow. Didn't produce much of anything, so he was happy to buy this farm when it came up. Besides, this isn't where I was hurt, was it? That was in the church. And this was where Sister Agnes had lived. She was a wonderful woman. Did I mention that she nursed me through that paralysis sickness."

"Polio?"

"Oh yes. Must have had four other people afflicted." She sighed. "Most of them died, God rest their souls, but she saved me. And those what passed on, why she was at their bedside, ministering to them like an angel, helping them to pass on to the Lord with a clean heart. Sister Agnes hated to see suffering. She knew how to make herbals and simples to help heal wounds and ease pain. Her mama taught her and she passed on most of what she knew to me."

Hargitt stood and went back to the ironing. "A couple years after Tanner died, Sister Agnes read from Matthew when Jesus told his disciples to go out and cure the sick and exorcise demons. She told us that we were also charged likewise. Said we had to exorcise our own demons before they took over us. That was a mighty day for me."

"That was when you forgave Tanner and made peace?"

She laughed. "That was the day that Daisy and I set fire to the church and burned it to the ground."

CHAPTER 35

Wren loitered around the entrance to the short C.C.C. trail, pretending to read the trail sign. She waited until the housekeeping mini-van left Cabin 7 and puttered up towards Cabin 8. Then she casually stepped onto the narrow road, walking as though she was out for a stroll. When Mrs. Dowd drove by, Wren waved and then broke into a trot to catch up to her.

"Hi, Wren. Enjoying the fresh air today?" The plump, middle-aged woman opened the rear doors and took out a bucket with cleaning supplies.

"Yeah," said Wren, "But it's kinda boring just hanging around. Hey! Maybe I could give you a hand?"

Dowd squinted at Wren, studying her with her head cocked like a bird. "I suppose it would be okay. You can carry in the sheets and towels." She pointed to a neatly folded stack.

Wren cradled the pile in her arms and followed the housekeeper down the stone steps to the cabin. Like all but Cabin 1, the base was built up of large, irregularly-sized stone blocks expertly fitted together to a height of two feet. Above that rose an outer wall of rough-cut wooden slats painted brown. A brass oak leaf knocker hung on the door. All the doors had keypads, but Mrs. Dowd slid a thin card into a slot above the numbers. A green light flashed and she opened the door, Wren following on her heels.

She'd never been in one of the guest cabins before and was surprised to see that it was constructed much like the one she lived in now only much smaller. It had the same pine-paneled walls, oak floors, and thick ceiling beams. The showcase of the cabin was the stone fireplace on the opposite wall. To her left was a double bed. To her right were three steps down into a kitchenette. Instead of a table, a counter divided the upper room from the lower with four wooden stools lined up beside it.

The upper room was divided in half with a sofa bed which faced the fireplace and a small television stuck in the far corner. A desk and chair on the left wall looked out a window onto the hillside. The only other furniture was a chest of drawers and a sliding rocker which waited near a door that led down another three steps into a bathroom.

"This is it?" asked Wren. "I expected something, you know, more fancy."

"This is one of the efficiencies, hon. It's made for two but the sofa opens out so a family with two children could stay here. I think it's kind of cute." She plopped down the bucket and inspected the room. "Just put those towels on the bathroom sink for me, dear and bring up the bag of dirty linens, please. My knees will thank you."

Wren deposited the laundry bag in the van while Mrs. Dowd busily spritzed and wiped the kitchen countertops. While the housekeeper was occupied, Wren took the opportunity of inspecting the fireplace. There was no closet behind it, no dark recess like in the journal.

I don't understand. She snatched up the sheets and started making the bed.

"You don't need to do that."

"It's okay. I don't mind. Like I said, I was bored and I'd never been in the cabins before."

"Aren't they special?"

"Uh huh, but I'm confused. Someone told me that this

cabin was bigger and had another whole room on the other side of the fireplace."

"They must have meant one of the other cabins and forgotten what number they were in. We do have some big ones that hold six or eight people."

Now Wren wanted to see every cabin in the park. Surely no one would just make up a story like that just to have something to write in the journal. She contemplated stealing the pass key, then immediately rejected the idea. She'd get caught and then she'd never find out the truth about this Ben Owen and Agnes Ellwood. If she did a good job helping, she'd at least see the rest of the cabins and maybe get invited to help from the start from Cabin one on another day.

Thinking of Cabin 1 made her wonder why it looked different from the other cabins.

"Mrs. Dowd," she said, stuffing a pillow into a case. "How come Cabin one doesn't have any stone around the bottom? It just sort of sits there at the top of the hill without any of the steps going up or down either."

"That one was built sometime in ninety-one so we'd have at least one handicapped accessible cabin. I think there'd been a trailer there for one of the rangers before that. It's got a much bigger bathroom than all of the others, guard rails, no steps. I guess whoever got the bid for building it didn't include the stonework outside. Probably kept the cost down."

Wren barely heard the rest of the housekeeper's story after the first sentence. Her mind focused on the fact that a new cabin had been added at the top of the run. That meant all the remaining cabins were renumbered. She needed to see Cabin 9. And that was the next cabin on the cleaning run.

CHAPTER 36

"Good morning, Phoebe." Jeannie Newcomb, the daytime desk clerk, looked up from the office computer. "How did your morning program go?"

"Fine. I had three families for a change." Phoebe poured a cup of coffee, took a sip, and decided it needed a dose of creamer. "I took them down to Sugar Run and got them into the water looking at stream life."

"Was the stream down enough to do that?"

Phoebe nodded. "Past the bridge it's broad and shallows out. The kids just like getting wet, but the parents seemed pretty interested in seeing the damselflies and mayflies under the rocks." She stirred the creamer in with her finger. "Well, most of them. One asked where we found the dead body. She wanted to see the spot. Ghouls."

"We get all kinds here, honey. This morning I had someone want to know if there was enough privacy for her husband to take a leak off the back porch of their cabin. I told her all the cabins had indoor plumbing and that we appreciated him keeping his business inside." She cocked her head and peered at Phoebe. "You look kinda wrung out, hon. You okay?"

"I'm fine. Just tired. A couple in Campground B have

been a pain. Last night they called in a woodchuck with their mess. I made them clean up, but this morning they left more food sitting out on a table and there was a raccoon into it. I chased the raccoon off, woke up the campers, and ordered them to clean up their new mess before anything else came in."

"Did they?"

"Yes, but only because I watched them. And this time I gave them a citation. They seem to think the park should reimburse them for a pack of hot dog buns and a box of cream filled cupcakes as well as a chewed up tent. And now I've got wildlife on a sugar high." Phoebe yawned and stretched. "At least they're leaving today. I just hope they don't file a complaint."

"Oh, nobody would pay attention to it even if they did. Are you doing a split shift again today?"

Phoebe nodded. "I'm going home now. Maybe catch a nap."

"You need someone to keep an eye on Wren? She can stay in here."

At the mention of Wren's name, Phoebe suppressed a sigh. Her daughter, usually uncommunicative, had pronounced an edict. She would spend the day in the park. She said that she had a chance to pick up some tip money making beds in the cabins. While Phoebe doubted that the park would hire a soon-to-be fourteen year-old as a part-timer in housekeeping, she didn't care to argue. If Mrs. Dowd was willing to let her tag along and restock towels in return for keeping a buck or two, so be it. All she wanted to do right now was go home and finally see what was in those pages she'd copied last night. She had no sooner crawled into bed with them last night when she fell asleep. But now she had time and, more importantly, privacy.

"She's got other plans in the park today."

"Oh? Maybe that cute boy lifeguarding at the pool?" asked Jeannie.

"If only Wren were so uncomplicated. I think it would be a relief to only have to deal with puppy love. But thanks anyway, Jeannie. I'll be back around three." She turned to go, remembering that she still hadn't gotten the lifeguard's prints. Crap! "Oh, Phoebe. I nearly forgot. You got some mail today."

Phoebe stopped in surprise. Personal mail was a rarity. With the state footing the bill on her electricity, sewer and water, she didn't even get that many bills. "Must be a chance to overextend myself with another credit card. Which reminds me, I think I'm going to splurge and get a satellite dish at the house. It's not fair to ask a teenager to give up television."

Jeannie handed her a long, white envelope. "Actually it looks kind of official. Are you still settling your husband's estate?"

Phoebe looked at the return address. "Walker, Whittenhouse, and Bromwell in Fayetteville. That's not the firm that handled his estate."

"Maybe it's good news," suggested Jeannie. "Maybe you have some old great aunt that died and left everything to you."

Phoebe could tell that Jeannie was dying to know what was inside the envelope and frankly, she felt the same way. Curiosity won over discretion. She opened the envelope, pulling out a single sheet of paper.

It was definitely not a prize or an inheritance.

"My in-laws are suing for custody of Wren. They're claiming I'm an unfit mother."

* * *

Boone had heard a few confessions over his terms as a deputy and later as sheriff, but none of them had ever caught him broadside like that one. His lower jaw dropped and hung for several seconds before he recollected himself and cleared his throat.

"You set fire to the church?"

Mrs. Hargitt nodded. "Yep. Me and Daisy." She leaned forward, her lips and face crinkling into a wry smile. "What'cha gonna do, Sheriff? Arrest me?" She sat back in her chair and giggled like a schoolgirl.

"Do you want me to arrest you?"

She winked at him. "Daisy's gone, so who else you got?" Her voice dropped to a conspiratorial whisper. "But if you promise not to, I'll tell you who burnt the barn out back."

"It wasn't you?"

Mrs. Hargitt shook her head. "What do you take me for, sheriff? I ain't no firebug. I told you that burning the church was exorcising my demons, just like Miz Agnes said.

"Uh huh. And now you're going to tell me that burning the barn was, too." He imagined the fire spreading fast in an old, wooden loft filled with hay and straw. Boone already knew that the Tanner clan was an alcoholic mess, but now it seemed that even several of the good congregation had resorted to arson to purge themselves of abusive memories.

What the hell happened to these people?

He turned his attention back to the smiling old woman holding a hot flat iron.

"That's right, sheriff." Mrs. Hargitt unrolled another white nightgown, and pummeled it with the iron, working it carefully around the decorative buttons on the front placket. "Things happened in that barn."

"Reverend Tanner again?"

She nodded. "Umhmmm. Man was the devil's own spawn."

"Did you see him do anything or did someone tell you?"

She put the iron aside and folded the gown, her gaze boring into his eyes. "One doesn't need to see to know. We're a country folk out this a ways. But Ms. Agnes always told us to stay out of the barn. Can you imagine that? Not letting young-uns go in to see a new calf or play up in the loft when people gathered here?"

"Perhaps she didn't want anyone to fall and get hurt?"

"Pshaw! If Jepthah had still been around I could understand her saying such. Everyone said that he killed her pa, not that I ever believed it but . . ."

"Wait a minute. Now you're speaking of the Reverend Elwood's death? Who was this Jepthah? I thought a horse kicked him."

"Jepthah was the horse. A big-un. Pushed him hard onto

the hay fork. After that, folks said he had a mean streak, but he didn't. Daisy and I used to slip him carrots. He was as gentle as a kitten. So I figure there was some t'other reason for keeping us out of the barn. I reasoned that Tanner might have done things to other young-uns there. Maybe to Miss Agnes' sister. I think she came back and set fire to the barn. Exorcising her own demons. Or maybe Sister Agnes did it herself, knowing what her husband did and how her pa died."

"Maybe," murmured Boone. He was liking this less and less. A family full of abusive history often turned abusive on their own children. One of them may have tried to molest George, killing him in the struggle. Then Boone's mind grasped another implication. "If you don't think that the horse pushed Reverend Elwood into the fork, what do you think happened?"

Mrs. Hargitt leaned across her ironing board. "Murder," she whispered.

* * *

Phoebe barely remembered driving home, unlocking her door, or sitting down. She moved as one stunned, slammed with a sense of betrayal just as when she got word of her husband's death. The mental fog hung low and thick, a denial that refused to leave and admit the truth which hovered like a vulture to the side, waiting to begin pecking away at the last dying shreds of reason in her life.

Why?

The truth fluttered in at last and hunched on her shoulder, taunting her in her ear. This is what Wren meant when she talked about other arrangements. She's behind this. She hates you.

"Oh, God." Her prayer came out as a groan. She slipped off the couch onto the floor, sobbing uncontrollably into the cushions. What had she done? Losing Charles had been hard enough and there were all those nights when she could hardly bear to lie in a bed without him beside her. If it hadn't been for Wren, she didn't know how she could have gone on living. Always, in her darkest pits of anguish, she knew that she had to be strong for her daughter.

And so she'd clawed out of the depression, forced the brave smiles, bullied herself through the school year until she found a way to build a fresh life for themselves; a life full of beauty and peace. She kept telling herself that Wren would come around. Like a plant that was uprooted, it would wilt for a short while until, nurtured by loving attention in a fresh environment, it would build even stronger roots and grow lush and beautiful.

She hates you. The taunting voice persisted. It's not the place, the lack of tv or phones, it's you! You did all this for nothing. No! You did it for yourself. And for what? So Burt can fire you anyway?

Her breath came in wracking sobs and a burning pain grew from the pit of her stomach up into her throat. She couldn't breathe, couldn't swallow.

No one will miss you.

It was true! Wren would be relieved. Her in-laws would be well rid of her like some unwanted, untrainable mongrel that wouldn't run away.

She reached around, unsnapped her holster, and slid out her Glock.

CHAPTER 37

"Aren't we going to clean Cabin 9?" asked Wren.

"No one stayed there last night, hon. My next cabin is number eleven. But you don't need to come along, though it was sweet of you to help me here." She handed the envelope of tip money left on the dinner counter. "Here, darling. You keep it."

"No," said Wren. "That's for you. You did the hard stuff. I was just hoping to see inside number nine, that's all. I've heard that it's really pretty in there. That the fireplace is huge."

"It is one of the nicest cabins, in my opinion." Mrs. Dowd loaded the cleaning supplies into the van. "Tell you what. Since you won't take the tip money, I'll give you another treat. I'll unlock number nine and let you look around while I go down to eleven. But make sure you turn out all the lights and pull that door shut good and tight when you leave. I don't need a cabin left unlocked or a door ajar for raccoons to get inside. Ranger Phillips would have my hide."

"Thanks. I'll be careful." Wren got into the van to ride to the next cabin.

Mrs. Dowd slipped into the driver's seat, picking up the radio handset. "X-5B to X-5A"

The radio crackled. "X-5A here."

"Finished with eight. Heading to eleven now."

"10-4. Take your break after that."

"You have to check in after each cabin?" asked Wren. "Bummer." The van pulled up to Cabin nine and Wren opened the door. "You won't get in trouble for this, will you?"

Mrs. Dowd shut the engine and got out, fishing the pass card from her pocket. "No. I'm going on to do my job." The housekeeper waved and Wren turned to see who was at the bottom of the hill. It was Shirley walking to her store; the dam and the lake visible behind her. Mrs. Dowd unlocked the door and let Wren in. "But mind what I said about the lights and shutting the door when you leave."

"I will. And I'll stop by Cabin eleven to let you know. Thanks."

Wren flicked on a light switch then quickly turned it off, afraid that someone would notice and come investigate. Enough daylight filtered through the window blinds, and she'd brought a flashlight with her. The big fireplace stood ahead and to her right, each perfectly fitted stone a testimony to the mason's skill. The mouth was at least two foot wide, but was now sealed with metal doors held shut with a padlock, waiting for fall. Wren slid her hand along the stone mantelpiece which ran as a solid block across the top, leaving a ledge wide enough to hold a photo or small bric-a-brac. She imagined it decorated with bittersweet for Thanksgiving and wondered if her mom had the same ideas about their own house.

Don't think about it. You're not going to be here."

She pulled the old journal from her pack and opened it to the page she'd dog-eared. According to the entry, the carving was in a tiny broom closet in the room on the other side. Wren stood in the living room, the sofa and two rockers behind her, the large kitchen and a bathroom to her left. Unlike the efficiency, this cabin's two bedrooms were separate, one entryway just to the right of the front door, the other on the far side of the fireplace.

She looked into the right hand bedroom first. It was just big enough to hold a double bed, a chest of drawers, and a caned chair. The other room was much larger. To Wren's surprise, there stood another fireplace in this room as well, sharing the same huge chimney. Like the one in the living room, this one was also locked up, but a note on the mantle informed guests that fire safety no longer permitted this one to be used. Unlike its counterpart, one side of the mantle ran behind a fake, knotty-pine paneling which didn't quite match the rest of the room. The closet.

Wren removed her flashlight and opened the door to a tiny area big enough to hold a mop, bucket, broom, and dustpan. She pushed them aside and wedged herself in, her light playing over the stone.

She found the carving on the third pass. B Owen + A Ell. She held the light closer, adjusting the angle to create more shadow. B Owen + A Ellwood. The last letters were much fainter, easier to miss. Wren caressed the carving, letting her fingers trace the smooth O and the delicate L's. Wren dropped her bag onto the floor and took out a piece of tracing paper and a pencil. Holding the paper over the carving, she carefully ran the side of the pencil over the paper, watching as the letters came to life. She folded the paper and slipped it into her notebook.

Wren imagined old Mr. Owen as a young man, finishing this fireplace and thinking about the woman he loved. She saw him suddenly overcome by a fit of romantic passion, dedicating his finest work to her, a promise of a home he'd build for the two of them.

Maybe they made love here. Right in front of the fireplace.

Whatever happened, something went sour in the relationship. Agnes never married him. She married a preacher instead and very quickly after her father died. Mr. Owen had hinted that she did it to keep him from being charged in her father's death. But that didn't explain why they didn't elope and run away. An idea popped into her head, one that explained why Agnes couldn't wait to be married. What it didn't explain was her choice in husbands.

Wren pulled the journal out of her pack and looked at the

journal entry one more time. The woman wrote about part of the rock holding iron stains. Once again, Wren played her light over the stone but it didn't give enough light to show much beyond shadows. Then she noticed the bare light bulb high overhead.

"Duh!" She found the switch and flicked it on, bathing the little room in sixty watts of glare which effectively hid the carving in the shadow of the mantle's edge. But it exposed the corner of the mantle. Sure enough, there was a faint trace of rusty brown on the corner. But Wren didn't see it as iron ore deposits.

It looked to her like dried blood.

* * *

Just do it. Just squeeze the trigger.

Phoebe cradled the Glock on her lap, trying to reconcile the brief agony of a bullet piercing her skull with the quiet oblivion that lay beyond the pain. How bad could the pain be? Probably nothing compared to the mental torture she was feeling now.

She lifted the gun and stared at it. Is this what Cleopatra did with that asp before letting it bite her? Did she wonder at the deadly beauty of the beast? Caress it first?

Don't be an idiot. No one believes that legend anymore.

Still, the gun's stark lines fascinated her, drawing her hypnotically.

Just do it. Put it in your mouth. Point it up. Squeeze.

Maybe she'd see Charles. She imagined meeting him in some ethereal location, comparing being blown to bits with blowing one's brains out. She raised the gun to her mouth and slid it past her open lips. The barrel felt warm. It stuck to her chapped lips, snagging as it went in. Her tongue licked it, caressing the harsh plastic.

The sensation made her blink. She'd been expecting a cold, metallic taste even though she knew that the gun's casing was made of a polymer. It didn't taste . . . real.

Phoebe pulled the gun barrel from her mouth and stared at it, bewildered by the discrepancy between her expectation and the reality. What else that she expected was wrong?

Maybe she wouldn't see Charles.

Her Sunday school training played out in her brain. This was a suicide. Suicides went to Hell because they played God and took the easy way out. Well, she was in Hell already, wasn't she? What could be worse?

Feeling like this for eternity, you idiot!

She quickly set the safety and put the gun on the floor, pushing it away from her. For several minutes she sat on the hardwood, her back against the couch, staring at the gun as though it might still decide to go off and shoot her.

What were you thinking? My Lord!

A cleansing anger rushed through her, running down her face to her fingertips, setting her jaw and clenching her fists.

I'm a raving idiot! I refuse to get fired. Who would take care of Spunky Chunk?

The anger quickly shifted from herself to her daughter. How dare Wren goad her grandparents into this? Who did the little bitch think she was? She remembered the sweet girl of two years ago and tried to reconcile it to the dark teenager that shared her life now. When did the real change occur? Wren was morose when Phoebe left her in her grandparent's care, but when Phoebe came home, it was to a sullen girl dressed like a carrion crow. Her grandparents turned her into this. They encouraged and funded that damned funereal wardrobe.

"Be damned to that! They want a fight. They're going to get one."

And Wren's choice of dress was going to be the first battle.

* * *

"Murder!" Boone was beginning to question this woman's sanity. Living without the benefit of television had given her too much time to invent stories. "What makes you think Elwood's death was anything but an accident?"

Viola Hargitt folded her last item, a faded blue pinafore, and motioned for the sheriff to follow her. "Come with me and I'll show you."

Boone followed her out the back door and across a weedy lot to the barn. From up close and at this angle, he could see the full extent of the destruction. One side of the barn had been built into the hillside, the stone blocks stacked to the roofline. This side remained standing, the stones merely blackened with soot and even that was restricted more to the south end where the fire had started. The entire roof was gone, and the last remnant of the loft had had long since collapsed into the interior. Mrs. Hargitt stopped midway inside, leaning on her cane near one of the tremendous floor to ceiling support timbers.

"Jepthah's stall was there," she said, pointing to the blackened debris on the packed dirt floor. "And this was where Reverend Elwood died." She nodded to the support. "You just go have a look at it, sheriff." She stepped aside, folding her arms across her chest.

Boone approached the area as he would a crime scene; observing without stepping closer, taking in the layout. The stall included the support post. There were even a few wooden slats attached to it. The opposite wall was built up of stone to the height of four feet. A singed, worn riding saddle lay in a blackened heat atop it. He nudged aside a few ruined two-by-fours lying beside the support post and found a charred pitchfork. "This is the fork that Elwood landed on?"

Mrs. Hargitt nodded.

Boone picked it up. Most of the handle was intact, the dense oak unable to burn. He regarded the four tines with interest. They were certainly sharp enough to have done the job. He was about to ask the woman where the fork had been when he saw the two square-headed nails sticking high out of the support less than two inches apart. Instead, he hoisted the fork and let the head rest on the nails, the handle hanging down. The tines tips were even with the top of his head, high enough that the average man would never have feared the points.

"It would have hung here."

"That's right, sheriff."

"Then it couldn't have been hanging there when the horse kicked him. Otherwise, unless he was extremely tall, he'd have hit his head on the metal base."

"He wasn't particularly tall," she said. "Normal height for a man."

"Then the pitchfork must have been leaning against the post or the wall. Was the reverend in the habit of leaving it lying around?"

Mrs. Hargitt shook her head no. "If you know barns, sheriff, you know they can be dangerous places. Reverend Elwood was scrupulous about putting tools away proper like."

Boone took the big fork down and tried positioning it in different ways, imagining how the scene may have played out. "Perhaps Agnes or someone else had used it and had forgotten. Elwood was stabbed in the chest?"

"In the back, below the shoulder blades," she said.

"And do you know how he was found? Did anyone ever say?"

She nodded. "I told you that people forget children are around and whisper things they don't think we hear. He was pitched forward. Pardon me, sheriff. I didn't mean no disrespect for the Reverend Elwood with that choice of words."

Boone nodded for her to continue.

"Anyways, he fell forward, so's his head was facing Jepthah's head. The fork handle was a sticking out of his back like he was a marshmallow for toasting."

"And Agnes, found him?"

"Yes. She said she was waiting for him to come home and heard the commotion. Not but a few minutes later, Tanner drove in. To call on her."

Boone filed that last bit of information away as he studied the scene. "The manger was over here, right?" He pointed in front of him, keeping the pitchfork to his left. "So Jepthah would have been facing this way and . . ." he put himself where the horse's rump would have been and swung his hip left as if he were shying. "So Elwood would have been caught about here and fallen this way." He leaned back, imagining the man's trajectory.

"He wouldn't have landed the way everyone said," said Boone more to himself than to her. He'd have been pushed back here," he stepped into position, "and then since the fork and wall would have kept him from going backwards, fallen forward so his head should've been near or under the horse's hind legs. And the only place I can see that the fork could've been braced enough so that it pierced him would've been here," he pointed to the corner where the support met the wooden timbers. "But then, the tines would've been facing up rather than out and . . ."

Boone looked over at the widow's knowing smile. "Someone had to have been holding the fork at his back. Reverend Elwood was murdered."

Mrs. Hargitt watched him through lowered lashes, the faintest hint of a smile on her lips.

And she knows who did it.

CHAPTER 38

The closet looked like a black hole, and Phoebe dove into it. She tossed items over her shoulder; a rainstorm of colorless t-shirts, shorts, and pants falling behind her. It might have been a mortician's casual clothes rather than a teenage girl's wardrobe.

"Enough is enough," she muttered. She hadn't bought any of these items for Wren, nor after she discovered the girl's predilection for black, did she supply any money for shopping. "It's all Fran and Jack's fault."

Wren had a job now and money. The only thing that kept her from getting more of this trash was that the stores in Wayside Springs had yet to discover Goth for girls, and that Phoebe refused to turn over any credit cards to Wren for on-line shopping on Shirley's computer.

Phoebe bundled the mess in her arms and strode back into the living room, heading straight for the fireplace. She dropped the clothes on the hearth and sorted them into two piles: flammable cotton and anything else. Wren favored nylon cargo pants. This one was bound for the trash. Everything else was flammable cotton. She tossed the assortment into the fireplace, opened the flue, and lit a fire under them.

When she picked up the cargo pants, she felt something

crinkle in her hand. Phoebe unzipped the pocket and slipped her hand inside, expecting to pull out a forgotten dollar bill. Instead she extracted a folded sheet of note paper. She draped the pants across her left arm and unfolded the paper, expecting to see some teenage poetry. Instead, she found a crude sketch of a stone archway, with the keystone labeled. Something Wren drew in art class? Only this didn't look like Wren had made it. The hand was too jittery.

She turned it over and found Wren's notes on the back. Check Cabin 8. Look at fireplace for initials. Ben O and Agnes E?

"Ben Owen and Agnes?" Ben Owen was the name of the C.C.C. man in the cabin journal; the one reportedly sitting outside of cabin eight. Where did Wren find this? The only thing else on the paper was Shirley's name with a question mark by it and the word, 'raVen,' the letter v in upper case like vulture wings. It made no sense.

She refolded the paper and put it back in the pocket. This pair of pants would stay for a while. At least until she could find out what Wren was up to. She lit the fire in the fireplace.

* * *

"You look a might confused, Linus." Grace Leewood leaned back in her chair. "It's been quiet here today. Why don't you tell me all about it? Talking aloud helps a body to think."

Boone dragged the wooden chair in front of her desk around to the side and straddled it backwards, his arms draped over the chair back. "It's this cold case, Gracie. The main reason I'm following it now is that I think someone killed Beulah Ingram before she could uncover the truth about it while researching the Tanner family. Only the research isn't making a lot of sense."

"No leads or suspects?"

"Hell, too many suspects." He spared a glance out open visitor window to see if Jo had heard him across the entryway. Grace was more tolerant of the occasional mild swear than Jo. "It seems that Noah Tanner, the grand patriarch, was an abusive son-of-a-bitch that not only beat his own kids, he violated some of the young girls in his church, possibly even his daughter and sister-in-law." He ran a hand through his hair, the thought of this monster making his scalp crawl. "By all accounts, his wife, Agnes, was a wonderful, saintly woman. After Tanner died, she kept the family and the church together. Probably healed a lot of wounds physically and spiritually, but even then, her older kids took to alcohol and to beating their own children."

"So it could have been any of them that hit that boy and killed him?"

Boone nodded. "But that doesn't explain the little girl. Why leave her to freeze to death? According to her cousins, this Ruthie was slow. If she saw anything, she might not have even understood what she saw."

"You're talking about a killer, sheriff. Common sense or compassion has nothing to do with this."

"Isn't that the truth," Boone said. "This morning I spoke with one of the last members of that congregation, a woman named Viola Hargitt. She was one that this senior Tanner abused and, after hearing Ms. Agnes talk about purging demons from the soul, she decided to torch the church where Tanner had violated her. Then she claimed that someone else, maybe Agnes's sister, did the same thing to the Tanner's barn. I wish I could find some record of her."

"Purging demons with fire," mused Gracie. "It's a wonder that they didn't just kill Tanner outright."

"He was already dead. Died of an apparent heart attack one spring day. Sitting on a porch working on a sermon and sipping tea one moment, dead the next."

Leewood's eyebrows rose suggestively.

"Yeah," said Boone. "The way Beulah died. The thought occurred to me, too. And that's not the only possible murder. Agnes' father, the Reverend Elwood, had died less than a week before she was married to Tanner. He was unsaddling his horse in the barn when it supposedly shied and shoved him back into a pitchfork where he was skewered."

"Ouch. But you don't think this was an accident." It

wasn't a question.

"Nope. And neither did Mrs. Hargitt. She showed me the crime scene, such as it was. If the pitchfork was hanging in its usual spot, it was too high. If it was leaning against the big post, it was angled wrong. Besides, Elwood was supposed to be careful with his tools like most good country folk. He wouldn't have left it lying around."

"Do you believe her?"

Boone considered the question for a moment. It was one he'd asked himself on the drive back to town. "Yes, I do. At least, she believes she's telling the truth. I think she knows or at least suspects who did it, but she wouldn't say. She spoke about people talking, but I got the distinct impression that she'd actually seen the body."

"She's lived at the old rectory for years."

Boone knew Gracie was prodding him, which was why he liked talking out half-formed ideas with her. "She has. She knew the barn and the horse that supposedly killed Elwood."

"Who found the body?"

"His daughter, this sainted Agnes Tanner. She supposedly ran out of the house and found him. Shortly afterwards, Tanner showed up. Then Elwood's wife, Rachel, came home, learned what happened, and suffered a seizure or stroke or something. She was never right after that."

Grace twiddled with a pen on her desk, working it round with her thumb and index finger. "Then they just have this Agnes' word for it. Could she have come up behind her father and stabbed him with the fork?"

Boone shrugged. "It would take a lot of force. I believe that a big old plow horse could have pushed hard enough to drive a man back against the tines."

"What if someone was bracing it against his back, maybe about to stab him? Only this person got an assist from the horse." Grace paused for a moment. "I guess your next question is, did Agnes have a motive? Was Elwood, her father, an abuser, too?"

"Not that I've heard. No one speaks ill of him when they

speak of him at all. He was their minister and that was about it. Agnes married Tanner shortly after her father's death, though I heard one story that she was being courted by a C.C.C worker at the park."

"So if daddy didn't approve," said Gracie, "she could see fit to finish him off."

"Only she didn't marry the C.C.C. man. She married Tanner." Boone thought for a moment. "Tanner was a deacon. He became minister after her father's death."

"So he had motive. And that C.C.C. man would have had motive, too, if he wanted this Agnes badly enough. Those men were strong from all that hard labor."

"Except that the C.C.C. man didn't get her."

"I wonder why?" asked Grace. "Maybe she didn't think she could leave her mother. You said she had some sort of seizure?"

"Yeah. Agnes might have felt she needed to stay for her, and her father's obit says there was a younger sister, too. But surely the C.C.C. man would have let her mother and sister move in when they got married." Boone tented his fingers and rested his chin on them. "If this Tanner was that big of a monster, he may have had some threatening hold over Agnes. Something to force her into marrying him."

"Blackmail? Maybe he knew who killed Elwood and swore silence if she'd marry him?"

Boone nodded. "He'd turn in his rival to the authorities unless she gave him up."

"Well, it's a hell of a story, Linus, but I don't know that it sheds anymore light on the murder of those two kids. Or Beulah," she added.

"No," Boone said, "But it gives me another angle to look at, besides the random transient and wondering how Burt McGowan's involved."

"Burt McGowan? Why in heaven's name are you suspicious of Burt?"

"Because he's lied and he's hiding something. George Tanner was supposed to be very inquisitive and very interested in bats. Maybe Burt caught him where he shouldn't have been and, in a struggle, the boy fell and hit his head. Problem is, that doesn't explain the little girl. None of this does. But Beulah had uncovered something or was about to. Something someone didn't want reaching the light of day. And she'd been researching the Tanner clan. So those older murders are my link to hers."

"You said that this boy was supposed to be inquisitive," said Grace. "What if he started asking questions at that reunion, family questions that someone didn't want answered?"

Boone slapped his palms on his thighs and stood. "So what," he asked, "did the boy find out? And who is alive today to try to cover it all up?"

"Oh, before I forget, Linus, you had a phone call from that librarian in Fayetteville. You're supposed to call her back."

Boone called from his office. "Ms. Robb, this is Sheriff Boone returning your call."

"Sheriff, great news. You were right. Noah and Rachel Tanner had two children, Agnes and another daughter named Dorcas."

Dorcas. It was what Mrs. Hargitt claimed Tanner called her. And Agnes had taught her all she knew about herbs, too.

The woman had a bad leg, but her arms were strong. Boone wished he'd gotten her fingerprints.

CHAPTER 39

"What the hell did you do?" Wren ran into her room and yanked open her drawers.

Phoebe followed, blocking the way out. "Listen up, girl. I have had it up to here with your morbid crap!" She made a slicing motion across her eyebrows. You think that you're the only one who lost someone? I lost my husband!

"You burned my clothes?

"Are you listening? Only that Goth crap, so yeah! Pretty much all your clothes. You can wear your old blue jeans or stay in your room naked for all I care. But you're done with this vulture impersonation. And that goes for that dyed hair. I swear it almost looks purple most days. You're going to let that grow out to your own color."

Wren folded her arms defiantly across her chest, her feet apart. "You have no right," she screamed. "You think you can tell me what to do, but you're wrong. Soon you won't be able to."

Phoebe pulled the lawyer's letter from her side pocket. "I suppose you're referring to this? Very clever. This was your idea, wasn't it? Did you email your grandparents from Shirley's computer? Of course you did. What did you tell them? That I was forcing you to hunt for your own food and bathe in icy streams?"

She wadded up the letter and jammed it back into her pocket. "The only reason I'm not burning it is because I will have to deal with it. But you're not going to win that fight. I am not an unfit mother and this is not an unfit environment. But you are a self-centered little creature and it's time you snapped out of it. You are not the only person to lose someone. Can you possibly be so hateful that you'd make me lose the only other person I love?"

"Oh? And who's that? The sheriff?"

Phoebe took three steps into the room. "No," she said softly. "You!"

Wren's only reply was a series of rapid blinks, but Phoebe thought she saw the girl's arms relax slightly, if only for a moment. Then Wren's body went rigid and on the defensive.

"If you don't think I love you more than anything in the world, Wren, then . . ." Phoebe felt her throat constrict. Her eyes stung and blurred as she fought back the tears. "Oh, Wren." She opened her arms, ready to receive her daughter in a tender embrace.

Wren turned her back and stared at the open drawers. "All I have left is a dark blue t-shirt and one pair of blue jeans. What am I supposed to do when that's dirty?" She pointed to the black nylon parachute pants she was wearing. "Can't I at least keep these?"

Phoebe's relief that her daughter hadn't started screaming threats was so great that she'd forgotten about the other issue, the strange paper from the other pant pocket. At the mention of pants, she remembered. "What you need now are some shorts. But until we get somewhere to buy some, you'll have to wear those blue jeans. You can turn them into cut offs, and I'll loan you some of my plain white t-shirts or buy a park t for you."

She retrieved and tossed the other pair of nylon pants to Wren, waiting to see if she mentioned or did anything with the paper. "I didn't burn these. Nylon just melts. You can cut them off into shorts, too, but only until we get you some new clothes."

She kept her gaze on Wren's face, waiting for a reaction. She saw a fleeting smile, possibly at recovering a favorite garment. Wren gave them the once over with her eyes and nose, as though trying to decide if they needed washing or not. For a moment, it seemed that the laundry pile would win, until a hand grasped the side pocket and froze.

She's remembered the paper in there. Will she take it out or hide it?

"Do they need washing?" Phoebe reached for the pants. "I can take them in to work tomorrow morning and use the park's laundry facilities."

Wren folded them quickly and stuffed them in a drawer. "They're fine. No sense wasting water for one pair."

"You're sure?"

Wren stood with her back braced against the drawers. "Absolutely. And actually, the pair I'm wearing are pretty gross. I'll just change into the others now." She retrieved the cargo pants and draped them over her left arm while she shucked out of the current pair and kicked them aside. "I'll cut the legs off now."

Phoebe picked up the discarded pair of pants, struggling with what to do next. Wren was hiding something, but was it worth risking another rent in their tenuous relationship? If she'd found drugs or even excess money, but a paper with a few names on it? Why the question mark beside Shirley and what did raven mean? Some code word? An attempt at an artistic signature?

She'd been expecting a far more horrendous confrontation over burning her daughter's clothes and challenging her about this custody nonsense. Perhaps that was all it took to snap Wren out of her defiance, a strong show of parental authority, like ripping the bandage off an old cut that needed light and air. Once the initial shock and pain left, healing could begin. Phoebe was no fool. She didn't expect a miraculous mother-daughter bonding. It might be best to just let this rest for a day. Address it later.

"I have a day off in three days. We can go shopping then."

Wren nodded, not looking up as she cut the legs off the cargo pants just below the zippered pocket.

"I have to go back to work tonight. Are you okay here alone? You can come with me."

"I'll be fine."

"Well, okay if you're sure," said Phoebe. "There's pasta salad and cold chicken cacciatore in the fridge for when you're hungry."

Her daughter peered up at her through her dyed bangs. "Okay."

Phoebe hated that hair more than anything else that Wren had done. "Maybe we can get a beautician to fade that hair dye."

"It's just Koolade, mom. I use grape and black cherry to get something dark. Do you mind? I kind of need to be alone for a while," said Wren. "I don't feel like doing this whole sisters and B.F.F. thing right now."

"I don't want to be your best friend for life, Wren. I want to be your mother."

Phoebe left her daughter to contemplate life and went to work. She stopped at the visitor's center first and used the computer to type a reply to the law firm informing them that, if they wanted a fight, she'd give them one. But as she printed it out, she decided she needed to be more immediate in dealing with her in-laws. She quickly called up her email account and typed in her password.

And that's when it dawned on her. The word "raVen" was a computer password. But for what site? There was no way of knowing. She focused on her email, informing her in-laws that they didn't have a snowballs chance in Hell with this suit, especially once she proved that it was on their watch that her daughter turned into a freak.

The room grew darker as a cloud covered the sun. More chance of thunderstorms again tonight. As far as Phoebe was concerned, she felt as though it grew out of her and that she could shoot lightning from her fingertips at her in-laws.

* * *

"Wren? I'm home." Phoebe spoke loud enough to be heard, but not so loud as to wake her daughter. It was only nine-thirty, but a bored teenager might easily opt for the oblivion of sleep rather than face a lonely evening with one spastic tv channel. She felt a pang of sympathy for Wren. It must be hell for her. Tomorrow, she'd see about getting a satellite dish.

Wren was in her room, door open, sitting on her bed reading. She wore the recently made pair of cut off pants and the navy blue t-shirt. Phoebe glanced at the book's cover. It was one of the books from the visitor center's guest library, a mystery by Sandi Ault called Wild Inferno. The sight was encouraging.

"I'm home, sweety."

"Duh. Way to state the obvious."

The response was not so encouraging. Phoebe took a deep breath, determined not to engage in a fight, but also not to bend over backwards to accommodate rudeness. She was beginning to understand that Wren responded better to a show of strength. If this was a battle for supremacy, Phoebe intended to come out as alpha wolf.

"Stow it, kiddo," she said. "Did you eat the supper I left for you?"

"Yeah."

"Well I haven't had mine. Come and sit with me while I eat."

"Uh, no!"

"It wasn't a request, Wren. You're not the only one around here who's lonely. Now haul your butt out to the kitchen with me. I've got some news that should interest you."

Phoebe turned and walked away, hoping that a young person's almost instinctive drive to follow a cool order would kick in. She made a side trip to lock up her hated Glock and put on a comfortable pair of gym shorts and a baggy t-shirt before heading into the kitchen. By the time she'd put the last of the chicken cacciatore in the microwave to reheat, Wren had plodded into the dining area and plopped into a chair. She still carried the book and immediately stuck her nose in it. Okay, so she also has an instinctive drive to try to irritate authority.

"Good book?" Phoebe asked. Wren grunted an affirmative. Phoebe had read Ault's first book, Wild Indigo so she was familiar with the premise: a BLM woman living in the wilderness with a young wolf. "Her house makes ours look like we're almost civilized, doesn't it. Imagine living with a wolf."

The microwave beeped and Phoebe removed her supper, setting it on the table. "I've been thinking. It is pretty rough doing without everything. I've decided to call the satellite dish people tomorrow and have one installed. I miss television. And we need also internet access here."

Wren looked up from the book, but said nothing. If Phoebe was disappointed, she didn't let on. "Anyway, I thought you should know. It is going to cut into the budget a bit, but I think if we give up canned sodas and chips, we can make it. What do you think?" She sliced into her chicken and waited. If Wren started spouting crap about not living here much longer, then she knew she had a full battle on her hands.

Wren didn't bubble over with enthusiasm, but she at least didn't argue. She shrugged and contemplated her thumbs for a moment. "I guess I can do without soft drinks."

"Not so sure about the chips, though, are you. Me either. I think the need for salt and grease is instinctive." Phoebe was rewarded with a fleeting hint of a smile. "Actually, it mostly means that I don't put as much away for retirement or rainy days as I'd like. You're not too bad off for college. I put all of your dad's insurance into that account. What there was of it."

Wren closed her book. "Daddy didn't plan to die, did he?" The question held no venom, just a mournful note of a little girl desperately missing her father.

Phoebe dropped her fork and reached across the table for her daughter's hand. "No, sweety, he didn't. God knows I didn't plan on it either."

Wren left her hand under her mother's for a few seconds

before slowly sliding it out. She reopened her book, never making eye contact. "Having a wolf sounds pretty neat, but a lot of work. I'd rather have television and internet. A dog would be kind of cool, though. Sometimes the noises outside at night creep me out."

Phoebe wondered what sounds in particular Wren heard that frightened her. "A dog, huh. Now that's an idea worth considering. Spunky Chunk doesn't make much of a protector, does he?" Phoebe continued eating her meal. Wren made no further attempts at conversation, and Phoebe attempted few, wary of stepping on some emotional, teenage landmine and destroying what tentative progress she'd made in this détente.

An hour later, Wren went back to her room. There were no goodnight hugs or wishes, but Phoebe still felt a stirring of hope. One way or another, she'd win this battle. And the best way, she decided, was to get everything else out of the way so she could focus on the two things that mattered right now, Wren and her job. She'd catch that life guard tomorrow morning at the pool before it opened and get his prints for Boone. Then she'd drop it off at the sheriff's office when she took Wren to town for her afternoon art lesson. If they left early, they could shop for clothes.

She climbed into bed and reached for the photocopied pages. Now, at last she'd see what was in that missing notebook. Maybe something useful to deliver to the sheriff. As nice as he was, it would probably be better all-round if Wren didn't see him at the house anymore. At least until she'd worked out some of her issues over her father's death. Like he'd be coming by to see you anyway. That was just business. Nothing more. She pushed aside any other thoughts of Boone and concentrated on the papers.

Monday Nov. 29, 1976. Spending day two of our anniversary. So romantic, all except for the resident mouse. The Ranger brought over some mouse traps this afternoon to set in the cupboards. Think we'll pass on that. Don't want to open a door and find a dead mouse any more than a live one.

Lovely cabin but short on blankets. That Ranger tells us

that the bed squeaks something fierce (he must get a lot of comments about that. Either that or he tested out the beds and gave this one a seal of approval.) And then this morning when I was looking for one of my slippers under the bed, I found a pair of women's panties. Gave them to him when he brought blankets. His face turned as red as the panties. Too funny!

The entry concluded with some comments on the joys of hugging in front of a warm fire and seeing some deer walk through the yard one evening when the snow was lightly falling. It was an amusing look at honeymooners, but nothing more.

Phoebe turned to the next page which was dated mid-March. It was a family's spring break trip; the parent's and their twin sons. Most of the page was used as a score pad for dominos and each of the boys drew some sort of funny, big-mouthed alien creature in the corner. The only other thing of note there was their first sighting of a pileated woodpecker.

She read entry after entry. By the time she'd finished the copies, she'd found only one entry that mentioned Burt. It was written by an eleven-year-old girl named Nancy who had been on a nature hike and apparently become smitten with the interpreter. Everything was Ranger Burt this and Ranger Burt that. It ended with a drawing of a park Ranger and labeled as "Ranger Burt" with a heart drawn beside it.

Cute but hardly damning.

Why, then, did Burt take it?

CHAPTER 40

Wren loved the tic tack noise that plastic keys made on a keyboard. She heard it as the sound of freedom, the sound the world made when one end talked to another. Of all the things she hated about living in this park, not having internet access was the worst. Worse even than no cell phone coverage. After all, she really had no friends to call.

It had been her one relief that both her grandparents and Shirley had internet and weren't troglodytes. She'd emailed the former over a week ago, complaining long and hard about the monstrous way they lived, focusing on the tiny school she was expected to attend, suggesting that mom had lost it and wasn't fit to take care of her anymore. She'd dwelt on the terrors of being left alone in an isolated cabin deep in the forest where a murder had taken place. She failed to mention that the murder, if in fact that's what it was, happened thirty-five years ago.

They responded the next day. They were going to take her away and have her live with them in Fayetteville. They were sure they could have her mother declared unfit and gain custody. It would probably never go to court. Her mother would just cave in and give her up.

Everyday Wren waited for something to arrive in the mail. Her mom would cry, would plead and beg, but Wren would stand firm. If her mom wanted to give up this nature crap and move to someplace civilized, okay. Otherwise, she was gone. She hadn't counted on her mom going all primal and burning all her clothes. Geez! Talk about being dramatic. Wren felt a twinge of guilt as she remembered her mom's plans to sacrifice some of her retirement money to get the very things Wren wanted. Her mom was more interesting than Wren cared to admit.

Today, she wasn't emailing her grandparents. Frankly, they bored her, following her every whim. No, this morning Wren was back on the hunt, prowling through births, deaths, marriages, and divorces. Ben Owen had confided a few tidbits the last time she saw him and she wanted to run them down.

The first time she used this, she'd started with her own family and her father's death. Then out of curiosity, she'd looked up Shirley to see who'd been her husband. The marriage to a Sergeant Fred Gracehill hadn't lasted a year. Shirley's father had been more difficult to locate. She typed in her password, 'raVen,' and went on from there. An hour later, just as Shirley was calling for her to restock the canned goods shelf, she'd found more than she'd hoped for.

"Coming. Let me print out this email, okay?"

She stared at the screen. There it was, the entire story. Well, maybe not the entire story, but most of it. From the other room, she heard Shirley running a box cutter across cardboard. Wren pulled the office door closed, printed out the final compiled sheet of information, and shoved it in her notebook. An earlier printout with potential names and her first attempts at tying them together was no longer needed so she shoved it deep in the stack of recycled paper. Whatever her boss thought of her, there was no way she'd appreciate this.

Wren had not only learned that Agnes Elwood had had a sister named Dorcas, but Wren now had a pretty good idea of who was Shirley's father.

* * *

Phoebe waited until the lifeguard went on break before approaching him. She hadn't paid much attention to the student employees in the park. One worked part-time for maintenance, picking up trash bags and recycling from the cabins and campgrounds. Another helped out in the laundry room for housekeeping. They were kids much like she'd taught in her previous career. This one looked a little older and carried himself with the self-entitlement one expected of an oil-rich, middle-eastern prince.

He was good looking in a blond, pretty-boy sort of way, although on closer inspection, Phoebe thought his features resembled a Pekinese more than a Brad Pitt. She wondered if he'd had anything to do with Wren's recent interest in swimming. She hoped not. Phoebe had run into his type before when she'd taught school; manipulative and slicker'n greased ice. The type that would suck up with 'yes ma'ams' to get something, then run her over with a car that cost more than her first house.

"Rick?" she called inquiringly to his tanned back. The vending machine in front of him rumbled and thunked, spitting out a cola.

"Yeah?" he answered, turning. He pulled the tab on the can and took a long swig, eyeing her the entire time.

"We've had a little vandalism problem recently. I was hoping you could tell me if you've seen this man around." She opened the file folder, displaying a color print of the sheriff's father.

Rick spared it a three-second glance. "Naw. Never seen him."

"Are you sure?" persisted Phoebe. She kept the folder mid-way between them, close enough to invite him to take it up, but far enough away to make viewing it more difficult.

Rick Cooper leaned forward, studied the photo for another two seconds and shook his head. "Dude's never been around here. Try the store."

He drained his soft drink and tossed the can into a recycling bin. It landed with a clatter as the lid swung back and forth. Phoebe cast a glance at the bin. There were a lot of cans in there. It would be hard to tell which one was his, but maybe

Boone could do it. She'd have to ask maintenance to save that bag for her.

"Thanks anyway," she called to his retreating back. *And if you touch my daughter, I'll be serving up your gonads as fried Arkansas oysters.*

He strutted away, giving a thumbs up without turning. Phoebe exited the pool area and nearly collided with Wren. "Oh, sorry, sweety. Hey. Are you done for the morning? We can leave soon for town. Maybe look for clothes before I drop you off at the library?"

"Didn't get him to touch the photo, did you?" Wren asked.

"What? How did--"

"I heard you talk about it and saw that folder when the sheriff was at the house. So . . . not being stupid, I assume that the sheriff wanted this jerk's fingerprints. What did he do?"

Phoebe blinked, taken aback by her daughter's perspicacity. No sense in lying to her. "The sheriff is trying to solve a robbery. He wants to clear everyone that's worked in the store. That's all." Just then she heard the clatter of cans and looked around the corner to see the summer help dump the entire bin into the back of a pickup truck. "Oh, no," she said, "there goes his prints."

Wren snorted. "One can in that whole bin? Seriously, mom. This is Caddo County, not C.S.I. Hicksville. You want the loser's prints? Leave it to me. He gets off work in an hour. I'll take care of it then."

"But, honey, I don't want you to get involved in this, and if we wait until he's done, we can't do any shopping before your art class."

Wren rolled her eyes. "Trust me. This will be my pleasure. Somehow I doubt that the sheriff is trying to write this guy off."

Phoebe left wondering just what that boy had done to make her daughter hate him more than she did her.

* * *

Wren didn't feel like helping her mother and she didn't hold any love for the sheriff, either. Who did he think he was, coming on to her mom, trying to make her forget dad? But at present, she loathed Ricky Cooper even more and desperately wanted to see him taken down a couple of notches. She had no doubt that, whatever the sheriff was looking into, this guy did it. She waited behind the store in the shadows, a plastic bag in her hip pocket. She saw him leave.

"Ricky, wait up," she called. When he turned, she sauntered over to him, doing her best to look cool. She wished she had some hips to sway, or better yet, breasts to flaunt.

"Oh, it's you. Hey, no hard feelings about whatever got you so steamed the other day."

"You really sorry?" she asked.

"Well, yeah . . . sure." He unlocked his truck, a brand new extended-cab Dodge.

"Then prove it. Make it up to me."

Ricky stood with one hand on the driver's side door and tossed his gym bag inside. "What are you talking about?"

"Give me your cigarettes," she whispered, glancing around to see if anyone was looking.

"What makes you think--"

"Listen, I've seen you smoke. I know you have a pack. Do you think I can get out of this dump or that anyone would sell me some even if I could? So give me yours. Come on, Rick. Whatever you have left. I really need a smoke."

Cooper's mouth broke open in a toothy grin. "You really are a wild one. Damn, girl, if you were only older. . ."

"I'm old enough. Come on. Before someone comes out and sees me here."

Cooper hesitated a moment, then reached into his glove box. "What the hell," he said. "Why not. But you're gonna owe me."

Wren opened up the plastic bag like she was trick or treating. "Just toss it in. Quick."

Cooper threw the half-empty pack into the bag which Wren quickly rolled up and stuffed in her pocket. "If it's in a bag, my pants won't smell like cigarettes," she explained. "Thanks." She turned to leave.

"Hey," he called after her. "I can take you for a ride in my truck sometime. Maybe show you a point of interest." He grinned, wriggling his eyebrows and his hips.

Wren walked away. "Can't today," she called over her shoulder.

Fifteen minutes later she found her mom and dropped the bag in her hands. "His prints are all over the pack inside. I hope whatever he did, he rots in jail for life."

* * *

Joe Owen examined the new wallboard in the store's office.

"I'll send a painter out as soon as I can," he said. "Then you'll be good as new, Shirley."

"Thanks, Joe," said Shirley. She ripped open a carton of 'Dead Man Hollow' coffee mugs. "I appreciate your taking time off from your other jobs to do this. While you're in there, how about taking my recycle paper for me."

He brought out the nearly full box. "Yeah, okay. Hey, a lot of this is still good on one side. I'll sort through it and pull those out. The grade school's using stuff like this to run handouts. You know, trying to cut down their paper costs."

"Whatever." She picked up the label price gun and started running a price tag onto the bottom of each mug.

"Shirley! What's the name of that girl who works for you. The one that wears black."

"Wren Palmer. Her mom's the new ranger interpreter. Why?"

Owen scratched his chin, his lower jaw jutting forward. "She's been sticking her nose where it doesn't belong."

Shirley filled the back row and started another in front of it. "She's a teenager. That's what they do."

"Did you know she was talking to dad? I saw her at the nursing home, leaving his room."

She paused, coffee mug poised on the edge of the shelf. "I know she's working on some history report. Maybe she wanted to ask him about the C.C.C." Her voice sounded doubtful.

"I don't think so. I heard her asking about Agnes. And when I left, he was asking me about Daisy and Ruthie."

"He's done that before, Joe. His mind wanders sometimes."

"Yeah, but this time he was really agitated. He rambled on about building a fireplace and carving stone. Then he started crying and talking some gibberish about barns."

"He's old, Joe. You're doing what you can for him. Can't do more." She finished placing the mugs and carried the empty box to the counter. "You want this box to put the good-one-side paper in?" She tossed it to him.

Joe leafed through another stack of inventory sheets, set them in the empty box, and continued sorting. Suddenly he stopped. "Shirl. Come have a look at this." He waited while she came to the counter. Then he handed her a paper covered in part with hand-drawn boxes and letters, and names connected by lines and question marks.

She took it, studying it with open-mouthed disbelief. "It's a Punnet Square. I used to teach that stuff."

Joe nodded. "That's what I thought, though my biology is none so good as yours. There are three of them. She scratched through the first two. Must have been trying to figure out how it worked before she hit on an answer she liked." He pointed to a few scribbles. "And look at the names."

Shirley sucked in her breath. "Oh, my lord. What has that girl gone and done? You found this in the paper box?"

"Yep. Tucked down deep where it wouldn't be noticed. Did you look at the back?"

She turned the paper over and scanned the paper. "I don't understand. This is from some genealogy website. It's just a list of census names and . . . oh crap!"

"Yeah," Joe said, "the little witch has broadened her field of interest, it seems. And we both know what happened to the last kid that did that. One of us had better do something about this and soon."

CHAPTER 41

"Who is she?" Grace leaned against the break room door as Boone hurried in for a cup of coffee.

"What do you mean?" Boone asked. He was hungry and drinking coffee seemed like the only alternative to shoving a cheeseburger in his mouth.

"I mean, you've shaved off that stubble you came in with this morning. And," she added leaning in closer, "you put on a fresh polo shirt. The one you wore this morning had a little spot of spaghetti sauce or something like that on just below the collar."

Jo joined them and picked up a donut. "He brushed the dirt off his shoes, too. Not to mention that in the last week he's taken off a couple of pounds. Not surprising with the lettuce and apples he's been eating."

"Can't a man just try to look decent around here?"

The two women looked at each other for a moment then shook their heads. "Nah," they said simultaneously.

"Hey, sheriff," said Jo. "We're not saying that this is a bad thing"

"That's right," added Grace. "Women are all the time bringing you cookies and pie and flirting with you. About time you found someone."

"I'm only following up on a lead with that lady ranger. She called me a while ago to say she's bringing in some possible evidence."

"Oooh," said Jo, her voice sing-songing. "The lady ranger is coming by."

"Don't you two have some work to do?" Boone said as he took his coffee back to his office. Why did they always think they needed to fix him up with someone? Then again, why, if he was only following up on a lead, did he feel like he had butterflies in his gut?

Sometimes they're better investigators than I am.

Twenty minutes later, Grace escorted Phoebe to Boone's office and mouthed "Nice" behind the ranger's back.

"Hi, Linus," Phoebe said, handing over a plastic bag. "That boy's fingerprints are on this pack of cigarettes. He wouldn't pick up the photo."

"How in the world did you--?" he asked, rising.

"Wren got them. I don't think she likes him very much."

Boone wondered what would have prompted the girl's assistance. He must have really pissed her off. Boone had learned first-hand back in college just how vindictive a woman could be. Hell hath no fury never quite covered the truth. "Are her prints on it, too?"

Phoebe shook her head. "No, she said she told him to drop them inside the so her clothes wouldn't pick up the odor."

"Well, that's great. Thanks. And thank your daughter for me, too. This should help us to eliminate some possible suspects."

"Good. And I found that missing journal in Burt's office and managed to sneak a photocopy of the whole thing." She placed a folder on his desk. "It's all in there along with that untouched photograph of your dad."

He pulled the folder to him and opened it up. "Anything interesting in it?"

She shrugged, "Not that I could see. Maybe he just picked one up at random to see what was in them. You know, for curiosity's sake. It just happened to be the one I remember seeing. I mean," she explained, "it was the only one with an orange cover. Probably attracted us both."

"Could be," said Boone, not believing it. "Have a seat. Can I get you a cup of coffee?"

"Thanks, but I have to pass. I really need to get back to the park. There are some Girl Scouts coming in to clean up one of the trails for a service project and working with volunteers is part of my responsibility. But, maybe another time."

"It'd be my pleasure. I'll walk you out."

He escorted her to the door, aware that both Jo and Grace were watching him. After she left, he rounded on his dispatcher. "Jo, get a hold of Garnett. Tell him I need him to get some evidence down to Little Rock asap."

He now had the prints of all the hardware store employees now as well as the one from the dead addict. The crime lab could not only try to match the print on the bottle with any of them, as well as run it through AFIS, but that would only work it the meth maker had a record. It would take a couple of weeks for the crime lab to get around to matching the prints, but unless something else turned up, Dick Cooper would have to be content with it.

* * *

That visit by the sheriff had been most unexpected. And most disturbing. To think that someone would take such an interest in solving that boy's death after all these years. Well, there was little to be learned thanks to the family either dying out or scattering like leaves in a storm. Soon he'd give up, especially if pressure could be made to bear.

But that girl! She was another matter entirely, motivated by morbid curiosity. She would have to be dealt with. Tanner would've known what to do with her. But it wouldn't be too difficult. Troubled teenagers disappeared all the time.

CHAPTER 42

"I'm sorry, but you can't see Mr. Owen." The administrator stood with high-heeled feet planted apart and her arms crossed. Her face no longer bore any trace of pleasantry. She reminded Wren more of a guard than a manager.

"But why?" asked Wren. "I thought you said it was good for him to have company."

"His son is afraid that Mr. Owen is getting too upset. He requested that, aside from himself, we allow no one else to stop in."

Wren looked at the woman's scowl. Her words said "no one else," but the eyes said "in particular – you aren't allowed in." So much for coming dressed in something other than black.

"And," added the woman, "I did some checking. I can't find any Church of the Blessed Carpenter, so I think you were lying on your first visit. Just what are you up to, young lady?"

Young lady? That was the death knell for sure. When an adult called her a young lady, it always meant she was in serious trouble, second only to having her full name recited. "This is some kind of discrimination," Wren said. "You should ask old Mr. Owen if he wants to see me."

"Absolutely not. So you just take yourself out of here and

don't come back."

* * *

Boone finished reading the photocopied journal and set it aside. Nothing in that journal connected with George or Ruthie. Once again, he ran through the most likely scenario. An uncle or his father, killed George in anger. He buries the boy under a stone ledge in an out of the way ravine, hauling rocks up from the creek bed to hide the body so everyone assumed the boy wandered off and got lost in a cave.

So what happened to Ruthie? It always came back to that. Was she actually left to die for a reason, or did the child in fact simply wander off, looking for her beloved cousin, clutching her most precious treasure, a teddy bear? The toy itself was problematic. No one remembered her having one. A little girl, so starved for affection that she clung to her fourteen year-old cousin, would've clutched a stuffed toy like a life preserver. So when did she get this bear and who gave it to her? The grandmother, Agnes, had arrived Thursday morning. Had she brought a stuffed bear with her as a gift?

And what happened to the bear after they found Ruthie? Tom didn't remember it being buried with her. Had it been given away? Was it considered evidence in an open case? The death was ultimately ruled as accidental, but by then the parents might not have wanted to pick up any belongings, choosing to drown their grief in alcohol instead.

Boone was running out of options. Barring a miracle on the few fingerprints he was sending off to match against the one on the boy's belt buckle, there was nothing more he could do. He'd turn the boy's body over to his older sister for burial. Yet someone had killed Beulah to keep this quiet. Suddenly he had an idea. He waited until Deputy Garnett came in.

"You needed me to courier some evidence?" Garnett asked.

"Yes, but I want to take a look at some old evidence first. It's this George Tanner case."

"That's pretty old, Sheriff. Evidence from old cases are routinely disposed of."

"I know. But I'm hoping that since this was an open case, anything put into evidence is still there. Actually, I'm more interested in anything pertaining to the little girl."

"Ah, hell, Sheriff," said Garnett. "Her death had been deemed a tragic accident. I can't imagine anything was kept."

"Only one way to find out."

"You're the boss. Anything over five years old is in the courthouse basement."

Nearly forty-five minutes later, they'd located the box buried in the back. The fact that Ruthie's death wasn't considered an official case was what had saved it from being purged later. It had slipped through the bureaucratic crack.

Finally, a bit of luck.

Inside was an evidence bag containing six-inch bear wearing a little backpack. The only other items in the box were a little pair of saddle shoes, a cotton dress that buttoned down the back, and a rock and feather which the girl had in her dress pocket. The parents had never picked them up from the coroner and they'd been stored in the locker for want of anything else.

Boone examined the bear through the bag. It had been brand new with the park's label and a price tag still attached. He signed for the bag. It would go to the State Crime lab, and hopefully they'd be able to pull something from it; a hair, a fiber, prints on the tag. Not that any of that would mean anything other than the fact that many people had handled the bear. But Boone was getting desperate to find something, anything, to connect the children's deaths to someone yet living. The trick would be to have prints to match against and he'd done his best to acquire a set; a set that would go down with Garnett along with the prints for the meth case.

Next he picked up the bag with the shoes. Like any kid's shoes, the toes were heavily scuffed, the laces more gray than white. He turned them over and looked at the soles. "Notice anything odd here, Ethan?"

Garnett looked at the shoes, so small that it was difficult to imagine feet ever being that little. "Looks like an old shoe, is all. I don't think anyone wears that style anymore."

"Look at the dress. Tell me what you see." Boone waited while his deputy examined the garment. "Again, old style of dress. Looks like something belonging to an active little kid."

"What do you mean?" asked Boone.

"Well, picture a kid sitting outside playing with something." He pointed to the skirt. "See, just what you'd expect, there's some ground in dirt and bits of leaves stuck here."

"It's dirty."

"Yeah. It's dirty," said Garnett. "But that's what you'd expect. I mean the kid had to have hiked a long way and then she fell asleep in the dirt outside that cave."

"So, if she hiked all that way, why are the tops and soles still clean? They're immaculate" asked Boone. "She'd cleaned her shoes earlier in the day according to her brother. That girl didn't walk to the cave. She was taken there and left."

CHAPTER 43

Wren headed straight for the library's science section. Since Beulah had died, she hadn't ventured to ask any of the other librarians for help. She didn't care to explain her interest to yet another adult. For a change, she was glad she was wearing more ordinary clothing. With her hair tucked under a ball cap, she was less conspicuous. She'd also discovered that black was hot. It was a bit of a relief to have a white t-shirt on, not that she'd have ever admitted it to her mother.

Her fingers traced the titles until she found one that looked promising. Biology and You. She pulled the book and flipped it open to the table of contents. An introduction to heredity started in chapter nine. Wren plopped the book on a table and thumbed to the chapter's start. From there she turned page by page until she found the section she wanted, sex-linkage. Strange how such a kinky sounding topic could be so dull.

She passed over the part about the Russian empire and some blood disorder, spared a glance at a photo of a calico cat, and found the section on color-blindness. This was what she wanted to check. Wren felt in her pocket for change. She'd photocopy these pages. Then she'd see about an earlier ride home rather than waiting for Mrs. Phillips. But only after she made a couple of sketches in her art book, just in case her mom insisted on looking. The rest of the class was outside, drawing flowers.

"Hello there, Wren."

Wren looked up, surprised. "Hello." The last thing she wanted was for another adult to see what she was doing and report back to her mom. She popped a dime into the machine and pressed 'print.' The copier flashed under the book.

"You're not wearing black today."

"No," said Wren. "It's a long story." Go away.

"I'm sure it is. A biology book?" The first sheet came out and was instantly snatched up. "Genetics? I thought you were researching Agnes Tanner. Did you give up on that?"

"Um, no. And actually, this is sort of part of it. But it's kind of hard to explain." Wren picked up her copies and folded them in half, shoving them into her notebook.

"How interesting. It looks like you're branching out in your research. Is your mother helping you get through all of that? Didn't she teach biology?"

"She did, but I'd rather not ask her. She doesn't know I'm doing this and probably wouldn't approve." Wren hoisted the pack onto her back. "See, she thinks I'm taking an art class right now. I don't need for her to find out that I'm not. Okay?"

"Such rebellion. I was probably that way, too, at your age. Don't worry. Your secret's safe with me. But, I think I know someone that could help you understand all of this. I could take you there now if you have time."

"Now? I can't go now." She looked at the clock on the far wall. I've only got an hour before I catch my ride home. Besides, I know someone else I could ask if I need help."

"You mean Shirley? I would not ask her if I were you. Not about this."

"Oh." Somehow this surprised Wren. But then grown-ups always confused her.

"Wren, I know that you've talked to Ben Owen. And some people get a might touchy about other people knowing a family's private business. I have an idea. Can you meet me here tomorrow?"

"I don't know. I--"

"Monday then. Nine o'clock? I'm sure you can find a way. I'll see that you get home before anyone knows you were gone."

Wren nodded, not knowing how she was going to pull this off. But her curiosity had taken deep root, and she really wanted to know the whole story. Otherwise, it was like having a tv series cancelled half-way through the season and no way to find out what happened.

"Okay, Monday morning. I'll see what I can do. And thanks."

* * *

Dick Cooper stormed into Boone's office, arriving seconds after Jo's head's up call.

"Well?" Cooper demanded. "Have you solved my robbery yet?"

"Working on it," said Boone. "Found evidence of meth production with fingerprints on it. My deputy is on his way with it to Little Rock for them to try and match it. But I have to warn you. It can take at least two weeks to get a result back."

"Two weeks? Is that the best you can do? I have it on good authority that you're still wasting the taxpayer's time over that dead kid. That's an old case. It's not important."

"I beg to differ with you there, Dick. It is important. I believe that a more recent death is related to it. And someone killed that boy – and the little girl. They deserve some justice."

"I deserve some justice. And the taxpayers deserve your time, not some long dead kid that no one cares about anymore."

Boone folded his arms across his chest and leaned back in his chair. "Who's this good authority you mentioned?"

Cooper jerked his head back in what Boone could only suspect was an effort to look down his nose on him as though from some lofty height. "What do you mean?"

"I mean," said Boone, "just a moment ago you said that you had it on good authority that I was wasting the taxpayer's time. So I'm asking. Who's this good authority?"

"That's not important. I get phone calls. People don't always leave their names. The point is," Cooper said, waggling a finger at Boone, "that you do the job you're elected to do."

"I'm doing that."

"Not running around on some old cold case, you're not. Now, I want some results on those fingerprints and I want them sooner than two weeks."

Boone leaned forward, his hands clasped on his desk. "Dick, if I could get those results back sooner, I'd be delighted. But it's out of my hands. The Crime lab gets inundated with evidence for processing, and those prints are going to end up in the queue along with everyone else's very important evidence. It will get done when it gets done."

Cooper's tightly drawn lips curved down on one side. "We'll see about that. I have some connections with our senators, and the Governor's my personal friend. I'm going to put in some calls and we'll just see about this nonsense." He jabbed his finger at Boone again. "But I'm warning you, sheriff. I want some action on those results as soon as you get them. Do you hear?"

"I hear you, Dick." Hell, the entire office probably heard him.

But just the same, he wondered which of the people he'd questioned about that Thanksgiving had complained to Cooper.

CHAPTER 44

There were never many participants for the weekly sunrise hike, but Phoebe enjoyed it most of all because the ones who attended truly appreciated the beauty. The first time she led a sleepy-eyed family up the steep Fire Watch Trail, she was amazed at how quickly everyone, especially the children, adapted to the silence. Often people felt inclined to force conversation on the hikes, but not during the pre-dawn walk.

For one, the trail, though wide and safe, climbed in a continuous switchback It cut up from the older limestone at the base, past black shale, and rose three-hundred and twenty feet through the oak woods and a belt of cedars to the sandstone overlook, stained a rich ochre with iron deposits. Most hikers quickly saved their breath for walking. For another, they often saw deer or other wildlife which hadn't returned from their nightly prowls and quickly learned that noise alerted the animals.

Weather permitting, participants were told to meet an hour before sunrise and bring water. This Friday, Phoebe carried a backpack containing sliced melon, strawberries, and some assorted packaged pastries. With a steady pace of two and a half miles per hour, they'd make the rim overlooking Sugar Run Creek before sunrise. Then they'd sit on the smooth sandstone overlooking Dead Man Lake and wait, facing southeast for the sun to top the ridge and transform the surrounding sandstone bluffs into gold. Afterwards, they'd toast the day with breakfast on the rim before walking back down.

This morning, Phoebe had only had two takers, Verl and Vivien Keck. She waited until they'd seen the sun rise and the lake below turn into a glittering turquoise gem before she began questioning them.

"This may sound like an odd thing to ask," she said as she opened the container of strawberries and honeydew chunks and handed around plates, napkins and forks, but has Sheriff Boone spoken to you yet?"

The couple looked at each other, passing along those unspoken communications that long-time couples were so expert at sending.

"This is about that boy you found, isn't it?" said Mrs. Keck. "We heard about that."

Phoebe nodded. "He's re-interviewing everyone who was here back then, trying to find out anything else, maybe a detail in your memory that's remained."

"Well he can't re-interview us because no one ever interviewed us the first time," said Mr. Keck. "Not that we wouldn't have been willing, mind you. We liked those children."

Phoebe passed the box of cinnamon cake donuts. "You talked with them?"

They both nodded. Mr. Keck was busy biting into a donut so his wife answered for them. "The first time we saw him, we were heading to the park store when he and his little cousin came out from it. It was all he could talk about. Bats this and bats that." She chuckled softly. "And that little girl, what was her name?"

"Ruthie," said her husband around a mouthful of donut.

"That's right, Ruthie. She was such a little doll. But so timid around everyone except George. She loved that cousin of hers and he seemed to dote on her."

"Timid? Not . . . slow?" asked Phoebe. She took a drink from her water bottle.

"Slow?" echoed the older couple simultaneously.

Mr. Keck snorted. "Pshaw. If anything, she was rabbity."

"Rabbity?" asked Phoebe.

"That's a country expression, dear," said Mrs. Keck, taking a strawberry. "Wary of danger. Spooked easily like a wild rabbit."

"What was she scared of?" asked Phoebe.

"Her mother probably," said Mrs. Keck. Despite their isolation on the trail's ledge, she lowered her voice to a conspiratorial whisper. Voices carried on the wind. "She drank and screamed something awful. Her father was pretty loud himself. I saw them. Children raised in those conditions learn to retreat into themselves."

"Anyway," continued Mr. Keck, "George just took to us like we were long lost friends and struck up a conversation. Told us all about the bats and how he wanted to go into the caves and see them. We told him it wasn't safe. That you had to be grown up and with someone trained as a spelunker." He bowed his head. "Always thought that I should have been more forceful. That he didn't listen to me."

His wife patted his hand. "He's been reading about bats in some book in the park store the day before it seems."

Phoebe nodded "Picture books on bats are supposedly a good seller, even now."

"Oh, I don't think it was a picture book," said Mrs. Keck. "I got the impression that George had gotten his hands on a biology textbook or something. He said the book had a lot of interesting things on DNA and cells . . ." She took a drink of water. "Said it was better than his high school biology book, and he was jealous."

"We thought it must have been a text book belonging to Shirley," said Mr. Keck. "She taught biology, you know, and she was home for Thanksgiving. I think she'd been doing some lesson plan in her mother's office early Wednesday morning and left the book behind."

"Did Ruthie talk to you?" asked Phoebe.

Mrs. Keck nodded. "She warmed up to us and wanted to sit on my lap, bless her heart. Children have a sixth sense about people. Poor child starved for a cuddle. Then she started jabbering about the green boats."

"We didn't know what she meant at first," said Mr. Keck. "Thought she saw some dead sycamore leaves floating on the water, but she was pointing to the red canoes that were stacked upside down for the winter on the dock."

Mrs. Keck chimed in. "George whispered to us that Ruthie was a little slow but we told him that she was probably just colorblind. I know it's rare for girls, but it does happen."

"George got really excited after that," said Mr. Keck. "He said his uncle, Ruthie's father, was color-blind. He was going to do a study of the family for a science fair project. He said the trick would be to collect data without their knowing what it was about. Something about making the results more accurate. I guess he worried that some of his relatives might tell him what they thought he wanted to hear rather than the truth."

His wife frowned. "Considering his family, I'd be more inclined to think that they wouldn't have cooperated at all. They were all part of some off-branch little church. Sometimes people like that don't approve of science."

One of the park's many black vultures soared overhead, riding a thermal updraft of warming air before gliding down to catch the next thermal. It was a lazy way of flying, requiring few wing flaps. Phoebe and the others watched it with appreciation until it drifted out of sight.

"So graceful," said Mr. Keck. He stood and assisted his wife in getting up after she and Phoebe repacked all the plates and containers. "We'll go into town sometime Monday and catch that sheriff. Tell him what little we know. The last we saw of those kids was on Thanksgiving before noon. The pair were heading up the road towards the store. We were starting on the trail around the lake then. George waved at us before he went into the store. Other than that, the only other person we saw that day was Burt. We'd finished our hike and saw him heading to one of those cabins. Looked like he was in a big hurry so we didn't call to him."

"It was that pretty cabin," said his wife. "Looked right down on the lake and the dam from the patio."

"Probably one of the guests had a stopped toilet or something," added Mr. Keck.

"I find it interesting that you didn't think the girl was mentally handicapped," said Phoebe. "From what I hear she was a sweet little thing, very fond of her cousin. I can just picture her tagging along after him, hugging her stuffed bear."

"Well she did tag after him, but we never saw her with a toy bear," said Mrs. Keck. "Though I did hear that she was found holding one when she'd died."

"Did either of you help in the search?" asked Phoebe as they started down the trail.

"Not officially. But once we knew the kids were missing, we got in our truck and drove around calling for them. That's when we saw Burt again, wasn't it, Verl?"

Mr. Keck nodded. "Yep, he was sitting on a rock in the A-Campground with his chin in his hands looking all introspective. We told him what had happened and he hurried off. Didn't see his truck nearby so he might have been on foot."

"I know Sheriff Boone will appreciate anything you can tell him. And if you let him know that I'll be back in touch with him soon, I'd appreciate it."

They walked down the trail in near silence, commenting only on a spring wildflower or on the identity of an unseen warbler, singing high atop an ironwood tree. But Phoebe's mind was turning over all the information, trying to make sense of a child so socially backwards that her own family thought she was mentally arrested. And to underscore it all, the fact that the park store had been open that Thanksgiving morning and that Shirley had been home at least a day earlier than she'd said, bringing her textbooks with her. Did she lie intentionally, or had she just forgotten? How would a person forget that?

She'd let the sheriff know the next time she went into town. Right now she needed to focus on her duties here. Burt didn't need any more ammunition against her. George and Ruthie had waited thirty-five years for justice and their murderer was likely long dead himself. A few more days wouldn't matter.

CHAPTER 45

On Monday, business usually slowed in the park, and Shirley Gracehill decided early to just close the store so the painter could finish the office wall. But she hated being un-busy, especially lately. It gave her far too much time to think and all she could think about recently was about that boy that had come into the store with a little girl nearly thirty-five years ago, asking questions and borrowing her text book. She'd left it open to finish lesson plans while waiting for her mother. History kept repeating itself according to people. Well, it certainly was doing that here. Another teenager, same set of prying questions. It made her nervous.

* * *

Wren staggered out of the bathroom, her eyes squinting against the early Monday morning sun streaming down the hallway. The hardwood floor felt cool against her bare feet.

"I'm off early today, sweety," her mom said. "It's coffee with a ranger morning in campground B. Then I have volunteers coming in to pick up trash on the Sugar Run Trail so I'll be gone all day, but I should be home by six. We can grill hamburgers for supper if you like."

Wren nodded, stifling a yawn. "Yeah, sure, hamburgers are fine."

"Are you going to work today?" asked Phoebe. Wren shook her head no. "Oh? The satellite dish people won't be here until Friday," said Phoebe, "Maybe you can get little Spunky Chunk to start coming to you. If you want, you can walk down to the pool and swim, or get a canoe. Just tell Shirley to charge it to me. But if you do go on the lake, wear a life preserver."

"I know, I know. I yell that at kids all the time." Wren flapped one arm in a combination half-hearted wave goodbye and gesture of agreement. Just go to work already.

"And if you need anything, you can call me on the radio. Anytime. Okay?"

"Jeez, mom. I'm not a child. I'll be fine." She wrapped her arms around herself in a defensive posture as her mother impulsively gave her a hug and kissed her on the forehead. Then her mom was out the door. Finally.

Wren stayed put until she heard the mini-van start up and pull away. Then she hurried into her room to dress. If she could get to the main road by eight-thirty, she could snag a ride with Ranger Phillip's wife into town. She slipped out of her cotton gym shorts and t-shirt and pulled on clean underwear, the cutoff jean shorts, sneakers, and a light brown Dead Man Hollow State Park t-shirt bearing an image of the Grotto Falls. On an impulse, she shoved the yellow bandana with the imprinted park map into her hip pocket.

She was no longer angry over having her clothes burned. If anything, having her mom pull that fireplace stunt got her into more comfortable cutoffs and t-shirts without having to admit that she wanted out of the other stuff. Black was hot. She'd also noticed how the boys working in the park had stared at her like she was some freak when she walked by, and it bothered her more than she wanted to admit. True, the lifeguard did turn out to be a jerk, but there would be other cute boys. She drank some orange juice out of the bottle, grabbed an apple, tucked her notebook under her arm, shoved a Dead Man Hollow ball cap on her head, and headed out the door.

Something thrashed in the greenery to her left. Wren

stopped, wary. It better not be a snake. The sound came closer, growing louder. Whatever it was, it was big. A fox? A deer? Suddenly the creature shot out of the vegetation and raced across the lane.

A chipmunk? A freaking chipmunk? She couldn't believe it. How could something that small make so much noise? The little ground squirrel bolted into the woods on the other side, and the crashing started afresh. Wren chuckled. She wondered if the little animal made all that noise to fool a predator into running away rather than pursue it. Clever. Okay, she admitted to herself, there were some parts of living out here that she enjoyed, like the chipmunks. She even thought it was fun that her mom was making a pet out of one. Maybe her mom would compromise; let her live in Fayetteville during the school year and hang out here in the summer.

She turned off her lane and hurried up the narrow dirt road, opposite the direction into the park. It meandered around a rising ridge for three-quarters of a mile before it joined with what was laughingly called a highway in the National Forest land. If she followed that two-lane road for another half mile, it would be joined by the dirt road from Ranger Phillip's house. Wren would wait there for Marsha to drive by. She'd wave her down and explain that her mom forgot to call and ask for a ride into the library. Even waiting to ride back with Marsha would get her back before her mom was done with those volunteers.

Wren finished the apple and tossed the core into the woods. The road climbed more steeply than she'd remembered, and she needed to pick up the pace. She'd only hiked to the side road that led back to the park's sewage plant. If she didn't hurry, she'd miss her chance into town. A few hundred paces farther on, Wren heard a vehicle come down the road from the maintenance area and turned to see who it was. If someone else saw her and told her mom, she'd be dead meat. She wouldn't get another chance.

The driver stopped. "Wren, where are you going all in a hurry?

"Um, I was going to go to the library. Mrs. Phillips sometimes takes me in with her."

"At the rate you're going, you'll miss her. Hop in. I'll take you to town. I'm heading in that direction."

"Okay, but don't tell my mom or she'll freak. I forgot to tell her I was going today."

* * *

"You're not going to believe it, Sheriff, but I think you hit pay dirt today." Graced plopped an overnight courier's envelope on his desk. "You might just have to buy Mr. Cooper a beer. Apparently he does have connections in high places."

Boone opened the envelope and read the cover letter. "Well, I'll be . . ." He slid the contents back into the envelope and stood at his open office door. "Jo," he hollered down the hall, "Call Judge Kilgore and get me an appointment today. I'm going to need a warrant."

* * *

Wren looked out the rolled down window, peering into the woods. Her initial reaction when they'd left town and headed into the hills was wondering why anyone who knew about genetics would choose to live out here. She thought about her mom. Maybe all biologists were like that. Parts of the road had looked vaguely familiar, like they were heading back to the park, but then Wren had never paid too much attention to the scenery. It all looked alike to her.

You've seen one tree, you've seen them all.

The vehicle brushed against a limb that hung out over the road, the branch slapping back into the open window. She felt the whip-like sting across her cheek and pulled back.

"Careful, there," said the driver. "Not much traffic down this lane anymore. The trees aren't quite as friendly as they are in the park."

Wren rubbed her sore cheek. They rode too close to the right, sometimes brushing into branches. "Where are we going?"

"I'm taking you to where Agnes Tanner grew up, although I still prefer to think of her as Agnes Elwood. If you're writing about her, you should see her home."

Wren felt some pangs of disappointment. She had expected to talk to someone who understood the genetic inheritance questions she still had; someone who could verify her suspicions. Instead, she was going to Viola Hargitt's house again. No wonder this place looked kind of familiar. "Did you know her? Agnes Tanner, I mean."

"Yes I did. A beautiful woman. She didn't deserve that beast for a husband."

"But she had to marry him, right? I think I know why, too."

"That's what I've been wondering. I know you've been asking a lot of questions. I want to make sure that you really do understand. I think seeing her home will help."

They slowed to a crawl, driving around to the back of the old house. They parked behind the remains of a shed, now covered in vines. Wren didn't let on that she'd already been here. After all, Mrs. Hargitt hadn't given her a tour inside.

"See that barn? Or rather, what's left of it? That's where her father died." They walked into the ruins and stopped at one of the stalls. "He was speared against that very pitchfork."

Wren gasped. "Gross." She'd read about it in a newspaper article, but somehow this made it more real. Maybe this trip wouldn't be wasted.

"It was awful. But the worst of it was that Deacon Tanner came to the house shortly after and saw what had happened. He wouldn't believe that it was an accident."

"But she didn't kill her dad, did she?" Wren asked. "I mean, everyone says she was this really good person." In the back of her mind, she wondered where Mrs. Hargitt was.

"No, she didn't kill him. Well, not intentionally. She fell against her father when the horse shied and together, horse and woman, they pushed him back against the fork. But Tanner, he knew Agnes didn't love him. He knew she wanted to marry someone else."

"Ben Owen," interjected Wren.

"My my. So you know about Ben, do you? Agnes was

going to elope with him that very night. He'd even given her a ring. But Tanner wanted to marry her. Oh, he didn't love her. Not certain he could love. But he knew he'd stand a better chance of becoming the new minister if he was married to the former minister's daughter. He'd been promised that."

"And threatened to turn her or Ben in if she didn't? That's rotten. How can a church man do that?"

"Wren, this had nothing to do with church or God, child. It had to do with power. People like to be in control, and a church man is no more immune to the lure of power than a dog catcher is."

Wren shook her head. "She should have run off anyway."

"And abandon her mother and . . . That poor woman wasn't well to begin with, and the Reverend's death devastated her. Agnes chose to forgo her own happiness to take care of her as best she could. Agnes always thought of others. It probably saved Ben Owen from being executed for murder."

"And she even married Tanner right away so that he'd think that the child was his." Wren heard a sudden intake of breath from her companion.

"My dear girl! Now just what makes you think that a woman as righteous as Agnes would have had a child by any man other than her husband?"

"I can't explain it exactly, but it has to do with DNA. See, Ben Owen was colorblind. I had a red notebook, and when he saw it, he said he liked green, too. And I think Ruthie, Agnes' granddaughter by her first child, Daisy, was color-blind, too. I heard that she didn't know her colors." Wren didn't say that it was Ben Owen who'd let that slip in one interview.

"What if she was? Her own father, Jessup, had difficulties with colors."

"See, that's what I thought, at first. But when I looked in some biology books on it, I found out that it's what's called a sex-linked trait. That means the DNA is on the . . . the chromosome that girls get two of. I don't have the picture with me to explain it." She'd realized that she'd left her notebook behind. "Ruthie had to get the DNA from her dad and her mom, Daisy. Daisy was what the book calls a carrier, not color-blind but that DNA was in her. And the only place Daisy could've gotten it from was her father."

"From Reverend Tanner then."

"No, see, he wasn't color-blind. I heard that he painted the church bright red to represent Christ's blood. So he knew red from green. But the book says that if men have one of those genes they're colorblind. It has something to do with their guy chromosome being all short and not having as much information. It doesn't have the color stuff on it. At least I think that's what it means. That's kind of what I needed to have explained by someone who knows about genetics."

"Then Daisy got some of it from her mother. From Agnes."

"I don't think so. I mean, everything I ever heard about the family was that Daisy's husband was considered kind of odd cause no one had ever seen that problem before. So I figure it had never been in the family until . . ." Wren stopped suddenly, feeling like she'd divulged too much. She decided to change the subject. Feigning ignorance, she asked, "Do you know who lives here now?"

"As a matter of fact, I do." Her companion gently placed a hand on her back and guided her towards the house. "This is all very interesting. Why don't you go inside. I told you there was someone I wanted you to meet. I don't get out here much anymore but I make myself at home here whenever I visit. I'll get you a glass of sweet tea, and we can all talk some more."

CHAPTER 46

Boone grabbed his cap. Finally! At least something was going right. Thanks to that insufferable pain-in-the-ass, Cooper, the State Crime Lab had pushed his evidence to the fore – all of it. Not only did he have a match to the methamphetamine bottle, the lab had promised to fast track the samples he'd sent down to the partial print on the boy's belt buckle and anything they could dredge up on the Teddy Bear's tag.

The irony was that Cooper's insistence at wielding his political clout was probably going to result in his own son's arrest. All Boone needed was the warrant to search the kid's room, his truck, and anything else Boone could think of when he'd filled out the affidavit.

Boone possessed some clout of his own, only his came in the form of his dispatcher. Jo had called the judge and used her amazing skills at handling people to get an appointment in the hour. The down side was that the warrant came back only for the youth's vehicle and whatever belongings he had with him. The warrant excluded the boy's home and his father's business. Boone hoped it was enough.

"Wish us luck, Jo," he said and left with Deputy Wells. They drove to the park in separate vehicles, pulling into the lot near the lake and close to the Cooper boy's truck.

"Stay by his truck, Gabe," Boone directed. "I'll get the kid." He marched to the pool and through the gate. A mother with a toddler in the wading pool looked up and immediately called to her older son who was preparing to cannonball off the diving board.

"Davey, come here now!"

Boone walked around the pool to the life guard's chair, a large gym bag hanging from the arm rest. "Richard Cooper?"

"Yeah. Is this about that guy in the photo? I told that ranger I never saw the dude before."

"Come with me." Boone turned to the mother. "Sorry, ma'am. The pool is closed." The woman snatched up her toddler, grabbed the older boy by the hand and hurried out the gate.

"Hey, man. You can't just come in here and close the pool like that. Look, I didn't know that girl was under age when I gave her those cigarettes. You should arrest her."

"Actually, I have a warrant to search your truck and your duffel bag there." He held up the warrant and nodded to his deputy who'd already snapped on a pair of latex gloves.

"Let me see that thing," Cooper said. The kid lifted his sunglasses and read over it, his pupils dilating despite the bright sun.

Nervous. Boone pulled on his own pair of latex gloves and picked up the duffel.

"I'm calling my dad. Your ass is gonna be grass, sheriff."

"Good luck getting a signal," Boone said as he herded the young man towards the truck.

Cooper frowned as he stared at the phone and lack of bars. "Damned park," he muttered. "Would it kill them to put up a cell tower?"

"Unlock the truck," Boone ordered. Cooper complied. Immediately, Garnett opened up a swab pack and started wiping down the seats.

"There's a sinus medication box sticking out from under the back seat." Cooper said.

"I have bad sinuses," snapped Cooper.

Boone didn't say a word as Garnett inserted the swab tip into a narcotics test pack with the reagent vials inside, and snapped off the ends leaving the tip inside. He sealed it and pressed on the first vial, releasing its chemicals. After a brief mixing, he broke open the second vial. The contents turned orange.

"Bingo, sheriff," Garnett said. He popped open the glove box, removed the maps, and opened them. A small baggy containing white crystal shards fell out.

"Hands behind your back," ordered Boone. "Richard Cooper, you're under arrest for manufacture and possession of controlled substances and for theft. You have the right to remain silent." He recited the Miranda rights, asked Cooper if he understood those rights, and put him in the back of the Tahoe. "Garnett, finish processing his truck, then get it towed back to base." Boone radioed Jo that he was coming in with a prisoner. As he put the truck in gear, he wondered if the ranger's daughter watched from somewhere.

* * *

Right now, Wren didn't want to visit or drink tea. She wanted to go back home. The statement that these trees weren't as friendly as those in the park had taken root and sprouted a nervous caution. "So you know the person who lives here," she said, trying to make casual conversation. "You come here a lot?"

"You don't think I just walk into stranger's homes, do you? I've known Viola Hargitt for a long time."

"It looks primitive," said Wren. She peered past the parlor to a bedroom cluttered with baskets of yarn and scrap fabrics. "I don't see any lights on the ceiling."

"The house hasn't been changed too much, but Ms. Hargitt is used to that. I pay her to look after my friend and do her laundry. Mine, too, sometimes. She'll be out collecting herbs today. Now, wait here just a moment and then I'll introduce you to my friend."

That grabbed Wren's attention. "Wait a minute! Mrs.

Hargitt isn't the friend I'm supposed to meet? I'm supposed to meet the person she takes care of?" When she and her mom visited, nothing was said about another person living here. Was that why she kept us on the porch? Wren held her peace, deciding that she shouldn't let on that she'd met Mrs. Hargitt already. Good thing we came here on a day when Mrs. Hargitt was off picking plants. For the first time, Wren wondered if Mrs. Hargitt was really Agnes Tanner's younger sister.

Maybe I should just leave. That notion was quickly dispelled by the fact that she had no idea how to get home. She wished now that she'd paid more attention when her mom drove her here and back, but the road turned so often and branched off several times. She heard footsteps returning. Too late to make that choice now. Just meet this friend and get this over with. She'd ask in the nicest voice to just drop her off where the county highway intersected the park road and she'd walk the rest of the way home. Home.

"Now, Wren. Who else knows about this fool notion of yours, that Agnes had an illegitimate child?"

Wren felt the fear inside of her grow a little more. "Why? What difference does it make?"

"Because, I've got to tell you, you may have poked a bit too far. Agnes held her family together in spite of all the hell Tanner put them through. People still speak her name in pious tones, and there are those that would consider it an outrage that there was even a taint on her memory. If they thought she had an illegitimate baby, they'd suddenly think that Tanner was a judgment on her, an atonement for her sin. And those that would protect her name wouldn't want that. Remember what happened to that boy that went snooping."

Wren shivered. "Does Mrs. Hargitt know? Would she kill me?" She thought about all the plants the old woman knew how to use. She probably knew as much about the ones that poisoned as about the one's that cured.

"Possibly. Did you know that Agnes had a younger sister?"

* * *

Phoebe entered the park office through the back door,

ready to stick her head into the McGowan's office. A solid oak door stopped her. "Sherry, do you know where Burt is?" His door was rarely shut unless he was out of the park for an extended duration.

"He never came in this morning. Maybe he had a meeting with the Regional Supervisor."

"Well, crap!" Phoebe put her fists on her hips and looked around the area.

"Why? What do you need?"

"I have a batch of volunteers cleaning a trail only I just found out that no one signed permission forms for the underage part of the group."

Sherry got up from her desk. "I got you covered, girl. Give me a minute." She pulled a master copy from the file cabinet and walked to the copy machine. "How many do you need?"

"Four." Phoebe listened to the machine's rhythmic whirr, punctuated by the "shoosh" as each sheet of paper slid out into the catch bin. "Funny that Burt didn't mention that he was going to be gone. He usually tells us."

Sherry picked up the finished stack and handed them to Phoebe. "I guess something just came up. He's had to leave a couple times these past weeks. Need anything else?"

Phoebe shook her head. "Just these."

"Wren going out on this clean-up with you?"

"Nope. She's taking the day off and hanging out at home. I think she may finally be adjusting to living in the park."

* * *

"Come in here, Wren."

Wren stood at the bottom of the steps in the doorway, letting her eyes adjust to the dim light filtering down through one, high, dirty window. The area closest to her appeared to be a sort of walk-in pantry, bigger than the bathroom in her mom's cabin. Besides rows of home-canned foods, there were canisters of flour and sugar, jars of peanut butter, and other staples. A thick darkness bathes the back of the room. Wren thought she saw something that looked like an old sewing machine in one corner. A disagreeable odor wafted from the far interior: a combination of stale sweat, ammonia, and a tinge of vinegar. It stung her nose, and she smooshed her upper lip against her nostrils in a futile attempt to block the stale stench.

"The person I want you to meet is in here. Don't be a ninny, child. She can't hurt you. But keep your voice down. And take your hat off. Be respectful"

Wren spied a long, low cot and one chair in the gloomy recesses. Something lay on the bed under a handmade quilt patterned in open fans. She plopped her hat on the chair back and tiptoed to the bedside, staring at a pale, wrinkled creature with wispy white hair. Something about the hair length suggested this was a woman. How could anyone be that old and live? It was as if she was looking at a living mummy, something out of an old horror flic. Wren felt a mixture of fascination, revulsion, and sympathy towards this being.

"This is Agnes Elwood Tanner."

"Ms. Tanner," whispered Wren. It made sense. She'd seen obituaries for her husband, but not for her. Yet no one else knew she was alive. "Agnes."

The ancient woman's eyelids flickered and opened.

"You have a visitor, Agnes. A young girl. She wants to ask you some questions."

"No, I . . . wait," stammered Wren. "I might upset her."

"Oh? So you're actually concerned that someone might become upset by your questions? Go ahead, talk to her. I'm going to fix your tea, and then I'll make some thin oatmeal for her."

Wren was left alone with the decrepit woman who stared at her with glazed eyes, her thin brows arched in puzzlement.

"D... daisy," Agnes said, her voice barely a breath.

"No. My name is Wren. Like the bird. You don't know me, but maybe you should go back to sleep now." This frail human, clinging to life by a breath, seemed like an animatronic corpse in a Halloween horror house. Even the woman's head looked more like a skull covered in a thin, bloodless parchment. Wren turned away, but the woman's bony hand gripped Wren's wrist in a movement as sudden as it was tenacious. Wren shivered at the icy touch.

A noise behind her startled her and she straightened suddenly. She felt something shoved in her right hand and looked at a wide mouthed half-pint canning jar.

"There's your sweet tea."

Wren tried to move but Agnes's skeletal hand gripped her other arm.

"Amazing how strong she still is."

"She should be in a hospital," said Wren. "Or a nursing home. She could be with--"

"Don't say his name. It upsets her. No, she's better off here, where we can take care of her. Now, I'm going to make her oatmeal. You sit down and keep her company. Just relax."

"I want to go home."

"Well, of course you do. After I feed her the oatmeal."

"I don't think Mrs. Hargitt should see me here."

"She won't. Don't worry." Her companion left again.

Wren sat down in a straight-backed chair with a caned seat, the canning jar in her right hand. Agnes watched her every move. Wren smiled, uncertain what else to do.

"My grandchildren," breathed Agnes.

Wren set the jar of tea on the floor beside her and leaned over, putting her ear closer to Agnes' lips to catch the words.

"It's all my fault." Agnes coughed, and Wren felt her own nerves tingle as though it racked her own thin body. "No one is safe."

Not knowing what else to do, Wren tried to ease the woman's mind. "Everyone is safe." Then curiosity got the better of her. "Safe from who?"

"From him. He'd hurt them."

"Reverend Tanner?"

Agnes nodded faintly. "God forgive . . . me. I had to end it. He was . . . evil . . ." A second hoarse cough racked her frail body.

"Shhh," said Wren, horrified at the revelation and Agnes might die from the stress.

Agnes's grip intensified, her milky eyes staring straight at Wren yet somehow looking through her. "But the others. Was it wrong to end their lives? So much pain. It was a mercy. Wasn't it? Mother taught me how. She would never do anything wrong, would she?"

Wren shook her head. "No. I'm sure she wouldn't." What others? Did she kill George and Ruthie?

Agnes' eyes flicked wildly from side to side. "They never found them, did they?" She moaned softly. "Oh, so innocent. The sins of the father were visited on them." Another moan. "The sins of the mother."

Another deep cough struck Agnes, and she released her grip on Wren's arm.

Wren reached down to the floor and grabbed the jar of tea, holding it to Agnes' lips, gently cradling her head with her right hand. "Drink this. Please."

Agnes took two swallows. "My daddy. Dead! Why?"

Wren's hands shook, fearful of what was happening, horrified by what sounded like a series of terrible confession. That question, "why?" reverberated in her own soul. It was one she asked every night when she looked at the picture of her own father. She had to calm this woman. "Don't talk anymore. Drink." She held the jar to Agnes's lips, urging her to take more sips.

"She was there. One of us was promised to him but she wouldn't--"

Then with a breath that sounded more like a dry rattle, she collapsed back against Wren's hand.

Wren dropped the canning jar as the horror of what happened hit her.

Agnes Tanner was dead.

CHAPTER 47

The canning jar hit the rough oaken floor with a hollow clink, splashing the remaining tea. Some washed onto Wren's leg. The rest spread out in wide fingers before soaking into the dry, unvarnished wood.

"What have you done?" The voice in the doorway was low and stern.

"I didn't do anything," wailed Wren. She kept asking about her grandchildren, were they safe. Was someone dead? She wouldn't stop." Wren felt sick to her stomach. Other than her own dad, she never really knew anyone who'd died. She'd definitely never attended a death much less possibly been the cause when it happened. Could they send her to jail?

"It wasn't my fault," she said as much to ease her own conscience. "Honest. I tried to calm her so I gave her some of the tea. But the excitement was too much for her. Her heart just quit." She faced her companion. "I'm sorry. I don't know why you insisted on making me talk to her. I didn't want to hurt her."

"Sit down!"

Wren obeyed, looking at her feet. She heard a deep breath, released in a long, slow shudder.

"She was old. Old people die."

Wren nodded. A tear spilled out of her right eye, and she brushed it away with a sniff.

"Did she have any dying words? Something that I should have heard? A last request?"

"Uh, huh," said Wren. She squeezed her eyes shut, trying to picture the scene so as to remember the words exactly as they were spoken. "She said, 'God forgive me. I had to end it. He was evil.' She kept asking if someone was safe now, but she never gave a name. Then later she asked if it was wrong to end their lives. I think she got all biblical with something about sins of the fathers and mothers getting visits. I didn't understand it." Wren paused for breath and to get firmer control on herself.

"Go on. What else did she say?"

"Well, finally she asked if they never found them and said something about their being innocent." Wren spoke slowly, thinking everything through. "She sounded like she was admitting something. I told her not to talk anymore, but she started on her father then. Said something about 'one of us being promised to him' and 'she was there.' She asked 'Why?' Do you know what she meant?"

Wren stared at Agnes's still form. Already the ancient woman's body seemed to have collapsed in on itself. Wren wouldn't have been surprised to see it simply melt away. She was also struck by the lack of emotion shown by her companion. She'd expected a look of horror or sorrow, something. It occurred to her that maybe this was not a surprise. "You knew all this?"

"I knew what Tanner was capable of, better than some."

Wren struggled to comprehend, but despite her attempts at being a rebel, she frankly had little solid information for understanding. Her life had been one of loving parents, a father who doted on her every whim. True, his brother, her uncle, was a drunk, but he'd never gotten violent. He'd never lashed out and beaten anyone or . . . It occurred to Wren that Tanner's crimes had reached a level of evil she'd never believed possible.

CHAPTER 48

"I want to report a hit and run." Donna Sherwood stood in front the open dispatch window, her blue vinyl purse clutched in both hands in front of her.

"Who got hit?" asked Jo. "Do I need to call for an ambulance?"

"My car. That's who got hit."

"Ah. Did you get the license number of who did it? Or see the make and model?"

"No. I was in the library when it happened. But when I came out to my car, there was a big scratch across the rear on the driver's side, and part of my tail light was cracked. Water will get in there when it rains and short out my light."

"I'll get a deputy. Why don't you have a seat." Jo pointed to a row of plastic chairs. "Can I get you coffee?"

"I'd rather have the sheriff."

"He had to go out of the office on duty. But deputy Chapman has lots of experience."

By the time Chapman was finished taking the lady's statement, he had nothing except the paperwork for the woman to take to her insurance.

* * *

"Have you seen Wren?" Phoebe felt as if she'd asked this

same question a dozen times already. With the large number of volunteers, they'd finished cleaning up the Sugar Run Trail in a couple of hours instead of the five or six that Phoebe had anticipated. After they left, Phoebe felt the need to go home and clean up. And that's when her search for Wren began.

Neither Sherry nor Jeannie had seen her. Jeannie was quickly adding up numbers and entering them into a tally sheet. "Shirley ought to know though," she said.

Phoebe shook her head. "The store's closed again today. I think there's still damage from that water leak to fix. At least there's a painter's truck parked in the lot."

"Was Wren supposed to meet you someplace?"

"No. I've been busy with the Friends of the Hollow, but they're done and gone. I told Wren I'd meet her at the house in time for supper."

Sherry looked up from her work, and gave Phoebe a look that said 'duh, then that's where she is.' Phoebe resented the look.

"I went to the house. She wasn't there. I've been calling or radioing the house for the last fifteen minutes. She's not answering. Phoebe picked up a half-finished injury report and slid it into her mail cubby. One of the volunteers had twisted her ankle on the trail during cleanup. "I'll just have to finish this later. At least with Burt gone, he can't get on my case about it. If Wren's ignoring the phone and the radio just to piss me off . . ." She looked around the visitor's center, taking in Burt's shut door. "Burt's still gone?"

"Yep," replied Sherry. "Did you try the lake? For Wren, I mean."

Phoebe ticked the places off on her fingers. "The lake, the store, café, pool, here. Did you know that the pool's closed, too?"

"Oh! You didn't hear?" said Jeannie. The sheriff came and arrested the lifeguard."

"Arrested the lifeguard?" So much for eliminating the boy from the list of suspects. Phoebe wondered if Boone had suspected the young man all along. It seems Wren had.

"She's probably just hiking one of the trails," said Sherry.

"Oh, please. This is Wren we're talking about. Anytime I mention taking a walk with me, she rolls her eyes and snorts."

"Well then, she's probably at home, Phoebe. I imagine you missed her when she was outside and called when she was in the bathroom or napping." Sherry pulled open a filing cabinet drawer and slipped the folder home. "And speaking of home, I'm outa here. Got a dentist appointment. It's all yours Jeannie," she added to her office mate.

Phoebe pointed to her mud-smeared shirt. "And I still haven't cleaned up yet. I doubt this is the appearance anyone wants projected around here. See you tomorrow."

She drove to her cabin, peering off the narrow road into the woods in case Wren was, in fact, wandering there. But by the time she pulled up to the house, the only creature she'd seen was one doe, standing in a thicket. A nutchatch called its nasally "nank nank" from nearby.

"Wren," she called as she opened the front door. "Wren?"

There was no answer. Phoebe slipped off her dirty boots and padded down the hall to her daughter's bedroom "Wren?" she said softly.

The bedroom was empty.

Where was her daughter? Maybe she'd gone back to that wild raspberry patch she'd found. It couldn't be far. Wren wasn't into hiking, hadn't been since her father had died. Phoebe searched the area for the path. She found the patch about one-hundred yards into the woods, but no sign of Wren.

She next made two complete circuits of the cabin, calling for her daughter the entire time. Knowing how stubborn her daughter could be, Phoebe assumed the girl either didn't care to have supper with her mother or that she'd forgotten and expected to meet with her somewhere for a ride home. The chipmunk sat near the step as though waiting for a treat.

"You seen Wren anywhere, Spunky Chunk?"

Phoebe went back to the visitor's center and made a fresh set of rounds. There was no sign of her by the lake or the visitor's center. The café was now closed. She drove through the park, making a circuit past the dam and around the campgrounds. Phoebe checked every restroom in the park including the men's, much to the consternation of one hiker.

Her daughter was not to be found. Most disturbing was the fact that no one had seen her all day. The scene over burning Wren's clothes and defying the girl's attempts to live with her grandparents loomed large. Phoebe fought down the panic that rose into her throat with an acrid taste. This was no time to cry. She had to think.

Where had she gone? Had she actually run away?

She called Marsha Phillips to see if Wren had ridden into town with her in the morning even though this was not one of her class days. The answer was a confused 'no.' Phoebe tried the library next in case her daughter had brazenly hitched a ride with someone else. The afternoon librarian said hadn't they seen her, but she had no idea if anyone in the morning had.

"I do remember the name," said the woman. "Skinny girl. Wears black? The art teacher wondered why she'd never showed up for any of the art classes and asked if she should expect her tomorrow or drop her from the roster. I'm afraid we can't give a refund, though."

She hadn't gone to her art classes? What the hell had she been doing in town?

Phoebe felt like she'd run out of options and self-control. It was nearly six and panic clenched at her throat.

She'd call the sheriff. Boone had a clear head. He'd know what to do.

The dispatcher put her through to him right away.

"Linus, It's Phoebe. Wren's missing."

"When did you last see her?"

"This morning. Early. Just before seven. I had a campfire coffee to get to. When I left, she was heading back to bed."

"Phoebe, try to calm down. Could she have just gone on one of the trails?"

"No. Wren doesn't hike any more. She made that abundantly clear to me."

"Where have you looked?"

Phoebe ran down the list, feeling her throat tighten and her pulse pound faster with each place she named. By the time she was finished, her voice was breaking. "Linus, I wouldn't be worried except she hates this place and isn't all that fond of me, either."

"Can you look around her room, see anything missing or out of place. Something that would give you a clue as to where she'd gone?"

Phoebe put the phone down and went into Wren's room. The bed was unmade, not too surprising, and the gym shorts she'd worn to bed were on the floor where she'd dropped them. The cut offs were gone as well as the park t-shirts that Phoebe had purchased for her. Wren's sketchpad sat on her desk.

"All I can see is that she got dressed," Phoebe said when she picked up the phone.

"What was she wearing?"

"If I had to guess from what's not on the floor, blue jean cut offs, white sneakers, and a brown park shirt. One with the grotto on it, not the bats."

"You sure?"

"Yeah. She didn't have a lot of options. I burned all her goth crap. I tried to call her grandparents, but they're aren't answering."

"Do you think she's with them?" he asked.

"Maybe. They're suing for custody. I got the letter a few days ago. I think Wren put them up to it. Like I said, she hates it here. And then . . ." her voice caught in her throat.

"Take your time."

"I'm fine. After I got that letter, That's when I burned her clothes."

"How did she take it?"

"Better than I expected actually. But maybe that was just a ruse, you know? Maybe she knew it didn't matter?"

"Give me the grandparents' names, address and phone number."

Phoebe recited the information.

"I'll notify the sheriff in Washington County to contact them. Sit on their house. Do you have any reason to think they'd hurt her?"

"No. Me maybe, but never Wren. But," she added, "She may not be with them. She could have run away on her own. She may be hurt somewhere."

"I'll put out a BOLO on her and be at the park as soon as I can. Where are you now?"

"At my house."

"Wait for me there."

CHAPTER 49

"You mean he . . . he attacked girls?" She couldn't bring herself to say the word 'rape.'

"Lots of them. He called me his Hagar, his wife's maidservant. Like I was his concubine."

Wren's stomach lurched and she fought back the urge to vomit. "But he was a minister."

"I told you, child, this had nothing to do with church or the Lord. It had to do with his being evil. The devil possesses whoever he likes, policeman, plumber, whatever."

"Is... is Shirley his..."

"You are a very clever girl. Not even Shirley knows that. She thinks that there was a wounded serviceman that fathered her and died before she was born, though she might have suspicions that she's Ben Owen's daughter. I went to him after it happened, hoping he'd marry me and claim the child, but he was still in love with Agnes back then. I'd hate to think what Shirley'd do if she found out. I told you, Wren, people don't much like for old family secrets to get exposed. That's how those two children died. Alive, they would have revealed these terrible secrets, including Agnes' sin."

Wren hugged her herself, trying to hold in her fear. Shirley, the one friend she had in the park, might actually try to kill her? Did she kill George and Ruthie just to protect a secret of her birth? Or had Agnes done that herself to keep her secrets; the death of her father, her love affair with Ben Owen. All Wren had wanted to do was pry into one little death, hoping for something exciting in her dull world, and it looked liked she'd stumbled into a nest of murders.

Wren remembered something. "Mrs. Campbell, you said Agnes had a sister."

"Yes, she did. Her name was Dorcas and she was many years younger than Agnes. Tanner was promised one of the two girls for a wife, a union that would bolster his standing as new minister. Agnes planned to leave with her lover. That meant Dorcas would be forced to marry Tanner and that was something she couldn't see clear to do."

Wren remembered that Mrs. Hargitt said she'd lived with the Elwoods, leaving later to work for the Hargitt family. Could that have been a story she'd made up? Who would send a girl to live with someone else just because they got remarried? Maybe she'd told the story so many times that she actually believed it herself. It would explain how she still felt enough concern for her older sister to take care of her in her old age.

"Did Agnes kill her husband? Was that what she meant when she said I had to end it, he was evil?"

"He was evil. How can you doubt that?"

"But if she killed him, it was in self-defense, right? I mean, if he was hurting people."

Mrs. Campbell shook her head. "The law wouldn't think so. No, it was murder. It was her lot then to live her life out atoning for her sin. Tanner was her punishment for succumbing to sins of the flesh. A sorrowful life struggling to save her family from their inner demons was her cross for murdering her lawful husband."

Wren felt she was slipping deeper and deeper into a quagmire, but there was something about it so bizarre that she had to know all or go crazy wondering. "How, did he die?"

"Poison. Lily of the valley makes water taste sweet so they

say."

And Agnes taught what she knew about herbs to Mrs. Hargitt. No wonder she said she doesn't like sweet drinks. More than ever, Wren wanted to leave before Hargitt returned.

Mrs. Campbell raised her face to the ceiling as though to heaven. "But only a few people knew about these things. Small sins in the balance against all the labor and good that this poor woman struggled to achieve. Do you know how many souls she tended through the polio epidemic? She saved some, she did. And others, she helped speed up their dark passage into heaven. Their deaths were a mercy. And in the end, her name has been kept pure and untainted. Have you noticed how no one knew she was still alive, yet there was no obituary? It fed her legend, making her seem like another Elijah taken up in a fiery chariot."

She dropped her chin and stared at Wren. "And now you know. Just like George did. He didn't know all, but he knew enough and he wouldn't see reason."

"I won't tell anyone, I promise," pleaded Wren.

"Hush, child. I told you, it won't be safe for you to go back there. But don't worry. I'll think of something. You aren't happy living there anyway, are you? No. So, if you don't show up, everyone will just think you're another sad runaway. Think of it like witness protection."

"No. My mom."

"Your mother will forget about you soon enough. Trust me. Parents don't always care as much for their children as the children think. Take Reverend Elwood, for example. He would have thrown his own daughter out as a harlot just because she'd been with Ben in the hay that night. And then he'd have thought nothing of giving Dorcas to Tanner."

"Did Mrs. Hargitt, I mean Dorcas, tell you about that?"

"Child, we were there the evening that Agnes lay with Owens. We saw it all from the loft." She winked. "And I was the one what held the pitchfork to ram into Elwood's back."

Before Wren could react, Mrs. Campbell left and shut the door. Wren heard the thick wooden bolt slide home, trapping her inside.

* * *

Mrs. Campbell sat in the kitchen, elbows on the table, her body slumped forward with her hands grasping the back of her neck. Agnes was dead. The woman she loved more than anyone, more than her mother, more than her own daughter, was gone. The sudden hole in her life stunned her more than she'd expected. She thought she was prepared for the inevitable, especially with Agnes' advanced age. She could still recall so vividly the day Agnes had seen her in the park. It was so unexpected and the surprise on Agnes' face should have been gratifying except for the knowledge that Agnes had organized the reunion not to see her but to meet another.

That and the fact that she'd cried out 'Dorcas," and ran from me like I had the plague.

Campbell's feelings were complicated by other emotions. Like seasonings simmered so long in a stew, it grew difficult to separate one from the other. She tasted guilt and fear along with the sorrow. Both of the former had had been present from the beginning. Neither would leave her alone. The fear at least had been useful. It had fueled her actions in the past when her fear of Agnes' elopement drove her to killing Elwood. Agnes' departure would mean that she'd have to marry Tanner. And I still ended up as his concubine. Fear of him still fueled her.

She could still feel the impact of her father's thin body against the fork's tines as she rammed it home, braced to meet his body. She'd been prepared to charge into him but Jepthah, bless him, saved her half the trouble, meeting her half-way. And she'd always been accounted as strong for her age. Hard work did that to a country girl, and what she'd lacked in physical build, her desperation more than made up for it. She could still hear Agnes's whispered question. "Why?" Equally clear was her unspoken response.

Why do you think? You're the eldest. It's your lot to marry the deacon, not mine. And if you try to run away, I'll say that your lover did it. That I saw him kill papa before he ran away.

We saw you rolling in the hay like some bitch in heat. If I tell Tanner, he'll back me up. You love this Ben, so I don't think you'll let them hang him.

She had watched, too, from the loft; Viola beside her. Viola hadn't understood, but she had. She heard their heavy breaths, watched every sensuous movement with the fascination of a budding woman. Oh, she'd seen the livestock mate before. Sex was nothing new, but this was different and somehow more primal than anything the rooster or boar were capable of.

It had made her hungry. Later, when Tanner seduced her, she'd actually given in more out of curiosity than duty or fear. But his rutting was like the boar and it had sickened her.

Well, all that and the ensuing daughter were in the past. She needed time to figure out how this changed things. She couldn't think, especially with that girl pounding on the door, demanding to be let out and taken home. The thickness of the door muffled most of the noise, but she could still hear it. She went outside to the porch.

Tanner's evil had been a poison in the community. She'd run away when she discovered that she carried his child and if she'd known any of the herbal purges she'd have used one. But her mother hadn't known about the things no decent woman would have used. So she'd run first to Ben Owen, hoping to seduce him in his grief and then pressure him into claiming the child. Only he wouldn't come to her. In the end she took the name Tabitha and invented a marriage to a soldier, one that was conveniently dead. And so she became respectable Mrs. Campbell without ever marrying. And, in the meantime, the church burned, the parish collapsed and people slowly forgot about Agnes.

Not Dorcas. She made a point of keeping her memory alive, partly out of love and partly out of a gnawing guilt. She slipped articles into the paper under various aliases, bolstering her sister's legend. And when Agnes' own children passed on, she saw to it that her sister was cared for. She owed her that much. She wouldn't allow her to become some drooling nursing home vegetable in adult diapers.

The fact that no one recollected Agnes' death only fueled her legend. Agnes had become immortal. And Viola, raised as a second sister for Agnes before Tanner's lust drove her to Ma Hargitt and her purgative cures, had been more than happy to care for her.

The greatest dangers to the legend's destruction turned out to be Agnes' own grandchildren. Bastard Daisy's backwards little girl was thought to be mentally deficient. But when the girl's cousin started snooping, he discovered that the terrified little Ruthie was only color-blind like her father. Then the damned boy had to read Shirley's text books and find out that it was impossible unless Daisy also carried the trait, a trait that Tanner never had to give. She knew if the boy carried out his project, he'd discover what no one else knew, that Daisy was Ben Owen's child; that she carried that gene for faulty vision and that she'd passed it on, not to her son, Tom, but to her daughter, Ruthie.

And George wouldn't listen to reason. He was too excited.

Still, she was grateful to him. If he hadn't uncovered the secret, someone else would have later. A teacher perhaps, some outsider with no business poking around the family history.

The big mistake was allowing the boy a proper burial, but wild hogs weren't as common back then and neither were the bears. She couldn't count on him being consumed. Besides, it made for a more convincing story for everyone to assume the boy had gotten lost in the cave and his cousin died waiting for him. Frightened little Ruthie was told to wait outside the cave until George came for her. The teddy bear and her trust in George cemented her obedience.

Why did that ranger have to find the body? Why did her nosey daughter have to go snooping? Worse, this girl had heard Agnes confess to killing Tanner.

If only she'd drunk the tea instead of giving it to Agnes.

They all had known about the lily of the valley. Tabitha always found it ironic that a flower known for purity could not only be so lethal, but deceptively so. Its sweet taste made it palatable unlike so many other poisons. Agnes had used a few times; once to put their poor deranged mother to rest, three times to relieve the suffering brought on by polio's creeping and incurable paralysis and once to kill a demon when Agnes discovered that his wickedness extended to raping his own, supposed, daughter.

Each of the uses had been counted as merciful blessings.

This girl needed to die. And making her disappearance seem like an ordinary runaway was not the problem. The problem now was age. Tabitha was still strong, but not strong enough to choke a healthy teenager or strike her down. She hadn't really been strong enough back then, either. Age had weakened her body but not her will.

The sound of a car engine disturbed her thoughts, and she hurried from the front porch to intercept the visitor. To her surprise, the car sported a Caddo County Sheriff's Department decal on the side. They couldn't be after the girl already, could they? She should have turned on the police scanner. Her stomach knotted up.

"What can I do for you?" she asked.

"Good day, ma'am. I'm deputy Peters. I come out here every Friday to check on Ms. Hargitt."

Mrs. Campbell smiled. "You need a new calendar, deputy. It ain't Friday."

"No, ma'am. I'm going to be off for four days come Wednesday. Thought I'd stop by today to see if there was anything she needed. Wood chopped, jars opened. Anything at all."

"Isn't that sweet of you. Viola's not here right now, deputy. I'll tell her you stopped by."

The big man didn't move. "I didn't think Ms. Hargitt could drive. Where is she?"

"I never said she drove anywhere, deputy. She likes to walk in the woods when it's pretty. Sometimes she collects herbs. Today I believe she said she was going to pick the wild raspberries."

"Ah," he said. "And you are?"

"I'm just a friend from church. Several of us in the congregation come out to visit. But it's so nice to know that she has others looking in on her, too." She put on her sweetest smile.

The deputy stepped back around to the driver's side. "I figured she had someone bring her groceries. Good to know. Tell her I'll see her next Friday again."

"I will do that." She waited until the car was out of sight down the lane before moving. Blast. She didn't know that Viola ever let the law on the premises. She wondered if he'd ever seen Agnes or suspected she was in the back larder. He didn't ask about anyone else, so probably not. Still, the encounter made her edgy. She needed to make a decision about that girl and soon.

CHAPTER 50

Wren sat on the room's only chair and hugged herself, trying to stop the shivering. Not two feet away lay a corpse. It was as though the powers-that-be mocked her previous fascination with death. She looked at the dead woman's face, trying to convince herself that it was just an old woman, nothing to be afraid of. The bloodless, ivory skin had already sunk deeper into the cheeks and the toothless mouth gaped, the lips pulling back around the gums. The eyes, milky with cataracts, stared at the ceiling.

She suddenly recalled every vampire or zombie movie she'd ever seen and expected to see the corpse rise up from its bier and come for her. Wren jumped up and pulled the quilt over Agnes' head.

Why was she still in here? What was Mrs. Campbell doing? Wren got up and pounded on the thick door. "Let me out! I want to go home!" No answer. She called again, louder, only to break into a dry cough. She hadn't had anything to drink since the orange juice and her throat was parched. Why did she have to drop the glass of tea?

Then it occurred to her, Agnes died right after drinking the tea. What had Mrs. Campbell said about Tanner? Something about a poison that tasted sweet? Sweet tea? Was the tea poisoned? Mrs. Hargitt said she didn't care for sweet drinks. Was that why? Did she keep this poison on hand? But Mrs. Campbell made that tea. Why would she try to kill the very sister she'd taken care of for so long?

She didn't get the tea for Agnes. She got it for me. Was it an accident? Did she know?

Wren backed up until her spine pressed against the outer wall, her hands over her mouth in horror. Maybe it wasn't just Shirley or Mrs. Hargitt that she had to worry about. Faintly, through the high window, she heard the sound of a car engine starting up.

"Help! Hey! I'm locked in here." Wren shouted up at the little window until her parched throat caught in a cough. When she stopped to catch her breath, she heard the engine receding. Whoever it was had driven away.

Tears rolled down her cheeks as she flopped back into the chair. For a minute she rocked back and forth on the hard chair, hugging her arms at the elbows, her sobs racking her chest. She wanted out, she wanted her daddy. Hell, right now, she thought, she even wanted her mother. Just not left in here to die with some shriveled up dead woman.

Wren's stomach growled and brought to mind her hunger and growing thirst. She turned her head away from the lump under the quilt and looked at the well-stocked shelves.

You're in a pantry, you idiot. There has to be something safe to eat in here.

She rummaged through the items on the shelves and came across a stash of canning jars filled with peaches. She'd eat a jar of those. The juice would help quench her thirst, too. Quickly she unscrewed the metal cap but to her surprise, only the outside of the cap came off. There was still a flat lid pressed tightly against the jar. How the hell do you open these?

There had to be some trick to it. She tried gripping the lid from the top, jamming her fingernails under the metal cap, but her stumpy nails were too short. A knife.

She set the jar on the chair and searched the shelves for anything remotely sharp. When she'd exhausted the shelves, she got down on her knees and peered underneath, looking for a tool box. She found what looked like a rusty fishing tackle box shoved in a dark corner.

Wren dragged it out, disturbing a spider in the process. Bringing it closer to the light under the window, she opened the box. Inside was a pair of pliers whose center bolt had rusted shut and one flat-head screwdriver. The screwdriver would have to do. She slid the box back under the shelves in case that crazy Mrs. Campbell came back in here. Then she attacked the canning jar lid. After stabbing it repeatedly, she heard a hiss of air and realized that she must have released a vacuum of sorts. Now her runty nails were enough to pry up the lid. She shoved the screwdriver into her rear pocket, tugging her t-shirt over the handle to hide it. After another pull, the jar top came off with a satisfying "spunk."

At first she drank the juice, greedily sucking it down until a peach half slapped her in the mouth. She opened wider to receive it and swallowed it nearly without chewing. Delicious. Wren devoured two more peach halves before slowing to chew the rest.

When she was done, she replaced the punctured cap and screwed on the lid. Then she hid the empty jar in back of the other jars, hoping no one would go snooping anytime soon. Finally she turned her attention to getting out. The door was bolted from the outside so that was no good. The window? It was high and small but perhaps by standing on the chair she could get it open and pull herself up.

Wren listened for any sound, a hint that either Mrs. Campbell or Mrs. Hargitt was returning. Both were dangerous as far as she was concerned. So far everything in the house was quiet. She positioned the chair under the window and stood on it. If she stood on her tip toes, she could barely see out. She decided that, once she had the window open, she'd put the tackle box on the chair seat and stand on it, gaining five inches in the process.

She cautiously slid her right hand along the lower window frame, feeling for a handle. Nothing. No, there was something, a little button of sorts. She couldn't tell what. Okay, time for the tackle box. She put it on the chair seat and stood on it. Now she could see the entire window. At the very top were two hinges, so the bottom didn't raise up, it swung out. It made the fit tighter still, but Wren was skinny and thought she could do it. She had to do it.

The button turned out to be a little slide catch. It looked as if it rotated to unlock the window but it was glued shut with a thick coat of dingy white paint. In fact, the entire window had been painted shut with what looked like several layers of heavy paint. There was no way she was going to get this open.

Wren clenched her lips together, fighting back the urge to cry again. Why was this happening to her? If daddy hadn't gotten killed then they never would have moved out here. Her mother would have never taken her to that stupid high school, she wouldn't have had to do this stupid history report, and she'd have never met these horrible people.

It's your own stupid fault for going into town and trying to dig up a murder case.

"Shut up!" she muttered to herself and pushed all thoughts of who to blame to the back of her mind. A new thought pressed forward. She had to pee.

"No way I'm going in here."

She stabbed at the paint with the screwdriver, chipping it away.

* * *

Mrs. Campbell had watched the deputy drive away. She wished this one hadn't seen her. True, he didn't know her name and he hadn't seen her car which she always kept well hidden, but where there was one deputy, another often followed.

She turned and looked into the woods beyond the barn. Viola wouldn't be back until nearly dusk. Walking was tedious enough for her, but when she rummaged for her herbs, she often took a lunch and made a long day of it. As a result, she'd be exhausted when she returned.

Too tired to fight back.

And the girl wasn't going anywhere just yet. So she had some time.

An idea germinated in her brain. A runaway teen, obviously troubled, intent on robbing an elderly woman, not realizing the woman has a .22 rifle. A struggle, an oil lantern tipped.

Yes, it would work. It would eliminate her problems. She just needed to gather a few supplies first.

She walked away from the house towards the galvanized shed and her hidden car, not noticing the girl at work on the window on the other side of the house.

CHAPTER 51

Wren wasn't sure how long she'd been stuck in the house. She never wore a watch and she didn't see a clock in the pantry. But the sun had shifted so that the shadows now stretched instead of shrinking as when they had when they'd first arrived. It reminded her of when someone pulled on a rubber band and she half expected the shadows to suddenly snap back, catapulting acorns and leaves into the air. She didn't know how far a shadow extended every hour but these told her it was getting late in the afternoon. She'd been at the window too long. That and her arms ached.

She tried the knob again. This time it jiggled in the casing. Wren wacked it with the screwdriver handle and the knob turned. With any luck, she'd be able to open the window now. After shoving the screwdriver back into her hip pocket, she tried for a more secure stance on her precarious perch and pushed. The window didn't move.

She smacked the wood with the heel of her hand, then with both hands. Once, twice. On the third try, the casing broke loose along with the window. The fragile glass shattered into pieces, raining down on her head and shoulders. It struck the floor, tinkling like rain.

"Damn."

She wondered if she should sweep up the mess. *Like she's not going to be able to tell you're gone already. Idiot. Should've just broken the glass to begin with.*

Wren shook the shards out of her hair and peeked at the opening. She could probably fit through the space but she didn't relish crawling over the remaining glass slivers. One more shove on the casing and the window swung out.

Her stomach rumbled again. Might as well take a jar of peaches for the road. She had no idea how far she'd have to walk to find someone she could trust and right now, she didn't think she could trust another adult ever. She pulled out her yellow park bandana and wiped her sweaty forehead, then hastily stuck the kerchief back into her hip pocket.

After climbing down and grabbing a canning jar, she scrambled back up onto the tackle box. Wren gave another look out the window to see if anyone was around. Convinced that the coast was clear, she set the fruit jar outside and, using the last of her limited strength, hauled herself up into the gap. Her fingers clawed at the grass and brush outside, digging into the muddy soil. Once her head and shoulders were out, her legs dangled free. She felt like a pilgrim she'd seen in history books, stuck in the stocks, waiting for someone to throw crap at her.

The last push off the chair upset the tackle box and Wren heard the jarring clatter as it hit the glass-studded floor. If anyone else heard that, they'd be after her in no time. She worked harder and stretched both arms as far as they would extend, hauling another few inches of her chest outside. The window casing, which had been resting on her head, slid off and slammed against her back.

She stifled an outcry and renewed her endeavors. Now she wriggled her stomach, undulating her hips like a snake. Mud squished under her armpits from where she'd ripped the grass out of the damp soil. A few more inches. Her thighs touched the wooden rim and the window rode across her backside, snagging the bandana as she squirmed forward.

"Ungh!" Wren's knees made the casing and, with two

strong pushes, she was out. Free! Free and coated with mud. She lay on the ground, panting, catching her breath. Was this was it felt like when she was born? Gross. She snatched up the fruit jar, kicked the window casing back into place behind her and ran for the woods, leaving the dirty kerchief behind.

* * *

Mrs. Campbell never told her daughter that she still owned a .22, but truth be told, she enjoyed a fricasseed squirrel once in a while. And ever since she was a girl, she was good at bagging one with her rifle. Most people took the easy road and sprayed shot at the head, but shot went everywhere, and she hated picking it out of a carcass. Viola wouldn't have a rifle in the house. She said someone would see it and ask questions. Now Campbell knew who she meant. Blasted deputy. How much snooping did he do?

Well, it didn't matter. Agnes was dead. Viola's usefulness had ended and her liability had increased. Mrs. Campbell pushed aside the latest growth of honeysuckle and trumpet vine, exposing an old tool shed and an older outhouse. She'd hated this outhouse and was never so grateful as when she learned that Viola's husband had insisted on installing indoor plumbing. But the buildings proved useful. They hid her car and her rifle, the car behind them, the rifle inside carefully wrapped in tarp along with enough ammunition to keep her in the occasional squirrel for the rest of her life.

She reckoned that she had about an hour, maybe two. The girl wasn't going anywhere, but it wouldn't do for Viola to get back and let her out. Not that Viola ever came home early when she was hunting herbs. The poor thing had to stop so often. Walking was hard enough with her lame leg, but Mrs. Campbell had noted of late that she also favored what she called her good hip. It would be a mercy for Viola to not have to live in that old house and endure that sort of pain. She intended to help her, just as Agnes had done for so many others beyond healing.

As she forced back the obstinate vegetation, Mrs. Campbell honed her plan. She'd make it look like the girl had invaded the house, intent on stealing, and Viola had defended herself with an old hunting rifle. In the panic, a kerosene lantern spilled over and ignited the house. At least, that's how it would appear when someone finally came to put out the fire.

Not that Viola knew how to handle a .22, but Mrs. Campbell did. She'd unbolt the pantry and tell the girl she was taking her home. When Wren came out, she'd shoot her. And later, after Viola was dead, it was a matter of putting a knife in the girl's hand and leaving the rifle in Viola's. The fire would cover any discrepancies. She was no fool. She'd watched those crime shows on television. People were always checking for powder residue and things like that.

Finally inside, she let her eyes adjust to the gloom. Ahead, on a rotting shelf, lay her bundled rifle. She unwrapped it, letting the tarp drop to the floor. Then she took a box of ammunition. It might help if she left the open box behind in the pantry, perhaps spilling out. It would look like Viola had loaded in a hurry before her attacker came at her.

And after that? What about Agnes?

Should she burn her body, too? No, she decided. Someone might question the identity. She'd take the body back here to the shed and wrap her in the tarp. The vines grew so thick that they'd cover the door again in a week. Then she'd go back to her little apartment as though nothing had ever happened.

Tanner won't like it, but Tanner be damned. She chuckled softly. He already is.

Mrs. Campbell was just a little sad to think she'd never get to hunt and eat squirrel again.

CHAPTER 52

Boone hated certain parts of his job: the senseless suicides, searching the back roads for a hidden meth lab, and the spousal abuse. He dreaded looking for runaway teens most of all. All of the former grew out of the county's poverty. Once known for timber harvesting, the county's current source of revenue was trading in on its scenic mountains, bluffs, and Big Sugar Creek. But not everyone in the county could run a bed and breakfast, outfit float trips, or sell souvenirs. The truth was, the very beauty of the land made it hell to eke out a living. And so people beat their spouses, tried to make and sell drugs, or just shot their brains out.

And some ran away.

He didn't know Wren Palmer well, but he'd seen the signs of a disgruntled, rebellious teen during their brief encounter. The clothes, hair, and the attitude didn't make a kid bad any more than it made them good, but this one wasn't happy with her mother or her life. If he was a betting man, he'd bet she ran away. The alternative was even worse, suicide.

Phoebe met him at the front door. Her reddened eyes told him she'd been crying.

"Phoebe, no word yet?"

Phoebe shook her head no. "Come in, Linus. I don't know

what to do."

"Do you have a recent photo? Something with the way she looks now?"

She picked up a picture from an end table. "I have this. It was taken the day we got here."

Boone took the photo. "I'll send this out. And I requested some dogs. They should be coming along with our search and rescue team. Since this is where she was last seen, we'll begin from here. She hasn't been gone that long, so try to relax. I know that sounds impossible, but I need you to remain calm. Can you do that?"

Phoebe nodded.

"Good. Ah, I hear trucks pulling up now. I'm going out to my mobile command unit, contact the Washington County sheriff, and get this search underway." He pointed to a large white trailer behind his SUV. "We'll find her. We'll get her back."

Within minutes, Boone had the searchers, which included the park's rangers, organized and on the move. Boone moved the unit near the park office, the better to take advantage of the buildings additional phones and fax machine if needed. He'd already used the latter once, to transmit Wren's photo to the State Police. Phoebe hovered nearby, unable to wait alone at the house. Instead, Boone left one of the citizen volunteers at the house in the off chance that Wren wandered back home on her own.

His radio crackled to life. "Central command, this is deputy Wells. The dogs have followed her trail along the road heading south. We found the apple core that she'd tossed, then the dogs lost the scent forty yards from the forestry road that cuts into it." He gave a map coordinate. "Looks like she got into a vehicle."

"Signs of struggle?"

"None. Can't see any scuff marks on the road where someone might have dragged her away. Looks like she went willingly."

"Her grandparents!" said Phoebe. "She must have arranged

for them to pick her up."

"If that's true, then we should know soon," said Boone.

Three minutes later they had their answer. Wren's grandparents had been playing bridge at the community center. They'd been there all day with dozens of eyewitnesses to prove it. Moreover, they were horrified that their daughter-in-law had left Wren alone at the house.

"They could have hired someone else to get her, but it doesn't seem likely," said Boone. "I've issued a Morgan Nick Amber Alert. Her photo has been faxed out. We will find her."

Phoebe's eyes watered up and her lips tensed as Boone watched her struggle to maintain control. "Maybe you should go home, Phoebe."

"No! I need to be involved. I'm a commissioned law enforcement officer, remember? I should be a part of this search."

A truck door slammed out in the parking lot. Boone looked out the open back and saw a forestry service man step out with a bloodhound. "I called back one of the dogs," Boone said. "I know it's a long shot, but I want to see if they can pick up the trail around here. It's possible that she merely stopped in a walk along the road, came back and walked into this area."

They watched as the dog sniffed the grounds, searching for a fresh scent. Another truck pulled in and Boone saw Burt McGowan get out. Just then, the dog pulled wildly on his lead, his jowled head snuffling strongly around the passenger side door.

Phoebe flew at McGowan and pummeled his chest with her fists. "You rotten bastard! What have you done with my d daughter?"

* * *

Wren ran, paying no attention to direction. All she wanted to do was put distance between herself and that house. After ten minutes, she felt a sharp pain in her side and realized that she'd been holding her breath much of the time. She stopped and leaned against an oak, letting it support her while she inhaled deeply. Her stomach felt queasy from swallowing air.

As she gripped her stomach, she looked around the forest.

Where am I? It occurred to her that she probably should have continued down the lane to the road instead. But she didn't think that road was well traveled which meant she'd only run into that crazy Mrs. Campbell. Wren tried closing her eyes for a moment to regain control of her emotions but, when she did, she saw Agnes' shriveled body and heard her death rattle.

Suddenly her entire body was wracked with shivers. She dropped the jar of peaches into a patch of yellow violets and collapsed to the ground beside an overgrown stone foundation.

You can't stay here. You have to find a way home or to town. Someplace with people.

The shivering subsided as exhaustion took over. For a moment, she fought against it before succumbing to sleep.

* * *

Phoebe pounded on her boss's chest again and again, oblivious to any physical pain as his brass cut into the sides of her little fingers. The tall man recoiled under the blows but didn't cry out which only fueled her fury. "Is that why you gave me Sloan's shifts? So you could have more access to Wren? Was probation just a threat to keep me too busy to discover your filthy little secret?"

"Phoebe, stop it," called Boone, reaching for her wrists.

She didn't. "Did you like boys, too? Did you kill that boy to keep him quiet?"

"Phoebe!" roared Boone.

She stared at Linus, blinking in disbelief. *Why wasn't he arresting this man?*

"Phoebe! Listen to me. You're out of control. Calm down."

"He took my daughter. He took my daughter!"

"And I intend to find out why and where." Boone gently moved her aside before turning to confront McGowan.

"What about it, Superintendent? Did you take Wren?"

"Yes, I picked her up this morning, but not to hurt her. For God's sake, Linus. What do you take me for? She was

331

trying to catch Ranger Phillip's wife to get a ride to town. I knew that she rode home with Marsha before so I assumed it was okay. I dropped her off at the library."

"I don't believe you," screamed Phoebe. She leaped for McGowan but Boone had an arm around her waist in a flash, pulling her back.

With his free hand, Boone took out his portable radio and directed one of his deputies to check the library again for any sign of Wren or anyone who could verify that she'd been there.

"Calm down, Phoebe," he coaxed. "I can't get to the bottom of this as long as you're in this state of mind." Phoebe stopped struggling and he released her.

"Come into the trailer, McGowan," Boone said. "We need to talk."

McGowan looked from Phoebe to Boone and back again. "I'd never hurt Wren, Phoebe. You should know that. I guess what I did was stupid, but I knew she'd miss Marsha and I didn't want to see her hitchhiking. I thought I was keeping her safer by giving her a ride myself. You have to believe me."

Phoebe didn't answer. All she could think of was that this man, her own boss for cripe's sake, had taken her daughter.

Boone motioned to the trailer's open rear door. "Let's go in."

"Wait a minute," McGowan said. "Wren left her notebook behind in my truck. I didn't notice it until I was coming back, mainly because it was on the floor. Let me get it for you."

"I'll get it," said Phoebe. She needed to distance herself from her boss before she did something that would warrant her own arrest. When she returned from the truck, both Boone and McGowan were in the trailer, its doors closed against her.

She turned her attention to the notebook.

* * *

Mrs. Campbell had lingered, sitting in her car, fine-tuning her plan and gathering strength of conviction. When she finally returned to the rectory, the sun had long since moved west, leaving the area in a long, lingering, late afternoon dusk that kept the house cool. One quick glance through the interior told her that Viola wasn't back yet. It wouldn't be long now. She didn't care to be out too late for fear of stumbling in the gloom. Mrs. Campbell thought about calling out the girl and shooting her before Viola came home, then decided to wait. If the old woman was close at hand, she might get spooked by the noise. Mrs. Campbell didn't want that. Killing her would be difficult enough since it had to be done face to face and violently to make it look like she'd been attacked by the girl.

Instead, she waited on the front stoop, listening to a few lingering warblers trilling their mating songs. She loathed this spot, her mind conjuring all that had happened here, including her daughter's conception in the barn. The irony of Shirley thinking that she might be Ben's child amused her. After all, everyone thought his bastard, Daisy, was really Tanner's daughter. And Ben should never have abandoned her sister. Or seduced her to begin with.

Now there's a man that needs to die. Twice he'd escaped her attempts and it galled her to no end. If I send him to Hell, Tanner will keep busy tormenting him rather than me.

She heard a crackling voice singing nearby.

"Lazy bones, sleepin' in the sun. How you gonna get your day's work done? Sleepin' in the noon day sun. Never get your day's work done."

Viola had returned. She would deal with her first.

CHAPTER 53

Wren woke with a start. "What?" she exclaimed before she remembered what had happened. She clamped her lips together. Someone could be out there. Listening. Looking for her. Unfortunately, she couldn't trust that whoever found her would be friendly.

Stupid! I wasn't supposed to go to sleep. How long have I been asleep?

Not for the first time today did Wren regret not having a watch. She tried to remember what her father had taught her about reading the sun's angle and the length of shadows, but it had been so long ago that the memory was fuzzy. Besides, she was in the forest. Shadows were hard to come by in here. Still, she didn't think she'd been asleep that long. She still felt too tired.

And she still had to pee. In fact, it was that need that woke her.

Wren went around the oak, relieved herself, then picked up the jar of peaches. Hunger and thirst took precedence now.

It felt like she'd run for miles, but in fact, it had only been about ten minutes so she hadn't gone very far. Maybe not even a mile. *Better get a little farther away first. But what direction? Where was she?*

She looked around at the stone blocks, sticking up out of the greenery. It looked like a foundation. Then Wren remembered that the church had stood somewhere down an overgrown path from the rectory. She must have found and followed it. Mrs. Hargitt had said something about this place, but Wren couldn't remember what. It wasn't worth going to see? No fancy headstones? All Wren knew was it wasn't far enough away from that house.

She opened the can of peaches using the screwdriver and sat on the foundation to eat them. While she ate, she looked around and saw where she'd stomped through a patch of ferns. Okay, that was the way she'd got here. So, go the opposite and put in some distance.

Maybe I should just try to find the road and follow it. No. Mrs. Campbell would look for her along the road. If only she could remember which way was supposed to be home, she'd try to cut cross country to get there. Just pick a direction! North sounded right. But which way was north?

There was some moss. Wasn't it supposed to grow on the north side of stuff? No. Her mom had talked about that at one of her myth buster ranger talks. Moss grows wherever it's protected from the wind or sun so it can grow on any side of a tree. She closed her eyes and tried to reason it out. The sun went from east to west. So shadows started out in the west and ended up in the east. When she looked at a map, east was to the right and north straight ahead. It had to be afternoon by now. Okay, she'd keep the shadows to her right. That should get her back to the park. Surely she'd stumble onto a trail then and just follow it to the visitor's center. And she wanted to get there before dark. The woods got scary in the dark.

It was like one of those stupid math story problems. If Wren can walk four miles an hour in the woods, how long will it take her to get the hell out of here?

She drained the last of the peach syrup and tossed the jar into a hole under the foundation followed by the screwdriver. No sense giving either Mrs. Campbell or Mrs. Hargitt a clue that she'd been there. Then she turned so the lengthening shadows were to her right and started walking.

* * *

The jar hit the snake's head with a solid "thwack" and it responded by striking at it, yellow venom spilling down the blue glass. The sensation of fangs hitting the glass did nothing to appease the irritable animal's temper. His tail vibrated rapidly, the buzzing rattle warning whatever was out there to steer clear or risk its wrath.

CHAPTER 54

At five-fifteen, Paul Bristol walked into the sheriff's office and said he'd seen a fender bender earlier in the day outside the library. After deliberating all day at work, he thought he should report it. This time Chapman got a make and model and a partial plate to run through the DMV records. The car was registered to one Tabitha Campbell. Bristol thought there'd been a passenger in the car, someone with a purplish cap.

* * *

Boone waited until McGowan was seated, towering over his erstwhile acquaintance. He'd known Burt since he was a deputy and never once had the man done anything remotely suspicious. Until recently.

"Linus, you can't possibly believe that I'd hurt that girl."

"Let me tell you what I've observed, McGowan," Boone said, purposely avoiding familiarities. "You've been holding back from the beginning of this entire investigation. You kept the names of that RV couple from me, the Kecks. You told me all the cabins were occupied that Thanksgiving of seventy-six and cabin eight wasn't. You were seen leaving the library the day Beulah died. And now as I understand it, this girl has been looking into the Tanner family for some report, and you take her out of the park. It does make one think that she found out something you didn't want anyone to know."

"You think I had something to do with Beulah's death, too?" McGowan's face went white. He bowed his head under Boone's gaze. "Oh, my . . . It's not what you think, Linus."

"What am I thinking?"

"You think I killed those kids and Beulah and kidnapped Phoebe's daughter."

"Did you?"

"Cripes, Linus, I had an affair." He flung his hands to the side. Deb was pregnant and sick all the time. The smell of food made her sick. You think I was coming home to a Thanksgiving dinner? She'd told me to go into town and find something to eat. Hodges had gone hunting and left his wife behind. I guess we were both feeling sorry for ourselves and . . . . well we sort of took advantage of each other. But only that once," he added quickly.

"In one of the cabins?"

"Yeah. Number eight. It had been reserved, but the person cancelled at the last minute. Funny thing was, the cabin was unlocked when we went in."

"And Deb doesn't know you cheated on her." Boone made it a statement.

McGowan shook his head. "No. And I hope she never finds out." He pointed to the phone. "You could ask Sharon Hodges. She'd confirm it."

"She didn't mention it when I talked with her."

McGowan hung his head. "You've talked with her? When?"

Boone didn't answer. "So that's why you removed that one cabin journal."

McGowan's head snapped up. "You know about that, too? Does Phoebe?"

Boone nodded. "She'd seen the opening date and read a little of the entry. Then when she got the box back to her house, that one wasn't there. It had to be either you or Shirley that took it. So what was in it?" He already knew, but he wanted to hear it from McGowan.

"The cabin was a mess. We left it in a bit of a hurry, and the next guests made note about it. They found a pair of women's panties under the bed.'"

"How would that point to you?"

"Because I was in charge of housekeeping staff back then. They'd called the office saying the cabin needed fresh sheets. I took the linens over because I didn't want the head housekeeper wondering why a cabin she'd left in perfect order should be a mess." His face turned a deep crimson. "I was an idiot. When I learned they were honeymooners, I actually told them that the bed was a real squeaker. And later the woman said they needed blankets. That's when she handed me the underwear. The way she looked at me and grinned . . . She wrote that the ranger must have tested out the beds and given it a seal of approval."

"Your name wasn't mentioned though."

"It didn't need to be. Like I said, I was in charge of the housekeeping staff then." He put his hands out imploringly to Boone. "You gotta understand. No one besides the visitors ever reads those notebooks. But when Phoebe planned on taking that box home . . . I was afraid she'd read it, maybe say something to someone else. Word could get back to Deb."

And the irony of it was, thought Boone, that Ranger Hodges was having an affair in a hunting cabin at the same time. Jeez, didn't any of these people appreciate what they had? Thoughts of the girl he'd been engaged to right after college flashed through his mind. She was no better and since then, law enforcement hadn't taught him to trust very many people. Phoebe had been true to her husband at least.

Someone pounded on the trailer door. "Linus!"

Speak of the devil. Boone opened the door. "What is it?"

Phoebe shoved a red notebook into his hands. "Read what Wren's been up to."

* * *

"Hello, Viola. Did you have a pleasant walk today? Find the herbs you wanted?"

"Why, good afternoon, Dorcas. Yes, it was a fine walk. Look, I found a bit of bloodroot along with a nice patch of berries." She raised the rectangular basket, handcrafted of white oak. "I should be able to make a good spring tonic for Miz Agnes." She eased herself up the porch steps, set her basket down, and rested against a post. "But it does get harder every time. I collected some fresh willow bark for myself to cut some of the pain in my hip."

"I'm most appreciative of the care you've given my sister all these years."

Mrs. Hargitt waved a hand. "No burden. I think after you took off she sort of looked upon me as her little sister. But I'm sure she's grateful that you come out once in a while to sit with her." She stooped to pick up the basket.

"You had a visitor today."

Mrs. Hargitt stopped in mid-bend and looked up, her head cocked like an inquisitive sparrow. "Why I can't imagine--"

"A deputy sheriff."

"But it's . . . oh," Mrs. Hargitt stammered as she straightened, her basket forgotten. "Dorcas, I've never said a word to him. The sheriff sends him round to check on elderly folk. I thought it would be more suspicious if I sent him away, but I don't understand why he came today."

"He's off duty later this week. Wanted to be certain that you were all right. Quite a nice young man."

"That he is, Dorcas. Sometimes he chops wood for me. But as I said, I've never told him about Agnes and he's never been farther than the kitchen. Why, even the sheriff doesn't. . ."

Mrs. Campbell picked up the basket. "The sheriff has been here, too? When did this happen? Why didn't you tell me?"

Mrs. Hargitt wrapped her hands in her apron and looked at her feet. "I know it bothers you to have anyone coming around. I didn't want to upset you."

"I'm not upset. But tell me about the sheriff."

"He came by a few days ago. He was looking for any relatives of the Tanner boy that disappeared all those years ago, and Daisy's little girl, Ruthie."

"You didn't tell him about me, did you?"

"Why, Dorcas. Of course not. I told him how my husband and I moved here when the family was gone. He wanted to know about them, so I showed him where the old Reverend died and told him all about how Agnes took care of her mother and helped me and others through all the sicknesses of mind and body." She looked shyly at Mrs. Campbell under lowered lids and smiled. "I knew it would please you to talk up Agnes that way. Keep her memory alive."

"Yes. Thank you."

"Then you aren't angry with me?"

"Sakes, no, Viola. What can you do when the law comes to your door? As you said, if you shoosh them away, they get nosier." She motioned to the door. "Stop fretting. I'm sure he's never suspected anything. Otherwise he'd have insisted on looking in on Agnes and maybe taking her away to one of those horrid homes." She gave her left arm to the younger, but frailer woman. "Come inside. You must be completely done in."

"Yes, the sooner I get a cup of hot willow bark tea in me, the better. But how has Agnes been today?"

They walked into the kitchen. Mrs. Campbell set the basket on the table, picked up a dishtowel and opened a drawer. Mrs. Hargitt took an iron rod and poked at the banked embers in the wood stove before adding in a few twigs to rekindle the fire.

"She's been very . . . quiet," said Mrs. Campbell.

"Poor old dear. Would you care for a cup of tea, Dorcas?" She turned to face her friend, a water kettle in her hand. "I--"

Mrs. Campbell rammed the butcher knife up into Hargitt's chest just above the lowest rib. To her surprise, it wasn't much more difficult than stabbing into a thick-skinned pumpkin. Less effort than when she'd speared her own father. An odd, strangling sort of gurgle came from Mrs. Hargitt's open mouth. Her eyes stared wide in shock.

"It's nothing personal, Viola," Mrs. Campbell said as she gave the knife a twist. "But Agnes is dead, and I don't need you anymore." She kept her towel-wrapped hand on the knife until the woman fell to the floor, then she let go, leaving the knife in the woman's chest. Mrs. Hargitt gasped, blood sputtering from her nose and mouth with every exhalation.

Mrs. Campbell stood watch as her sister's caregiver bled out, gasping. "I'm sorry it has to be this slow, Viola, but I need you to live long enough to shoot someone. Not that you will, dear. But it has to look that way. "

That's why she struck for the lung, slicing into the diaphragm. Mrs. Hargitt would eventually drown in her own blood but she'd live long enough to have fired the rifle. Of course, if all really went as planned, there wouldn't be much for a forensics expert to look at anyway, but one could never tell. It would probably help to put the weapon in Viola's hands and squeeze off a second shot just to be sure. After the girl was dead, though. While Mrs. Campbell waited, she turned on the police scanner and listened with interest as a search team reported in.

So they know the girl is missing. That's fine. Wait until they find that she stabbed an innocent old lady and got shot for her pains. As she watched Mrs. Hargitt gasp out her final breaths, she wondered if Wren had heard anything. It was quiet down in the pantry.

"Rest easy, Viola. Not much longer now. And you won't be bothered by that painful hip anymore. It's not the way Agnes would have done it, but you never drink sweet tea. One would think you didn't trust me."

Mrs. Hargitt gagged once and mouthed "why?" Then her body relaxed.

Why? It's just what Agnes had asked when their father died. The repetition of the question befuddled Mrs. Campbell for a moment, causing the past and the present to intertwine and tangle like that confused mess of trumpet vine and honeysuckle. For a moment, she couldn't recall who was locked in the pantry. That boy George? Ruthie? No, some other girl.

She went to the bedroom and pulled the rifle out from under the pillows where she'd temporarily hidden it. It was the girl's turn now. But when she opened the pantry door, the girl was gone. Only the ball cap remained where she'd hung it on the back of her chair. She spotted the broken glass on the floor. "Damn!" There was no longer time to remove Agnes and bury her. Instead, it was time to go hunting.

Luckily a girl was easier to hit than a bushy-tail squirrel.

CHAPTER 55

Phoebe tapped the notebook. "She's been investigating those murders, George and Ruthie's."

Boone quickly read through the girl's notes. "And having more luck than I've had." He held the book open to one page and pointed to an entry. "Look here, she found something else in another journal about Cabin 8. A carving in the fireplace."

"I never saw that journal entry. That's the cabin where Ben Owen was seen during the reunion," said Phoebe. "But I don't understand. He was looking at the lake, and you can't see the lake from there. I checked."

"Cabin 8?" said McGowan from the trailer doorway. "What year?"

"Nothing you need to worry about, McGowan," said Boone. "You're off the hook. Go on back to your office and wait for my word. If I have to leave to follow up on a lead, I'll be putting you in charge of the search here."

"But, Linus, we renumbered the cabins at the end of ninety-one. We'd just finished building a new one where Hodge's trailer had been. Cabin 8 became 9." McGowan looked from Boone to Phoebe. "Phoebe, I never harmed those kids back then, and I sure as hell would never do anything to Wren. I just took her to the library so she wouldn't hitchhike."

Phoebe couldn't think of anything to say that wouldn't come out hurtful and, at the moment, she felt as much to blame for Wren's disappearance as anyone. More so. She looked at Boone for confirmation.

"He's got an alibi for seventy-six."

Phoebe nodded. She was finding it harder to trust anyone, but if the sheriff said that her boss was clean, then she believed him. McGowan look like some kid not picked to play on a team but he didn't go into the park office, opting to stay in the background.

"Come inside, both of you," said Boone. "I need to look at this more closely."

As she sat down in a folding-wooden chair, she overheard Boone replying to a deputy's report. They left the trailer door open, admitting a cool breeze into the stuffy container.

"Deal with it, then," said Boone. "It's a fender bender. We've got bigger problems here."

Phoebe's right leg jittered up and down in short, rapid movements. "What happened? Did they find her?"

Boone shook his head. "There was a report of a minor accident with a parked car. Someone turned in the partial plate and the car make. It looks to belong to Shirley's mom, Mrs. Campbell. Shirley'll probably be pissed. Deputy thought I should tell her."

Phoebe put her hands over her face. "Where could she have gone?"

"We've got the Amber Alert out. That means every law enforcement official in the state is on the lookout as well as utility workers and a good many socially minded citizens. And my deputy in town is still passing her photo around and asking for help. Someone surely saw her. She's . . . very noticeable." He shifted his chair closer to Phoebe. "Now, explain this to me." He touched what looked like a torn out page from another book.

Phoebe took the notebook. "This is from one of the journals. I gave Wren some of the newer ones to read.

Thought she might find it interesting and maybe it would give us something to talk about." She knew what Boone was doing. He knew as well as she did what that entry meant, but he was trying to involve her, keep her from slipping into panic. She clutched at the chance as if she were clinging to a thick root, trying to keep herself from falling off a cliff face. "Apparently, there's a hidden carving in cabin eight. Something covered by a later remodeling. You can see by Wren's notes that she believes the letters stand for Ben Owen and Agnes Elwood."

"Agnes Tanner's maiden name."

"Right. Wren said she was researching Agnes Tanner, Beulah got Wren interested in her Said she was a very important woman for the area. I thought it was a strange coincidence since we found George, but I'm wondering if Wren had initially tried to write about his death."

"And Beulah gently shifted Wren to another part of the family," said Boone. "It looks like Wren wasn't settling for the saintly Agnes story. She wanted more."

Phoebe frowned. "So it seems. Wren has never been a moony romantic girl, but then, she was never almost fourteen before. Maybe she was trying to prove a hopeless romance." She looked at Boone. "A Romeo and Juliet sort of situation, only without the . . . oh dear."

"What?"

"Well, I was going to say, without the deaths, but if she had her heart set on finding a murder to write about, she may have used Agnes as a means to look farther afield."

"I'm interested in these names," said Boone, taking the book again. "This was Agnes' family." He ran a finger down the other names. "Joshua Elwood, Rachel Elwood, Noah Tanner; Agnes' immediate family and husband. They all have death dates."

"But there's none by Agnes' name. She's got a big question instead. Does that mean she's alive?"

Boone shrugged. "At least she was alive during that big reunion. And she was here then."

"Could she have killed the kids for some reason?"

"Maybe," said Boone. "But she couldn't have killed Beulah. Even if she's alive she'd be extremely old. Someone today is willing to kill to keep it a secret."

Phoebe's eyes widened. "What do you mean?"

Boone rubbed a hand across the back of his neck. "Beulah Ingram didn't die of natural causes. She was poisoned. And it's no coincidence that she was working on getting information for your daughter when it happened."

Phoebe pressed her hands to her mouth. "Oh, Lord. Poor Beulah." Then the full reality sank in. If someone killed Beulah to stop her from learning something, they wouldn't hesitate to kill . . . "Wren!"

Boone didn't respond, and Phoebe was grateful that he avoided all the usual platitudes and hollow promises. People who'd had no control over her husband's fate had told her that he'd be fine when he went overseas. He wasn't. She knew that the sheriff was doing everything in his power to find Wren. She couldn't ask for more. Instead, she tried to involve herself even deeper into the investigation in the hopes of uncovering some nugget of information to help him.

"Who's this Dorcas," asked Phoebe, looking over his shoulder and pointing to the names.

"Dorcas was supposed to be Agnes' little sister. The girl left home at some point and no one ever seemed to know what became of her. She's been a dead end. No social security record, marriage license, or obit. You'd think an unusual name like that would stand out."

"It's biblical," said Phoebe. "She's mentioned in Acts. The name means gazelle."

Boone's head snapped up. "Did you say gazelle?"

Phoebe nodded. "Why?"

"I talked to a Viola Hargitt. She said that Tanner had called her his little gazelle."

"Then you think she could actually be this Dorcas? That she changed her name so no one would recognize her?" asked McGowan.

"It's a possibility that I plan to follow up on."

"I met her, too," said Phoebe. "I talked with her about wild plants for medicine and food. I took Wren along hoping she'd get interested in writing about Mrs. Hargitt rather than about Agnes Tanner. At one point Mrs. Hargitt sent me to look at her ginseng garden and kept Wren behind. Wren had just asked her about Agnes and Tanner. Wren said later that they didn't talk about much, only about a king snake that lived under the porch, but I wonder if that was all."

"If she knew about herbals and medicines, she might have known how to poison someone," said Boone. "But she has no car. She couldn't have taken Wren from town."

"And I don't think she was here in seventy-six. Not in the park," said McGowan. "Look. That boy was wrapped in a blanket, right? Well it just occurred to me. In that journal I took, the woman said there were no blankets. Maybe someone stole them to wrap George's body in."

"But no one was staying in that cabin over Thanksgiving, right?" asked Boone. "Except for. . ."

McGowan blushed. "Yeah, except for me and Sharon. But someone could've gone in after we left it. Or even before. I doubt we'd have noticed if there was a blanket there or not. My point is, you had to have a master key to get in there. Only the park people had those."

Boone picked up Wren's notebook again. "There must be something else in here to help."

He turned the page. A folded sheet of paper slid onto his lap.

"What's that in the margin?" asked Phoebe. Her stomach was in a knot, and she wanted to scream but she forced herself to remain calm. Panic wouldn't help find her daughter.

Boone peered more closely. "This looks like something I had in a biology class."

"It is," said Phoebe, coming around to stand beside him. "It's a Punnet square. It's used to do basic genetic problems. But what's Wren doing with one of those?"

"She's copied this from someplace else," Boone said. "See how neatly it's done. No guesswork. But look here. She's trying different alternatives."

"Let me see that," said Phoebe. She took the notebook from him as Boone turned his attention to the folded papers. "Why this is for sex-linked traits! Red-green colorblindness to be precise."

"You're certain?"

"Absolutely," she said. "I taught high school biology before I came here." She raised an index finger, signaling that she wasn't through with her thought. "Friday morning I had a breakfast hike with Verl and Vivien Keck, an older couple that RV here a lot. I told you about them. Did they talk to you yet? They said they would."

Boone shook his head no.

"Well, I asked them about that Thanksgiving. They said that they saw George and Ruthie Wednesday by the lake. George was all excited, which was probably par for the course with the boy. He'd been looking at some books in the gift shop about bats, only they seemed to think he'd seen one of Shirley's textbooks. She was already home for Thanksgiving. But the really interesting thing was that this couple claimed that Ruthie was not mentally handicapped. She was just incredibly timid, like a child that's afraid. They called her rabbity."

"Her mother, Daisy, was an alcoholic," said Boone. "She screamed a lot."

"That's what the Keck's said, and that would explain it. They went on to say that Ruthie, who seemed to warm up to them, pointed to a stack of red canoes and called them green boats. George explained that Ruthie was slow, but Vivien told him that she was just colorblind. It was rare, but it could happen to a girl. George got really excited after that. He told them that he was going to trace that in his family for a science project."

"So Wren got onto this somehow as well," mused Boone. "And that project may be why George was killed?"

"It could be," said Phoebe. "Either he just annoyed the hell out of one of his relatives or he was about to uncover something that no one wanted uncovered."

Boone leaned forward, for the moment ignoring the papers in his hands. "Explain this to me. My biology was a long time ago. From what I learned, Ruthie's dad was color-blind, so I don't see why this would be a big deal."

"Okay, condensed version. A woman has two x-chromosomes. A man has an x and a y. The gene for colorblindness is only on the x-chromosome. Since a guy's only got one of those, he gets whatever traits are on it. But a female has two x's so the only way she can be colorblind is if both of her x-chromosomes have that faulty gene. You with me so far?"

Boone nodded. "What you're saying is that Ruthie's father would pass a copy of that colorblind gene to his daughter. But, she also had to get another one like it from her mother, Daisy, right?"

"Correct. And the only way for Daisy to have had even one gene to carry would be if she got one from either of her parents." She pointed to Wren's notes. "According to Wren, Reverend Tanner wasn't colorblind. So he couldn't give Daisy the gene."

"He wasn't. Mrs. Hargitt said he painted the church red to remind people of the blood of sacrifice. She also told me that Agnes had been given a ring with a red glass setting that she jokingly called her emerald, but it didn't come from Tanner."

"Wren has written down 'Ben Owen'." Phoebe snapped her fingers. "Ben Owen, the stonemason from the C.C.C. was colorblind. Remember, in one of those notebooks was from a camp reunions and a friend of his wrote about that. How he couldn't tell his shirt colors. "

"Owen was supposed to be courting Agnes," said Boone.

"What if Daisy was Ben's child?" asked Phoebe. "That would explain her carrying the gene. And that's a secret someone in the family wouldn't want out. But who besides Agnes would have known?"

"Maybe Agnes killed the kids," said McGowan. "You said she was here at the reunion."

Phoebe stood and paced in the confining van. "None of this is telling us where Wren is."

"I'm not sure that this will either." Boone held up the other papers. "But it does shed some light on what she'd learned." He handed the papers to Phoebe and waited until she'd looked over them.

"I don't understand."

"She was tracking down some genealogies," said Boone.

"Yes, but this is about Shirley and Mrs. Campbell and. . . oh my stars. Shirley's dad wasn't this Campbell soldier. He died too early and there's no marriage license." Phoebe put her hand to her mouth and fought back the rising fear. "I wonder if Shirley knows about this."

"About her parentage? Or about Wren's investigations?" asked Boone. "Either way, I need to talk to her."

Phoebe placed a hand on Boone's shoulder to both steady herself and to keep him in place. "The store's closed today. Linus. I never checked to see if she was inside, though. Oh my Lord. Maybe she picked up Wren in town."

Boone sent a deputy to the store to find Mrs. Campell. "If she's not there, look for her."

"Linus," Phoebe said, "I never knew Mrs. Campbell's first name. I'm kind of old school that way. You know, the whole Mr. and Mrs. thing? You mentioned her a while ago as being in a fender bender. What is her first name?"

"It's Tabitha."

Phoebe groaned. "Remember when I said that Dorcas was a name out of Acts? Well it goes on to say that Dorcas was also known as Tabitha. They're really the same name. But which one of those women was Agnes' sister; Mrs. Hargitt or Mrs. Campbell?"

"And which one of them people killed Beulah to keep her quiet?" finished Boone."

CHAPTER 56

It didn't take Wren long before she was hopelessly lost. It took a little longer before she would admit it to herself.

The feeling began when late afternoon clouds put an end to the shadows. At first, she maintained her direction by focusing on a distant rock. Later a wide, curving ravine blocked her way. When she thought she'd finally gone around it, she tried to pick out the rock again. Time and again, the foliage blocked her view or her path, making her guess at her ultimate direction. Only later did she realize that the far hillside was loaded with rocks and they all looked alike to her. There was no way of knowing if she'd been following the same one.

She listened for voices carrying over from the park or from a house but the only sounds she heard were from the occasional woodpecker or a spring warbler trilling its love song. There was no road noise, no whoosh of passing cars or groan of a truck downshifting to make a steep curve. Nothing to point to humanity.

Her only consolation was that neither Mrs. Campbell nor Mrs. Hargitt were nearby.

Wren suppressed a sob, wiped the tears from her eyes and kept on moving, trying to follow the ridge.

* * *

Shirley Gracehill could hardly stand still. At least the painter was finished, but the fumes would keep the store closed for the rest of the day anyway. She hung around, keeping her ear to the park radio and the police scanner. She knew that Wren was missing, that she'd gotten as far as town and then disappeared. She also knew what Wren had been up to and now she was more afraid for her mother than she was for Wren.

There was little love lost between the two grown women. Shirley's mother had hardly been affectionate, but at least she'd never abused her. It wasn't long before she understood that there was something about her father that her mother wouldn't tell her. As far as she knew, they had no family, only a long revered woman named Agnes, a friend for whom her mother had a deep devotion. A woman she saw in the park thirty-five years ago talking with a man.

But Shirley was no fool, and it wasn't long after she'd gone away to college that she started hunting down old records, trying to discover her ancestry. Somewhere in that search she met Joe Owen. Together, they suspected that the story of the injured World War II soldier was a lie and that they might be related. Neither had the extra cash to do a DNA test to prove it.

It was something she could never ask her mother. The woman went as mute as a statue over some things. But Shirley was no fool. She had her own ideas about her parentage. It was why she made sure the store inventories never revealed the missing teddy bear and cast iron dutch-oven lid hook. Shirley felt obligated to protect her mother.

She heard the radio call for patrolling deputies to watch for a black Chrysler New Yorker that had swiped another car in the library parking lot while leaving in a hurry. Shirley didn't need to hear the license plate to know what had happened, especially since she realized that the passenger with a purplish hat was probably a teenage girl with purple-black hair. She switched off the office radio and left.

History was going to repeat itself.

* * *

Mrs. Campbell stared down at the body on the floor, the woman's blood staining her faded pinafore, soaking into the raw oaken floorboards. She kicked her once to make certain that she was dead. From behind her, she heard the police scanner crackle to life. There was an Amber alert on that girl.

She scowled. She'd hoped to have more time. Now she could barely afford the time it took her to yank open the bureau drawers and make it look like the girl had robbed the place. No time to move Agnes. At least the girl had left her cap behind in the pantry. That would incriminate her in this mess. She'd leave it on the floor near Viola. For an added effect, she fired the rifle into the wall opposite the dead woman to look like she'd shot at her assailant and missed. And if she found the girl too far away to drag her back, she'd make certain no one ever found her body.

If only that damned girl had drank that tea instead of giving it to Agnes. Then she would've dumped her corpse down the old outhouse hole or deep in the woods where there were wild hogs. That had been the problem with George. Bones left to find. Hogs left nothing. But then, she reflected, thirty-five years ago, the wild hogs hadn't been such a problem.

The burial place hadn't been her idea even though she was grateful for the help. Hauling those rocks would've been too hard even for her.

And now the girl's fingerprints won't even be on the knife.

For a moment, memories and emotions became muddied, as the sediments of the past muddied the flow of the present. Who was that lying on the floor? Someone Agnes couldn't heal? There was too much that Agnes couldn't mend. Was it Daisy?

Daisy was Tanner's last victim.

"I did what I could for you, Agnes!" she screamed. "I did my level best to make it up to you. I took care of you. I made you a legend. But I just couldn't let you leave me behind to marry that monster." She sobbed. "Why didn't you kill him sooner?"

Agnes' voice whispered in her head. Let it go. Let it all go out of you. Purge the demons inside!

"Purge the demons! She tried to do it once but the demons stayed. She'd try again."

She staggered into the parlor and tipped one of the oil lanterns, watching as the flame licked the curtains.

Then she got in her car and drove down the road, looking for Wren.

CHAPTER 57

When Jeannie Newcomb told Phoebe that someone was in the office waiting to talk to her about Wren, Phoebe assumed that one of the librarians had driven out to the park with news of Wren. Instead, she found her in-laws. Fran and Jack Palmer stood by Assistant Superintendent Sloan's office, their faces livid, arms folded across their chests. Both slender in build and with short, silvering blond hair, they looked like an ad for a fashionable seniors' cruise or for a nutritional supplement drink.

"A sheriff's deputy came to our bridge club and wanted to know where Wren was," said Fran. "He as good as accused us of kidnapping our own granddaughter."

"We drove here as fast as we could," added Jack. "Now we demand to know what's going on."

Phoebe herded them into her tiny office, pulling the door shut behind her. "You were planning on taking her away from me. Kidnapping her seemed the next likely step."

"Our getting custody of Wren is for her own best interest," snapped Fran, wagging a finger at Phoebe. Her diamond rings flashed. "You are clearly not considering the child in your decisions."

"That's right," chimed in Jack. "She sent us an email telling how frightened she was by strange creatures outside her window at night."

"And how terrible the schools are," added Fran. "And now we find that she's missing! What kind of a mother would leave her daughter alone in this horrid place?"

"Not a fit one, that's for sure," chimed in Jack. "So if you think for one instant--"

"Shut up!" snapped Phoebe.

Their blue eyes opened wide in shock and consternation. "I beg your pardon," said Fran.

"Well, you should," said Phoebe.

"That's not what I meant," said Fran. "I--"

"I don't give a rat's ass what you meant." Phoebe fumed inside, all the years of putting up with having every decision she'd made as a mother from the brand of diapers to this last grab for a good life, all second-guessed by her in-laws. The frustration, the longing for approval, all of it had lain pent up inside of her, fermenting over the years. Now it gushed out in one cathartic geyser of anger.

"Now listen up, you two, and listen good. You are the problem. Not me. You indulged her whim to dress in black and dye her hair. You're the ones that let her keep wallowing in her grief instead of helping her move on. You've built up that idea that I made Charles re-enlist and you know it's not true. It was all his idea. So if there's a rift between my daughter and me now, it's because you encouraged it. And if she's tried to run away from here and gotten in trouble, it's your fault. And once I get her back, I'll let every damned lawyer you've got know it, too."

They stared back at her, wide eyed, mouths agape. Phoebe read past the shock to see a smattering of fear. This was clearly a side of their daughter-in-law they'd never seen before.

And whose fault is that? She knew it was her own. All she'd ever done was try to curry their favor or, eventually, just cave-in to avoid conflict. Might as well have tried to rake the forest's fallen leaves. It would have been less futile.

"Now, you two are welcome to wait in my house if you like.

I'm sure you're too worried about Wren to want to go back to Fayetteville, but stay the hell out of my way and the sheriff's. We're running a search here, and we don't have time for you. She tossed them her keys. "The lady at the desk can tell you how to get to my cabin."

She turned her back on them and marched out to the mobile command vehicle to demand a set of orders. Halfway there, she had an idea of her own and ran for her van.

* * *

Deputy Chapman contacted Boone by radio, using a secure frequency.

"Sheriff, special courier from the Crime Lab just arrived with an envelope. Seems that when Dick Cooper got the governor on their case, they took it to mean expediting all the evidence you'd sent on to them."

"Tell me about it, Jack."

"We've got matches on a print found on that girl's teddy bear tag and one on the thumbprint on the boy's belt buckle."

Boone listened to the results just as his other deputy came back empty handed in his job to locate Mrs. Gracehill and bring her to the command trailer.

"She's not in the park, boss. And her car's gone."

"Find her! Now!"

* * *

Mrs. Campbell figured the girl would head straight for the road and high-tail it back to town. Surely she couldn't have been gone too long or gotten too far. One mile, maybe two at most. No matter, it was a good fifteen miles to town on a nearly deserted road. She drove slowly down the country lane with her windows down, scanning both sides for any sign or sound of movement in case the girl decided to keep to the trees. Her car bounced and jolted over the rough spots and potholes. She'd always been glad for every one of them, too. It kept people off this road, especially the sightseers and fall leaf gawkers. And that meant that the girl had very little chance of picking up a ride until she'd joined with the county highway another ten miles on.

The closest neighbor was Ethan Burdett at the top of the next ridge, but his farm sat on another, more heavily frequented road. Unless the old man was spending his days staring down into this valley from his barn loft, she was as good as invisible and it was unthinkable that this city girl would try to find her way home straight across the Dead Man Hollow.

Less than two miles down the road she heard a branch snap somewhere to her right. Couldn't be a deer. Not at this time of day. Besides, they rarely make noise.

She stopped the car and peered into the forest, scanning the dense foliage for movement.

"Blasted eyesight's not what it used to be," she muttered to herself and reached below the passenger seat for a pair of binoculars. Once again she searched the woods, panning the area where she'd heard the noise. She caught a glimpse of something pale and zeroed in on it. It was the girl's arm.

Campbell got out of the car with a slight groan as she eased out her stiff back. "Should've let Viola fix me a tonic for this arthritis before I killed her," she muttered. She left the car door open, not wanting to risk the noise of it shutting. Instead, she rested her rear against the car and tracked Wren's movements through her binoculars. The girl was too far away to hit with the .22 but that didn't mean she couldn't herd her. The old church grounds weren't far. It would be a good place to lie in wait once she had the girl turned. And once she was down, she could dump the rifle and the girl's body and into the church's outhouse pit where no one would ever find her.

"Sending you a gift, Tanner. A young one, just like you like them."

CHAPTER 58

The mud had dried on Wren's arms and shirt, wicking away her body heat. At first she hadn't minded as the June day had leaned towards hot, but with the cloud cover came with a cool front. She wrapped her arms around her slender body and hugged herself against a shiver. She'd long since given up any idea that she knew where she was going, hoping instead that she'd bump into somebody's farm before too long. Hopefully they'd be friendly and have a phone.

A stray tear rolled down her right cheek, leaving a pale stripe in a muddy smear. Did anyone even know she was gone? Was anybody looking for her? Maybe Mrs. Campbell was right. Maybe her mom would be happy to be rid of her.

She swallowed hard, fighting back the urge to just sit down and cry. She was hungry, thirsty, and tired. Her feet hurt, and her legs were scratched from passing too close to a patch of wild blackberries. It seemed like ages ago since she'd devoured the handful of fruit including the unripe ones. And mom was going to grill hamburgers. Her stomach rumbled. *Just try to move in a straight line this time and get out of here.*

Two steps later, she heard a loud "crack" followed by a "thwack" as something hit the ground ahead and to her left. *Somebody's shooting at me!*

She turned and ran. The rifle cracked again behind her.

* * *

Ethan Burdett took the last two rungs of the ladder slowly. It wouldn't do to slip on the worn wooden spindles and fall. Sixty-four years had made him more than cautious, and if his mind forgot his age, his bones took care to remind him; especially his right hip. Next time he'd store his hay bales in the spare stalls at the end of the barn and leave the loft to the sparrows and the owls. Hell, maybe he'd just get rid of the horses. He was too old to ride anyway.

Naw, he thought. He couldn't do that. They were like old friends, something alive to come home to. Besides his grandkids still visited over the summer and maybe if the horses were gone, they'd find a reason to stay away. He'd just toss down a few more bales this time and save himself a couple of trips to the loft.

After pitching three bales down the open space to the bottom floor, Burdett took a moment to look out the gap in the big window. Always a fine view, another reason for hauling his sorry carcass up that ladder. He leaned a gloved hand against the sliding door frame and stared out at the hollow. The last time he'd been up here, the redbuds and dogwoods were in bloom and the distant hollow had been a resplendent show of purple and white with that pale, ephemeral green of early spring. Now everything was in full leaf.

A twist of smoke caught his attention and he peered farther out. Looked like that old Hargitt woman was still burning wood in the wood stove. Judging by the amount of smoke, it wasn't well seasoned either. He hadn't ever had much truck with her. Most people out here kept to themselves, and she more than others. Seeing smoke there was a sign of life at least. He turned to go back when a sharp crack echoed across the ridge. Now who was hunting? Curious, he looked again and spied a black car on the old dirt road on this side of the hollow.

"Ms. Hargitt ain't got no car." Burdett remembered the deputy picking up a dirty bottle and telling him that someone had been making drugs out here. He wondered if they were at it again. Maybe that smoke was from some meth shack. He heard those places burnt sometimes.

"We'll just see about that."

With a little more speed than caution would dictate, Burdett shinnied back down the ladder and high-tailed it to the house to call the sheriff's office.

* * *

Shirley took the main road out of the park with the intent of cornering her mother and demanding to know what she was doing with the Palmer girl. Trouble is, she really had no idea where to look.

Maybe it's all a mistake. Maybe she's genuinely interested in helping Wren.

Maybe pigs will fly south for the winter. If her mother was involved with Wren, then there was an ulterior motive. Tabitha Campbell was not the giving, loving sort. Oh, true enough she read to what she jokingly called "the old folks" at the nursing home, but Shirley suspected it was because it allowed her to swipe the occasional pain pills or antibiotics from the patients.

She'd check there first on the off chance that she'd taken Wren to see Ben Owen. Two miles out of the park, she turned on the radio scanner in the car.

Ten minutes later, she heard the deputy announce that he was going to check on a black car on the dirt road north of county road seventeen running south of Dead Man Hollow. He termed it a possible meth manufacture but Shirley knew better. Her mother had taken Wren out to see that crazy old Hargitt woman. She made a u-turn at the next crossing and raced back, taking the suggested forty mile per hour curve at sixty.

* * *

Phoebe knew that the sheriff would be angry at her abrupt departure, but it was clear that he was deliberately leaving her out of the search. Call it protecting her or whatever he liked, she wasn't going to put up with it. Especially now that she had a hunch where Wren had gone.

The girl hadn't been too interested in meeting with Mrs. Hargitt the first time, but Phoebe suspected now that her attitude stemmed more from being there with her mother. It became very obvious that Wren wanted to know more about Agnes and Reverend Tanner, questions that a mother's presence stifled. Phoebe wondered how much Wren asked while she was off inspecting the ginseng bed. It was very possible that she'd convinced someone to drive her back out to Mrs. Hargitt's home so she could complete her interrogation.

What if it was Mrs. Campbell?

Surely none of them meant to harm Wren. But it was a thought Phoebe didn't want to dwell on. Someone had killed Beulah for aiding Wren, poisoned her. And who knew more about natural poisons than someone who knew natural medicines?

Maybe I should've left a message at the office.

Noah Tanner had called Viola his Dorcas, his gazelle; seemingly to mock her lameness. But could she have actually been Agnes' sister? It would have been easy for her to change her name back then, before many of the rural people had social security numbers locking their lives into a channel of government documentation. Heck, many of them didn't have birth certificates.

Phoebe tried to focus on her driving. The dirt road hadn't fared any better for the last rainstorm which had gouged and eroded it in a network of drying channels. The van jerked and bounced and one of the seeming ruts turned out to be a black snake, sunning itself in a dry spot. She jerked the wheel in time to avoid hitting it, and the snake, its peace disturbed, insinuated itself into the ragweed patch by the roadside.

At least it wasn't a rattler.

She found the inconspicuous little side track that led to Mrs. Hargitt's house. Judging from the fresh tire imprints in the soft ground, at least one other person had been here recently. When she pulled into the clearing, she saw Shirley's Honda parked in front.

The sight didn't fill her with relief.

Phoebe pulled back and left her van in the lane, blocking anyone's exit. Every nerve in her body screamed at her to get out and find Wren, but she knew if there was trouble, she'd need more solid backup. She forced herself to radio the park and let them know where she was and what she'd found. To her surprise, it was Burt that answered the call.

She didn't wait to hear him tell her to stay put. She had no intention of it.

* * *

Shirley hadn't been to this house in nearly thirty years and then it was only in curiosity. Burt had told her about the woman who lived in an old parsonage and collected herbs. Her mother, in one of those rare moments when she wasn't nagging to restock or re-price something, mentioned that she sometimes took some of the canned goods that had sat on the shelf for a while to Mrs. Hargitt in charity. Shirley had offered to go along and help out, but her mother told her that the woman didn't care for much company and would get scared of new people.

If her car was seen nearby, then this is where she came.

It was possible that her mother had taken an interest in Wren and offered to take her to see where the famed Agnes Elwood Tanner had grown up. Sometimes maternal affection skipped a generation and with no grandchild to nurture, maybe she'd heaped her care on Wren.

It was possible, but highly improbable. Her mother was not a giving woman. Even those canned goods were a way to keep fresh stock on the shelves for customers and write off the unsold as a donation. Nothing altruistic about it at all.

And when she went into the house and found the body and the remains of a smoldering fire struggling unsuccessfully to burn a mildewed couch in the cool, humid room, she feared the worst. But neither her mother nor the girl was in the house. She poured water on the fire.

After a brief search, Shirley found impressions where small sneakered feet had headed off into a nearly overgrown footpath. She hurried as quickly as she could after the girl.

* * *

When Boone found out that Phoebe had driven off without informing him, he immediately called for her in-laws to tell him what had been said between them. Nothing they told him had any bearing on Wren's current situation.

That was when Jo notified him about the black sedan seen on County Road seventeen, the road to Mrs. Hargitt's house. Boone didn't believe for a moment that this was a meth manufacturer and neither, for that matter, did his dispatcher. Jo'd noted the similarities to the car involved in the fender bender, a car which the deputy had found belonged to Tabitha Campbell. When he questioned his crew, Deputy Peters replied that there had been another woman at the house when he stopped earlier to check on the old lady. His description matched Tabitha Campbell's.

Boone left McGowan in charge of the rest of the search, unhooked the trailer and sped off towards the Hargitt house.

CHAPTER 59

When a forest is left to its own devices without human advice; the trees stretch tall, keeping the shady understory in ferns and violets with an occasional mid-sized dogwood or redbud to keep them company. But where humans have hacked and pruned and dug, the woods take on a different form after the site is abandoned. Thin, scraggly cedars and hackberry branch out for space rather than height. Poison ivy finds a foothold along with any seeds left behind in bird droppings. Briars tie it all together like living barbed wire.

As a result, Wren had initially found much of the forested area remarkably easy to walk through, but now she fought wild raspberry canes, gooseberry bushes, and small upstart saplings, all with thorns or a surplus of snatching, clawing branches. They grabbed at her, like a mob, hindering her progress as she stumbled forward. She emerged with her legs, face, and arms were scratched and bleeding. Like sharks when there's blood in the water, swarms of mosquitoes fought for a place at the table. The struggle made the sight of an open glade ahead all the more precious and when she recognized it, made her despair all the deeper. It was the old church grounds. I've been going in a circle!

She leaned back on the remains of a headstone, tears

welling in her eyes. She knew she needed to keep moving, find shelter and water. Her head told her to get up and follow the lane to the dirt road and trust that some passerby would take pity on her. But her legs shook, and her head ached. The grounds were empty. No one was looking for her. She could rest for a moment.

Then she heard footsteps approaching from two different directions at once. From the distant house they came with rapid, heavy footfalls. From the nearby woods ahead, the tread was more stealthy.

Wren forced her legs to work and ran to the back of the foundation where a bit of stonework stood a few feet high. She did her best to crouch behind it, hoping to heavens that she wasn't visible. At least until she could figure out if these people meant to harm or help her.

* * *

Phoebe didn't bother to knock. Instead, she yanked open the screen door and rushed inside. Smoke hung heavy in the air, a rank fog as from a smoldering trash site. She listened but didn't hear the crackle of flames. Whatever had been burning had worn itself out by now.

The front parlor was empty. In fact no sound came from any of the rooms. No sign that someone was napping or working anywhere. Phoebe would have assumed that Mrs. Hargitt was simply out in her garden except for that pall of smoke. She took in the charred remains of the curtains and the soot-stained sofa, finishing with the overturned lantern on the floor. The sofa arm dripped and she knew that someone had put out the fire recently. But who? She glanced into the bedroom then headed for the kitchen.

She found Mrs. Hargitt, her pinafore bloodied and torn, the butcher knife sticking out from beneath her pendulous bosom. Flies droned around her face and chest.

"Wren!" she called loudly. There was no answer beyond the flies. "Wren!" she repeated with more force. Nothing. But her daughter had been here. There was her navy blue ball cap on the floor, sporting a bat and Dead Man Hollow State Park in gold embroidery.

Phoebe stopped a moment to recall the proper procedure as she'd been taught during training. She didn't want to contaminate the crime scene, yet she needed to get around the body and check out the room beyond. Her eyes scanned the floor, observing the blood pattern. The body had fallen where it lay. On the floor opposite Mrs. Hargitt were some plaster chips. Phoebe looked up to the wall and saw the hole where a bullet had struck. But where was the weapon? Who took it?

She edged her way carefully around the perimeter of the room, avoiding the side with the bullet hole. Several steps led down to a heavy door. When she reached it, she took out a tissue from her pocket and used it to turn the knob so she wouldn't add her own prints to it. It opened into a dimly lit pantry. The late afternoon sun did very little to illuminate the room.

But it was enough. Enough to see the broken window glass on the floor beside a wooden chair and a toppled tool box. Someone, perhaps her daughter, had stood on the rickety structure to reach the window and escape.

As her eyes adjusted, Phoebe noticed the bed against the far wall, covered over in a crazy patchwork quilt. Something about the lumps under the quilt told her that it wasn't just a made bed waiting for someone to rest on. She pulled back the quilt and gasped when she saw the aged face underneath. Another dead body. The fact that neither one belonged to Wren didn't go too far to dispelling Phoebe's mounting hysteria.

She left the house and ran around to the side that held the pantry window. When she spied the soiled bandana wedged in the window frame, she wanted to shout. Wren had escaped.

But so had a killer.

Phoebe took her Glock from the holster and checked it. The magazine was full and one bullet was already in the pipe.

That's when she heard the scream.

CHAPTER 60

"You're not fooling anyone, child. I see you sticking out from behind those stones."

Wren didn't move except to peer cautiously with one eye to one side of her scanty protection. What she saw made her knees quiver. Sweet old Mrs. Campbell was striding out of the far tree line, a rifle in her hands.

"You can come out of there. I'm not going to kill you," the woman said. "I need to take you back to the house."

"If you're not going to kill me, why do you have that gun?" asked Wren. "Why did you lock me in that cellar with a dead person?"

"I told you that it wasn't safe for you to go back home. That I needed to find time to think of a solution. I told you that my daughter would be plenty upset to know you'd snooped around where your nose didn't belong. I've got the rifle for my own protection. There's snakes around here, you know."

The mention of snakes reminded Wren of Mrs. Hargitt's earlier warning. She'd said there was a big rattler that lived around here. Wren had thought it was just a story to keep her from investigating the headstones, but now she wasn't so sure. Weren't they supposed to warn people away with their rattle?

She listened carefully, trying to hear beyond her own pulse pounding in her ears but all she heard was a soft "shooshing," like the pebbles in a rain stick or softly singing cicadas. Even the sound of heavier feet had stopped. The shooshing wasn't too far from her, just behind and to her left.

Wren tried to turn while still crouched, inching around on her knees to keep her chest and head protected by the short wall. She was half way around when she saw the rattler and screamed.

To Wren, any snake was big, but this one bordered on monstrous. He lay partially coiled four feet from her, his head raised, his tongue whipping in and out as he tasted the air. The snake's tail ended in a vibrating rattle over two inches long. The animal was clearly unhappy at being disturbed.

"There's a snake here," Wren whimpered. "Please shoot it."

"Get up slowly," advised Campbell. "He doesn't want to bite you. That wastes his venom and he needs it to hunt. Just move slowly and you won't disturb him."

Wren could barely control her leg muscles. They felt gelatinous; quivering masses stuffed inside a skin casing around dissolving bone. She also couldn't take her eyes off the snake. She needed to know that the reptile hadn't moved, that it wasn't striking. Her right hand reached for the top of the short wall as she braced herself.

"Okay," she said in a cracking voice. "I'm getting up slowly."

She was half way up when Campbell fired the rifle.

CHAPTER 61

The rifle crack and Wren's second scream melded into one explosive burst. She expected to feel a blossoming of pain before all feeling stopped, but the bullet plowed into the ground in front of her, sending up a spray of dust and gravel, which flew into her eyes. She instinctively staggered, trying to step away from the onslaught.

"Stop!"

A new voice, female, shrill in barely controlled panic, erupted from the path to the house. Wren recognized it. Shirley? But it was too late.

She stepped right in front of the snake.

The rattler, irritated beyond endurance by the spray of gravel, struck with blinding speed, sinking its fangs into Wren's soft calf.

She screamed again, a long, keening shriek of pain and terror which reverberated against the woods and was echoed by the frightened caws and cries of a pack of crows and several jays. Then she ran three steps forward and collapsed in a heap on the ground.

* * *

For Phoebe all sound stopped. There were no birds, no pounding of her feet, no hard intakes of breath – nothing but

371

the hellacious outcry, ripe with pain and terror. When she burst though into the clearing she saw Shirley Gracehill standing between Mrs. Campbell and Wren, "Stop it, mother. Put the rifle down and help me get this child to a hospital."

"Don't be foolish, Shirley. I can't let her go. She knows too much. And even you can't say that I killed her. As far as you know, I tried to shoot that snake and missed. It wasn't my fault. Now move aside and let nature take its course. Did you know she stabbed poor Mrs. Hargitt? Is it my fault she ran off and got herself snake bit?"

"That's not true, mother. I don't believe it. Maybe you didn't mean to hurt Wren, but if you let her die, then it will be murder. We can make this right."

"You know, you look just like him when you're angry, daughter. Same chin. Same nose. There were days when I couldn't abide to look at you."

Phoebe took in the scene quickly, training her Glock on Campbell. "Put down the rifle, Mrs. Campbell," she shouted. "Put it down now or I'll shoot." Phoebe's attention was split between the two dangers; the motionless old woman and the snake, still coiled and vibrating with fury not two feet from her daughter. It tightened its coils, tensing for another strike.

"Do what she says, mother." Shirley took one step towards her mother, her hands outstretched.

"I hated him!" Dorcas Campbell fired one round, hitting her own daughter in the chest.

The rifle crack and the soft "thwack" of bullet smacking flesh melded into one. Shirley's eyes widened in shock, her mouth agape as she fell, her blouse darkening with blood.

Campbell turned the rifle on Wren.

Phoebe fired repeatedly, shot after shot finding its mark until the hideous old viper was no longer a threat. The last two shots were for the rattler.

* * *

Boone wasted no time with going into the house, not after hearing the shots fired from somewhere down the overgrown path. Instead, he raced along the old footpath, his weapon drawn. He found Phoebe kneeling beside her daughter. Both Mrs. Campbell and Mrs. Gracehill were down, blood pooling around them; neither had a pulse.

"She's been bitten," cried Phoebe. "The timber rattler got her." Phoebe had taken off her belt and tied it tightly above the bite, trying to reduce the flow of venom to the rest of Wren's body. The girl's eyes were closed as though she'd fainted. Or worse.

Boone scooped her up in his arms, turned and raced to his vehicle, Phoebe running behind him. "I'll get her to the hospital," he said, laying her in the back seat. "I know this will be hard, but I need you to stay here and call for my deputies. As soon as they get here, give them your statement and then you can come to the hospital."

"My daughter..." she protested.

"There's no time to waste!" It was an order and Phoebe knew it. Knew also that her daughter's life depended on the speed at which she could receive the anti-venom. No time to radio and wait for an ambulance, and Boone knew these roads better than she did. He sped off, lights flashing and siren wailing, leaving her alone to wait and to pray.

* * *

"How is she doing?"

Phoebe looked up from the bedside and saw Boone. He held a little bouquet of daisies in a clear glass vase and a plush, cream-colored teddy bear. "I thought . . . I mean I know she's nearly fourteen, but . . . oh heck, I just wanted—"

"She'll love them," said Phoebe, taking the offered gifts. "Especially the bear." She put the flowers on the end table next to a larger bouquet of yellow roses and helium balloons and tucked the teddy bear beside her sleeping daughter. "The doctor said the worst is over. The anti-venom saved her, and she survived the anti-venom. Her leg looks like hell, but she's young. It will heal fine. She just needs rest now."

"Your in-laws still here?"

Phoebe nodded. "They do love her. They're staying in a bed and breakfast in town. They won't . . ." her voice broke and she paused to collect herself, swallowing hard. "They won't speak to me."

"Well at least something is going right for you," said Boone with a grin.

Phoebe laughed, stifling it with a hand to her mouth lest she wake Wren. "I needed that. Thanks," she added, taking his hand and giving it a gentle squeeze, "for saving my daughter's life. I can never repay that."

"Ah, cook me dinner sometime."

"I can't believe Mrs. Campbell shot her own daughter," said Phoebe, shuddering.

"Shirley was Noah Tanner's daughter and I don't think Tabitha Campbell, as she called herself, had any affection for anyone but her sister, Agnes. Has Wren talked much about it?"

Phoebe nodded. "Some. She said Mrs. Campbell, or Dorcas as it were, killed her own father. He would have cast off Agnes and that meant Dorcas would have had to marry Tanner. But I think Dorcas felt some guilt for forcing her sister to stay on. And eventually, Tanner had his way with Dorcas like he did with Viola and even Daisy. I wonder if Tanner knew she was Ben Owen's child and not his."

"Jeez," said Boone. "He may have suspected but as far as Daisy knew, Tanner was her father. No wonder she drank. And killing those kids was all just to keep Agnes's reputation pure and unsullied."

"Apparently," said Phoebe. "All part of that wracking guilt or fear. Do you know how she did it?"

"Speculation is all I have. George with Ruthie in tow came into the store on Thanksgiving, hoping to talk to Shirley or look at her books again. I imagine . . . Dorcas, I still have a hard time thinking of her by that name, tried to talk him out of it but the boy was nothing if not persistent and enthusiastic. So she hit him on the head. The skull still had some burrs from a new cast iron implement. We've checked the things that the store carried in the inventory back then. Looks like it was one of those pot hooks used with a dutch oven. You know, to lift up the lids. She probably took it home."

Boone fingered the bed rail. "I also talked to Joe Owen. He said that Shirley once told him she suspected her mother had done something rash because when she took inventory and checked the books, there was a pot lid hook and a teddy bear unaccounted for at the time the kids disappeared. When she'd asked her mother about it, Campbell clammed up. She might have eventually given the hook to Mrs. Hargitt. There's one in the old house, but any evidence is long since degraded."

"Then what was all the connection to Cabin 8?"

"She needed to get rid of the body. So she went to Cabin eight. It was unused that day, officially at least. She didn't know that Burt had been there having a tryst. Ironically, it's also where Ben Owen had carved his testimony of love to Agnes. Not sure how she got in, but she took one of the blankets to wrap him up in before she hauled him off in her car. The little girl had to die, too, but even Campbell couldn't just kill a little child outright. So she gave her a teddy bear to keep her quiet and left her outside that cave, telling her to wait and George would be back for her."

"And Ruthie waited until she froze to death." Phoebe shuddered. "Poor baby."

"The lab results came back with Mrs. Campbell's fingerprints on the boy's belt buckle, probably when she rolled him into the blanket, but it was Shirley's on the teddy bear's tag. Of course, if she did any restocking..."

"I can't imagine that Shirley actually had a hand in any of this. She tried to save Wren."

"No," agreed Boone, "but if she suspected all these years, she was complicit. She paid for it though, didn't she? Still one has to wonder. Mrs. Campbell was a strong woman, but that was a lot of work toting a body and all those rocks alone."

"Did Mrs. Campbell kill Beulah?"

Boone nodded. "That we're sure of. We found a couple of canning jars in her pantry at the retirement home of what looked like water. It tested positive for the cardiac glycoside. There were lily of the valley growing outside of her bungalow and it looked like some had been cut recently. Put those in water and the resulting liquid is deadly."

"So much hate and guilt," said Phoebe with a sigh. "Even to killing her own daughter." Boone nodded. He looked from the sleeping girl to Phoebe and she read the comparison of the two families in his eyes.

"Families can be difficult."

CHAPTER 62

Boone parked the Tahoe on the old logging road, nearly in the same spot that he'd put it in mid-June when he came to investigate the crime scene. Phoebe stepped out of the passenger side, then helped her daughter out of the back seat. The girl still moved stiffly, but every day gave her more energy.

The sound of another vehicle on the packed and rutted dirt made her turn. Her boss pulled up behind them in a park pickup. She watched as Burt got out and assisted a woman from the passenger side. Elverna Keefe cradled a small wooden box in her arms. They walked together down the steep slope, slowly and carefully, keeping to the easier paths and sturdy rock ledges until they were just above the ravine where Phoebe had first found the boy's remains.

"Is this the spot?" asked Mrs. Keefe.

"Yes," said Phoebe. She pointed to the fallen hickory which had been dragged to the side of the trail. "That's the tree that grew out of your brother's . . ." She stopped herself before she said "body" and hastily amended it. "Your brother's pocket."

Mrs. Keefe took a cotton handkerchief from her purse. She unwrapped it to expose a belt buckle, now cleaned of blood and fingerprints. "Can I leave there here, too?"

Phoebe read the questioning anxiety on her face. People couldn't be buried in the park, but she knew that ashes got scattered with or without permission often enough. But the buckle? To her surprise, Wren spoke up.

"I kind of got to know George when I was studying his Grandma Agnes. If you don't mind, I'll keep it in his memory."

Mrs. Keefe handed the buckle to Wren who pulled her new yellow Dead Man Hollow bandana from her pocket and carefully rewrapped the buckle in it. Mrs. Keefe smiled. "That's a right fitting kerchief for him," Mrs. Keefe said. "Thank you."

The stood in a solemn line, heads bowed in silent prayer as Mrs. Keefe walked to the hickory and sprinkled the powdered bone on the bark. "Rest in peace, George."

In the distance, a pileated woodpecker hammered loudly on a tree, beating a fitting drumroll for the ceremony.

"It's a beautiful spot," Mrs. Keefe said after a few moments of reflection, then allowed McGowan to escort her back to the truck.

Boone, Phoebe and Wren waited a moment more. Wren looked around the woods, her eyes wide and pained, as though she expected at any moment for something to emerge from the forest and assault her. After a few moments, Phoebe felt her daughter's hand tentatively take her own and hold on. Phoebe gripped it tighter, her throat tightening in the realization that her daughter was finally bridging their differences, that they could heal and become a family again.

Burt no longer talked of a probationary period. Her job was secure now.

"I'm building a run for Spunky Chunk," said Phoebe, "to keep him safe. Want to help?

"Maybe. I still hate it here, mom," Wren said softly. "And now I'm afraid."

"I know you are, sweetheart. We'll talk about it. But your father would've been so proud – is so proud of how you escaped and handled yourself. When you're ready, there are some things of your father's that we can look through together. Things I haven't even looked at.

Wren squeezed her hand. "He's probably proud of you, too, mom."

EPILOGUE

"How are you feeling today, Dad?" Joe Owen stepped into his father's room and pulled up a chair to sit beside him. His father looked paler, his eyes more distant. Joe could only think of him as looking empty. Hollow. He wondered if the news of Mrs. Campbell and Shirley Gracehill had hit the old man hard. They had been acquaintances at least and possibly a lot more, though Joe never had any proof of a closer relationship. Had he lost a sister now?

"The nurses said you went out to the garden again this morning. They were glad that you didn't try to wander off again."

"Wanted to pick some flowers," mumbled the old man. He pointed a calloused finger at a plastic cup with a few daisies and a mass of elongated green leaves. "Not much out there."

"They look nice," said Joe. "You want me to go and let you sleep? You look kind of frail today, Dad."

Owen reached for his son's sleeve and grabbed hold. "No. Have to talk to you."

Here it comes at last. Joe knew that his dad had loved another woman before he married, but he wouldn't talk much about her. Well, if it gives him peace, so be it.

"You know that I wanted to marry before I met your

mother, son?" Owen didn't wait for an answer. "I got her pregnant, but she went and married someone else."

"It's okay, dad. I think I know what you're trying to say."

"No, son. You don't." Owen closed his eyes and when they reopened, it was as if he was looking into the past. "I saw her again a long time ago, at the park. You know, the one I helped build."

Joe imagined his father going back to visit, possibly at that C.C.C. reunion. He saw him walk into the store, unsuspecting, and being confronted by his long lost love.

. "I thought we could finally come together," Owen said. "Your mother was dead. It would've been okay. I reserved a cabin – our cabin. Used a fake name but I cancelled at the last moment so no one else could get it. Didn't want anyone to know I was there. Didn't want to spread any gossip that might sully her. You see, I still had my pass key from when I had to go in and finish the stonework."

Joe patted his father's hands. "Dad, maybe this isn't such a good time. You're getting too worked up."

"No! I have to tell you."

"She had a sister she hadn't seen for years. And when she saw her, it upset her. She told me it was too late for us." Tears welled up in Owen's eyes and spilled down his gaunt cheeks. "I went into the store later to try to see if there was anything I could do or say . . . there was a boy there. The things he was saying. . . About my Agnes." Owens fingers made fidgety motions in the air. "Dorcas goaded me. She put. . . she put it in my hands. I couldn't help myself. I . . ."

Joe's eyes opened wider as he realized what his father was confessing.

"Dorcas, she was Agnes' sister, she got my key and got some blankets from the cabin. She bundled him up in them and told me to dump the body. And then I saw my Ruthie, my own granddaughter, hiding behind a counter, crying. Dorcas told her that George was sleeping and to be quiet. She said she'd get the girl to quiet down while I got rid of the boy. So I did. But she…. She killed my little grandbaby!"

"Dad . . ." Joe couldn't say anything more. His mind was too overwhelmed. Shirley wasn't his sister. It wasn't Mrs. Campbell that he'd loved. It was this other woman, this Agnes. And he killed that boy. Joe's stomach churned from the horror.

"Dorcas is why I couldn't marry her. But she's dead now," said Owen. "Finally that horrid woman is dead. And now I've confessed my sin and I can be free."

Owen's hands shook as he reached for the cup of flowers. He tossed the two daisies and the slender lily leaves onto the floor and drank the water.

ABOUT THE AUTHOR

Suzanne Arruda, a zookeeper turned science teacher and freelance writer, is also the author of the Jade del Cameron mystery series, several biographies for young adults as well as science and nature articles for adults and children. An avid hiker, she spends as much time as possible hiking in the Ozarks with her husband. You can reach her on Facebook (Suzanne Arruda, Mystery Writer).